Readers are falling in lov

My Super Sweet Six

"*Just what I was looking for in a YA time travel novel... Don't miss Rachel Harris's debut. It's a totally fun and totally satisfying read.*"
—Lisa T. Bergren, author of the River of Time series

"*Fresh and funny, Harris's detail-rich writing makes for a truly charming debut novel.*"
—Holly Schindler, author of *Playing Hurt*

"*A book that demands to be read in one sitting... Once you start traveling through Italy with Cat Crawford, trust me, you won't want to stop!*"
—Stephanie Kate Strohm, author of *Pilgrims Don't Wear Pink*

"*Harris's debut is a knockout. Her characters are charming and wonderfully entertaining, and they're set in a unique and well-defined world that will capture your imagination from the very first page.*"
—RT Book Reviews (4 1/2 stars)

"*Rachel Harris has skillfully crafted her debut novel.* My Super Sweet Sixteenth Century *covers a breadth of issues, all in a fun-filled, thoroughly enjoyable package.*"
—NY Journal of Books

"*Light and charming, this debut novel will appeal to those who want to leave the real world behind for a while.*"
—SLJ

Also by Rachel Harris

My Super Sweet Sixteenth Century

For adult romance readers

Taste the Heat

A Tale of Two Centuries

Rachel Harris

Entangled Publishing, LLC
2614 South Timberline Road
Suite 109
Fort Collins, CO 80525
Visit our website at www.entangledpublishing.com.

Edited by Stacy Abrams and Alycia Tornetta
Cover design by Alexandra Shostak

Print ISBN   978-1-62266-012-4
Ebook ISBN   978-1-62266-013-1

Manufactured in the United States of America

First Edition August 2013

To my husband, Gregg, for the weekends away so I can write and always believing in me, and for the Flirt Squad, the best group of cheerleaders an author can ask for.

Chapter One

I close my eyes against the gentle breeze and twirl, my green silk surcoat swishing around my ankles in glorious abandon. The warm sun seeps into my skin, and it is as if the very air I breathe is saturated with happiness. Fourteen years of grooming to become a wealthy merchant's wife, two years toiling to suppress my sinful desires, and it all culminates in this moment.

Pray let it be today!

Five long days ago, Matteo—as he allows me to call him in private—asked me to meet him here so we could discuss our future. A future I am eager to begin. Every prayer and every thought since has been spent in anticipation.

The scent of freshly cut flowers from a merchant's stand fills the air as Mama's wise words float in my mind: *Nature is but a sign of Signore's provision, Alessandra.* My eyes open to the vibrant blue of the iris petals, a certain premonition of good things to come, and a giggle springs from my throat.

"The sun's light holds not a candle to your radiance today, Less."

With a delighted smile, I turn to the sole person besides my beloved cousin Cat who refers to me by that peculiar name. "You and your flattering tongue are agreeably met, dear friend," I tell Lorenzo, maintaining one eye on the crowded piazza. "Care to keep me company while I await Signor Romanelli?"

My brother's best friend sets down his easel. "It would be my pleasure." He props his foot against the sandstone building behind us and rakes a paint-stained hand through his golden curls. "Last week you believed he had intentions of betrothal in mind. Have you seen each other since last we spoke?"

An inkling of disquiet blooms, but I whisk it away. "No, but it is my suspicion he has spent the time in preparation to meet Father when he returns."

Lorenzo nods, and we fall into a companionable silence, taking in the bustling life around us. The Mercato Vecchio is as noisy as ever, a cacophony of yelling, laughter, babies crying, and donkeys braying. A group of children races past, bumping into a nearby servant and jostling the basket she carries. A single red apple rolls to a stop by my feet.

A vision of our fairy-tale performance that day in the countryside plays before me, unbidden and poignant. The poisoned apple, the evil hag, the chance to shuck my dutiful daughter role and become someone wicked. I adore my cousin Cat for many reasons, but the gift of that afternoon most especially. Despite the church's strident opposition to female actresses, she gave me the opportunity to experience the rush of performance. To live the dream I once thought sinful.

Unfortunately, it was after my dear cousin departed that sadness adhered to the memory as well. When Cat returned to the future, she left three powerful words in her wake: *passion*, *equality*, and *freedom*. Maidens of the twenty-first century may hold these ideals dear, but they are most unacceptable in the sixteenth—as much as I wish it otherwise. As a result, I have spent the last two years in turmoil, battling between my expected duty of propriety and my newfound desire for passion.

Lorenzo kneels to pluck up the apple, and I meet his gaze.

He, too, is remembering.

As he returns the apple to the woman, mouth set in a tight-lipped smile, I marvel again at the impossibility of it all. For a reason neither of us has come to understand, fate left Lorenzo and me alone in the ability to perceive the noticeable differences between Cat, my future descendant, and Patience, my sixteenth-century cousin—the girl Cat temporarily took the place of. Of course, there are the similarities that come from being blood relations. Hair near the same shade, lips just a touch wide. But gone are all the unique qualities that made Cat so wonderfully vibrant. There is no denying that the true Patience is lovely in her own right, but who could ever compete with such a dynamic, time-defying person?

I have never explained all the details surrounding Cat's implausible tale, but then, I have never needed to. With the fiery passion that only a true artist can understand, Lorenzo just *knows*. Eventually, he discovered an outlet for his misery, using the pain of Cat's departure to fuel his art, studying under a variety of masters, earning public commendation and creating masterpiece after masterpiece.

I stuffed mine into reinvigorated attempts at marriage.

Lorenzo gazes over the bustling piazza, and his previously sad smile becomes genuine. "I believe your suitor has arrived."

Giddiness bubbles inside me as I follow his gaze.

Matteo.

He has yet to spot me, so I take the opportunity to drink in the sight of him. The broad line of his strong shoulders displayed in his dark doublet. The enticing tilt of his mouth I can see even from this distance. Absent are the lines of stress that far too often mar his handsome face, and I watch as he laughs with someone to his right. My heart hammers.

He is truly *yummy*, as my fair cousin would say.

At twenty-eight, Matteo is eleven years my senior. He is a bit young for marriage, but our families are old friends, and a union will bring increased prosperity. We will make a good match. Being with him will quiet the rage inside me, the need for more. It has to.

The crowd between us parts, and I spot a young woman beside him. I tilt my head and squint.

"Novella d'Amico," I say, my voice barely above a whisper. Formerly Novella Montagna, daughter of one of the wealthiest families in Florence. Courted and desired by all the men of marriageable age last year, she married a Venetian nobleman and moved away that winter. I turn to Lorenzo, my ribs an iron vise around my lungs. "Why has she returned to Florence?"

He shakes his head, his eyebrows furrowed. "I am not sure. But I shall find out."

Lorenzo marches over to a band of women pretending

to shop, obviously using the pleasant fall day as an excuse to prattle incessantly. As he approaches, Signora Benedicti, Signora Cacchioni, and Signora Stefani pause their chattering to gaze over his features as if he were an expensive piece of Venetian glass or a new onyx cameo. Completely undignified, but sadly, not uncharacteristic.

If gossip is desired, Lorenzo could not have chosen a better group.

I look away in disgust and fix my gaze on Matteo, willing him to glance my way. A few minutes later, I get my wish. My insides squeeze, but I force a smile, pushing every stolen moment and whispered promise into the gesture.

He does not return it.

Matteo reaches to clasp Novella's hand, his once-warm eyes now emotionless stones.

All excitement and hope drain away. Air ceases to be a necessity. Time stops, and cold dread washes over me. The market fades away as my gaze locks on their interlaced fingers.

From the corner of my eye I see Lorenzo turn away from the gossiping horde, his amiable face etched with pity. But I already know.

When he reaches me, he looks down and scowls. "Signora d'Amico returned home a widow last week, her full dowry intact." He inhales sharply, and I close my eyes, steeling myself for the truth to come. This is not how I envisioned this day unfolding.

"They met with the notary just yesterday."

Good leads to good. Somehow, the lesson from my childhood does not fit this new reality. I always do—have always done—the right thing, the proper thing. I do my duty. There should be a reward.

He is supposed to love me back.

Lorenzo clears his throat, and I know he is waiting for me to meet his gaze. With burning tears threatening to escape, I compel my eyes to open.

He places a gentle hand on my shoulder. "Alessandra, Matteo and Novella are married."

The *click-clack* of footsteps on the cobblestone road muffles my sobs. After pleading with Lorenzo not to follow, I make my faltering escape from the piazza, away from the prying eyes of Mama's friends and the smirk of triumph on Novella's contemptuous face. Tearing through the streets of my beloved city, my gaze blurred, I pray my feet will somehow find their way home. And as my eyes alight on the familiar four-story, tan stone building, my knees nearly buckle in gratitude. Fate may not have ruled in my favor in matters of the heart, but it appears to have taken pity on my sense of navigation.

My toe catches on the cracked stone floor, and I stagger through the arched opening of our courtyard. I set myself to rights and press on, the quiet solitude of the garden beckoning me onward, and sink to my knees in a corner covered in shadow. But today, the darkened retreat does not soothe. The scent of fragrant flowers and the melodic bubbling of the nearby fountain do nothing to ease the stabbing pain of Matteo's betrayal.

I still cannot bring myself to believe it. Months of secret

assignations and declarations cannot end in such a way. Surely I must be in the midst of a nightmare. At any moment I will wake up, get ready again, and leave to meet Matteo, where he will whisper words of our future and how much he loves me.

I blink rapidly, but nothing changes.

With a trembling hand, I wipe at relentless tears. I cannot help but think that Cat would be stronger. In my place, she would have stormed across the crowded piazza, flung a cutting remark at Novella, and demanded an explanation from Matteo. Then she would have kicked him.

The image of my near betrothed's eyes popping out of his head eases my spirits a little, and I hiccup a laugh. Cat had been a storm of unquenchable strength, challenging the rest of us to either match her in vivacity or be left in the dust.

But alas, I am not my dear cousin.

In Cat's world, in the future, a girl is free to live with passion and blatant disregard for propriety. She can ignore the rules of etiquette and society and follow her dreams—even when they led her here, five hundred years into the past. Fate, mixed with a little gypsy magic, granted Cat the opportunity to experience the impossible. She glimpsed another way of life and, for a short while, was given rest from the worries of her own.

Crumpling to the ground, for once not caring if my surcoat gets soiled, I close my eyes and let fresh tears fall onto the damp earth beneath my cheek. "How I long for a gypsy adventure of my own."

As I lay there, unmoving, willing the world to end, a faint tinkling sound rings near my ear, yanking me from my despair.

A slow shiver creeps from the base of my spine. It quickly

gains speed before bursting across the rest of my body. My eyes spring open to branches and petals dancing around me in a sudden breeze, a few snapping and fluttering away as the winds grow stronger. Ribbons of my auburn hair blow across my eyes. I clamber to my feet, fighting against the abrupt gust stealing my breath, and hold down the hem of my gown. The wind shoves me forward, and the storm swallows my shriek.

Then, as suddenly as it began, everything stops.

When I find my voice, I ask the stillness, "What, in Signore's name, was *that*?"

Unsurprisingly, the now calm and quiet courtyard does not reply.

Glancing down, I brush away the debris clinging to my surcoat—but the sharp *crack* of a twig behind me causes me to freeze.

"*Buna ziua*, Alessandra."

I spin around, and my gaze lands on a girl near my age. Her long raven hair is unruly and tousled, her costume one of bright-colored skirts and sheer veils. Her arms are bare, as is a slice of bronzed skin around her midsection. I avert my eyes as a whisper of a memory taunts the edges of my mind.

How does she know my name?

A small smile, unnatural and amiss on an otherwise somber face, plays upon the girl's mouth as she says, "The stars have heard your plea."

Chapter Two

"Reyna."

The whispered name passes my lips as recognition slams into me. I shake my head, unable to comprehend what my eyes are seeing. For months after Cat's return to the future, I imagined the young gypsy appearing before me. I held tight to the belief that one day she would come back, perchance with a message or sign from the future. A clue as to how my fun-loving cousin is doing or, selfishly, to grant me a magical adventure of my own. And now she is here. Standing a mere foot away, no longer in the drab servant frock she wore during her stay but looking just as she did that brief moment I last saw her, when Cat followed her into a mysterious green tent and disappeared from my life.

Reyna's magnetic gaze twinkles as she takes a step back and waves her arm in the air, sending the dozen bracelets wrapped around her slender wrist clanking in unison. Poised like one of Michelangelo's statues, she hitches a pointed sable brow heavenward as if waiting for a response to an unasked question. Confused, I shift my gaze beyond her...and my breath seizes.

There stands that same green tent—the portal that sent Cat home.

I jerk my gaze back to my cousin's gypsy girl, a wild stirring of hope building in my veins. She nods, and her feigned smile turns devious. Then she disappears inside and crooks a finger through the open flap for me to follow.

My previously halted breath escapes in an audible *whoosh*.

All of the servants are upstairs. Mama is traveling as companion to Patience on her journey to London, and Father is returning from visiting my uncle in Venice. My brother Cipriano, the one person who could truly dissuade me from such a course, is in Milan, having left a few short months after my cousin. There is no one here to stop me. I am depressingly alone, even more so now than this morning.

The chance to be as audacious as my fearless cousin, even if it is just for a moment, propels me forward. I fly across the cracked stone ground, throw back the folds, and boldly enter the darkened space.

But once the canvas doors seal closed behind me, apprehension dawns. Darkness is everywhere.

I lift my palm an inch from my nose and cannot see it. The only thing I *can* see is a curved path of sporadic candlelight, seemingly with no end. The reassuring fountain from the courtyard no longer bubbles, and the harsh sound of my labored breathing escalates to fill the void.

A word my cousin taught me from the future springs to mind: *creeptastic.*

Taking a trembling step, I tentatively call out, "Reyna?"

I squint, then widen my eyes, lean forward then back away, hoping to see the space before me better. But my efforts do nothing to illuminate my surroundings. Or to comfort me. I take another step, and a cool hand closes around my wrist.

"Ahh!"

"*Chavaia.*" The low, rough hiss in my ear sends my already galloping heart into my throat. "First you must remove your slippers."

My slippers? Pressing a palm against my chest, I glance down at my feet.

It is not right for a lady to walk barefoot — a suitor could see her ankles. Since Reyna masqueraded as a servant in my home during Cat's stay, she would know the rules of propriety, but a glance at her shadowed yet stern expression confirms she does not care.

I yank my bottom lip between my teeth and gnaw like a rabbit. My head rocks back and forth, the vexing tug of war beginning again between what I *want* to do and what I know I *should* do.

No gentlemen are present, I tell myself, even as a voice sounding suspiciously like Mama's whispers, *A lady must always follow society's expectations.*

But Reyna and I are alone. No one would ever have to know.

I stare at my slippers again, and a new, more daring voice joins the festivities in my crowded head. *Just think of it as a simple experiment, Less.*

And that decides it.

Smiling, I lift my chin in the air the way I imagine my cousin would, kick off my slippers, and wiggle my toes on the cool, gritty stone. The sensation is scandalously splendid. And *deliciously* wicked. I wiggle them again and giggle.

Reyna's snort of amusement snaps me back, reminding me where I am. She bends to place my slippers on the bottom shelf of an elaborate wooden structure, dusts her hands twice, then gives a curt nod. "Come."

With that, she tromps ahead. I tiptoe in her wake, my wide eyes growing accustomed to the flickering candlelight. On either side of the dotted aisle are never-ending shelves, one side boasting jeweled mysterious objects and the other unlit candles, pottery jars, and numerous labeled vials. It reminds me of an apothecary, though I doubt Reyna traveled five hundred years in time to prepare a remedy for my occasional head pains.

Smoke curls from a jar beside me, and the earthy scent of pine floods my senses. We stop at a small table covered with a black silk sheath, lit by the glimmer of a large sapphire candle. Reyna takes a seat and patiently waits for me to do the same.

Swallowing past the pebble lodged in my throat, I realize I have no idea what will happen next, whether it be good or evil, safe or treacherous. But I cannot continue as things are, always wishing for more. Maybe at the end of this journey, blessed peace awaits. And as for fearing Reyna herself…well, the joy on Cat's face when she stepped inside this very alcove to return home was unmistakable. Cat trusted her gypsy girl. So shall I.

Reyna tilts her head to study me. "You clearly crave

adventure, Alessandra. But I have to wonder if you are brave enough to grasp it."

I wince, both at the raspy edge to her voice and the woefully accurate assessment. She is right; Cat did not inherit her fearlessness from me. Bravery is a virtue I have never quite grasped, though it has not stopped me from wishing it were otherwise.

Perhaps this will change that.

Though I do not know if Reyna is here to send me on an adventure or is simply asking me a question, in this moment, I *choose* to be brave. Or, at least to pretend to be. Steeling my spine and stiffening my shoulders, I jut my chin forward and confidently proclaim, "Y-yes."

Or perhaps not.

Frustrated with my telltale stammer, I close my eyes. For all my desire to become a stage actress, that performance was severely lacking. I count to three, will my betraying voice to strengthen, and try again. "I mean to say, yes, I am." I meet her eyes as brazenly as I can. "I am no longer the timid girl you once knew." Palms glazed with perspiration clench at my sides and I strain to keep my expression neutral.

After a moment, Reyna's mouth twitches into a shadowy semblance of a smile.

"Misto," she says, and though I cannot comprehend the foreign word, I sag in blessed relief.

The table wobbles when she stands, and as I watch Reyna's bare feet glide to the wall of shelves, the glint of a golden band around her toe catches my eye. Mesmerized, I find myself wondering why anyone would adorn a part of the body hidden from the world.

"I am sure you are wondering why I am here," she says as my mind wanders, envisioning the scandal I would cause walking slipperless within the public square. "I admit my visit surprised me, too. After Caterina and I returned, I thought my purpose was over. But not twenty-four hours later, the goddess Isis gifted me with another vision."

At that, my guilty smile withers, and icy fingers of foreboding jerk me to attention.

As Cat would say, her implausible time travel *rocked my world*. I have always believed in the divine and trusted in forces like fortune, fate, and *destino*. Since I was a little girl, I have faithfully attended daily morning mass and evening vespers, I rarely travel on Saturdays, and I never leave home without my talisman. Yet when my cousin returned to the twenty-first century, my belief in a benevolent power was shattered.

How could anything that taunted me with ideas and freedoms I could never hope to experience possibly be *good*?

Unaware of my emotional upheaval, Reyna says, "At first I did not understand it. The second vision differed so much from the first. But after consulting with my *puridaia*"—she glances over her shoulder—"my grandmother, I was at last able to decipher the prophecy."

A prophecy.

Strange how such a simple word could send pinpricks of fear over my entire body. Wringing my hands, I watch Reyna dig through her sundry of items and wait for her to continue. When Reyna finally turns, she waves a golden object in triumph. "Ah-ha!" She palms a candle, then lowers her chin. "My vision,

Alessandra, was of *you*."

The tent spins. Or perchance that is my head. A peculiar squirming wriggles in my belly—from fear or excitement, I do not know. The singular thought my fuzzy brain contains is a repeat of her words: *of you, of you, of you.*

Reyna strides back to the table with a smirk, the shiny object and a small white candle in hand. She sets them down with a *clank* and a *plop*, and then gives me a wink. She lights the wick.

The unexpected, and quite enormous, blaze knocks me backward.

Rebounding in my chair, I watch in rapt horror the glow double, then triple in size. The core of the flame flashes blue, then green, then shocking vivid purple.

"Th-that is not possible," I whisper.

Reyna does not argue. Instead, she chants. *"Tatum, tatum, tatum vel."* Her eyes reduce to slits of liquid mercury. "Sit," she commands in a low, steely voice. When I do nothing but stare dumbly at the unworldly flame, she says, "You asked for this, Alessandra."

At the reminder of my claimed bravery, I clamp my molars together and stuff the urge to take back my foolish declaration. For two years, I have cried out for adventure, for change. For release from the turmoil my cousin left in her wake and the knowledge there could be more in life than simply marrying well and being a submissive daughter.

Skittish limbs notwithstanding, I do want this.

"Is Cat content now?" I ask.

If my question surprises her, Reyna does not show it. She

nods thoughtfully. "Yes, I believe she is. Caterina's destiny took her on an adventure that answered many questions. It did not solve them all, for only she can do that. But if you were to see her again and ask, I trust she would say the trip was worth every *hiccup* she encountered."

A laugh bubbles from within at the amusement in Reyna's eyes. The memory of Cat's many missteps plays before me much like the magical box of *movies* she brought in her satchel, and I recall her horrendous performance at a society dinner, her continual use of strange vocabulary, and the passionate way she did just about everything

With a brusque nod, I return to my chair. "I am ready."

"Khushti." Reyna does not waste a moment. She draws a steady breath and closes her eyes, rolling her head in a slow, controlled circle. Without lifting her lids, she says in a low whisper, "Close your eyes, Alessandra."

Bunching the fabric of my surcoat in my damp hand, I comply. Instantly, sounds grow sharper. I hear a ringing, followed by a metallic rattle. When Reyna speaks again, her voice is louder. "In your mind's eye, I want you to visualize the happiness you called upon the stars to seek, whatever it is your heart most desires."

In my mind, Matteo bows before me, as he did so many times, clasping my hand and flashing his enticing smile. I had been convinced we were happy, that he would be my salvation. I was foolish, and that realization hurts worse than his betrayal. The pieces of my heart splinter a little more.

The memory blessedly fades, but in its place springs a surprising one of the afternoon performance in the countryside.

Why that memory chooses to taunt me for the second time today I am not certain, for it will do me no good. The joy and release of our fairy-tale play may be what my heart desires, but it is not my destiny. It is not written in the stars for a girl like me, born in this time.

Even so, I watch the vision play out before me, and the sense of longing that overwhelmed me in the piazza consumes me anew.

"Good," Reyna says, as though she, too, can see my thoughts. "Hold tight to that vision, Alessandra. Do not let it go. But now imagine a locked door materializing in front of you, keeping you from the vision. From the happiness you deserve."

At her words, a heavy wooden door appears and slams shut. The faint sound of Cat's laughter seeps through the crack underneath. Though I know it is just a vision, pain lashes inside my chest, and sweat trickles down my back.

I have to open that door.

An eerie breeze suddenly sweeps through the interior of the tent, reminding me of the squall from the courtyard. My auburn hair flies back and my eyes fly open. Reyna latches onto my wrists.

"Stare into the flame, Alessandra," she orders. Her voice is deeper than I have ever heard it before, as though it is coming through the *earbuds* Cat kept in her satchel with the singing box. "Concentrate. Look into the flame!"

The wind picks up, whipping the sheath on the table and the sides of the tent, whistling around us and competing with her booming commands.

"Do you see the locked door?" she yells, and I nod fiercely, blinking against the sting of my long hair lashing my eyes. The vision dances within the glowing flame. "Now, in your mind, walk toward it…unlock it…and step through it!"

The scene unfolds exactly as she describes. Within the vivid purple core, I watch my palms press against the smooth wood and push open the heavy door. But on the other side, I no longer see Cat, Cipriano, or Lorenzo. I only see myself.

"Pour your passion into the vision!" Reyna's voice grows louder with each word spoken. And though I want to ask why the vision changed, I do not speak. Whether from fear I messed up the spell or needing to see the vision play out, I bite my tongue and throw open my heart, letting myself feel all the emotions I have kept locked inside for so long.

A large stage appears below the version of me dancing within the flame. A beam of light brighter than the sun suddenly shines over me, and the thunderous sound of applause breaks around me. Instinctually, I know they cheer for me. Pleasure washes through my core, and the Alessandra in the flame closes her eyes, savoring it. Triumph and rightness fill me to overflowing, even though I do not understand it. But when the girl in the vision opens her eyes again, the light no longer shines on her. The stage is eerily silent. And a young man enters the vision.

I cannot see his face, but his clothes are like those in the colorful pictures from the future. Dark pants hug his long legs. A faded black shirt frames his broad back and strong arms. And even though I am certain we have never met, he reaches out to embrace the Alessandra in the vision. Warmth pools in my belly.

"Send your desires to the stars!"

This time I jolt at Reyna's shriek, and her grip tightens on my wrists.

Scared the image will disappear if I lift my eyes to the sky, I silently pray for the only desire I can think of in the moment and hope it is enough: *I want to be there. On that stage. With that applause. And I want to be with him.*

The fact that I do not know who *he* is does not matter.

"Did you do it, Alessandra? Did you speak your heart?"

I nod frantically, and her nails embed themselves into my flesh. She tugs me toward her, chanting, "Gracious Lady Moon, ever in my sight, kindly grant the boon I ask of thee tonight."

Reyna repeats it two more times, each time her voice growing louder and louder until her chant echoes in my ears. The ground under my feet rumbles. The table shakes.

Then every candle in the tent snuffs out.

The room is engulfed in black.

Chapter Three

My heart convulses against my rib cage as though it wishes to leap from my chest and run back to the pleasant safety of my bedroom.

Just like the rest of me.

Reyna releases my hands from her painful grip, and I draw them close, shivering with panic, fear, and strangely enough, excitement. Though I have never been more scared in my life, I have also never done anything quite as thrilling.

The table jostles, and I hear Reyna walk away, hopefully to light another candle. Gentle tinkling of crystal soon promises just that, and I tap my leg, eager for an end to the all-encompassing shadows. Her feet scuffle toward me, but before she strikes the match, a harsh, repetitive hum emanates from the other side of the tent. A peculiar deep, vibrating commotion follows, tickling the wisp of a memory. Somehow I have heard that unworldly sound before.

Light springs to life on the table, carving a hole in the darkness, tickling my nose with the smell of burning sulfur. A third sound, a piercing shriek, comes from just outside the tent. So close, it could be in my very own courtyard.

Throwing my hands over my ears, I crouch low in my chair. "What are those horrifying noises?"

Reyna ignores my question. "Alessandra, the adventure that you seek is full of possibilities," she says in a serious, thunderous voice. "But always remember where your *real* strength lies."

Tentatively, I remove my cupped palms from my ears, relieved to hear the shriek silenced, and blink up at the gypsy girl.

Another cryptic message.

Cat spent the whole of her time in Florence trying to decipher Reyna's riddle about lessons to learn, yet my cousin left before getting any answers. Any that I knew of, that is. I have often wondered how it was she was able to return, if she managed to solve the elusive problem on her own, or if Reyna merely took pity.

Then I stop and realize…*I received my own message.*

I am on my own gypsy adventure!

A sharp squeal outside tempers my enthusiasm. Wincing, I swallow nervously and look to Reyna, hoping for guidance. What she gives is an impatient nod toward the front of the tent, wordlessly telling me it is time to go.

Well, then.

No longer timid, my inner voice mocks. *Is that not what you said?*

Rising from my crouch, determined to silence that voice,

I plaster a wide smile onto my face and take a shaky step forward. Then another. And another. Soon I am just inside the tent, the fluttering flap the sole thing concealing me from the scary world waiting outside.

Where have you sent me? I want to ask. *What do I do now?*

Instead, I turn and curtsy. "Thank you." It is not much, and my voice wobbles, but she seems to understand my distress, because she offers a small smile.

Without another word, I slide my feet into my slippers. When I stand, Reyna is suddenly right beside me. She hands me a folded piece of soft paper. "Give this note to the man waiting outside. He will take you where you need to go." My hand closes tightly over the missive.

Reyna pulls back the flap, and blinding sunlight shoots through the opening. "Be brave, Alessandra. Reach out and take the adventure that you crave. On your journey, three signs will mark your time: an angel will speak, a soft-rose songstress will captivate, and life will imitate art. I will return at sundown when the third sign is revealed. Use your time wisely." She looks deeply into my eyes as she says this, and I nod, knowing that I can live a lifetime of adventure in whatever time fate grants me. She watches me a moment more, then with a slight twinkle in her amber eyes, she whispers, "*Latcho Drom*, Less."

Before I can react to her use of my nickname, or ask what the foreign phrase means, Reyna gives my shoulder a gentle shove.

· · ·

Glaring sunlight permeates the thin veil of my eyelids. Even though it is noonday, the light is exceptionally bright, at least in comparison to the shelter of the tent. I shield my brow with a curved hand and force my protesting eyes open. At the sight before me, I promptly shut them again.

There is no need to fear, I tell myself. *It is all but a fantastical illusion.*

Regrettably, my escalating pulse begs to differ.

Sounds become crisper in the darkness. Rumbles, shrieks, wails, and hums. Unfamiliar chirps and impossible beeps. Piecing together my wilting courage, I take another peek and find nothing is as it should be.

Where my palazzo usually sits is an enormous structure with golden doors and red columns, a metallic roof, and a massive mounted dragon. A pair of terrifying sculpted beasts guards the entrance. The ground is no longer one of cracked stone or even the damp earth of my garden, but assorted gray blocks etched with handprints, slipper prints, and a series of strange markings.

I stare at the mysterious shapes on the stone before me and gasp as they all at once become clear: *Harry Potter, 7-9-07. Rupert Grint. Daniel Radcliffe. Emma Watson.*

While a few of the letters are different than I am used to, it is as if my mind is faster than I, readily making sense of it all. Stooping to see the words closer, I set down Reyna's missive, place my hands in the indentations below the word *Emma*, and marvel at the fit.

"Reyna," I call out, raising my voice over the myriad of noises. "What brand of *crazy* magic is this?"

The voice that leaves my mouth is in a foreign tongue. My words echo back through my memory, and something pops in my ears like air escaping. New sounds trickle through my unclogged ears, people talking and singing like the music Cat played in her tiny box, but this time, I actually understand them.

I twist my neck around, hands still pressed into the cool hollows, wanting to share the astonishing news with Reyna. But she and the tent are gone. In their place, an overwhelming crowd in varying degrees of scandalous dress swarms the square, each costume more shocking than the last.

Exposed ankles, exposed legs, exposed *stomachs…*

I avert my eyes heavenward, twin flames of heat burning up my throat and into my hairline. Clutching the note, I press my hands against my knees and prepare to stand. The rough texture beneath my palms causes me to freeze.

A horrible unimaginable truth tries to be acknowledged, and I reluctantly run my hands along my thighs, hoping, praying my fingers will brush against the soft, cool silk of my surcoat. But when they follow the curve of my lap and meet in the middle, mortification demands a glance down.

Gentlemen's trousers!

Gracelessly and clumsily, I push to my feet, searching for a place to hide. If Mama's friends were to see my legs encased in trousers, I could be ruined. Shame would come to our family name, and Father would be disgraced.

Scanning the boisterous square, wildly jerking my head from left to right, I stumble over my own feet, lose my balance, and crash into a solid wall of rock behind me.

"Hey!" the wall growls before shoving me forward. "Better watch yourself, little girl."

I swallow to push my heart back where it belongs and turn to the owner of the disagreeable voice which I can unfortunately comprehend. A scowling brute of a man lifts a scarred lip, exposing a golden tooth. The sun glints off a ring puncturing the middle of his nostrils, and I cringe, hearing Mama's voice again, this time warning me never to leave home without a chaperone.

The world is full of danger, Alessandra. Especially for unescorted females.

It never occurred to me to ask what forms of danger the world holds. Now I wish I were more prepared. The man takes a step, and I shrink into myself, bracing for the harm to come. "My-my apologies, sir. Please do not hurt me."

In reply, he grunts. I wait with firmly sealed eyes, but when the pain fails to come, I crack them open and see him shouldering his way through the crowd. I wrap my arms around my stomach, as if I can somehow hold the squirming mass together, and exhale.

If this is the start of my gypsy adventure, I believe I am quite ready for it to end.

A person dressed from head to toe in red and blue with a giant spider emblazoned on his chest walks past, followed by a man wearing all black and a flowing cape. I gawk at a huge man painted green. Is this the future or a strange, altered world?

On the fringe of the square, closer to the bustling road, a flash of crimson catches my eye. I waggle my head around the ever-moving crowd and spot a woman in a long, flowing surcoat.

Finally, someone like me.

A man holding a bright yellow sign leads a long line of people between us, and anxiety pulses through me. I cannot lose her. Pushing through the crowd, my weak apologies swallowed in the commotion, I fly past maidens sprawled on the dirty ground posing with various handprints. *Clicks* from boxes like the one Cat called a *camera* go off on either side of me. The chunks of gray ground give way to a smooth strip of road oddly marked with stars, and I stretch out my hand to reach the woman, the tips of my fingers just snagging her right sleeve. "Pardon me."

She turns and eyes me strangely, glancing at my tight grip on her gown, and I hastily let go, rubbing my fingers together at the unusual feel of the fabric. "I am sorry," I say before clearing my throat. *How do I ask this without appearing completely mad?* "It was my hope that you could perchance tell me where I am?"

The woman, dressed as *I* should be, bestows upon me a sweet smile. I am surprised to see her teeth lined with shiny metal. In a noticeably unnatural accent, she replies, "Ah, dearie, behold the world-famous TCL Chinese Theatre."

Despite hearing the word *theater,* my hopes of rescue plummet. This woman is not like me, after all. She is an impostor.

Heaving a sigh, I turn around to behold the madness from whence I came.

It is *not* as splendid as the woman believes.

Towering buildings across the street capture my attention. A white sign sitting atop one proclaims it as the *Roosevelt Hotel,* and opposite me, past where all sorts of strange carriages seem to fly over a paved road, a colossal structure houses a variety of merchants. I smile at the happy orange *Hooters*, finding it an odd but intriguing location for an owl shop, and then pause at *American Apparel.*

The woman remains beside me, watching me curiously. I ask her, "And the city in which this famous theater resides?"

My question elicits a slight waver in the woman's pretend smile. "Why, Hollywood, of course."

It takes a moment for the foreign word to sink in. But when it does, the weight of fear and anxiety that has nearly crushed me from the moment I discovered Reyna gone lifts, and relief streams in like a glorious sunrise.

Hollywood.

Cat spoke often about this land of actors and actresses, plays, and *movies.* Her satchel contained glossy portraits of such things and a device that allowed me to witness one of her father's films.

Now understanding that the woman's use of a false accent marks her as an actress, I curtsy in awe. "Yes, Hollywood. Of course." I wiggle my fingers in anticipation and ask one final, important question. "And pray, can you tell me what century we are currently in?"

She fists her hands on her hips and tilts her head, now abandoning her role altogether. "Honey, are you all right? Do you need some water or something?"

I shake my head, impatient for her answer. Cat never confided the exact year she was from, but I know the era. And if by chance Reyna sent me to my cousin's time, it is possible I could have a helpmeet through this worrisome journey of the unknown.

The woman scrunches her nose, and when she replies, her voice is high-pitched and questioning, as if she herself is not quite sure of the answer. "The twenty-first?"

Just as I dared to hope.

I clap my hands and do a little dance, enjoying the comfort of the peculiar slippers on my feet. Reyna's cryptic message flashes in my mind, as though the very words are floating in the air, and I grin so wide it hurts.

Alessandra, the adventure that you seek is full of possibilities. But always remember where your real strength lies.

Cat's time is a time of opportunity, freedom, and passion — a world full of possibility.

And now I am here, too.

Overcome with emotion, I throw my arms around the woman's neck and kiss her ruddy cheek. She pats me awkwardly and leans back, a wobbly smile on her face. "And you're sure you're all right?"

Looking at the world around me with new eyes, I nod emphatically. "I am perfectly and wonderfully happy. Thank you for asking."

A beep blares from the frenetic road, and the woman bobs her head toward the sound. "That your ride, honey?"

A disgruntled man waves his hand from inside a yellow horseless carriage, then pins me with an annoyed gaze. "Meter's running, lady. Done enough sightseeing yet?"

With a glance behind me to confirm no one is there, I point to myself. "Are you referring to me, sir?"

He exchanges a look with the actress beside me that I cannot read, and the woman smothers a grin. She pushes me toward the carriage. "It *is* warm for January. Maybe it's best you get along home now and rest."

Though the word *home* sounds comforting, the idea of getting inside the modern form of transportation is positively terrifying. I clench my fists, and Reyna's missive crinkles. I swallow. "I-I believe I was told you would take me where I needed to go," I say hesitantly.

I slide him the visibly trembling note through the open window, and he yanks it from my fingers. He reads it, scowls, and juts his thumb at the back of the carriage. "So? You getting in or what?"

I frown. The future appears filled with unpleasant people whose manner of speaking is even stranger—and more improper—than my cousin's was.

The woman squeezes my shoulders and mutters a good-bye. Determined not to give way to feelings of desertion, I stare at the door and wait for the coachman to come around and help me in. When he merely settles deeper into his seat and a footman fails to appear, I realize he expects me to get in by myself.

Well, then. Perhaps chivalry cannot exist in a world of female equality, I ponder, studying the unfamiliar frame of the carriage. But if women of this time can do this, so can I.

How hard can it be?

Lifting my head high, I run my hands along the cool, solid frame. I cannot find a door pull. I press harder against the metal and scratch at the glass window to no avail, then squat to study the apparatus closer. My driver sighs from the front.

I choose to ignore his ill manners.

On closer inspection, I discover a hand-sized metal indentation. The intricate detail is impressive, a truly modern marvel. With a triumphant grin at my discovery, I curl my fingers around it and yank. My reward is a gratifying *creak*.

"Aha! Figured it out," I proclaim, climbing onto the springy, cracked seat.

My coachman does not appear sufficiently impressed.

The cloth inside the carriage reeks with a disharmonious blend of sweat, food, and something undefinable, and the floor where I place my feet is filthy. But neither the coachman's aloofness nor the unappetizing smell and dirt surrounding me can quell my pleasure.

I am well on my way to acclimating to this strange new world. My cousin would be so proud.

Keeping my back straight so as not to lean against the seat, I watch the man turn a dial, causing the music pouring from the front of the carriage to increase to an uncomfortable level. He grips a tattered wheel with both hands and looks to the left. The carriage lurches with a sudden powerful jerk. My head slams into the greasy window.

My pleasure dampens.

A shrill shriek emanates from below our carriage, and we advance with a jolt, moving faster than should be humanly possible. I brace my right arm against the dank seat in front of me and clench the stinky cloth of the seat behind.

"Sir, must we travel so fast?"

The coachman meets my gaze in the mirror above his head

and rolls his eyes. I lick my lips and try again, raising my voice to be heard over his dreadful music. "Surely this is unsafe! Kindly remember you have a lady as a passenger."

If it is possible, the horseless carriage actually gains speed. Deciding it best not to antagonize the man any further, I clamp my jaw and watch as my cousin's world flies past my window in a dizzying blur of confusing gadgets, scary transportation, and indecent clothing. I hold on for dear life.

Chapter Four

What feels like hours later—but what is probably much shorter—the stomach-roiling ride ends. Exactly how long we careened through the hazy streets of Hollywood I cannot say. I was too busy keeping the contents of my stomach off the already grubby floor and doing my best not to notice the distressing speed, sights, or *creeptastic* sounds of the future.

After the first few minutes within the flying carriage, I fastened my eyelids shut and centered my thoughts on Cat, praying as my body jerked back and forth that her home was our final destination. And as we now roll to a stop, it is with a heavy heart that I slowly crack my eyes open to take a peek. A large, pointed gate sits in front of us, a swirling letter *C* inscribed in its center.

Joy floods me. If he were not so vile, I would kiss my maniacal coachman.

Crawford.

Cat's last name is Crawford.

Before the notion is even fully thought, I yank the metal handle and throw open my door. Peeling my feet off the sticky floor, I practically leap from my seat, eager to feel solid ground beneath me again. Beyond the gate, a two-story white building looms tall and proud, and instinctively I know my cousin waits inside. I take a step toward it.

"That's gonna be twenty bucks, lady."

And lurch to a stop.

The man extends an open palm, and his meaning becomes clear. "Ah, yes." I pat my shiver-inducing trousers and shove my hands inside a pair of pockets I find on either side. I am certain that I do not have any *bucks* on my person as even one such animal would hardly fit in the carriage with us, but perhaps fate has left me with something. Then I pause. "*Twenty*, you say?"

In my time, twenty florins could buy a home. Things have certainly changed in the last five hundred years.

When my hands leave my pockets empty, I am not surprised. Mama never allowed me to carry florins in town, and it appears as though I am fresh out of any *bucks*. The coachman's eyes narrow disdainfully, and I chomp down on my lip. "L-Let me just step inside and get that for you."

The gentleman—if that term even applies—watches, suspicious, as I stagger to a small gate off to the side. If this is not Cat's home, then I can only hope it belongs to a benevolent stranger with currency to spare.

I hesitantly close the gate behind me and cross the paved ground to the front door. Lines string across the sky from wooden posts, and two glass-encased torches glow from the exterior walls. I have no idea what any of it is, but it is all extremely fascinating.

I lift a hand to knock on the red-painted door and spot a small, circular torch embedded into the stone. Just like the larger torch affixed above it, the blazing flame somehow remains contained within, and before I can think, before the possible consequences of touching fire can spring to mind, I extend a finger and press. Fortunately, the surface is cool and does not burn—but as the torch sinks into the stone and a series of *ding*s rings out, I snatch my hand back as if it had.

From inside, I hear the rhythmic *clack*ing of footsteps approach. I push my hair behind my ear, pull down the exceedingly tiny tunic that comes nowhere near my hips, and fretfully tap on my leg.

The door *creaks* open...and there stands my beloved cousin.

Thanks be to Signore above.

"Alessandra?"

Cat's dark brown eyes look as though they want to pop from their sockets. Her mouth gapes, and she shakes her long brown hair as if to clear her head. She looks just as I remember, exactly as she did when I saw her last—except in lieu of the crimson, cut-velvet surcoat she wore then, my cousin has on dark trousers and a loose, flowing tunic. It is much longer than my own. I yank down my top again and meet her startled gaze, and a knot forms in my stomach. As it takes a leisurely path up to lodge in my throat, I cannot help but wonder, *Is she pleased to see me?*

It has been two years. Perhaps she wants to keep our time together a happy memory left in the past...or worse, has not missed me at all.

Forcing a smile on the outside while restlessly twitching within, I say, "Greetings, *cousin*. I know my unforeseen presence must come as a shock, but I pray the surprise is well met?"

Cat blinks, either still in awe or severe discomfort, and I twist my fingers together behind my back. Her mouth opens and closes like a fish a few times before she says in a slightly dazed voice, "Well, of course it is. I mean, I've missed you sin—" She cuts off and grasps my arm, raking her gaze over me as if she, too, can barely believe this is happening. "Wait, did you just speak English?!"

Relief pours in, and I laugh aloud, happy and grateful to have a familiar face in the chaos. Pulling her into a hug, I say, "Is that not how gypsy magic works? After all, *you* do not speak Italian anymore."

Cat laughs into my hair. "Touché."

I inhale the sweet scent of rose clinging to her skin. Guilt for ever doubting our gypsy girl twinges, but it is hard to hold onto it in the midst of so much happiness.

After a moment, my cousin pushes me to arm's length, smiling as she looks over me again. "To answer your question, of course I'm stoked to see you. But how is this even possible?" She shakes her head again. "What in blazing Hades are you *doing* here, girl?"

I lift a shoulder and grin. "Is it not obvious? The fates have sent me on a time travel adventure of my own."

"Ah, yes. The fates." Cat smiles, and with an audible exhale, her shoulders visibly lower. "I got a note from Reyna about a half hour ago, telling me to expect some kind of delivery, and

I've spent the last thirty minutes totally freaking out. I didn't know what or who was gonna be on the other side of my door, but I have to say—*this* is my exact brand of gypsy mojo."

My cousin's delightfully strange vocabulary, spoken in her native English, makes me grin like a giddy simpleton. It has been a long time without her.

As though she can read my mind, Cat's eyes grow misty, and I feel my own begin to fill. She clears her throat and squeezes my shoulder. "Well, let's not just stand around gawking on the porch. Get your butt inside, girlfriend."

She takes my hand and pulls me back to the open door, but an impatient *beep-beep* stops us in our tracks. Cat lifts an eyebrow.

"Ah. That would be the ill-mannered coachman of my yellow horseless carriage. He requires payment for escorting me from the chaotic theater of etched handprints and strange creatures, but I am afraid my new trousers did not come lined with money." He beeps again. "Any chance you have a deer or goat lying about?"

A squiggle appears on Cat's forehead. "Deer or goat?"

"Hmm, is that not right?" I ask, pulling on my ear. I was almost certain that was what he said. "He informed me the ride was twenty *something*—I thought he said bucks. Could it have been ducks?" I scrunch my nose. "Are waterfowl a popular currency in the twenty-first century?"

My cousin's sudden boisterous laughter is my first clue that I have made a cultural error. The second is the two pieces of green paper emblazoned with the number twenty that she pulls from her pocket.

Oops.

When Cat's merriment ends long enough for her to catch a breath, she says, "No, no waterfowl or mammals. That would be awesome to see, but it'd unfortunately make shopping pretty difficult. Nope, we here in the good ole US of A circa 2013 use cold, hard, boring cash."

Her continued giggles trail behind her as she traipses down the paved walk. She hands the *cash* to the coachman, who in turn gives her a shred of a smile that looks horribly amiss on his disagreeable face. Then he leaves in haste.

Cat grins as she walks back to where I stand waiting, her dark eyes surveying my outfit. She throws her arm around my shoulder and says, "You know, I never thought I'd see you in anything so scandalous, Less. Whatever will the neighbors think?"

. . .

Cool air blows from a vent in the ceiling. Cat's soft mattress sinks below me, and a pleasing aroma wafts from her purple coverlet. A long white pillow lying across a sea of purple declares the bed *Heaven*…and I have to agree.

Cat's room is not what I expected, though truly I had no idea what to imagine. Her walls are a cool shade of green, the wooden floors bare and reflecting the golden light from an array of *light fixtures* and *table lamps* (see how well I am learning?) around the room, and a row of glass doors runs along one wall. Her bedchamber is neat and tidy and, surprisingly, not at all shocking.

My cousin comes out of the huge room she calls a closet,

arms folded. "Looks like the extent of my feminine wardrobe, or at least what *you*'d consider feminine, consists of a handful of fancy premiere dresses, a crazy long skirt Nana got me to wear to church at Christmas, and a frumpy frock that was shoved at the back for God knows why." Her lip curls in disapproval as she holds out the garment in question, her thumb and forefinger extended as though it were made of poison.

I actually like it, but I dare not say so.

"Of course there's also the dress I wore to my Renaissance-inspired sweet sixteen," she continues, pulling out a long amethyst gown with clear reluctance.

I shoot from the bed to grab it, but Cat whisks it behind her.

"First the rules, Miss Forlani," she says, eyes twinkling at my new name.

Once she processed the shock of my arrival, Cat quickly set to work on how my time here should unfold. First on her list was bestowing upon me a new identity. Apparently, if we divulged our familial relationship to anyone, her father would most certainly flip his pancake—whatever that means—so I have been rechristened. I am now Alessandra Forlani, foreign exchange student and budding actress.

The foreign part certainly fits.

"You can wear this dress around the house," my cousin continues, "when we're the only ones here. Unfortunately, although Jenna, my stepmama-to-be, is in New York until tomorrow, my dad should be home from the set any minute now. But either way, trust me when I say that unless you want everyone thinking you're a crazy person, it's best just to go with the flow. If I had to wear five pounds of scratchy clothing and a freaking corset when I lived in your time, you can put up with a little skin showing here."

I gulp at the revolting image those words conjure, and Cat shakes her head. With an exaggerated sigh and teasing roll of her eyes, she hands me the next best choice, the gown she deemed a *frumpy frock*, and I eagerly snatch it from her fingers. The fabric is smooth and silky. I hold it up, judging the size and length, and declare it perfection.

"Now unlike you, we don't have fancy lady servants to help get us dressed, though as modest as you are, I'm shocked you even let them, anyway. But this is the bathroom." She opens a door to reveal a second room attached to her bedchamber, this one containing a wall of mirrors. "Feel free to get changed in here."

I tiptoe inside, awed by the abundance of light and variety of basins. A box of glass and a huge white tub take up most of the space. It smells like the satchel of future items Cat brought with her during her stay with my family, and I close my eyes and inhale.

Behind me, the door closes, but Cat continues to talk, her voice easily distinguishable through the thin wood. "I still can't believe you're here," she says as I set the gown on the smooth counter. I grab the hem of my tunic and lift, still in awe myself, and she adds, "But why do you look so much older? It's only been, like, what? Two months since I left Florence?"

Arms in the air, tunic over my head, I freeze. I catch sight of my reflection, turn five shades of crimson, and spin away. "Dear cousin, either my English translation skills are defective, or your mathematics are. I believe you mean two *years*."

Silence on the other end for a moment, then, "Uh, no. I mean two months."

Holding the top against my chest and cracking the door open just enough to see one of her eyes, I ask, "But that cannot be possible. I assure you, when I entered Reyna's mysterious green tent this morning, it was the year 1507."

Her head snaps up from the row of books she is perusing on her shelf. "Did you say 1507?" she asks, emphasizing the last number. When I nod, she tightens her mouth and tilts her head to the side. "Have there been any interesting developments or, err, any *changes* in the last two years?"

As her sharpened gaze flitters about me, oddly focusing on my face and hands, I reply, "Other than that I was once fourteen and am now sixteen, no." Cat nods distractedly. Obviously something is consuming her thoughts. "And last I saw you, you had just turned sixteen. How old are *you* now?"

"Still sixteen." Cat nods slowly. "We're the same age."

The fact that I am now an equal with my older, wiser, daring cousin is not lost on me. My spine straightens with pride.

She blinks her eyes as if to clear away her thoughts, then grabs a thick tome and begins pacing the length of her room. "Since Reyna's all about the cryptic, I'm assuming she didn't give you an idea of how long you'll be here?"

"In a way," I answer with a shrug and wry grin. "It was Reyna, after all. She said that three signs would mark my journey—an angel speaking, a soft-rose songstress captivating, and life imitating art. When the third sign is revealed, she will return at sundown." Then my grin turns into a frown. Now that I am here, with my beloved cousin I have missed so much, I know that however many days fate has granted me, they will be over in the blink of an eye.

The matching frown on Cat's beautiful face tells me she is thinking the same. She forces a smile and says, "Okay, definitely in keeping with the cryptic, but I'd expect nothing less. By any chance, did she include a riddle-like message to go along with your gypsy adventure?"

Choosing to focus on the time that I will have with her instead of the heartache of leaving again, I nod, and then close my eyes to concentrate, wanting to ensure I repeat it verbatim. "She said, 'The adventure that you seek is full of possibilities, but always remember where your real strength lies.'" I open my eyes and grin again. "As cryptic messages go, I do believe that is a good one."

Undeterred by my wit, Cat chews her lip, deep in thought. "Well, the strength part at least is easy," she says with a wave of her hand. "That's acting. You rock at it, and there's no better place—except maybe New York—to explore it than Holly-wood." She plops down on her bed, bouncing as the temptingly supple mattress springs up underneath. "But possibilities…what could that mean?"

I lift my shoulder in response. Knowing she has more experience with gypsy riddles than I, I close the door and focus again on getting dressed. I toss my tunic on the ground and tug on my trousers. After a moment, I call out, "Cousin? I appear to have a bit of a problem."

"What kind of problem?" she asks, her voice muffled and distracted.

"A trouser problem. It seems they do not want to be

removed. I yank and yank, yet they refuse to budge."

Seriously, how maidens manage to get dressed alone with clothing such as this is beyond my comprehension. I shove my thumbs beneath the rough band at my waist and wrench.

A lengthy pause from my cousin, then, "Did you try unzipping them?"

"*Unzipping?*" I ask, not at all familiar with the word or the action.

"Yeah, with the zipper. The metal thingy with teeth?"

Wrinkling my nose, I take a look and indeed see a track of metal trailing down the front of my trousers. At the top is a little latch. As I grab it, I feel it sink lower. The pressure around my hips eases. I tug it back up and then down again. "A *zipper,* you say? Cat, I must tell you, the future is filled with interesting things."

She laughs.

After my zipper fun, I peel the trousers down my legs and step out of them, seizing the gown before I can catch another glimpse of my bare flesh in the mirrors. I slide my arms through the soft fabric and instantly feel at home.

When I open the door, Cat is where I left her, sitting tall on her mammoth bed. "I think I got it." With a victorious grin, she holds up a leather tome, the words *Roosevelt Academy* written on the cover. "Reyna said an adventure full of possibilities, right? That means options, choices, potential. Things you can't experience in the sixteenth century. And at our age, in the twenty-first, there's no better way for you to get all that than by enrolling in school."

I jerk my head back. "School? Do you mean to send me to

a convent?"

Cat scrunches her nose and blinks in succession. "No, not a convent, you beautiful weirdo. High school! With me. And it just so happens that the spring semester starts tomorrow, so it's perfect timing." She laughs. "Actually, that's probably not a coincidence, huh?"

My cousin appears positively giddy with her discovery, but apprehension begins to squirm and knot in my stomach. If today's jaunt to the theater was any indication, crowds from this time and I do not mix well. So I clear my throat and ask, "What precisely does one do at a high school? You should know that I have already learned my letters, music, and art, as well as how to dance and be festive. Truly, what else is there?"

"You mean besides boys?" She gifts me with a cheeky grin, and my jaw drops. It is not possible that boys and girls attend to their schooling together. Cat's grin grows wider as if she can read my thoughts. "Oh, my time-traveling chica, I have so much to teach you. And your first lesson, darling ancestor of mine, starts now. We need to work on how you talk."

Chapter Five

My jaw hangs agape. If she had suggested I prance around naked, I think I would be less shocked.

"The way I *talk*?" I ask. My cousin certainly never conformed the way *she* spoke when she was in *my* time. "Cat, are you implying it is *I* who needs to learn to speak properly? You—you who speak with half words and improper grammar? I will have you know—"

"Whoa." Cat throws up her hands to halt my outburst. "Chill, chica. I come in peace, I promise." The strange phrase diverts me, as was probably her intention. She smiles softly. "You're right, you do speak correctly. And personally, I love the way you talk—you're like my very own BBC special come to life. But see, that's my point. If you go to school tomorrow and talk like that, you're gonna be the only one…well, except for a couple stuffy English teachers. Those half words you say I use? They're called contractions, and that's the biggest thing you have to learn."

I wrinkle my nose. "Contractions?"

Sometimes it is as if Cat speaks her own language—beyond the English I can now somewhat comprehend. Listening to her talk has always been a touch unsettling, but back in my own time, I could brush off her nonsensical comments as mere rubbish. Here, in the future, where everyone I have encountered seems to utter the same words and phrases, it is a mindboggling struggle to feign understanding. It is as if there is English…and then another unique dialect, reserved solely for locals.

"It's a way to take two words and combine them so it's quicker and easier to get out." She shrugs. "What can I say? We're Americans; we're lazy. But no one goes around saying things like *cannot*, or *it is I*, or even *going to* anymore. We say *can't* and *I'm* and *gonna*."

While the concept of shortening words is nothing new, the general practice has never been encouraged, much less the expected norm. I roll my tongue around the word *gonna* and cringe.

Cat nods in approval, apparently having missed my distaste. "I'm jotting down a quick list of the most important stuff before my dad comes home. You can begin trying some of these out tomorrow, and then you'll have an entire weekend to learn them before Monday."

My gaze shifts to the writing on her lap where a thick line divides the writing on the page into two neat columns. At the sheer amount of blue ink on the page, my eyes grow wide.

Can language truly have changed that much?

My cousin glances up and, misunderstanding my shock,

rushes to reassure. "Less, I swear it's not that I want you to change or even think you need to. I think you're a bag of awesome just the way you are…but if you really want to fit in here, I'm just saying, you might wanna work on the speech a little."

I concede with a nod and plop onto the springy bed beside her. Tucking my legs under my gown, I eye the growing list in her hand. "I shall endeavor to learn these contractions before nightfall. Is there anything else?"

Cat chews on the tip of her pen and narrows her eyes in thought. "Well, we do need to work on getting you an acting gig. When Dad gets home, I'll see if he has any hookups with auditions. Judging by how long my time travel adventure was, I'm thinking something smaller. Maybe a commercial or walk-on part, at least to start with."

I circle my head in a nod, pretending to follow the jargon. "Will your father be angry that I am staying with you?" I pause and squint at the page, attempting to read upside down. "I mean, that *I'm* staying with you." Cat flashes me a grin in approval. "Will he not find it strange that a foreign exchange student is unexpectedly living in your home without prior warning?"

"Are you kidding?" She gives an exaggerated shake of her head and laughs. "Jenna's got him so twisted up with wedding plans he'll assume he just forgot. Honestly, the timing couldn't be better."

Cat turns again to her list, and I lean back onto my elbows. Despite her kind assurances, my stomach of butterflies remains in full flight. According to her, Mr. Crawford will arrive any minute expecting to pick up his daughter for a nice, quiet dinner, and instead will discover me—an extra mouth to feed and another woman he has to shelter and protect.

Could it really be as simple as my cousin believes? Will he just welcome a total stranger into his home and family?

To distract myself from thoughts of being turned away, or worse, becoming an inconvenience, I scan the expanse of Cat's walls and catch sight of a painting tucked to the side of her bed. I gasp as a feeling of home envelops me, and I lean closer, sure that my eyes are playing tricks.

The rushing waterfall. A woman wearing a crown of daises and white linen. The folds of the fabric draped around her slender body, gathered and dipped in such a way as to expose a mysterious pear tattoo on her hip.

"Lorenzo's painting," I whisper in awe.

Beside me, Cat stiffens. She swallows visibly and focuses on the faded masterpiece before us. "I found it...the day Reyna sent me back." A small smile plays upon her lips. "You don't even want to know how much buying this set my dad back—or the creative linguistic gymnastics I had to pull off to explain why the girl looks so much like me..." Her voice trails off then, and her gaze turns wistful.

Not wanting to open what I hope is a healing would, I temper my voice and say, "I remember when he completed it last year. A year after you left," I add, a gentle reminder of how long it has been. For her it has been but a mere handful of weeks, but for those of us she left behind, it has been considerably longer. "Lorenzo poured his entire heart and soul into that painting, Cat. He has never forgotten you."

Pain washes over her face, and her eyes close. After a

moment she whispers, "Me neither."

For someone who seldom enjoys sharing her emotions, Cat's are written all over her face. I turn away, disconcerted at the rare display, allowing my cousin her privacy.

The door to Cat's room vibrates, followed by a hollowed *thump* down the hall. A loud male voice calls out, "Peanut?"

Cat starts, as if coming out of a daze. "In here, Dad!" My hands fly to my hair, smoothing and flipping the loose strands, and she plasters a grin upon her face. Winking at my sudden wide-eyed panic, she shoves the tablet under her pillows. "Just showing my *roomie* her new digs!" Quieter, she says to me, "That should get his attention."

Sure enough, a tall man with dark blond hair and kind, quizzical brown eyes materializes at the bedroom door. "'Roomie'?"

Forcing my feet not to bolt in fear, I swallow down the lump of guilt for my part in the upcoming deception, for Cat does have a point. The truth is hard to believe. Plus, I have never been very good at denying my cousin anything.

"Yeah, you remember, don't you, Dad?" she asks, confusion wrinkling her brow. *And she says I am the actress?* "The semester foreign exchange program we signed up for? You said it'd be okay. I did forget to mention Alessandra was arriving today, though. I hope you don't mind."

To be honest, watching the deceit roll off her tongue so effortlessly is both awe-inspiring and a tad worrisome.

But Cat's father should be commended for his agreeable nature. His look of puzzlement deepens for a brief moment before smoothing out into a welcoming smile. "No, of course

I don't mind. Alessandra, is it?" I nod, and his smile broadens. "Glad to have you here. Where is it that you're from again?"

Oh, about five hundred years into the past. "Florence, Italy, sir."

His mouth opens in surprise. "Is that right? Did Cat tell you we recently returned home from a visit to Florence? Beautiful city. What an amazing coincidence."

Coincidence indeed.

I nod in response, biting my lip, not wanting to ruin the ruse for my cousin. I have never been proficient at maintaining falsehoods. Cipriano stopped telling me about his illicit exploits long ago in well-deserved fear I would let something slip to our parents.

Mr. Crawford claps his hands and rubs them together. "Well, I planned to take my daughter for a dinner date with her dear old dad, but I'd love to have you join us. I take it Italian's okay?"

. . .

My cousin's gentle snores keep me company as I again pore over the notepad she gave me after dinner. What started as a series of contractions became a growing list of unique words and phrases, some I have—*I've*—heard her use, and others completely original. For instance, the phrase *oh em gee*. Or the words *dude, douche bag, peeps, duh,* and *legit.* Under "technology," she has *iPad, iPhone, texting,* and *YouTube.*

And then there are entries like *tool* and *sick* and *hot*, which all seem clear enough, but their inclusion implies they must have a double meaning I *don't* grasp.

In truth, Cat should have included definitions.

As if this daunting list were not enough, my mind is still reeling from dinner. After the nice man delivered a free basket of bread to our table, Cat snatched one and then went straight to asking her father about upcoming auditions. My hand froze mid-reach.

Mr. Crawford put down his menu and pursed his lips in thought. "Marilyn Kent recently took over leadership for this year's weekend winter workshop at The Playhouse. Lending her name added a lot of buzz, and a lot of bigger names are expressing interest," he told us, dunking his bread stick in the delicious marinara.

Again, I had to feign complete understanding, this time over what a buzzing bee had to do with anything. I wiped my hands on a napkin and took a sip of safe, clean, non-contaminated water. *Amazing.*

Mr. Crawford swallowed and continued. "From what I hear, a ton of on-the-cusp actors and B-list stars are flocking to be attached, and auditions already started, but I'll make a call in the morning and see what I can do." He grinned and tweaked Cat's ear. "If I can't use nepotism on my own kid, I may as well use it on my temporary one."

The easy affection between them and his willingness to include me made my heart hurt a little, but in a good way. I may be away from my parents and brother, but I *am* with family.

Then he looked at me and lowered his eyes, wincing. "It'd probably be a minor role at best, though. The workshop is a series of snippets from Shakespeare's plays, so there won't be an obvious breakout role or anything."

I wrinkled my nose, wondering if I should know who *Shakespeare* is, and Cat jumped in. "Hmm, a late sixteenth-century playwright who loved flowery words and old-world formalese. I think my girl Less can handle that."

Mr. Crawford picked up his menu, oblivious to Cat's double meaning, and we shared a grin. I remained hopeful and eager throughout dinner about the opportunity, but when we returned home and Cat handed me a few volumes of Shakespeare's work, apprehension set in.

So here I lie, tucked under Cat's coverlet with a helpful *flashlight*, interchangeably obsessing over my need to learn modern jargon to fit in at the high school and poring over Shakespeare's plays—which actually make much more sense than Cat's list of gibberish—so I can excel at my upcoming audition. I blink my heavy eyelids in an attempt to stop the words from swimming on the page, and fight to open them again.

Perhaps I will just rest them for a moment.

In the dark, behind my veiled eyes, the maze of confusing words part to make way for a tall young man with dark hair. The features of his face are hazy, but his clothing is quite clear—dark pants I now know are *jeans* and a tight black shirt.

It's the boy from the second part of my vision with Reyna.

Though I do not know who he is, it is as if my soul does. All my tightly contained disquiet dissipates, and in its place, peace… and a delicious warmth in my belly.

Clinging to those feelings and my vision of the boy for as long as I can, I surrender to the wave of serenity and drift to sleep.

Chapter Six

Cat hands me a large bowl of multicolored circles drenched in milk and grins over a spoon. "So did you enjoy your marathon shower, Ms. Time-Traveler?"

I bite my lip and cast my eyes to the table. "My apologies, dear cousin. I *couldn't* seem to help myself."

Even my correct contraction usage cannot stir me to look up.

Truly, out of all the modern inventions I have encountered thus far and wish I could bring back with me, the glass box *shower* is my favorite—even better than the marvelous *toilet*. Inside the stall, wonderful warm water flows from a silver spigot, like a waterfall bending at my will. After staying up late and waking early this morning so I could study the seemingly endless list of words, the temptation to luxuriate under the spray was just too great.

Unfortunately, my cousin failed to mention the limited

supply of warm water.

Wincing, I lift my head. "Is your father quite angry with my tarrying?"

Cat closes her mouth around a heaping spoon of cereal, and the harsh sound of crunching fills the air. She swallows and says, "Nah, Dad's a guy. He can hop in and out in less than a nanosec, whereas I, on the other hand, got to experience the joy of shaving my legs with goose bumps." She winks. "Lucky for you, I still love ya. Now eat up. We gotta leave in five minutes if we want to sign you in before first period."

My stomach knots up, and I push my bowl of untouched breakfast away. Cat reaches over to clasp my hand. "Less, you're gonna be great. Just think of it as a performance—one big acting gig. If it's stressing you out, forget everything I said last night. You're gonna do great."

I grin at the encouragement, but then bite my lip. "And if I mess up?"

"It doesn't matter. Today is just the first day back, and it's a Friday. I bet half the school won't even show up, and the other half will probably forget anything that happens over the weekend, anyway. So don't worry about it. Just go in there and have fun." She pumps my hand. "And if anyone messes with you, you let me know, all right?"

Her gaze narrows, as if she's already mentally berating invented hecklers, and I cannot help but smile. *Signore be with anyone who dares ridicule me today.*

Cat leans in and waves me closer, as if she wishes to impart a secret. "A very wise woman once said that no one can make you feel inferior without your consent. That's my motto, and it's gonna be yours now, too. I want you to walk into that school today with your head held high, ready to soak up every memory and experience you possibly can, okay?"

My cousin's impassioned words of inspiration, though a little shocking, achieve their purpose. They embolden me, add a touch of fire to my veins and steel to my spine, and remind me *this* is why Reyna sent me here. *This* is what I need—room to breathe again, a moment in time where I can live and search for more, and the grace to make many mistakes as I do all of the above.

I can do this.

I look at Cat again and with conviction say, "*I'm* ready."

. . .

High school is nothing like I imagined. In fact, it is like nothing I could have even dreamed. I had thought the theater where I arrived was chaotic, but *this?* This is mass hysteria.

Boys and girls loiter together in the halls, all without chaperones. Several couples openly engage in scandalous embraces, and exposed skin is everywhere. Odd-shaped brown balls are lobbed from one end to another while all manner of talking, singing, and screaming echoes off the line of metal cages Cat calls *lockers*. A distinctly strong medicinal smell permeates the air, along with a host of other scents pouring off passing bodies, and as my nose twitches, I fight the intense urge to sneeze and run back to the relative safety of Cat's bedroom.

Having successfully registered, a feat made easier by a copy of a birth certificate and foreign exchange paperwork that *magically* appeared in my school file, I now clutch my new schedule firmly in my hands as I follow my cousin through the constant stream of moving bodies. A piercing *ring* erupts overhead, and I jump at the fresh sensory onslaught.

I shall *not* miss the terrifying noises when I return to my time.

"That's the bell," Cat tells me over her shoulder, winding her way through the labyrinth-like jumble of fellow scholars. "Which means we gotta book it."

Book it. This expression was not included in Cat's list, nor was it one of the double meaning selections she explained in detail this morning. Yet somehow I know that she does not mean we must act like the notebooks contained within the satchel on my shoulder. However, what she *does* mean remains a mystery. I expel an exasperated breath.

Cat twists around, laughs, and hooks her arm through mine. "Book it, as in move it, as in hustle." She shoots me an amused look as she pulls me forward. "As in we must make *haste.*"

Ah, a word I comprehend. I laugh and increase my speed to match my cousin's frantic pace, shouldering my way through the crowd, too, and trying not to notice the appraising looks from both the male and female students. I bunch the brocade fabric of Cat's long skirt in my hand and sink lower into my borrowed knit cardigan.

Breathe, Alessandra. Just breathe.

Being the youngest in the family—and a girl—I have never been the center of attention. Perhaps that is why I love the theater. But onstage, performers are watched for their characters, the roles they are playing...not because they so obviously fail to fit in.

I glance back, unable to help myself, and end up plowing into my cousin, who has stopped outside an open door. She grabs my shoulders to steady us both, then nods to the room. "American government," she says. "I wish we had more classes together, but like I said, you're gonna be fine. Just—"

She breaks off and jolts me back as a massive boy pushes through the door. I freeze in place, letting more of the crowd flow past me as Cat mutters a few unladylike words under her breath. Despite the blanket of tension, I grin.

Staring intensely at the back of his retreating shaved head, she continues. "As I was *saying*, just remember what I told you. Sit in the back, slink down in your seat, and don't make eye contact with the teacher. It'll be a piece of cake."

Even with the unexplained food reference, I detect the false confidence in her voice.

I take a deep breath, and in the quiet absence of my pounding heart, I realize the boisterous hall has hushed. When I turn, I find it practically empty.

This is it. The moment Reyna may or may not have sent me here to experience—an adventure full of possibilities.

Concentrating on not fainting, I take a shaky step toward the daunting classroom. "I-I shall meet you after?"

"I'll be right here waiting the second you get out."

With a nod, I straighten my shoulders and then bound through the door before I can change my mind. Behind me, Cat calls out, "Good luck," but I do not turn. I *can't*. I place one foot in front of the other, feeling every gaze following my movements but refusing to look up, and make my way to the back of the room. Drying my wet hands on the folds of my skirt,

I slide into a vacant seat.

I shall not faint, I shall not faint.

I chance a glance up and see more than a dozen pairs of eyes glued to my person.

Or perchance I shall.

Luckily, a young woman chooses that moment to stride purposefully across the front of the room, and I focus on her instead. Small wire spectacles frame her intelligent golden eyes. Although she appears to be not much older than I am, she holds herself with unparalleled grace and poise. My tension ever so slowly sinks from my shoulders.

Then her perceptive gaze travels over the students assembled, hesitating and stopping to rest on me. Terror fills me anew. My cousin warned that I could be called on to introduce myself, and I hastily try to remember the intricate story we created last night.

My mind goes blank.

I wet my lips, knowing it had something to do with being an exchange student, but for the life of me, I'm unable to recall any of the specifics, when the instructor blessedly nods, a small smile playing on her lips, and continues her appraisal of the class.

I cannot—*can't*—contain my sigh of relief.

This may not be so bad, after all.

She concludes her survey of the room and sashays over to close the door. Upon her return to the desk, she leans a hip against it, eyes alight with amusement. "Good morning, everyone. And welcome back. My name is Miss Edwards. Your former teacher, Mrs. Spano, is on maternity leave, and I'm happy to be taking over her classes for a few months. I trust you are all eager to dive right in. This semester—"

A young man bursts through the doorway, stealing the rest of her words…and the collective air from the room.

With nary a care for disrupting the instructor's lesson, he tromps in, his heavy boots thumping against the tile. He lifts a chiseled chin in prolonged greeting as he crosses the room, and I find that I am unable to drag my gaze away.

Our young instructor folds her arms, and the boy brushes past, barely managing to avoid whacking her with his tattered green pack. He pauses to select and then maneuver down the long aisle beside mine. He has yet to look at me, but as he draws nearer to where I sit, I feel my pulse rate increase in tempo, contrasting with his controlled, leisurely stride. And when he comes to a full stop at the empty chair to my left, my breathing outright stalls.

My skin feels flushed and tight, my mouth parched. Restlessness stirs within, and I find it difficult to remain still.

I have no idea what is happening or why, only that every sense I have seems to be attuned to this beautiful boy. And he has yet to even acknowledge my existence!

Look up, I silently plead, sneaking glances at him through wisps of my hair. *Notice me.*

He plops his pack on the ground, and a stripe of something blue tumbles out the open flap. I lower my gaze to a messy writing pad littered with haphazard papers shoved inside, the name *Austin* spelled out in bold black writing on the cover.

Austin. A derivative form of Augustine, yet the boy before me bears no resemblance to the great saint and man of faith. If anything, he resembles one of Lucifer's tempting, sinful brethren with his disheveled raven hair and mischievous, beguiling eyes.

Austin folds his long legs under the desk and leans back to slide his hand into the pocket of his dark jeans. He withdraws a pair of earbuds, much like the ones Cat brought during her time-travel stay, and soon the faint sound of music floats in the air.

Our instructor calls out, "That was quite the entrance, Mister…." She pauses and stares at the boy beside me.

"Michaels."

She consults a paper on her desk and nods. "Oh, yes, Mr. Michaels," she says, not sounding at all impressed—or surprised. "Well, I'm Miss Edwards. Maybe the next time you join our class, you can add prerecorded fanfare to spice things up." Austin lifts two fingers to his forehead in a mock-salute, and she sighs. "Now, back to American government…"

She turns to the large whiteboard behind her and begins writing. Austin places the buds in his ears, bobbing his head to the beat, completely ignoring her…*and* me. I slump farther down into my seat.

I try to tell myself it *doesn't* matter, that I do not want attention from someone who feels the need to be so disruptive, regardless of how beautiful he is—but I *don't* believe myself. Pushing thoughts of my rude neighbor away, I try to focus on foreign words like *electoral college* and *congressional district,* anything other than the frustratingly rude boy beside me, but my gaze keeps flitting back. His bouncing knee rattles the desk, dragging the metal feet along the hard tile, and the pen in his hand taps rhythmically to the music seeping from his ears.

How can anyone concentrate with such boorish behavior around?

Indignation on behalf of my instructor—and all right, perhaps a bit over my bruised pride for failing to elicit even a neighborly smile—churns inside me. A mixture of heat and odd tingles flows up and down my arms and legs, and I clench my hands into fists.

Tap, tap, tap-tap. Tap, tap, tap-tap.

The skin on my scalp itches and I shove a section of hair behind my ear. A girl in front of him turns, and a grin stretches across my face. Good, she is annoyed, too. *She'll* tell him to be quiet, give a scathing remark like Cat is always able to deliver, and he will be thoroughly chastened.

Righteous triumph builds in my chest as I lean closer to hear.

She bites her lower lip and rolls her eyes—but not in a mean way. She does it playfully, with a smile, as though Austin is an adorable pup or childish imp. Austin lifts his chin, tossing the girl an impudent wink and saucy grin.

And *that* is when I snap.

Before my movement registers in my brain, my hand is across the aisle, snatching his pen from his tight grip and flinging it across the room. My elbow accidently hits the book on his desk and sends it clattering, loudly, to the ground.

Now I have his attention.

Austin finally turns to me, treating me to the slow once-over he just gave the girl in front of him. She turns, too, curling her lip as if she has discovered something disgusting on the bottom of her shoe. My skin burns under their joint scrutiny.

"Problem, Princess?"

I jerk my head back, eyes wide. Not so much at Austin's words, though I can tell he does not mean the term affectionately, but the way he delivers them—scornfully, tauntingly.

"Me?" I squeak in protest. On some level, I realize the room is strangely quiet, but I have yet to gather why. My faculties are wholly consumed with the infuriating individual before me. "*I'm* not the one causing the problem!"

My voice echoes off the tile below our feet. Austin lifts a dark brow…and suddenly, I realize that I am.

Panic sears my cheeks as I look around and notice all prior conversation, even the young instructor's lecture, has halted.

The girl in front of Austin purses her lips in a cruel sort of grin, and I see the instructor watching me, waves of disappointment pouring off her. Every eye in the room is turned in our direction, which for some reason ultimately prompts Austin to give me my coveted grin.

My mouth goes dry.

I have never—*never*—held myself with anything other than complete decorum, public or otherwise, yet spending less than five minutes in Austin Michaels's presence has led to complete and utter depravity.

"I-*I'm* s-so very—" I begin, only to feel Austin's warm hand close around mine.

"My fault, Miss E. Pen slipped." He looks to the floor and grins. "Book, too."

Miss E's dark brow hitches heavenward as she studies us. After what feels like an eternity she says, "While I have no doubt that you somehow share the blame, Mr. Michaels, I will still need to see the both of you after class."

All I can do is nod, my cheeks and neck burning in humiliation. The fight, my anger, and all perplexing bodily reactions have left me. In their place remains nothing but a surreal feeling of disbelief. Miss Edwards sighs, and the class continues.

"That's some sexy accent you have there," Austin says in a hushed voice—but not *that* hushed. A few people around us snicker at my evident discomfort, which of course only serves to spur him on more. "Italian, right? Mmm. Say something else— how do you say *blush* in Italian?"

When I ignore him, he says, "You sure do have that rosy glow going on. Normally I have to work harder to inspire something like that. Like what you see, *Princess*?"

"D-don't call me that," I stammer, blushing all the more from his brazen question. "And I do *not* blush."

That earns me my wink. "Sure you don't."

Austin looks to the front of the room, and I follow his gaze. The teacher has her back turned, drawing what appears to be a map of sorts on the whiteboard. My eyes flick to the large clock mounted on the wall. Class is nearly over, and I have managed to follow exactly nothing of the lecture.

Alas, my experience thus far as a modern-day student has not been exemplary.

Though I do not wish Austin to know the effect he has on me, I cannot keep my eyes from snapping back. And when I do, I find him practically in my seat. His long torso is stretched across the aisle, and his face is ever so close. Warm breath fans across my cheeks, and I catch the scent of mint. Soulful blue eyes drill into mine as he dares to touch a lock of my hair, twisting it around one long, tanned finger. My heart pounds at his blatant familiarity.

This must be what rage feels like.

Under his breath, Austin says, "It's too bad that wasn't a blush. I thought it was kinda hot."

A shocked puff of air and saucer-like eyes are my only response—having learned from Cat's list of words the double meaning of the word *hot*—and the left side of Austin's mouth lifts in a smile of victory. He settles back in his own seat and reinserts his earbuds. The pen tapping begins again, only this time louder and with more force.

I raise my chin and stare straight ahead, vowing to keep my eyes from straying to the ill-mannered *jerk* beside me for the rest of class. I count the seconds in time with his taps.

I do believe I hate Austin Michaels.

Chapter Seven

The bell rings, and I longingly watch the rest of my classmates file from the room, inexplicably eager to sit for another hour in an uncomfortable chair surrounded by insufferable boys such as the one beside me. The main door opens again, and I meet my cousin's eye. Cat checks the watch I complimented her on this morning and mouths the words *let's go,* but I shake my head. I cannot leave—though nothing would make me happier— thanks in large part to the embodiment of evil who has joined me in front of the instructor's desk looking annoyingly unaffected and quite honestly, *bored.*

Is it possible he genuinely does not care about being in trouble?

Miss Edwards finishes scribbling a note and flicks her amber gaze up at the two of us. A sense of familiarity washes over me, but then she says in a clearly frustrated tone, "You know, I had hoped my first class would go a tad more smoothly."

Distressed, I shove my hair out from behind my ear in an attempt to shield my face. I lower my lashes and see Austin shuffling his feet.

Hmm, perhaps he is nervous.

When I lift my head, Austin is watching me, a strange, almost soft look in his eyes. It does even stranger things to my stomach.

Austin holds my gaze for a long moment before turning to our teacher. "Look, Miss E., it really was my fault. I was just messing with the new kid." He tosses her an impish grin. "Didn't Mrs. Spano clue you in on how exasperating I can be?"

More shocking than him taking the full blame for the incident is him taking any of it. For the last forty-odd minutes, I have rehashed and relived every horrifying moment, coming to the sad conclusion that the disruption was entirely my doing. No one else seemed disturbed by Austin's boorish actions, nor did anyone else feel the need to fling his pen across the room. That was all me. But it does not mean I plan to hinder his surprising act of gallantry now.

Chivalry may not be dead in this era, after all.

Austin's long lashes sweep across his cheekbones, and I turn to our young instructor, wondering if his bewitching magic can work on her as well. She tilts her head to the side and purses her lips, then slides her gaze to me. "Miss Forlani?"

Wrinkling my nose, I stare at her blankly, knowing the name sounds familiar but unable to place it. She consults a sheet of paper on her desk with a raised eyebrow. "You are Alessandra Forlani, correct?"

Fiddlesticks.

"Oh, yes! That is me—Alessandra Forlani." I bob a curtsy, and two different sets of eyes narrow in my direction.

Oops.

Flustered and fervently wishing my cousin could send me just a dash of her confidence and possibly a few words from her quick tongue, I push on. "I—I recently transferred here. From Florence. And I'm staying with the Crawford family. Beautiful family, really, and their home is quite splendid, filled with such enchanting things I never would have thought possible. It is amazing—"

I cut off here, realizing my rambling is only causing more harm. At least I did squeak in a contraction.

Miss Edwards squints at me long enough for my heart to threaten to stop beating altogether, but then the lines on her forehead smooth out, and she nods. Austin, however, turns his torso more toward me, continuing his quiet scrutiny with clear, shrewd eyes.

If he had but devoted such attention to the lecture, perchance we would not be in this predicament.

Trying my best to ignore him, I go to shove my hair from behind my ear and notice it already is. Instead, I brush it behind my shoulder, then fidget with the folds in my skirt.

"Wow, Florence," Miss Edwards says, studying me with impressed focus. "Glad to hear you're settling in. I hope you'll like it here, though I can imagine it's a big change."

Feeling Austin's perceptive gaze still on me, I offer a small smile, trying not to convey just how big a change it truly is.

The instructor sighs. Sliding her glasses off with one hand, she pinches the bridge of her nose with the other and says,

"Alessandra, it's like this. It's the beginning of a new semester — and for you, a new experience in a new country. I don't know if Austin just has a unique talent for challenging patience, or if things were different in your old school, but I can't have interruptions like that in my class. And—" She lifts a hand at Austin. "Before you argue, Mr. Michaels, I'm not only talking about the pen and the book. There was palpable tension radiating from the pair of you for the remainder of the hour, distracting the students around you and, quite frankly, *me*."

She shuffles through a stack of papers on her desk, obviously searching for something, and I meet Austin's eyes, knowing my own are filled with panic. His lips twitch into a semblance of a smile at the same time his bright blue eyes seem to say, *it will be all right*. And for some reason, my frantic pulse eases.

Then the instructor speaks again.

"It's no secret that this is my first teaching job, and I would like to begin it on a good note. A mentor advised during my student teaching that when two people clash as quickly and strongly as the two of you, there are a couple options I can take to ensure incidents like this don't happen again: I can either separate you or force you to work together."

The hint of reassurance in Austin's intense gaze vanishes as he laughs. "And when you say student teaching, do you really mean kindergarten?"

Although that particular word was not included in Cat's teenspeak list, I can decipher from the condescension in his tone and the tensing of Miss Edwards's fingers that Austin's comment was not at all helpful.

"Make all the jokes you want, Mr. Michaels, but I believe I'm here to do more than teach government. I didn't become a teacher to just open a text book and regurgitate information about a subject that you, of all people, already know so much about."

A muscle in his jaw clenches and his gaze sharpens. They share a brief, mysterious look. I glance back and forth between them, frowning, knowing I am missing something important, and wishing I had paid better attention to the lecture.

What could Austin know so much about?

"I think I'm also here to teach life skills," she continues. "To get you ready for college and life in the great beyond. So, knowing that, I've decided to go with the latter kindergarten principle. Here's your first lesson."

She holds out a paper, which Austin makes no move to take. Reluctantly, I grab the sheet, noting *Modern-Day Leadership* written in bold letters at the top...a subject I know *nothing* about.

"As of now, the two of you are partners for our first class project. Congratulations! All the particulars are included on the sheet, it is due in two weeks, and you're more than welcome to come to me—together as a team—with any questions before then. With an entire weekend stretching before you, may I suggest you get a head start?"

I blink and Austin rubs the back of his neck. Behind us, a stream of students pours through the open door, preparing for the next class, and I catch sight of Cat standing just outside, looking rather impatient. If we do not leave now, we will both be late for our next class. I swallow and grasp the paper tighter.

"Thank you, ma'am. I shall look forward to completing the assignment."

Austin chokes on a laugh, and I shoot him a look of death. His presumed humor is decidedly *not* advantageous.

Miss Edwards nods her dismissal, and Austin follows me through the door. Leaning close to my ear as we enter the hallway, he says, "Looks like you got some work to do."

I freeze mid-step, causing a dainty girl looking even more lost than I am to ram into me. Without even stopping to hear my apology, she weaves around us and breaks into a sprint. I take a breath and twirl to face my new nemesis.

"*I* have work to do?" I shake the paper in my hand, unable to believe that he intends to leave me—someone not even from this time—in charge of our shared project on twenty-first-century government! "I do believe you mean *we.*"

Cat stands to the side of us, watching with unabashed interest.

Austin rakes a hand through his already disheveled hair and says simply, "Yeah, I don't really do the whole school thing. But hey, good luck with that."

And with those parting words, he spins on his heel. Instantly the frenzied crowd swallows him whole, leaving me gaping in the eye of the storm as harried classmates rush past down the hall.

Well, so much for chivalry.

My skin prickles with righteous ire, and I draw in a ragged breath. Staring at my cousin, and then at the empty space Austin inhabited just moments before, I say, "Have you *ever* met anyone so rude...so infuriating...so completely... Oof!"

Evidently, simple words will not do him or this situation full justice. So instead, I shake my head and tighten my fists. "Can you *believe* him?"

Cat clamps her lips together. If I did not know better, I would swear she was stifling a laugh. "Honestly? No. I can't believe Mr. Laidback and Never Shows Up actually made it to class, much less provoked you in the hallway. I also can't believe he got my straitlaced, proper cousin all tongue-tied and crazy."

On instinct, I open my mouth to defend myself, but after a moment's hesitation, close it again. As much as I would adore denying my cousin's accusation, I cannot. This only serves to make me seethe even more.

So it would seem that, along with inducing depravity in an otherwise respectable female, Austin Michaels can also add erasing my ability to speak properly to his irritating list of inherent powers.

Cat shakes her head and tugs me onward. "You know, as much as I'd love to hear what it is he did to get you all riled up, your next class starts in, like..." She widens her eyes at her watch, then picks up her pace to a slow sprint. "*Crap*, in a minute. But don't think you're off the hook. At lunch, you are totally spilling how all *that* just happened."

I trudge along behind my cousin and think, *If I am able to make it that long.*

Yet somehow, by the grace of Signore, the stars above, or more likely, the lack of Austin in my next two classes, I get through the rest of my morning. Biology proves surprisingly interesting, though I overhear rumblings of an upcoming fetal pig dissection and take a moment to pray it occurs *after*

Reyna returns me to my own time, and then comes British literature—a subject that primarily discusses works created after my time, but I am still able to semi-follow. But through it all, my mind keeps flashing back to American government…or more specifically, to a particular insufferable classmate.

The bell rings again.

I gather my notebook and pen, place them inside my satchel, and follow the line of eager students fleeing through the door. The moment I step out into the cluttered chaos of the hall, Cat materializes near my elbow. "Spill it."

It takes the entire journey to our midday meal, down the stairs and outside the building, sidestepping gossiping students, for me to share the sordid story of my first high school experience. Pausing outside the large double doors to the cafeteria, I catch a whiff of something delicious. My stomach rumbles. From the corner of my eye I see my cousin's lips twitch at my tale, and with a huff, I say, "The rest you witnessed yourself in the hallway."

Cat nods. Her lips twitch again, and in an obvious attempt to transform her amusement into sympathy, she places a hand on my shoulder. "Wow." She clears her throat. "That was… wow."

She clamps her lips around her teeth, but unfortunately the gesture does nothing to stop the laughter shining in her big brown eyes. I sigh the sigh of the weary and grin despite my embarrassment. I guess the situation *is* rather amusing in retrospect.

Cat's dazzling smile bursts through her composure in answer to my own. "Now *that's* what I call a first impression."

Shaking my head, I strive for the positive. "At least it cannot be said that I am forgettable."

"Nope, you're definitely not that."

She laughs, then tugs open the doors, enveloping us both in an intense wall of sound. I widen my eyes and take a hesitant step inside, openly gawking.

The chaotic maze of hallways has nothing on this room. Bright multicolored papers litter the walls. Undistinguishable foul scents mingle with mouth-watering temptation. Loud music meets a cacophony of yelling, laughter, and utensils clanking, all melding into one elongated roar.

Lining the periphery of the space are various food stations, each boasting their own delectable choices, and each wafting a unique, overpowering aroma. Rows of students stand before them, choosing items before shuffling away laden with trays to the eating area in the center. Here, tables and chairs are squished together for seating, but apparently also for leaning, standing, and in one odd case (and what should be impossible, considering the noise level), napping.

Squeezing my throbbing temples between my hands, I ask, "Where does one even begin in this bedlam? How do you even *think*, much less choose what to eat or where to sit?"

"Well, I usually just follow my nose, or when I'm lazy, the shortest line," Cat replies, leading me to a station labeled *Panini*. "In this case, the line is both short and the choice particularly yummy. Now, as for where to sit, *normal* people clump together in their group of status."

Selecting a Sicilian panini from the menu, a fun nod to my homeland, I wrinkle my nose at her word choice. Cat sees my confusion and explains. "I don't really have a group…or a social status…or even many friends." She pins me with a look. "Mama Dearest—aka Caterina Angeli, the vixen of Hollywood, and the reigning queen of tabloids everywhere—pretty much kept me friendless until my little time travel escapade. When I got back, I started hanging out with this girl Hayley, but she eats during the second lunch period. So peeps like me kinda just float wherever the spirit moves us. And today, it's leading me over there." She points her elbow to a semi-empty table toward the back.

As we maneuver through the confined aisles, I try to process this latest piece of information. I have always envisioned my lively cousin at the center of every room, every party, every possible social sphere. The fact that she is without a large group of peers is astonishing. And yet another modern American occurrence I cannot fathom.

Cat plops her tray onto the table, and I take a seat across from her, cringing as my feet stick to the floor.

"So back to Austin," she says, shaking her carton of orange juice. "I don't know what to tell ya. I mean, sure, the guy's great for a laugh, and he occasionally shocks everyone with a semicoherent thought—when he bothers to even show up—but, dude, I can't imagine having to work with him."

She punctures the top of her carton with a straw and slurps loudly. I take a sip of my lovely water loaded with ice and agree with her assessment. I cannot imagine working with Austin, either. If this morning was any indication, prolonged exposure in each other's company will only lead to inappropriate flirtation, the inability to speak or hold my temper, and most likely, a severe headache.

I take a bite of my panini. Marvelous gooey, cheesy flavor explodes in my mouth. Cat laughs. "Good, huh?"

I nod and take another bite, my eyes rolling back in bliss. They flutter open and land on a group of boys gathering at the table behind Cat. They are all wearing matching shirts with their names written above a bright red number. I am unsure if their clothing marks them as uniformed guards or a band of students unable to remember their own names, but I am fascinated, staring at the writing and dreaming up possible meanings. A boy with the name *Daniels* written above the number thirty-two slaps the boy beside him on the back, jostling him forward, and I catch a flash of blond curls at the table beyond.

An eerie feeling crawls in my chest.

Bobbing and weaving my head around so I can see past the boy's massive arm, I struggle to get another glimpse.

"Less?"

Can it be possible?

A hand waves in front of my eyes, and I crane my neck, knowing it cannot be him, but excitement spurs me on nevertheless.

"Earth to Less, come in, Less."

A faint, familiar rumbling laugh reaches my ears. Cat tenses across from me, then twists her head. The boys take their seats, my line of vision clears, and I gasp.

Lorenzo.

Confusion colors my world. Cat turns back to face me, and I stammer, "H-how is he here?"

She gives me a wobbly smile. "Less, that's not Lorenzo. It's Lucas."

"Lucas?" I shake my head.

"Lucas *Cappelli*, to be precise. Apparently Lorenzo is Lucas's ancestor." Cat's voice wobbles, and she looks down at her hands. "Freaky, ain't it?"

I turn back to the boy who could be Lorenzo's twin and nod. "The word *freaky* seems to fit the situation amazingly well."

Lucas is two tables away, but even so, I can clearly distinguish his dark brown eyes, curly golden locks, and the dimple slicing through the bronze skin of his cheek.

Across from me, Cat pulls apart her sandwich, shredding the crispy bread into minuscule pieces. The slight tremor of her hands and the unnecessary mutilation of her food are the sole indicators that she is upset—otherwise her countenance remains as cool and collected as ever.

Unsure if I should pry or leave it be, I take a bite of my still intact panini and wait.

I do not have to do so for long.

"I met him at my sweet sixteen a few weeks ago." She glances up, and I am struck by the vulnerability in her gaze. My cousin is *never* vulnerable. "He's a junior, a year older than us. His family just moved back here from Milan, and Jenna's planning his sister's party." She pauses. "Angela's sweet. You'd like her."

She stares intently at her tray, and I do not rush in to fill the silence. I do not ask what happened at the party or any day since. Instead, I watch her lick her lips and crack her knuckles.

Though I want to scream for her to finish her tale, I want her to *want* to tell me.

Finally, Cat breaks the silence. "We danced…"

My stomach turns, remembering another dance, one I witnessed her sharing with Lorenzo. Cat's ball was magical for many reasons, but seeing the way they looked at each other that night changed something inside me. I have always wondered what it would be like to be on the receiving end of such adoration.

Cat drops her head and scratches her neck, using the action to steal a subtle glance at Lucas's table. Lowering her voice to a whisper, she says, "And now, it's like he's everywhere. I can't escape him, Less, and believe me, I've tried. I even went to my nana's house in Mississippi for Christmas break, but distance doesn't stop him from texting or calling."

A stunning blonde in a short skirt bounces up behind Lucas and brazenly wraps her arms around his neck. I hear my cousin's sharp inhalation as the girl leans in to whisper in his ear, blocking Lucas's face from our view. Cat emits a close impersonation of a growl.

Though I feel fiercely disloyal to my friend back home for doing so, I have to ask. "Cousin, perhaps this is another cultural thing I do not understand, but why are you so desperate to avoid him?"

Cat slaps the table in clear frustration. "Everything's just so confusing. I mean, he looks like Lorenzo, but he isn't. And I get that I'm never gonna actually *see* Lorenzo again, but it doesn't make it hurt any less, you know?"

She shoves both hands through her hair, and I nod in encouragement, because I do understand.

But then she says, "I have to tell you, though…there's a part of me that wonders if Lucas being here, looking so much like Lorenzo, if it's like a cosmic sign from Reyna, telling me I need to move on. That it's okay. That it's not horrible to like him and I should go for it. But then, I don't know." She laughs humorlessly. "Maybe it *is* just a random, crazy fluke. And I'm just pathetically fickle."

Her eyes are dark brown pools of self-condemnation and confusion, imploring me to give her an answer I simply do not have. So I shrug, as clueless about gypsy magic as she is, even as I wish I could do so much more.

At the back table, the blonde raises her head and says, "Oh, Lucas," giggling in such a way that manages to sound girlish and incredibly annoying at the same time. Cat grits her teeth, intentionally avoiding the scene behind her. "Plus, all of it…it just feels wrong, you know?"

I push my tray away, no longer having any interest in food, cheese-filled or not. "What feels wrong?"

"You know." She swallows. "Having feelings for someone else. At the party, when Lucas asked me to dance, I honestly didn't see the harm—it would've been rude to say no, and it was a chance to kind of relive my dance with Lorenzo at the ball. But it ended up being more than that. And then it got weird." She bites her lip and squints at me. "There was…a connection."

I cannot help it; I flinch.

Cat hangs her head. "I know! After an entire month of not being able to think about anyone else but Lorenzo, all Lucas had to do was slide his arms around me on the dance floor and my insides melted like in a freaking romance novel."

Shoving her own plate away, she bangs her head onto the table in an obvious display of berating herself. My heart feels torn. I so badly want to ease her distress, to pat her shoulder and say everything will be okay. But my hand hesitates midair.

Since Cat transported through time, Lorenzo has been my only real friend. Granted, he was and will always be more my brother's friend than my own, but he has looked out for me, protected me. And I know he would be devastated to know another man was trying to steal Cat's heart—much less someone who looks so much like himself.

But Cat is my family.

I stare at her long brown hair for a beat and then place my hand on her shoulder.

From the table behind us, a bubbly giggle breaks out. Cat twists around in time to see the blonde practically throw herself into Lucas's lap.

"And that would be Desiree. It took her long enough to find the fresh meat. School started what, a whole three hours ago?"

My cousin shakes her head in disgust and turns back to me. "Here I am all conflicted on what I should do while there're girls like her around, more than willing to introduce him to American ways. And I swear, it's like he's everywhere. I can't even get a moment to think, to process, without turning around and finding him behind me. Lucas is even in my art class, my sanctuary, of all places. And of course he's awesome, which means we have that in common, too. You should've heard Mr. Scott going on and on about how impressive Lucas's technique was and his stupid use of negative space."

She plucks the straw from her carton and attempts to snap it. When it refuses to break, she tosses it down the table. "If the boy's not teaching the class by the end of the year, it'll be a freaking miracle."

I study my lap to hide my smile. Not at the situation, but at my cousin's surprising reaction.

Never have I seen Cat show such straightforward agitation—not even when battling for her freedom during her stay in my time. Then she kept her distress and planning neatly contained, at least around my parents and brother. She never expressed her frustration in public…though the fact that Lucas has the power to make her so openly distraught now is telling in itself.

The realization is sobering, and my heart hurts for Lorenzo. But I know more than anything he would want Cat to be happy.

Back at Lucas's table, I see him gently but firmly move Desiree off his lap. She does not appear fazed. She continues to prattle beside him while a pained smile crosses his handsome face. He transfers his focused gaze about the room as if he's searching for something—or *someone*—and when it lands on Cat, Lucas's pained smile becomes genuine.

As if of their own accord, the corners of my mouth lift at the sight.

Chapter Eight

It is the second to last class of the day, thank Signore, and as destiny, the scheduling gods, and our mysterious gypsy girl would have it, I enter drama class. According to Cat, this is one of the most highly sought-after electives in the school, and I am fortunate to have been admitted.

We both know there is much more than mere luck at play.

Almost as soon as I enter the small theater where the class meets, a pretty brunette sidles up beside me. She looks over my outfit and the hands I have clenched into anxious fists at my sides and says, "You've gotta be Less."

"And you must be Hayley," I say, smiling as I take in her outfit. She has paired a bright blue hat with a yellow T-shirt and red skirt, a skirt that is both long and modest in the back and chopped scandalously short in the front. Cat told me her new friend desires to be a fashion designer one day, and after seeing what society deems "fashion" today, I silently wish her luck. "I was hoping we would soon meet."

Hayley nods her head toward the front of the classroom where a large stage awaits, and I fall in step beside her. "So, Cat tells me you're quite the talented actress."

Heat fills my cheeks, and I shake my head. "I fervently wish to be an accomplished performer, yes, but I am afraid my cousin is overzealous in her praise. I have only been in one play."

She gives me a look over her shoulder. "Living around here, you learn pretty quickly that experience has very little to do with talent. Trust me, with that girl's background, Cat can spot talent. And if she says you've got it, then you've got it. Thank God, too, because heaven knows this place could use some fresh blood."

When we arrive at the front row, she tugs down the bouncy bottom of a dark blue chair. She takes her seat and waits for me to do the same. With a grin, I pull my own chair bottom down, and then on a whim release my hold, watching it snap back up. I bite my lip to contain my laughter. Life here is filled with hidden amusements.

I am still standing, smiling at my latest discovery, when a bored voice dripping with condescension asks, "Never used a chair before?"

A tall blonde sashays past me, not bothering to wait for a reply to her rude question. She marches up the four steps leading to the stage and comes to a stop in the very center, thumbs flicking over the screen of her phone.

Taking my seat, I whisper, "Please tell me she is not the teacher." The girl does not appear much older than I am, but the way she commands the stage with her presence implies a sense of expertise.

"Oh, heck no," Hayley says with a roll of her eyes. "*That* is Kendal Williams, Wicked Witch of Roosevelt Academy and a star in her own mind if no one else's. She's the main reason we so badly need new blood in here. She thinks she's a bag of awesome because her résumé's filled with lame commercials hawking tampons and a half dozen forgettable walk-on sitcom roles." She looks at me and says with complete earnestness, "She's the teacher's pet and the source of all that is evil in the world."

Having learned the fine art of sarcasm from Cat, I smile and casually cast a glance at the back of the theater, wondering when the real teacher will appear. That's when I spot the *true* source of evil in the world tromping through the open door.

"Him again," I mutter.

Hayley follows my gaze and laughs. "Don't tell me. Your first day here and you've already fallen for the Michaels charm?" I scoff, and she shrugs. "Don't get me wrong, the boy's a hottie. I just wouldn't waste my time or heart on him."

I abruptly turn back around and busy myself with smoothing the wrinkles in my skirt. "Certainly not. The boy is insufferable." Austin stomps down the center aisle, the tread of his heavy boots sounding even louder as they echo off the theater's walls, and tosses his bag on the ground. I wait until he slumps in his seat and closes his eyes, again failing to notice my existence, to ask, "But purely for the sake of curiosity, why not?"

She laughs. "Inquiring minds, huh? Well, for one, you could do better. I don't really know you that well, but you seem like a sweet girl. Plus, Austin's not the *relationship* type. You see

Wicked Witch over there? As far as I know, she's the only one he's ever actually dated, and that was years ago."

My gaze snaps back to the stage. Kendal, the wicked witch, has looked up from her phone to watch a napping Austin, a line creasing the skin between her eyebrows.

"It all happened before I got here," Hayley continues. "But from what I hear, they were pretty hot and heavy. Up until she cheated on him in front of the whole school. Since then, girls fawn all over him, drawn to the whole bad boy thing he's got going on, but he ignores it. The surf is his mistress," she says dramatically, flashing me a smile.

Despite Austin's obnoxious behavior, I cannot help feeling a sense of sadness listening to the tale. I do not know what a *surf* is, but I *do* know what it is like to be betrayed by the one you care about most. Did Kendal give him any warning, or was he caught as unaware as I was? I fight the urge to go to him and offer him a hug. To let him know that I understand his pain.

But then he opens his eyes.

I try to look away, even though I know that I have already been caught, but it is impossible to do so. The deep blue depths of Austin's gaze ensnare me. The rest of his face is a mask, hiding away his secrets from the world…but in the eyes riveted on mine, there is an unmistakable flash of emotion.

Anger.

It is there and then gone in an instant, but my breath catches at the intensity. I blink my eyes and spin back around.

"Holy cow, girl," Hayley whispers under her breath. "That boy looked like he wanted to eat you for dessert."

"We had a disagreement earlier today," I explain as my

heart attempts to beat out of my chest.

"Must have been an epic one."

A woman with curly brown hair and large spectacles enters through a side door, and Hayley pulls a notebook out of her bag. Scooting low in her seat, she whispers, "Looks like Satan's spawn saw that little eye showdown, too."

Looking to the stage, I see the previous squiggle between Kendal's eyebrows has transformed into a series of deep grooves between narrowed, hateful eyes. Centered on me.

"Girl, you sure know how to make a first day interesting."

"It does seem to be a talent I possess," I confide, already wishing the day were over.

As our teacher, Mrs. Shankle, goes over all that the drama class has accomplished in the last few years, I quickly learn that Hayley was right. Kendal *is* the teacher's pet—a title she seems to hold thanks to a succession of starring roles.

Shuffling a stack of papers in her hand, Mrs. Shankle says, "Last semester our classes concentrated on set design and costumes, but this spring our focus is on performance! We'll explore what it truly means to be an actor. How to prepare for an audition, how to block a scene, and how to improvise as well as the various methods you can use to get into character. And what characters will those be, you may ask?" Expressive eyes land on each of us as she extends the anticipation. "Our play this semester will be...*Back To The 80s: The Totally Awesome Musical!* by Neil Gooding!"

The room erupts in enthusiastic chatter, and Hayley jots down the words *bubble skirt* and *parachute pants.*

"This is a high-energy play that is fresh and unique, and I

know you are all up to the challenge. Eighteen speaking roles will be open for audition, with the two main stars being Corey Palmer and Tiffany Houston. I have copies of the script here for everyone's perusal. Take the rest of this class to look it over and begin thinking about which part speaks to you."

With a flourish, she sets the papers on the edge of the stage, sends the class a maniacal grin, and then ambles off into the darkened space beyond the curtain.

Hayley and I look at each other and burst into laughter.

As we walk to get our own copies of the script, Hayley addresses the rest of the class. "Guys, I've heard about this play. Imagine every awesome cliché that exists in high school, set against retro music, big hair, and slouch socks. It's supposed to be hilarious." Jabbing an elbow into my side, she grins, lowering her voice to say, "And from what Cat says about your acting skills, the part of Tiffany is yours if you audition."

Sensing her suggestion has more to do with dethroning a certain teacher's pet than it does with me, I smile and say, "I believe—"

"Now, Hayley," a voice dripping with false sweetness interrupts. The murmurings of fellow students cease. "Are you trying to get the poor dear's hopes up? A starring role? From what I hear, the girl can barely speak English."

A sensation as though I have been struck steals my breath. Kendal strolls in front of me, pinning me in place with an expression that is at once innocent and cruel. "I'm sure you'd be more comfortable with a role closer to home. I don't know, one of the outcasts, perhaps?"

I blink once, twice, then look at the papers in my hand.

The roles for the musical are divided into groups—the regular kids, the popular girls, the cool guys, and finally, the nerds and outcasts. *Nerd* is a new word for me, one that Cat left off her list last night, but I am well familiar with the other term—and Kendal's intent.

Tingles crawl up my skin, gathering at the base of my skull where cold hits my veins. The weight of my classmates' stares crushes me. I am like one of Michelangelo's sculptures, frozen and powerless.

I have never been so embarrassed in my life.

Under my lowered gaze, a tattered brown boot appears. I raise my head and collide with Austin's intense stare, wordlessly daring me to stand up for myself. A glance at Hayley proves she wants me to do the same. But I am not Cat. As much as I wish it were in my nature to be bold, to say what is on my mind without worry over decorum or propriety, that is not who I am.

I lift a shoulder in silent apology and compress my lips together.

Hayley offers an understanding smile. Austin shakes his head in disappointment.

Grabbing his copy of the script, he stops in front of Kendal and stares at her. After a tense moment, she looks away.

Austin hops down from the stage and returns to his seat in the front row, closing his eyes and effectively shutting me out. The rest of the class seem to act as one, breaking off into groups and pairs, discussing the various roles and, if I were to guess from the blatant glances in my direction, *me*. And as for Kendal, there is no guessing required. Her singular focus remains on me.

Hayley hooks her elbow around mine and tugs me toward

our seats with an apologetic smile. "Remember what I said about you making a first day interesting?" I nod, and she tilts her head in Kendal's direction. "My dear, I do believe you just became Enemy Number One."

Chapter Nine

"Remember what I said before," Cat tells me. "The name of the game is confidence."

A huge gulp of air fills my lungs. On the other side of the clear glass, a packed room of aspiring actresses—otherwise known as my competition for the afternoon—wait restlessly. I reflect back to Reyna's tent and my claim that I was no longer the timid girl she once knew…and wonder if perhaps it is not too late to change my mind.

The second I stepped out of French—a subject I thankfully did not share with Austin or Kendal but did share with the much-discussed Lucas—Cat grabbed my arm, squealing over a text she received from her father. That should have been sign enough, for my cousin never squeals. But when she shoved her cell phone into my hand and I glimpsed the reason, I could not help but scream as well.

Twenty-first century nepotism is apparently a force equaled

only by gypsy magic, because Mr. Crawford did not merely get me an audition for the Shakespeare Winter Workshop—he got me one for this very afternoon!

Through the wide window, I assess the other actresses, girls with much more experience than my sole performance as a wicked queen before a whopping audience of three.

"Confidence," I repeat, squaring my shoulders, my spine, and even my teeth.

I can do this.

Cat moves to open the door, but I quickly beat her to the task. It may seem silly, but performing this small action gives me a much-needed sense of control. She steps back with a wink, waving me on, and I push into the room before I can change my mind.

Almost every head lifts to scrutinize the latest adversary/auditionee, but at least this time the blatant appraisal is not personal. Under the collective weight of their stares, perspiration beads, then trickles down my spine.

Cat takes my hand and pulls me away from the relative safety of the exit and into the interior of the tension-filled room. "Welcome to Hollywood," she whispers under her breath, and if I were not so terrified, I would laugh.

Welcome, indeed.

We take a seat in a pair of unoccupied chairs near the door, and I complete my own inventory of the room from beneath my lowered lashes. There are so many young girls and women here, and though I have thought of nothing else for the last two years, it still amazes me that they are openly free to audition, to act, and to pursue their dream of the stage. It is truly wonderful, though in the shameful, secret part of me I cannot help hoping that in just this one instance, they all fail miserably.

Along with a copy of *A Midsummer Night's Dream,* a Shakespeare play Cat declared the perfect choice for my audition, I withdraw the yellow tablet of contractions and teenspeak. According to my cousin, if I am to succeed today, I must find a way to blend them together.

On the ride over from school, she informed me that some directors—her father included—dislike actors who never seem able to separate themselves from the role they are given. "Your background is already gonna add authenticity to your lines," she told me with a wink, "which, believe me, Marilyn's gonna totally eat up. So since you have that going for you, I think it's important that you show a different side when you're not reading your part. That way, in their eyes, you appear to be an even more accomplished actress."

It is with these wise words in mind, and the comfort of Titania's speech being so similar to my own, that I choose the list of teenspeak to study now.

That is, until a tall, thin girl with smooth blond hair stalks across the floor and drapes herself over the empty seat beside me.

"What the hell is that, *English for Dummies*?" Kendal asks, sneering at the notebook. I should have expected her presence here at the audition, considering she is both an actress *and* apparently determined to make my life miserable. Lifting her pert nose in the air, she says, "It's probably for the best you're not *really* preparing, anyway. Don't want to get your hopes up since you're clearly out of your league."

Just as frozen as I was in class, I begin the mental countdown from five, knowing what will happen. I make it no further than the count of four before Cat is leaning over my lap with a ferocious look. She has no need for biting words—she simply smacks her lips and clears her throat. Austin's former girlfriend huffs, but returns to her seat.

Cat Crawford: cousin, friend, and constant defender.

"Do *not* let her get to you," Cat tells me in a low voice near my ear, a hard edge infusing the lyrical tones in her voice. "She thinks she's better than everyone because of her pathetic walk-on roles. The only semidecent thing she's done was play a two-bit part on a CW show, and her character was a bitch, too. No worries, girl, you so have this."

A chuckle that breaks into an adorable snort emanates from the row of chairs opposite us. I look up and lock eyes with a sweet-faced girl who tilts her head toward Kendal and rolls her eyes with a playful grin. I smile back in reply.

Recognition tickles the back of my mind, but I know I have not seen her before. The combination of her long raven hair and bright blue eyes is striking and unforgettable. Regardless, she is a kindred spirit, and her gentle smile in the midst of the emotional onslaught is a welcome sight.

"Forlani?"

A balding, pudgy gentleman waits at the door, staring at the list in his hands with as much interest as one would give to washing a pile of bricks.

Cat squeezes my arm. "It's showtime!"

I force a smile. It is that. It is also time to prove myself and validate this entire excursion to the future. Standing on wobbly legs, I blow out a long breath. The amiable young girl across the aisle lifts her thumb in encouragement.

"Here I go," I say, handing all but my copy of *A Midsummer Night's Dream* to my cousin. She whispers, "Good luck," and I follow the bored-looking gentleman through the door, down a never-ending hallway, and onto a wide, open stage.

A scuffed black floor is beneath my feet. Soft curtains hang on either side. An empty yawning cavern where an audience usually sits is now dark, save for a lamplit table near the front. I inhale air filled with possibility and exhale sixteen years of believing this would never happen.

Standing on this silent stage is every daydream, every fantasy, and every fantastical wish I have ever had come to life.

Someone hands me a thin stack of papers, and I nod absently in gratitude. I cannot help wishing Mama or Cipriano were here to watch me, though I doubt even they would fully understand how much this means to me. It has been my long-kept secret desire…well, until my fearless cousin stepped into my world.

A feminine cough snares my attention. I trace the sound to the small table, illuminated by a few lamps on either end, in front of the stage. Two women flank the bored, balding gentleman behind it, their features barely discernible in the dim lighting.

"Miss Forlani," the taller woman in the middle says, "my assistant handed you a scene from *Romeo and Juliet*. I realize you may have already prepared your own selection, but I prefer watching your process. It gives me a better grasp of how quickly you are able to think on your feet. This workshop is going to be a whirlwind, Miss Forlani, and I need actors who can keep up with me. You have five minutes to review the new material. Good luck."

My copy of *A Midsummer Night's Dream* thumps noisily on the hard floor as I snatch the stack of papers closer to my nose. My poor heart takes residence in my ears, and I can hear nothing other than my racing pulse.

If ever there were a time for one of those colorful words I have heard Cat mutter under her breath, now would be it.

My knowledge of *Romeo and Juliet* consists of knowing it is set in Italy and is about a pair of star-crossed lovers who take their lives. At least that is what the first page said, which is as far as I got last night before sleep overtook me.

The highlighted monologue Ms. Kent selected is from Act Two, Scene Two. As I anxiously pore over the words, the familiar cadence of the language rushes over me. My tense shoulders and rigid spine lose some of their starch. I find myself in those few emphasized words, in Juliet. Particularly in the line, *I'll prove more true than those that have more cunning to be strange.*

Yes, Juliet was a kindred spirit, too.

With a smile, I step into the circle of light in the middle of the floor. Remembering my cousin's suggestion to act more modern, I lift my chin and say, "I'm good."

"Begin when ready, Miss Forlani."

I take a deep breath and let the light falling on my skin infuse me with warmth. I close my eyes and the sounds of the wide, open theater fill my head: the creak of a chair, the stomp of a shoe, the gentle murmur of voices waiting. I imagine the space filled with people, all there to see *me*. I open my eyes and begin.

• • •

Walking back into the well-lit waiting room, it feels as though my feet are walking on air, like I am floating and am no longer in need of solid ground beneath me. Cat jumps up and pulls me into an embrace.

"So," she asks, her head still buried in my hair, "how did it go?"

At first, I cannot find my voice. Describing such an experience seems an impossible undertaking. But then I meet the contemptuous smirk on Kendal's face, still in the same seat I left her. "They asked me to stay for the next round."

The smirk falls, and a look of pure hatred washes over her face. Somehow, and it is wretched to admit, it makes me feel even happier.

Cat's laugh borders on the demonic as she leans back and pumps her fist in the air. "I knew it! I told you—didn't I tell you?" She hugs me tightly again and pulls me down into our seats. "Never doubt me, girl. You're a natural."

I shake my head and grin so big, I am sure Mama can see it back home.

The next two hours trickle by in an endless stream of hope-filled people walking in to audition and then leaving the theater despondent or in tears. And as each person leaves dejected, it is even more wretched to say, my confidence and belief in myself lifts a little more.

What kind of person does that make me, a person who finds joy and confidence in another's misfortune? My cousin seems to think it makes me *normal*. I, however, am not so convinced.

After the last girl leaves, tissue in hand, and all that remains in the previously crammed waiting room are a handful of hopefuls, my eyes meet my cousin's. The pride in her smile fills me nearly to bursting.

"They're gonna call you back again soon, but remember that you've got this. You *own* this. I can say without a doubt that no one else here is a better fit for these roles than you." A haughty laugh erupts from beside me, and Cat's eyes narrow. "No one."

When the door opens again, they call all five of us back together: loathsome Kendal, the sweet girl in front of me, two others who seem pleasant enough, and me. We fall in line, of course with Kendal taking the lead, and file down the long hallway and back onto the marvelous stage.

The man hands us each another stack of papers. When I look at mine, I am relieved to see the same words from my previous round. I sneak a glance at the two scenes on either side of me and realize they have given us each something different. The younger girl from the lobby has a scene from *Hamlet*, with the lines from Ophelia highlighted, and my neighbor to the right is reading Olivia's lines from *Twelfth Night*.

A graceful woman crosses the stage, the one who had until now sat in the middle of the table, and at once I know it must be Ms. Kent. She meets each of our eyes with an encouraging smile, and though I have lost feeling in both my fingers and toes, the act of support bolsters my spirits.

"Ladies, this round we would like to see how you interact with other people. The chemistry you can create with another actor, one you probably have no relationship with or have ever seen before. In addition, depending on the scene we have selected for you, we will be looking for a particular trait or skill. Since the male casting call won't be held until tomorrow, a few brave volunteers have stepped up to help."

She tilts her head, acknowledging a group of people sitting in a nearby row. I squint, but can barely make out their vague outlines in the darkness.

"Don't worry. We'll only be judging *you* in your scene, not how well our good-natured assistants perform. They are simply here to give you something to react to and play off in your scene. Sound good? All right." She glances at a clipboard in her hands and then back up, directly at me. "Miss Forlani, you're first."

And just like that, my bolstered spirits plummet.

First?

With everyone watching?

In the small part of my brain that is still thinking logically, I realize that the four other actresses and the handful of volunteers seated in shadow are hardly an audience. But I am still terrified.

I hear a snicker and know without having to look that it is Kendal.

Ms. Kent motions to someone in the wings, and I hear footsteps approach. This must be my Romeo. I scan my page and see a much larger section now highlighted. As my eyes skim the wildly romantic banter, my cheeks start to warm. And when I glance up to see the volunteer step out of the shadows, my blush turns into a full-on inferno.

"Austin?"

Bathed in the glow of the overhead light, Austin's bright blue eyes look deeper. His gaze bores into mine, and my heart begins pounding against my breastbone. My body tenses. Heat pools in my stomach. My breathing escalates. Again, I am overwhelmed by the wealth of foreign sensations and am shocked to discover this is what rage feels like...strangely, it is almost pleasant.

"Miss Forlani, this is Mr. Michaels. He will be your Romeo for this scene, reading the highlighted section on your pages. This is an extended sample, so for this round you will be allowed to use your script when needed. You have five minutes to familiarize yourself with both the lines and your partner. Good luck."

The first time she expressed the sentiment, I had been gratified. This time, however, I find myself a touch annoyed, as I will need far more than *luck* to salvage this audition.

I sidle up to my so-called partner and whisper tersely, "Are you here just to vex me? I assure you, you did quite a thorough job earlier today. There is no need for you to follow me so."

Austin blinks. "*Vex* you? Did you really just say that? Damn, you take this Shakespeare stuff seriously, huh?"

He smirks, and my gaze is inexplicably drawn to his mouth. I shake my head and move it back to his eyes, berating myself for my verbal weakness. His continued presence today has me so disconcerted, I am forgetting to watch my language.

"But no," he continues, "I'm not here to *vex* you. I'm here for my sister." The muscles in his stubble-covered jaw clench as a rapid-fire series of emotions washes across his face: affection, anger, sadness, and then back to cool aloofness. "My dad's assistant got stuck on the freeway, and Jamie needed a ride. So here I am."

Struck by the surprising insight his facial cues gave me into this perplexing boy, I follow where he points—past Kendal, who is visibly incensed—to see the young girl from the waiting room. Now the tickle of recognition from earlier makes sense. Their dark hair and soulful blue eyes are almost identical.

Jamie smiles and waves, and Austin gives her an indulgent smile in return. The sardonic angles and strong features of his face soften. He transforms.

And in this moment, he is the most beautiful thing I have ever seen.

Then his gaze shifts to me, and aloofness wins again.

"Please take your places and begin," Ms. Kent calls out.

My body locks in fresh fear. Impulsively I reach out, grabbing Austin's arm. Muscles flex beneath the firm, warm skin, and my mouth goes dry. His free hand closes around my fingers, giving a quick squeeze before removing them from his body. Then, in a loud voice only *slightly* laced with arrogance, he says, "I'm ready."

I shake my head and take a hurried glance at the pages in my hand. The highlighted section begins with two words from me and then a short speech from Austin—er, Romeo. I should be able to read the material ahead while he says his lines. I look out into the crowd and straighten my shoulders. "So am I."

Inhaling through my nose, I watch Austin from the corner of my eye. Outwardly, he appears calm, but I can see the worn toe of his boot scuffing the floor. The action somehow reassures me and with a smile, I turn to him and say, "Ay me!"

My plan *had* been to read my next speech as Austin reads his, but that is not what happens.

Because Austin does not look down at his page.

"She speaks: O, speak again, bright angel! For thou art as glorious to this night, being o'er my head as is a winged messenger of heaven…."

Although Austin is but a volunteer and has no need to be familiar with the script, he recites Romeo's speech as though he wrote the words, as if he believes them…and as if I am truly his *bright angel*.

Reyna's confusing riddle from the tent springs to mind, disrupting my romantic musings as I realize I have just met the first marker.

An angel speaks.

Two more markers remain until I am sent back to my own time. My pulse pounds in my ears.

Austin stops speaking, and I snap back to reality to see him wiggle his eyebrows, indicating it is my turn. Flustered, I tell myself to focus as I look down and read my next part. "O Romeo, Romeo! Wherefore art thou Romeo?"

And as I read those lines, I leave behind the tent, the riddles, and even my own identity. And I become Juliet.

So we continue, each reciting in turn, and with each line uttered, I become more enchanted. Yes, my faithful blush rises at the talk of Romeo taking me and at his being left unsatisfied—much to Austin's distinct enjoyment—but somehow as the scene unfolds and Austin stares into my eyes, I forget the audience. I forget the fight we had earlier in class.

I stare at Austin, and he *is* Romeo.

And I am in love with him.

Offstage, another volunteer acts as the nurse and calls for me, yanking me from my imagined world where I stand on a balcony in my Verona courtyard. I stumble on my next line. I look around, see the darkened theater and the director's table, and then glance back at my page.

"I hear some noise within," Austin whispers, giving me my line.

I glance up, grateful, before finding my place and beginning again. But the magic is gone. I say the next few lines, and Ms. Kent calls, "That will be all."

Austin bows and I bob a curtsy, and as we walk out from under the bright spotlight he whispers, "All this is but a dream."

A line from Romeo's next speech.

He continues on, back to the shadowed row of volunteers, and I slow my stride, curious how much of the Austin I just witnessed is the dream and how much is the hidden reality.

Chapter Ten

The soft, buttery leather of the backseat hugs me as our driver steers us away from the theater and away from confusing boys who spout Shakespeare. Cat, however, is still beside me, not letting me forget.

"How was that even possible?" she asks me again, pushing the button to raise the divider, separating us from our driver. She turns her body toward me so she can better scrutinize my every facial expression. And she has reason to.

Ever since I walked off the stage, I have been in a daze. The rest of the auditions were spent sneaking not-so-subtle peeks at the row where Austin sat, unable to pay attention to anything else. I know this because somehow I failed to notice Cat just a few rows away, watching not only my onstage performance, but also my equally interesting offstage one as well.

"I don't know what's crazier, seeing my Renaissance-period cousin spouting Renaissance lingo while dressed in designer clothes, or watching her optically make out with a Shakespeare-quoting Austin Michaels!" She throws her hands up in disbelief. "The boy who can't even find his way to English class was reading the lines like he was from the sixteenth century, too. How is that *possible*?"

That has to be the fifth time she has asked me that question, and I still have no answer. But she is right—Austin did recite the lines as if he were from my time. Perchance that is why my heart and brain are in such conflict. My heart wants to believe that the Romeo version is the real one. But that was an illusion, "too flattering-sweet to be substantial."

I just have to keep reminding myself of the very words Austin whispered as he walked offstage, that it was all but a dream and the real Austin is the boy who taps on his desk, listens to annoying music instead of hardworking instructors' lectures, and sends silent, brooding glares but otherwise ignores the pleasant-enough-looking girl sitting and gawking beside him.

I wrinkle my nose.

That last part may be a bit personal. But the rest is definitely accurate.

"I do not know," I tell her honestly.

Cat tilts her head, watching me for a moment more, and I see the instant she decides to give up the inquisition. I sag in relief.

"Well, as exciting as all that was," she says, digging in her purse, "the fun's not over yet. Jenna got back today, and apparently Angela and her mom are coming over to talk sweet sixteen plans."

She whips out her cell phone, showing me the text from her future stepmother. Modern communication is nothing if not convenient. She pockets her phone and stares at the plush gray carpet beneath our feet, the corners of her mouth turning up wistfully. "I wonder if Lucas will tag along."

Maybe it is remembering the soft smile on Lucas's face when he spotted Cat or the romantic scene I just read with Austin, but I surprise even myself by saying, "You know, he seemed rather nice in our French class."

Cat's head shoots up and her gaze sharpens, and I realize I failed to mention our shared subject.

Eagerly hiking a foot under her, she twists toward me on the seat and starts worrying her bottom lip with her teeth. In her eyes, I can see the battle brewing as she fights asking the question I know she wants to ask. Finally, she gives in. "Did he say anything about me?"

As soon as the question is asked she shakes her head. "No, don't answer that. It'll only make it worse. Ugh, why am I turning into such a girl?"

I cannot help but grin at the theatrics. It is a shame she is so against claiming her acting lineage; clearly, she has a gift. "And is it so bad, being a girl?"

"Yeah," she answers automatically. "It is."

Silently, Cat pats her hip, just over the spot where her pear tattoo lays. The night my cousin told me the truth, that she was not Patience D'Angeli from sixteenth-century London but Cat Crawford from twenty-first-century Beverly Hills, she also confided the details of her unfortunate past. I remember at the time it seemed almost impossible to believe that a mother would abandon her family, leaving behind a five-year-old daughter and loving husband, to chase a selfish dream. A *forbidden* dream in my world. The dream of the stage.

But getting to know Cat then and being here now eliminates any trace of uncertainty. And watching her deliberately seek out the representation of her pain, the symbol she told me she chose to remind her that the heart cannot be trusted, slices *my* heart in two. There are many reasons to loathe the woman who gave birth to my beautiful, audacious cousin, but the wounds she inflicted when she left have to be the biggest.

Aloud Cat says, "Less, being with your family taught me a lot. I'm not the same person I was before Reyna sent me on my gypsy adventure. I have a relationship with Jenna now, and I have Hayley. I'm even slowly giving up my constant need to be perfect. But I'm still scared." She shrugs. "There doesn't seem to be a magic button for that."

"And Lucas scares you?" I ask, now thoroughly confused. I have been unsure if I should encourage her obvious feelings for him, but if Lucas is dangerous, it makes my decision much easier.

She sighs. "With Lorenzo it was different. It didn't matter what I wanted or wished; I knew our relationship couldn't last. Eventually I'd find my way home again. So even though being with him was amazing, it wasn't real. Not really. Lorenzo was safe. Lucas isn't."

I gently nod, wanting her to continue, wanting to understand. In my world, in my social circle, people rarely marry for love. It is not that the marriages never lead to love, but freedom to pursue whomever you choose does seem to complicate matters a bit more.

Cat leans her head back against the seat, suddenly looking tired. "Lucas lives here, Less. In *my* time. And unless his family moves again, he's always gonna be here. But if I give in to this feeling of connection and explore the possibility that he and I could ever have what Lorenzo and I *almost* did, then what happens if Lucas stays here but leaves *me*? What if he gets to know me, the real me, without my mom's tabloid craziness and my dad's glitz and glam, and loses interest?" She gives a self-deprecating laugh. "People have a tendency to do that."

A bump in the road jostles us, and Cat throws an arm out, instinctively protecting me. When she looks up, I see that rare vulnerability back in her eyes.

Outside my darkened window, the world passes in a blur of green and blue, reminding me of the horror of yesterday's ride. So much has changed in the last twenty-four hours, and if my time-travel experience is anything like my cousin's, more change is to come. But it will not solve everything—Cat's fear is proof of that. I guess some things take a little more time...and perhaps one of the reasons Reyna sent me here is to help finish the work fate began.

A Cat-like plan starts forming in my brain.

I wrap an arm around my cousin's shoulder and squeeze her tightly. "You will always have me." She looks up, a rueful smile on her face, and I shake my head. "It matters not whether I'm here in body or merely in your heart. We are family, Cat."

All through the drive back home, I think through the night ahead. And the more my plan comes into shape, the more

excited I become. Now I just have to ensure that Lucas is worth
my efforts. And hope that he joins his mother and sister at the
meeting tonight.

The moment we open Cat's front door, an effervescent
woman with big blond hair and a bigger smile envelops us both
in a generous hug. Cat gives me an indulgent grin, and I know I
am finally meeting the infamous soon-to-be stepmother.

"You must be Alessandra," Jenna says, stepping away to
close the still-open door. "Peter has told me all about you, and
I'm just so sorry I wasn't here to welcome you."

Guilt washes over me anew at the deceit. It would have
been difficult for her to be present when she had not even been
aware of my arrival. "It is perfectly all right," I tell her. "Mr.
Crawford has been more than accommodating."

"Yes, well, I'm sure he has, but there are some things
women are just better at, am I right?" She wraps her arm
around my elbow, then repeats the gesture with Cat and begins
leading us to the dining room. "But now that I'm here, we'll get
all caught up and become instant friends, I can tell."

She jumps into an energetic retelling of her recent travels,
and I try to follow their conversation, but my chest grows
tighter and tighter. Jenna is everything I expected her to be.
She is jovial, welcoming—and reminds me so completely of
my own mother that an overwhelming sense of melancholy
crashes around me. In a way, I am grateful. It is as if fate put
her here to provide me a sense of comfort in the midst of chaos,
a bittersweet reminder of home and all that I am missing.
But watching the spirited way Jenna converses, smooths her
hand along Cat's hair, and repeatedly finds ways to show her

affection, it also prompts an intense longing for home.

How I wish Mama could be here with me.

The doorbell rings, making me jump. Aware that there are no servants to answer the door as I have at home, I say, "I'll get it," hoping the walk to the entryway will shake off my unhappiness. I can't spend my time here wishing for home. I *need* to embrace every moment I have while I can—before the other two signs are revealed.

With a decisive nod at my encouraging internal speech, I stroll through the atrium, choosing to focus on thoughts of how my mother would react to the scandalous clothing I arrived in instead. With a wide grin, I open the door.

On the other side of the threshold stands an adorable girl fidgeting with the strap of her handbag. And behind her, instead of the mother who was to bring her, is Lucas.

Smiling at the way fate works, I glance around to see if they came alone.

Lucas nods to the rumbling vehicle parked behind him. "Mom's on the phone in the car."

The trace of an Italian accent takes me aback. Cat did say he spent a few years in Milan, so I should have expected it. Misjudging my reaction, Lucas quickly adds, "She'll join us in a few minutes. Angela was just excited to get started."

Lifting an eyebrow, I look at the girl who appears fascinated with the flower doormat. Cat told me she was shy. Being nervous around strangers myself, I offer a smile of solidarity when she glances up. She grins in return.

Angela seems very sweet…but, if I had to guess, I would have to say the *other* Cappelli sibling was the one eager to get inside.

Stepping back, I motion for them to enter. "*Prego, vieni.*"
Angela's small smile grows as she steps over the threshold.

As I lead them to the dining room, I go back over my plan.
Tonight's agenda is simply to observe. In true Cat style, I have
fashioned what she calls a *checklist*, and I will (hopefully) mark
items off as the night progresses. In determining if Lucas is a
proper suitor for Cat, the first attribute I will be looking for is
his heart. Though my cousin never sees these qualities in herself,
she is the kindest, most loyal, and most loving person I have
ever met. She deserves to have someone who cares about her
just as ardently as Lorenzo did and who has as much love to
give her as she will give him.

After ascertaining the condition of Lucas's heart, since I
already know about his talent and shared interest in art, I will
watch how he interacts with others. In particular, his younger
sister, a person with whom he spends a great deal of time and
undoubtedly knows him best. I will also watch how he behaves
around his mother and Jenna.

Mama always said you could tell a lot about a person by the
way he treats his elders.

And finally, I will pay close attention to both Cat and Lucas
and how they interact with each other. If I am to support his suit
to win her heart, I must see a hint of the sparks and smiles I saw
her share with Lorenzo.

Truly, it is a tall order for one evening.

The sound of laughter guides our path to the dining room.
When we enter, Cat is looking at Jenna, the future stepmother
she once despised, with a radiant smile. The shell she sometimes

erects to protect herself from the outside world is gone.

Launching into my self-assigned role, I turn to Lucas and am gratified to see the soft look in his eyes again. The one I felt across the chaotic cafeteria, and the one that got my begrudging admission that perhaps there could be another for Cat.

Lucas's heart, check.

Then Cat turns and sees us, and her smile falters—not in an angry or upset-that-Lucas-came way but in a sad, regretful way. The taut muscles in her neck work as she swallows heavily, as if she is repressing the words left unspoken between them, and she shifts her attention to Angela. "Hey, Ang. Good to see you."

The shy girl from the threshold blossoms under my cousin's attention, and her rounded shoulders straighten. She skips over to Cat and throws her arms around her—and judging by Cat's wide eyes, the action is a surprise for her as well.

"You, too," Angela says, pulling back. "As much as Lucas talks about you, I thought I'd see you over the break. Guess Christmas got a little crazy, huh?"

A touch of pink glows under the bronze of Lucas's skin, and I rub my mouth to hide my grin. As for my cousin, she appears both pleased and guilty over Angela's inadvertent slip. Lucas clears his throat, and his sister scrunches her forehead, seeming confused over the sudden tension in the room.

"I have some great ideas for your party, Angela," Jenna says, her voice pitched a bit higher that before. She pulls out a chair and ushers the future birthday girl to sit in it, and the rest of us follow in turn, taking seats around the large oak table. Patting the girl's hand, Jenna smiles and says, "I think the first thing we should do tonight is pick out a theme."

Lucas takes a seat next to his sister and grabbing a scrapbook in front of him, begins flipping the pages. "Are all sweet sixteens costume parties?"

"No, but that's a great question. Cat's was because she wanted a Renaissance-styled gala, so the theme dictated cost-umes," Jenna explains. "But oftentimes a theme just gives us a direction for decorations, vendors to choose from, and occa-sionally, the suggested style of dress."

Lucas nods respectfully, then turns a page and grins. He elbows his sister and whispers to her under his breath. Angela's face lights up as she laughs and whispers back, and I have to add another check to my Lucas-as-suitor list.

Cares for sister, check.

The last on my list, watching for sparks between him and Cat, will not be easy, for not only is Cat determined to hide any interest she has for him, but she also has her future stepmother in the room.

As if the very thought of mothers conjures her, the doorbell rings again. Lucas stands. "That's my mom. I'll go let her in."

Jenna nods from her place on the other side of Angela and pulls the girl into a conversation about a picture in one of the books. Cat watches Lucas leave, then catches *me* watching *her* and looks down at her book.

When Mrs. Cappelli joins us in the crowded dining room, I am pleased to see she is nothing like Lorenzo's mother. *That* woman was an evil hag who was even worse than Cat's archrival Antonia was. This Mrs. Cappelli kisses Jenna on both cheeks and ruffles her daughter's hair before taking the seat Lucas holds out for her—the one he previously sat in, allowing him to walk around the table to the only other empty seat...the one beside Cat.

Very crafty.

And I can add another check: *displays respect for elders.*

As Lucas takes his seat, my cousin gives a valiant effort... but she cannot hide the hint of a pleased smile, the subtle shift in her posture to bring her closer, nor the discreet way her eyes keep drifting toward him.

Seeing them together, side by side, is a bit jarring, to be honest. But the visual does help me understand better why my cousin is fighting her feelings so hard. Having him here seems a little too easy, a shade too convenient, even for fate. But there is no denying the palpable attraction between them.

Lucas turns a page, and a dimple flashes in his cheek. "See, this is what I love about America," he says in a teasing voice that has Cat laughing before he even delivers the humorous line to his joke. "You pay all this money for a huge event and tell people to arrive in their underwear."

Her eyes widen, and she pulls the book he is looking at toward her. "That's not underwear, you Italian weirdo. They're in bathing suits. See, it's a beach theme."

Lucas shrugs. "You say potato, I say *potahto.*"

Cat laughs again, failing to realize the rest of the table is watching their interaction with various degrees of pleased smiles.

"Yeah, you would say *potahto,*" she says, shaking her head. "Now say vitamin."

"*Vit-amin.*"

The different pronunciation, delivered in the exaggerated

notes of his accent, sends my often serious, sometimes crazy, but rarely silly cousin into a series of infectious giggles. And the triumphant look on Lucas's handsome face for causing Cat's happiness answers any question I had about potential sparks.

Cat lifts the back of her hand to her forehead and pretends to swoon, seeming to forget, even if for just a moment, all the reasons she should not let herself like him.

"What is it about a guy with an accent?" she asks playfully, and I add another mark to my list.

Sparks, big check.

Chapter Eleven

I ring the Michaels's doorbell and turn to wave at Jenna, fighting the yawn building in my chest. After watching the tension between Cat and Lucas all night, though she blatantly denied it later, I laid in the soft cloud my cousin calls a bed for hours, memorizing my teenspeak list and thinking of Austin—and the conflicting version of him I met onstage.

This morning I pulled out Cat's copy of *Romeo and Juliet* and discovered that in Act One, Scene Five, the titular couple kisses. And although I was shocked, my stomach muscles tightened at the thought of what would have happened had Ms. Kent given Austin and me *that* scene to perform.

Would he have tried to kiss me?

Would I have let him?

Would I have enjoyed it?

I still don't know the answers, but the thoughts led me to ask Cat for help in obtaining Austin's address—so we could work on our American government assignment, *not* so he could kiss me. Of course Cat suggested I call him on the telephone instead, but that is not how we do things in my time. Granted, maidens do not usually visit unchaperoned and uninvited, either, but at least face-to-face communication would put me on some semblance of an equal footing.

So here I am, dressed in the "frumpy frock" from Cat's closet (an outfit Austin is sure to mock) arms laden with books from the Crawford library, ringing the Michaels's doorbell for the third time, and hoping that at least someone is at home.

Perchance I did not quite think this plan through.

Thankfully, just as I am about to give up and run back to the safety of Jenna's vehicle, the door opens.

Austin's sister Jamie greets me, her surprise evident in the tilt of her head, the wrinkles in her nose, and the lack of invitation to step inside.

"Juliet?"

I grin and bob my head. "Alessandra, actually."

"What are you doing here? Not that I'm not stoked to see you or anything," she quickly adds. Jamie glances at the large load of books in my arms, and her nose crinkles. "Is this about the workshop?"

"N-no," I stammer, no longer feeling as though the sneak attack approach was the best course of action. "I go to school with your brother—Austin? By any chance is he home this afternoon?"

Honestly, I am unsure at this point how I wish her to answer.

"Oh, sure, come on in." She widens the opened door, allowing me to step inside the cool entryway, and takes a few books off the top of the teetering pile. "You know, you really did great yesterday. Totally pissed off Kendal." She closes the door behind me and sighs. "Watching her fume was totally worth all of the preparation, even if I don't end up snagging a part. I can't believe I used to look up to her. And I really can't believe my stupid brother used to date her. Speaking of which, AUSTIN!"

I jump, at both the subject change and her sharp bellow up the stairs. A door closes somewhere above. Eyes on the ceiling, I swallow down my mounting apprehension. "But you were so good yesterday," I assure her. "I am certain you will be chosen." Then, sensing an opening, I add, "Your brother appeared quite comfortable with the material as well. Acting must run in the family."

Jamie snorts. "Austin act? That'd take way too much time away from surfing." She glances at the curved stairway a few feet away and then leans in conspiratorially. "But he was good, huh? He must've read that scene at least a hundred times helping me get ready for the audition. I knew it would be one of the pieces they'd have us do—I mean, come on. It's the *balcony scene*. It's a given, right? And I read *Romeo and Juliet* in school this year, so I was kinda gunning for that part. But it's totally no biggie. I dig Ophelia, too."

Trying to keep up with Jamie's excited, bountiful chatter makes my head spin. I grasp the insight buried within her speech and say, "So Austin helped you prepare?"

She nods. "Yeah, he's so good at languages and stuff like that, and the words in those plays just go right over my head. Man, people talked crazy back then, huh?"

I smile but withhold a comment in reply.

But then I think about Jamie's words and the fact that Austin supposedly has a talent for "stuff like that," and I find myself even more confused than I was before my arrival. Cat told me Austin rarely even makes it to class, and when he does, he does not spend that time impressing the professors with his scholastic aptitude. But the boy Jamie describes sounds intelligent and talented.

So the nagging question remains: which Austin is the real Austin?

At the sound of heavy clomping, I lift my head and see the mysterious boy himself coming down the stairs. His hands glide across the smooth banister, stretching his worn black shirt across the width of his shoulders. A wisp of a memory begins to surface, but before I can place it, Austin's eyes cut to mine. He freezes.

"What are *you* doing here?"

The accusation in his tone scares any reply right out of my head, but Austin does not—*doesn't*—wait for one. Instead, he continues his trek down the stairs and through the adjoining dining room to the kitchen beyond, leaving me with a heavy pile of books and a mouth still open.

Jamie winces. "Sorry about that. He's not usually so *rude!*" She yells the last word, but when no reaction comes from her brother, she rolls her eyes and leads me into the kitchen.

Austin lifts his head from the open refrigerator door and takes out two bright red cans of soda, my cousin's beverage of choice. He meets my gaze and lifts a can in question.

I place the books on the smooth, granite countertop and accept his offering with a smile of gratitude. I take a sugary gulp and nearly choke when he says, "Don't you look nice today."

Pleasure flows through my veins. I swallow and begin to say thanks—but then I see the taunting gleam in his eyes and realize he is mocking me.

I glance down at my outfit and suddenly feel silly.

Did I forget the Austin from class yesterday?

I rub the soft fabric of Cat's cardigan sleeves and hear the sound of Jamie mouth something to her brother before turning on her heel and stomping from the room. As I listen to her retreating footsteps, anger replaces my fleeting embarrassment. Just because I don't dress like my modern-day peers does not give him the right to disparage me for it.

A true gentleman, at least one from *my* time, would never treat a lady in such a manner.

I raise my head to tell him that very thing and am startled to find Austin's face so close to mine. The words die on my lips.

"I can see through you, you know," he says, his voice low, eyes flashing. "You're not as innocent and perfect as you want us to think. No one is. I can see that you're dying to break out of the prim and proper prison you've built for yourself, but you're too scared to admit it. You want more." He pauses. "Don't you, *Princess*?"

There is that nickname again, delivered this time with such derision that I take a step back. And in the face of such blatant antagonism, my blood begins to boil with an emotion that is anything but prim and proper, although nothing I have felt since meeting this exasperating boy is.

Breathe, Alessandra. A true lady does not display fits of anger.

I glance at Austin and see red.

Even when the gentleman so greatly deserves it.

To keep from lashing out in an unladylike fashion, I turn to my stack of books, preparing to carry on with my reason for today's visit…but then Austin laughs.

"What, no comment? No Shakespearean reply?" He compresses his lips into a thin line. "Guess I was wrong. I thought I saw some fire hidden in you the other day, but maybe you *are* just a sweet, spineless little angel."

Though he does not mean to compliment, in reality I should be pleased. In my time, those are often the characteristics most sought after in a wife…the very role Mama has groomed me for since birth.

But instead, I spin around and spit, "Well, I see through you, too!"

Austin's eyes widen, perhaps both by the content of my declaration and the vehemence in which I delivered it. To be honest, I am rather shocked myself. But I press on.

"You like to pretend you *don't* care about anything, but I see you. I see how you are with your sister. How you stood up for me in class. And how you were at the audition—I was on that stage with you, Austin. I know you are a lot smarter than you want people to believe. So perhaps I am not the one who is scared! *You* are the one who is hiding."

And at that, I collapse against the counter.

A flash of heat erupts under my skin, and my head begins to throb. The edges of my vision darken and the sounds of the kitchen—a slow tick, a low hum, a soft clanging—dim to a faint garble.

Oh, Signore in heaven, what did I just do?

Lifting a trembling hand to my mouth, I look to the boy

who is able to bring forth such fervent reactions from me. "I cannot believe I just said that." I swallow and push against the counter, thrusting my full weight back onto my feet. "My sincere apologies for my lack of manners. No matter how you behaved, it is no excuse for my actions."

A squiggle appears on Austin's forehead, and he watches me with shrewd eyes, as if I'm a puzzle to figure out. The edges of his mouth twitch, and then, wonder of wonders, he laughs. Genuinely this time, not in ridicule, and it must be said, the sound is glorious.

He lifts his chin and asks, "You really care about that stupid project?"

My mind spins at his confusing reaction and change of subject, but I nod. "About doing well on it, yes. And I need your help. I grew up in Italy and am unfamiliar with the ways of American government."

Or even modern Italian government, but I do not say that aloud.

Austin crosses his arms against his chest, flexing the muscles in his strong arms. My mouth goes dry.

"All right, then," he says slowly. He nods once as if making a decision. "I have a proposition for you—a *challenge*. When it comes to government I know way too much, but if I'm gonna pick up your slack and actually help you with this, you're gonna have to do something for me."

He pauses, dragging out the suspense, and I wrack my fuzzy brain for any situation in which *he* could possibly want or need *my* help. I bite my lip as Austin crowds me against the counter.

That inexplicable heat builds in my core again, along with a delicious twist in my stomach.

Placing both hands on either side of me, trapping me between the cool granite and the warmth of his body, Austin's gaze lingers on the lip I am worrying with my teeth as he says in a low, sensual rasp, "You need to loosen up."

My breath comes out in stilted, ragged bursts, and an uncomfortable giggle escapes.

The right side of Austin's mouth kicks up at my reaction, but he does not back away. "You need a guide," he continues. "A tutor to teach you how to take a chance, grab what you want, and not give a damn. And if after a couple weeks with me you're not convinced you need to break out of that sheltered, prim and proper, *fake* life of yours, I'll back off. I won't say another word about the way you dress, the way you act, or the fact that you sound like an eighteenth-century novel."

More like sixteenth, I almost say, but I stop myself in time.

The part of me that is insulted at Austin's classifying my life as *fake* is lost in a rush of excitement, curiosity, and a voice screaming in my head that this is what brought me here—my cry, my *need*, for adventure. Austin lifts an eyebrow, challenging me to reach out and take this adventure, to experience all that the twenty-first century holds. My pulse pounds in my chest, and I fight for breath.

I don't know if I do it to get space or to see if I affect the boy before me anywhere near as much as he affects me, but I boldly place a hand over Austin's heart and smile when I feel it beating just as fast as my own.

Absorbing his intoxicating heat and his promise of more, I grin and say, "Deal."

Chapter Twelve

"The string goes *where*?" I ask incredulously, dropping the garment from my fingers as if it holds the plague. My heart pounds in my ears, its pulse already heightened from my shocking meeting with Austin earlier and the crowd in this land of chaos my cousin calls a mall. It is Saturday, apparently the day teenagers descend upon this enormous building, and we are shopping for clothes for me that will somehow strike a balance between what she calls dorky and what I call common courtesan attire.

"You heard me," Cat says with a wicked smile and a pointed look to the scrap of fabric. Heat creeps into my scalp, and if it were possible for hair to defy all wisdom and burst into flame, mine would. Holding this conversation in public as people bustle past us is horribly and wholly improper.

"It's called a thong," she clarifies with glee, "and by putting the string up *there*, you avoid ugly panty lines. Trust me, no one wants to see that business."

I take a hesitant step toward the overflowing bins, peering down at the perplexing items again. "But surely it is uncomfortable to be lodged...in such a...spot?"

Cat shrugs. "You learn to live with it."

That is where my dear cousin is wrong. Despite my agreement to wear modern attire, I certainly do *not* plan to learn such a lesson.

Nevertheless, I cannot keep my twitching fingers from lifting another offending thong, either, this one with the words *No Chance* emblazoned across an area no one should have access to read. I wrinkle my nose.

"But if it does not even cover the entire, um, bottom area," I say in a choked voice, "why bother wearing one at all?"

Cat laughs and snatches the thong from my hand, replacing it with a brightly colored one with (thankfully) a tad more material. This latest selection declares the wearer to *Love Pink*.

"Less, I know you don't have this stuff where you come from, and I get it. That was a big adjustment for me, too, when I was in your time—walking around commando. But here's the deal: if you don't want to inadvertently cause a Britney Spears TMZ incident, these things are a must." Then she grins again and lifts an eyebrow. "Just remember: corset."

Again with her self-declared new mantra. Ever since we stepped foot inside this land of chaos, she has been repeating it, reminding me of the constrictive undergarment she had to wear while visiting *my* time, and brandishing it as her one-word form of instant guilt.

I roll my eyes but clasp the thin fabric. The intimate item is unbelievably tiny. And handling it in view of the other patrons is without question inappropriate. But as I rub my fingers along the delicate fabric, I must admit it feels luxurious.

"Very well," I say, snagging a nail on the wide lace band. I disentangle myself, then grab a few pairs in bright animalistic patterns. "I shall wear the undergarments. As long as they remain hidden by something much more appropriate for public viewing, you shall win this round. But," I quickly add before she can gloat much more, "I refuse to wear *that*."

Her gaze follows my pointed finger to a headless human form wearing a pair of dark trousers similar to the ones I was in when I first arrived, but these appear to have met with an unfortunate dagger incident. They are ridiculously short.

"Yeah, I already figured that one out. Don't worry—I have a whole other store in mind for your Pollyanna attire. We're just working from the inside out. A little faith, if you please, Miss Forlani." She grins and with a playful shove, steers me to the front of the store where a small line has formed.

Two girls stop chatting to sneer at my "dorky" attire, and I fidget with my sleeve. My cousin's cool hand closes around my squirming fingers, and I recognize the squinty, overprotective look in her eye. It is the same look from my vision in the courtyard, when I imagined her confronting the disloyal Marco and wretched Novella.

A jolt of pain lances through my chest.

Could that really have happened only two days ago?

I wince at the memory, and Cat's fingers tighten around mine. I cannot bring myself to tell her the true reason for my distress, so I watch, somewhat guiltily, as she waves her free hand dismissively at the girls in front of us, leans toward them, and hisses like a cat in their faces. "Turn. Around."

Their collective eyes bulge, and their heads snap forward.

Cat winks and continues as if nothing happened. "I'll spare you the dressing room experience here—I'm pretty sure I can guess your size, and Lord knows if you get spooked seeing yourself in this stuff, I'll never get you in the mall again."

The woman behind the booth calls, "Next," and the girls in front of us leap in their haste to get away. Cat's amused gaze meets mine, and I stifle a giggle. It is comforting to find my fearless cousin audacious as ever.

After several hours and rejecting more than a *bazillion* selections, we at last make our way home, bags brimming with a half dozen dresses and an array of ankle-length skirts. Our quest to find items that cover both my calves and elbows proved to be a tad time consuming, but the true reason for our extended excursion was my complete and utter awe over the vast display of ready-made clothing. Modern women no longer have a need to select fabrics and patterns and hire a tailor— they simply step inside a store, choose an item off a *rack*, and bring it home. Preparing for a ball or dinner party in this era would be effortless. It is too bad I cannot bring this marvelous improvement back with me.

Traipsing through the atrium of Cat's beautifully modern decorated home, I slurp the final remains of my creamy beverage and grin. On the way home, my cousin insisted that she needed a "sugar fix," so our kind driver stopped at a building with bright yellow arches filled with all sorts of delectable delicacies. A chill seeps down my throat, and I close my eyes at the blissful sensation.

This is a recipe I must have Cook try to copy.

Of course, thoughts of Cook turn to thoughts of Mother. And Father. And Cipriano. How much they would enjoy this modern delicacy and how much I wish they could be here experiencing this with me. My longing for them is the one thing hampering my joy. It feels as though it has been forever since I left home—so much has happened, yet it has been merely a couple days.

A warm, enthusiastic voice calling my name pulls me from my homesick ruminations.

"Yes, Marilyn, she's right here." Mr. Crawford holds out the telephone, eyebrows lifted and smile matching the one splitting my cousin's face. From their mutual expressions, I decipher that the gatekeeper of my one and only dream calling is a good thing, but I hesitate to take the device from his outstretched hand.

I have never used a phone before—other than to play one of Cat's magical movies during her time-traveling jaunt, that is. But when Mr. Crawford's eager smile turns curious over my hesitation, I gather my wits, figuring there is no time better than the present to learn. With a nervous glance in Cat's direction, I mimic what I have seen her do so many times before and speak into the air, "This is Alessandra."

As if by magic, Ms. Kent's voice rings in my ear, saying words I never thought I would hear. "Congratulations, Miss Forlani, you have been selected to play Juliet in this year's winter workshop!"

If Shakespeare himself had delivered this message, I could

not be any more shocked. Or elated.

Only my family's noticeable absence keeps this from being the best moment of my life.

If only I could share this accomplishment with them. I close my eyes, and it's as if I can actually hear Cipriano's booming, euphoric laughter. I can imagine Father's face glowing with pride. And as I wrap my arms around my middle to hold my warring emotions within, I can almost pretend it's my mother's slender arms clutching me in delight.

The rest of the conversation flies by in a blur of dates, requirements, and information. I learn that I am to return to the Playhouse in the morning to retrieve my script and be fit for my costume, and that Reid Roberts, an up-and-coming—whatever that means—teen actor, will be playing opposite me. I hand the phone back to Mr. Crawford in a daze of disbelief, and my cousin grabs me in a bone-crushing tackle hug.

My eyes close as profound gratitude, awe, and happiness overwhelm me.

Chapter Thirteen

The next day, I sit up tall in the soft leather seat that begs me to slump and meet my cousin's jubilant grin with one of my own. We are on our way to my first official task as an actress, and it is difficult to tell which of us is happier. Cat presses a button to raise the barrier behind the driver for privacy and asks, "You're sure you don't want me to stay?" My triumphant grin fades into a grimace at the touch of wishful interest in her voice.

It is not that I don't want Cat to stay. Along with the support she always gives, I could certainly use her backbone. For all of Kendal's wicked behavior at school and at the audition Friday, she read her lines flawlessly. There is no doubt in my mind that she earned a part and I will be graced with her presence today. But at least I can count on one friendly face to be there.

Shortly after hanging up with the director, the Crawford phone rang again, this time with the name *Michaels* appearing on the caller identification box—much to Cat's and my shared astonishment. For an out of town—and out of *time*—guest, I certainly felt popular.

After exchanging pleasantries, which consisted of *me* being pleasant and Austin being, well, Austin, he informed me that Jamie would be playing Ophelia in the workshop (huzzah!), and then declared he would be picking me up for the commencement of our agreed-upon week of adventure directly following today's meeting.

Cue the butterflies of anxiety—a whole swarm of fretful, restless, *dancing* butterflies.

I shake my head, willing the remaining insects to shoo, and squeeze my cousin's hand. "It simply does not make sense for you to wait through all the costume fittings and rehearsal announcements and then return home alone. Go to the mall with Hayley as you planned, and I promise to tell you about everything the moment I return."

Cat sighs. "Fine, I guess that'll have to do." Then she nudges me with her elbow. "I'm teasing. Really, I'm still shocked you're getting Austin Michaels to bring you to a library, and on a Sunday when the sun's out and the waves are killer. You must've worked some kinda mojo to get him to study on a day like this." Then she pins me with a worried, maternal look. "But no mojo was exchanged, right? You two just studied yesterday?"

And therein lies the main reason Cat cannot stay today.

She is unaware of my Austin Challenge.

If I were to share this portion of my gypsy adventure with her, I know what would happen. She would say that I don't know Austin. That it is unsafe to gallivant around town on a whim with a practical stranger, engaging in whatever *un*sheltered, exciting proposition he may suggest. She would attempt to talk me out of it...but I need this.

Cat is wonderful—a loving force unrivaled—but she treats me as if I am still the younger cousin she left behind and not the equal that I am today. Though truthfully, my overwhelmed behavior since my arrival has not aided my cause.

But Austin does *not* treat me like a child. Even with his ill manners and boorish behavior, he treats me as an equal. No different from any other person he shows contempt to, and certainly not like someone who requires gentle handling. And I know that I *am* safe with him. Austin Michaels has many faults, if my own witness and Cat's testimony are to be believed, but I know instinctively that he would never let anything happen to me.

My mind flashes to the feel of his warm chest beneath my palm and the length of his arms caging me in against the counter. A full-body tingle explodes across my skin.

Our car pulls to a stop outside the theater, and the driver walks around to my door. I turn to Cat with a feeling of seasickness churning in my stomach and force a smile. "Wish me well."

"Nah," she says, shaking her head, her lips pursed. "Break a leg."

Ignoring our sweet driver's proffered hand, I reach beside me, slam the door he just opened, and ask, "*Excuse* me?"

Cat laughs and playfully bumps my shoulder. "It's a showbiz expression, Less. Actors are crazily superstitious creatures, and for some random reason they believe wishing someone good luck will actually bring *bad* luck. So instead, they wish the opposite."

I wrinkle my nose. "Such as breaking a leg?"

"Exactly." Cat pauses. "Now that I think about it, it *is* pretty barbaric."

I nod in complete agreement and rap on the window of my door. When our driver opens it again, wearing an expression of exasperation, I shrug and slide out into the cool, January morning air.

"Perhaps I should add *break a leg* to my yellow tablet of words," I say, turning back with a grin. "You know, now that *I've* mastered all the others."

Cat rolls her gaze toward the heavens.

Standing on the sidewalk, I watch as the car drives away, the darkened back window growing smaller and smaller as it travels down the road. It turns a corner, and panic spikes in my blood.

Why have I never asked for a cell phone of my own so I can call them back?

For the first time since those frantic, terrifying moments outside the theater of etched handprints, I am alone again in this foreign, new world…not to mention outside another frightening theater, only this time for an entirely different, yet equally distressing, purpose.

"You look lost, gorgeous."

Pulled from disturbing visions of me winding up scared and alone in this confusing city, I twist around and stare at a boy who could be from my own.

He smiles, flashing a set of straight white teeth, and bows regally. "By chance I gazed out yonder window and glimpsed your ravishing beauty." He straightens from the waist and winks. "So I felt I best come out and introduce myself. Reid Roberts," he says, holding out his hand. "Your love-struck Romeo, Lady Alessandra."

I look from his outstretched hand to the line of his broad shoulders, clothed in a remarkably accurate dark brown doublet. I dare a glance at his toned legs encased in matching tights, confirming the costume department's impressive knowledge of historical fashion.

Returning my Romeo's grin, highly amused at considering myself history, I accept his hand and fall into a curtsy. The excuse to converse in my natural manner is just too tempting to ignore.

"Ah, good pilgrim, you flatter too much, for I am no ravishing beauty." Standing again, I attempt to withdraw my hand from Reid's grasp, but the firm pressure from his own increases.

I raise my eyes and see mischief sparking in his gaze. The distant rumble of a car engine brings into sharp awareness the fact that the two of us are outside alone, without a chaperone. Every word of warning Mama ever gave me about situations such as these swirls in my head. "And may I ask how you knew who I was, my lord?"

Reid runs his free hand through the spikes of his dark blond hair and grins as if he were a child caught sneaking a marzipan cake from the cook. "I may've asked around." At my wide-eyed look of disbelief, he laughs. "Okay, I totally asked around. But hey, anyone who has Marilyn Kent saying things like, 'raw, natural talent' and, 'find of the year' deserves my Mystery

Machine skills."

He gives me an expectant look, and when I fail to recognize the reference, scratches his chin. "Scooby-Doo? Band of teenage detectives and their adorable, treat-loving dog? No? All right, then."

At his look of bafflement, I vow to add *Scooby-Doo* to my list of modern lingo. At this rate, the list will soon become a book.

"*Anyway*, since everyone else is pretty much accounted for inside, I took a chance that the lovely lady stepping out of the black Mercedes was Alessandra Forlani, AKA my Juliet." Reid pauses. "And you were wrong, by the way." I squint, and he strokes his thumb over my knuckle. "You *are* beautiful."

Unaccustomed and embarrassed from the unexpected compliment and attention, I lower my lashes. Reid chuckles softly.

"After you, milady." I look up to see him wave his hand toward the theater doors. He lifts his chin, indicating that I should lead the way, and I bolt toward them.

Although my costar seems perfectly amiable—*and quite charming*—sixteen years of parental lectures on never permitting myself to be alone with a flirtatious suitor (and remembering how badly the stolen moments with Matteo turned out) are difficult to ignore.

Quickening my steps, I cover the remaining distance to the entrance of the theater at a near jog, hearing Matteo's deceitful claims of love with each footfall. I know now he never loved me—though in truth, I do not know that I genuinely loved *him*, either.

In preparation for my role, I've been reading more of *Romeo and Juliet*, and in response, thinking a lot about true love. I believe it was the hope of Matteo I loved more than the man himself. The dream that our union would quiet my growing discomfort with the role and skin I had been born into, the idea that a man could honestly care for me, not out of duty, but for who I was as a woman.

My heartbreak is not over Matteo's betrayal. It is over the death of that dream.

Blinking away the burn of tears, I throw open the double doors, eager for the diversion of the bustling crowd. Across the sea of bobbing heads amassed in the lobby, Jamie catches my eye and grins.

I sidestep my way through the assembled actors and meet my friend in the middle of the floor, the center of a world of chaos and excitement. "You ready for this?" she asks, eyes wide as she bounces on her toes.

I was born ready, I think, letting the moment settle over me. Aloud I answer, "As ready as I'll ever be."

Jamie laughs and opens her mouth to say something, then shuts it abruptly as her gaze transfers behind me. Turning, I find Romeo—er, Reid, near my shoulder.

"Sorry to interrupt, ladies, but I have to change." He motions to his costume with an exaggerated frown. "Sadly, as sexy as I make this look, they won't let me bring it home. But come find me after your fitting, Alessandra. There's something I need to ask you." His head dips down to meet my eyes, and I nod mine in promise. He grins. "Don't go disappearing on me, Juliet."

Reid disappears down the long hall, leaving me curious as to what he could possibly have to ask me. Watching his retreating backside, Jamie sighs. "That boy is scrumptious."

A snicker erupts behind us. "And way out of your league." I need not turn to know who the vile voice belongs to, but I do so, anyway. And when I do, I find a sneering Kendal, looking me over from head to toe. "So I hear *you* got Juliet." I nod, and she sucks in a breath. "What other work have you done?"

Jamie taps my foot, I assume in solidarity, and I answer truthfully, "Besides one minor, exclusive performance"— *if a meadow performance with an audience of three can be considered as such*—"*this* will be my first role."

At that, Kendal's jaw drops, and if it were possible for steam to escape one's ears, it would be pouring from hers now. Perhaps honesty is *not* always the best policy. In shocked, punctuated phrases she asks, "And *you*…got the main role….over *me*?"

I nod, torn between glee and trepidation. Though the workshop will consist of several scenes from Shakespeare's most iconic plays, roughly all the same length, *Romeo and Juliet* is the understood main performance.

And according to my cousin, Reid and I are the understood main stars.

For a moment, Kendal appears to be shocked speechless—a noteworthy event. But alas, the incident is short-lived. "What did you do?" she asks, hitching a blond eyebrow, arrogance returning to her sharp eyes. "Sleep with the fat, bald guy?"

Horrified at the thought and implication to my virtue, I shake my head and gape, unable to find words. I look around us and notice that while the flurry of activity has not stopped, it has indeed slowed down. Several pairs of eyes are watching our exchange, and though the majority of my fellow actors and actresses appear either unfazed by Kendal's slanderous remark or mildly amused—Jamie is noticeably incensed—a few of them cast curious glances in our direction.

I want to tell her—to tell them—that I earned my role because I was better, that Marilyn said I have *raw, natural talent.* But under the weight of the amused, doubtful gazes trained on me, my coherent response dies.

How did I *really* get the Juliet role? Did I truly earn it because of my glowing performance at the audition? Or is my proud achievement merely a fortuitous blend of Mr. Crawford's nepotism mixed with a gentle touch of Reyna's gypsy magic?

A clipboard-holding woman barks Kendal's name. Reluctantly, and not without apparent disgust for my lack of response, she follows in the woman's wake. For everyone else, it seems as though the fleeting curiosity over how I obtained my role is lost in the excitement of scripts as interns start passing them out. A young man calls my name and hands me mine. I run my fingers over the cover and release a ragged breath.

"Chica, that girl is the founding member of the bitch patrol, and everyone here knows it. Do not let her ruin this for you." Jamie puts her hands on my shoulders and shakes them back and forth. "Come on, this is gonna be awesome. We'll hang out at rehearsals and practice at my house—whenever Austin's not being an ass. We're totally gonna be besties. And let's not skip the fact you're paired with Reid Roberts, arguably one of the hottest celebrities in existence. That's the reason Kendal's so pissy. If I know her—which I unfortunately do—she expected to hitch her wagon to his megawatt star and ride on into glory. You totally stole her thunder!" A rather evil-sounding laugh escapes her throat before she quickly sobers and says, "I swear I'm not a bitch. I just hate that girl."

Smiling at my new friend's boundless enthusiasm and refreshing honesty, I lean in and confide, "I believe I despise her, too."

Chapter Fourteen

"This is really important to my career," Reid says, raking a well-groomed hand through his spikes. "With Marilyn involved and the early buzz around my indie film premiering in a couple weeks at Sundance, there's gonna be a lot of eyes on our performance. I need this to be a hit."

Nodding to show I am listening, though still unable to comprehend most of his bizarre use of jargon, I glance at the parking lot for Austin. He promised to be here at one o'clock, and according to my helpful costar, it is now one fifteen. Fortunately—or perchance not, depending on how you look at it. Mama would certainly think *not*—Reid is more than happy to wait outside with me.

I peek again at the emptying lot.

It's not that I am ungrateful for Reid's attentiveness. Being alone out here would be much worse. But if Austin does not appear as promised soon, all my fellow actors and actresses will be gone, and I will be left again in Reid's company without a chaperone.

It is odd that I am not similarly concerned with being alone with Austin.

"Maybe we can grab some lunch and run lines?" Reid suggests, interrupting my faulty logic. "I know you said someone's coming to get you, but I'll be happy to bring you home later." When he speaks again, his voice is nearer to my ear. "Besides, I'd really like to get to know you better."

His words, and the unpleasant reminder of Matteo they bring, get my attention.

My gaze snaps up, and Reid gives me his child-who-got-caught grin. "We *are* playing history's most beloved couple of all time. I think we should at least grab some coffee."

Though the offer of a hot beverage is innocuous enough, at least in light of the more aggressive twenty-first-century courting rituals I witnessed Friday in the school hallway, it is the way Reid says it that makes me nervous. The jut of his chin, the teasing lift of his eyebrow, and the melodic rising of his voice imply he means much more than a mere sharing of refreshment.

Swallowing hard, I wet my lips and stammer, "Oh, well, I-I very much appreciate the kind offer—"

"Sorry, man," a familiar voice cuts in, laced with humor and a distinct edge of possession. "But this one's mine."

The voice registers a second before a strong arm slips around my waist. Reid's eyes widen. I turn to the boy beside me and watch Austin's face twist into a sardonic mask of challenge, daring me to argue with his claim. I subtly shake my head.

I couldn't argue if I tried. My ability to speak left the

moment he tucked me in tight against him.

"Hey, sorry, dude," Reid says, lifting his palms up as he takes a step back. "Didn't know she was taken."

Although I am sure Austin is only pretending to be jealous for his own purposes, they so happen to align with mine. Reid believing that I already have a suitor will ensure future rehearsals stay neighborly. But had Austin and I *truly* been betrothed, and any of this were actually real, I think I would take severe umbrage with the both of them. A woman being thought of as a man's possession may not be too far from the truth for *my* time, but from what I've witnessed in my short stay and learned from Cat's many tales, it's certainly not how things are done now.

Austin shrugs and leans his head down to place a swift kiss on the tip of my nose. A tingle explodes from the point of contact and shoots shivers over my entire body, making me gasp audibly. He smirks.

"No problem," he says, "I'm just glad I got here when I did. Alessandra has a habit of being a little *too* nice—" He says this while giving me a pointed look, but I'm too busy hyperventilating over his unanticipated kiss to make any sense of it. "So I see where you could've gotten the wrong idea."

The two continue talking about me over my lowered head, while I remain in an Austin-just-kissed-me daze. A series of questions runs through my mind: where did Austin come from, why was he late, why did he kiss me, and most importantly, *why* did it have that shocking effect?

I'm not so sheltered to believe we shared the sort of embrace for which poets write sonnets, but it's the closest I have ever come. Even when Matteo brazenly pulled me into seclusion at a dinner party or social gathering, he only did so to whisper promises of our future. He was never so bold as to take me in his arms and show me what a true kiss of passion could be like.

And now that I *have* gotten a taste—granted it was on my nose, but still a taste—I decide I would very much like another.

Austin shakes me, jarring me from the fog. "Anyway, thanks for looking out for her until I could get here. I'm taking her to my family's place in Malibu, so we better get on the road." He looks down at me and winks. "Ready, baby?"

I stare into bright blue eyes twinkling with false affection, and my stomach clenches.

What would it be like to have a boy really look at me that way?

A cough pulls my attention back from my melancholy thoughts, and I find Reid watching me intently. "See you at rehearsal tomorrow?"

I nod. "I look forward to it."

Austin grumbles something under his breath and pulls me toward his hastily parked red truck. The driver's side door is ajar, and the engine is still running. As I climb in the passenger seat, I realize his truck is another example of the duality that lies inside this complicated, clearly intelligent boy. Cat told me that although she and Austin are in the same grade, the school held him back due to insufficient grades two years ago. Unlike her, he doesn't have to worry about bothering parents or hiring kind drivers when he desires to go somewhere—he is free to take me in his own car wherever he'd like.

On his own, without the need of a chaperone.

Stamping down the unfamiliar burgeoning heat in my core, I risk a glance back at the theater, knowing Reid is watching. His lips lift in a mischievous grin and he waves. Twisting fully in my seat, I wave back and Austin slams on the gas pedal, reversing abruptly. My head lurches toward the hard dashboard.

"Oof!"

As I rub my temple, I glare at him with everything in me, sending forth as much venom as I can muster.

To which he replies, "Oops," and attempts to look innocent, but fails miserably.

Any lingering heat in my veins from his shocking kiss turns to red-hot fury. I know he drove in such a manner on purpose—I only wish I understood boys better as to know *why.*

Sinking into my seat, I vow to ignore Austin for the rest of the trip. If he can be maddening to the point of complete exasperation, well, so can I.

I see him look at me from the corner of his eye, and his lips give an infuriating twitch. Then he pulls the truck forward, whistling a happy tune, as though he has not a care in the world. I clench my teeth to keep from growling.

As we drive pasts the front of the theater, I glance out my window to meet Reid's friendly gaze....and notice the gentle smile that graced his face before has grown.

• • •

The Michaels family beach house in Malibu has been transported from the pages of a storybook, adding only the wonderful modern convenience of electricity. Perched on the bluff over the ocean, the house is framed by towering trees and elegant stone work. The crashing sound of waves greets me as I step from Austin's truck and the scent of the salty air erases all the tension and confusion from the interminable drive. I close my eyes, take a deep breath, and cannot contain a small squeal of excitement.

Austin shakes his head and tromps to the front door. He unlocks it and walks through, and after a short pause on the threshold, foolishly waiting to be escorted or at the very least *welcomed* inside, I kick my shoes off at the entrance—as I have learned is a polite thing to do when entering someone's home. Truly, twenty-first century-people have no issues with ankle viewing—and follow in his wake.

The atrium opens up into a long, wide corridor, filled with elegant touches. As I walk, I lift my head to the soaring ceiling and accidently brush against a vase of flowers atop a polished mahogany table. It wobbles, then rights itself again. Up ahead, Austin turns right at the end of the hall, but I choose to take my time, soaking in the energy and sweet scent of the space and marveling at its secrets.

Family photographs line the walls, but it takes me a moment to recognize the boy who brought me here. The frames tell a story of a different Austin, one with close-cropped hair who wore suits and collared shirts. Who won awards—*lots* of them—and who appeared very close with his family.

There is his father, interchangeably wearing a stern expression in a handful of photos and an inauthentic smile in others, and then an attractive, frail woman I assume is his mother. Her gentle spirit seems to leap out from behind the frame, and I softly touch the glass. And, of course, I recognize Jamie right away. Unlike Austin, she looks almost the same as the girl I left an hour ago, except possibly a few years younger, and appears as smiling and jovial as ever. If I had to guess, the most recent photographs are a glimpse into Austin's world about three years ago—a time when he clearly had a much different approach to school. And fashion.

But as I stand before the wall of photographs, gaping at the transformation and wondering what could have caused it—along with why the timeline appears to stop three years ago—I notice another difference.

It's in Austin's eyes.

Their usual lightness, their playfulness, the sarcasm they naturally exude…it's all gone. The hints of vulnerability I have seen mere glimpses of are there, only magnified, as well as a palpable anxiety. When the family of four is posed together, Austin is seldom by his father's side. And when he is—like the one of them in front of a *Michaels for State Senate 2008* sign— the tension in his shoulders and jaw is unmistakable.

"Alessandra?"

I jump at the sound of Austin's voice echoing off the wood surrounding me. Twisting around, feeling guilty for being caught poring over something so personal, I breathe a sigh of relief when I discover I am alone.

"Are you coming or what?"

This time I realize his voice is carrying from down the hall. Leaving the surprising peek into Austin's past behind me, I dash around the corner and find the boy in question standing in the center of a room filled with luxurious white fabrics and a wall of windows highlighting a spectacular, deep blue ocean view.

It's all so beautiful…

So open…

I look back at Austin.

So…*secluded*.

A nervous giggle escapes.

"Th-this is enchanting, Austin," I say, taking a step toward him. My feet sink into the soft white carpet beneath me, and my toes practically sigh in response. "Thank you for bringing me here."

"This isn't a date, Alessandra," he tells me rather sharply, squelching any benevolent thoughts I may've had for him after seeing the family photos. "I don't do dates. This is a challenge."

"Of that I am well aware," I say, forcing a smile. If I were Cat, I would toss back a witty retort, but instead I ask, "And for my first unsheltered test, what am I to do? Ride a bike? Rollerblade?"

Both of these are activities we passed on our drive through the neighborhood and Austin had to explain, adding to his opinion of my sheltered life. Although I'm unsure how I will manage riding a bike in a skirt, I am eager to try.

The corners of Austin's mouth twitch—my first sign of foreboding—and then he tilts his chin at the open water beyond. My eyes widen in horror.

Not possible.

He would not *dare* to take me into the ocean…would he?

My cousin has assured me, repeatedly, that water is safe now, and though I've been taught entering a public pool of any kind is equivalent to asking fate to bestow the plague upon you,

I accept that things have changed.

But they haven't changed *that* much.

As scandalous as this century has proven to be, this is not Sodom and Gomorrah. Surely bathing with a boy who is not your husband is still considered *highly* inappropriate?

Then a photo flashes in my mind from Jenna's sweet sixteen albums. It's the one Lucas found so amusing, a party with a "beach" theme where the guests arrived in *bathing suits.* Realizing that must be what Austin intends for us to wear in the water—*not* going in nude—only slightly eases my stress.

The vivid image of the guests displaying so much flesh burns brighter in my memory.

And I'm scandalized at the thought of showing my elbows!

Staring through the window at the endless water, I know I cannot simply back down from this task. The challenges will stop, and this *is* what I want. Adventure and excitement. But since bathing suits appear to be a modern social convention, I cling to the possible out with everything that exists within me.

"Sadly, Austin, I am without a swimsuit." I sigh dramatically. Acting really does become easier with practice. "I thank you for the idea, however, as it does look refreshing. Perhaps another time?"

I offer a sweet smile, knowing that another time will never occur but not sharing that aloud. Austin smiles back. "Not a problem." He opens a door and steps back, folding his arms. "Dad's assistant stocks this place with guest suits, in every color and size you can imagine, all complete with the overpriced tags still on."

He pauses, and even from my distance away, I can see the

muscle throbbing in his jaw. Then he blinks, and the look from outside the theater is back in his eyes, daring me to give him another excuse. "So I repeat, not a problem."

My head begins to throb. *Fine,* I think, even as ice shoots down my back. *I can do this.* Inhaling deeply, I briefly close my eyes. *Forgive me, Mama.*

With a nod and walking tall, I push past him into the room. The door closes behind me. Not even the thick wood can hide the rich tones of Austin's laugh.

Gritting my teeth, I stand before the small open closet and survey my options. Austin is right—every color of the rainbow is represented, all in various styles, and all of them incredibly tiny. I remember noticing in Jenna's book that a handful of girls wore one long suit (in lieu of the itty bitty scraps of cloth the others did) and thinking if I were ever forced, at the consequence of death, to clothe myself in such a costume, that would be the style I'd choose. Unfortunately, but not surprisingly, that is not an option today.

I cautiously take down a pink *bikini* and hold it against me.

Fear and an intense loathing for the man who created this form of clothing churn in my stomach. I cannot wear this in front of Austin. But just when I feel tempted to give up—before even embarking on my first challenge—or give in to a dead faint, Reyna's words from the tent ring in my ear: *You clearly crave adventure, Alessandra. But I have to wonder if you are brave enough to grasp it.*

When I emerge from the changing room, cold and drafty, I cannot feel my feet, yet somehow they carry me onto the plush carpet. Austin is leaned against the counter, fingers flying on his phone. I must make a noise because he abruptly lifts his head, instantly causing my suit to feel as though it is shrinking on my body. My nails pierce the flesh of my palms, fighting the urge to cover myself...but then I notice Austin's slow appraisal.

His eyes skim over my exposed skin, heating it where a moment before it felt numb, and the muscles of his neck work as he swallows. Although he is careful to keep any emotion from his face, his approval radiates from his tense shoulders all the way to the fingers twitching at his sides. The realization emboldens me.

I wanted adventure. I wanted a taste of more, of what confident women like Cat experience every day. And here it is.

I straighten my shoulders and sashay forward, even venturing to add a sway to my hips as I do so. When Austin's eyes finally widen, I want to do a dance of triumph. Instead, I grin and let myself perform my own assessment. I've been so caught up in worry about *my* clothing that I did not pause to consider what *Austin* would wear. Now I know...a pair of long shorts molded to the thick muscles of his thighs, and that is all.

His strong, contoured chest is utterly and altogether bare.

I pause midstride.

Austin shirtless is a glorious sight.

My mouth goes dry, and an irrepressible grin springs upon my lips. I force my gaze to meet his, now back to aloof and unbothered, and begin to chide myself for my wanton behavior. But then I remember this is a challenge. And although I am certain the main test lies in the water itself, I am equally sure my behavior now is just as vital.

Recalling the impudent wink and saucy grin he tossed his

admirer Friday, I give him the same and repeat the words he asked me. "Like what you see?"

Perhaps my voice shook during the delivery, but I give myself an internal hug at the evident shock my audacious words create. Austin's mouth opens slightly, and his gaze sharpens as if seeing me for the first time.

But alas, my victory is short-lived. He recovers and moves toward me, closing the distance between us with quick, determined footsteps. He stops so close, I have to look up to meet the predator's gleam in his eyes. Running a callused fingertip along my collarbone slowly and seductively, his minty breath fans across my lips as he says, "Yep."

And time goes still.

Oh, Signore in heaven, now what do I do?

If it was not evident before, it is now—I am not meant to flirt. All I can do is stand here, breathing in the smell of his warm skin, with no clue how to react, what to say, or how to fight the extreme need to take at least a dozen steps back to a safe distance.

The silence stretches. Austin watches me, no doubt seeing every insecurity highlighted on my face. He lifts his hand and begins to reach out, and I forget to breathe.

His hand hesitates near my shoulder…and then shoots past it.

And he laughs.

Opening the glass door leading to the patio, he grins and walks out, leaving me alone. Again. Frustrated—and if I am to be perfectly honest, disappointed.

He was teasing me, testing me. And I failed.

But I will *not* fail again.

With renewed purpose, I march through the door, close it behind me, and gain speed to catch up with Austin's retreating back. I follow him down the stone path to the private beach and a weird object near the waterline. He turns and gives me a knowing look. "I thought we best start easy—ever been on one of these before?"

Not even knowing what *this* is, I shake my head.

"Didn't think so. Alessandra, this is a Jet Ski."

His condescending tone is not lost on me. Lifting my chin, I walk up to the object, flip my hair like I have seen girls do at the high school, and ask, "And how does it work? What do we do?"

Austin's eyes flicker down my body again. The late-afternoon sun has warmed the cool January morning air, but my skin prickles under his gaze. He takes a corner of his lower lip between his teeth and then says, "*You* get on, wrap your arms around me, press your chest against my back, and hold on tight. I take care of the rest."

The intimate image his words conjure steals my breath.

Picking up some sort of black clothing from the ground, he steps into it. "I'm guessing you never wore one of these before, so Alessandra, this is a *wetsuit*." His eyebrows rise as he condescendingly annunciates the word and tugs the slick fabric over his muscular legs.

I try not to stare as he tugs the tight suit over his hips. He first slides one arm inside and then the other, hiding me from the view of his chest. He reaches behind, and I hear the now-familiar sound of a zipper working as the fabric molds to his body.

Austin circles his arms, stretching the fabric, and it isn't until he stops and smirks that I realize I did not meet my goal of not staring. I shove my hair behind my ear and lean back on my heels.

"Now that you've seen how to do it, this is yours." He bends to pick up a second suit. Every move of his muscles is on display, and after only a slight hesitation, I avert my gaze. "I'm guessing you're about Jamie's size," he adds.

Not trusting my voice to keep secret my inappropriate thoughts, I nod and take the suit from his outstretched hand.

Since I watched every second of Austin tugging on his, this should be easy to put on. But when I step into the first leg hole, my big toe catches on the inside of the material, and I lose my balance. He catches my elbow and saves me from falling face-first into the sand. While his warm grip steadies my feet, the unexpected touch on my bare skin has the exact opposite effect on my knees.

Breathe, Alessandra.

"Thanks," I choke out, not able to meet his gaze. I make quick, embarrassing work of wiggling and tugging my wetsuit into place, bending and squatting for the proper fit, just wanting to be covered again. When the arms are in place, I reach around, trying to locate the string of the zipper, and feel Austin's hand close around mine.

"Here, let me."

He gathers my hair in his hands and tucks it to the side. My eyes close. The zipper starts its ascent up my back, and I proceed to listen to the pound of my pulse as Austin's fingers skate across my skin. When the garment is closed, he slides my arms through a sleeveless black vest, then turns my body to him so he can latch it. His hands falter as they hover over my chest. We gaze at each other for a long beat.

Then, clearing his throat, Austin snaps it closed and backs away.

He pushes the red-and-black Jet Ski into the water, past the first few crashing waves, then throws a leg over the side. He turns to me, extending an upturned palm, but as I watch the water pound against his legs, I slowly shake my head and inch away. Forget the confusion of the past few minutes or my concern whether riding wrapped around Austin is appropriate…are Jet Skis even *safe*? So far, my experience with modern machines has taught me that they travel at terrifying speeds. What if I were to accidently let go and fly off?

Austin's face gentles, and he curls his fingers, coaxing me closer to the watery death trap. "I've got you, Alessandra," he says. "I promise nothing's gonna hurt you. You can trust me."

The sardonic guise he hides behind drops for just a moment, but it is enough.

I say a quick prayer and place my hand in his.

With my legs straddling the seat, my arms wrapped tightly around Austin's firm stomach, and my chest and face pressed against his back, I do not need the extra layer my wetsuit provides. I am quite warm without it. Under me, the engine rumbles. Austin grabs my clasped hands, ensuring my death grip.

And then we are flying.

Fear is left behind me on the beach. My laughter is swallowed by the wind. And I hold onto Austin. The rest of the world falls away as he powers the machine forward. A whistling sound envelops us, yet there's also silence in the midst of the roar. Out here, there's no room for worrisome thoughts about the future or about the past. No time for concerns over when I will return or how much I miss my family. In this bubble of Austin, wind, and water, all I can do is live and breathe and smile.

Austin spins us in circles, and then we fly forward, free as the winged creatures overhead. He bounces us over a swell, and a spray of water splashes my face, tickling the skin left exposed by my wetsuit. I squeal, and under my clasped hands, I feel his taut stomach muscles shake with laughter. Then he takes off again in another sharp turn, racing in the opposite direction of which we came.

Excitement has me screaming, asking him to go faster. I close my eyes against the sting of the salty air and the lash of my hair and tilt my head back, feeling more uninhibited than I ever have before.

More free, more alive…just *more*.

Chapter Fifteen

As our car glides down the tree-lined street for my first full week of school, my thoughts are not where they should be. I *should* be reciting Cat's list of lingo along with the new references I searched and added myself last night—it turns out *Scooby-Doo* is an amusing program. I ended up watching (and enjoying) several episodes and laughing at the *gang*'s comical high jinks. My cousin, equally amused by my merriment, was impressed with how quickly I acclimated to using her laptop, and I must admit, so was I. It is amazing how much information is available at one's fingertips in this world. But in all honesty, right now I couldn't care less about talking dogs, the World Wide Web, or any of those things, for my thoughts are turned to Austin and the mysterious transformation he appears to have undergone three years ago.

Yesterday I learned that asking him directly about his past does nothing but make things worse. On our way out of the beach house, I made the mistake of stopping before one of the pictures of his family and inquiring why there weren't any recent additions. The temporary truce we struck out on the water vanished, the scales fell back over his eyes, and he walked outside without a word.

Obviously if I want to discover the truth, I must do so on my own.

"Cat," I say, turning away from the parade of homes outside my window. Beside me, my cousin lifts her head and opens her sleep-dazed eyes. A happy early riser she is not. "Do you know anything about Mr. Michaels, Austin's father?"

I know as I ask that a much easier way to uncover the truth would be to mention the family photos I found yesterday at his beach house; however, Cat still believes we were at the library all day. I'm unaccustomed to the pressing weight that the guilt of lying causes. If it were a perfect world, I could stop with the deceit altogether, but I can't, especially not after experiencing the rush of the wind and water on the back of Austin's Jet Ski. If I tell her the truth, she will likely ask me to stop the challenges.

And nothing is keeping me from whatever task he has planned for us next.

Cat scrunches her mouth. "You know, it's weird. In middle school, Austin was, like, king, totally set to follow his dad's footsteps to the White House. He was a year older than me, but I still knew who he was—everyone did. He led the soccer team, won all the assembly awards, was student council president... Then, when I was in the sixth grade, his dad won the senate election, and I remember him coming to school a couple of times. The man was a complete and utter tool, but you could see that Austin worshipped him."

Out of everything Cat just said, this surprises me the most. *Abhorred* seems a much more apt choice of verb, at least based on Austin's reactions around me whenever the subject of his dad came up.

"When Austin graduated," she continues, "I totally expected to find him on top of everything at the high school, even as a sophomore. But instead, I found him in *my* class because he failed an entire year." She shrugs. "I don't know how that happened. Even weirder is that when his dad campaigned for reelection a couple months ago, the news coverage just kinda skimmed over Austin. It was like he didn't exist. His sister Jamie was at all the events, at least according to the pictures, anyway, but Austin…well, if I were to guess, he was off surfing."

At the onslaught of information, I massage my temples, hoping that maybe *that* will help me process it all. Our car stops, and I glance out the window. We are at a light, a block away from the white stone building of the high school. Only a few minutes left to ask two more nagging questions. I tuck my leg under me and decide to go with the easier one first. "What about Austin's and Jamie's mother? I notice you didn't mention her."

Cat winces. "She died."

Horrified, I slap my hand over my mouth. Austin's mother had looked frail in the more recent photographs, but it never occurred to me that she could have been sick. Hurting for the young boy who lost his mother, I whisper, "How long ago?"

Cat tilts her head and stares at the ceiling, thinking. "I want to say two or three years ago. At the time, it was a big deal. She'd been battling breast cancer, and for a while, people wore pink ribbons and organized walks, and our health classes focused on prevention. But then, I guess people moved on to other causes." She frowns, and the car rolls again as the light turns green.

Austin's loss reminds me of how very much I miss my own mother, miss hearing her words of wisdom, and how devastated I would be if I ever lost her. As the high school comes into view, I take a breath and ask the final question I had been holding, wondering if in the light of everything else, it still even matters. "And Kendal?"

Cat narrows her eyes at me, suspicion rolling off her in waves, but she answers as we come to a stop in front of the school. "They were together when his mom died, but the cheating scandal broke not too long after that."

With a heart torn between wanting to run and hide and needing to find Austin and throw my arms around him, I step out from the car, up the front stone stairs, and into the frantic hallway. It would appear that fate has made the choice for me. Austin meets my gaze over the shuffle of students from where he stands, waiting beside my locker. He shoulders a bag that looks suspiciously stuffed—beside the one notebook I saw on Friday, I'm under the distinct impression he doesn't own any other supplies—and bestows an even more suspicious grin upon my cousin.

She, I notice, seems to be just as wary. "Good morning, Austin. You're here shockingly early. Did someone remember to take his good-student pills today?"

Austin's lips twitch with amusement, and he shifts his eyes to mine. "Just had a question to ask Less about our *project*."

I widen my eyes in silent annoyance but luckily, Cat doesn't catch his double meaning.

Out on the water yesterday, I told Austin about my need to keep his challenge a secret. Also, in a moment of adrenaline-filled weakness, I somehow divulged my peculiar nickname. From the look Cat gives me, she finds this very telling.

Austin smirks, apparently catching the same look. "I'll make sure she gets to class on time."

She chokes on a laugh. "That's interesting because I wasn't totally sure you knew how to get there yourself." Then she leans close and whispers, "Do you want me to leave?"

Not wanting her to see my excitement at Austin's proposal and what it could potentially mean, I lower my lashes and nod.

Cat smacks her lips. "O-kay then," she says, not sounding at all convinced. "I guess I'll just see you at lunch...*Alessandra*."

At her overt attempt at provocation—my cousin never uses my given name—I lift my eyes. "Yes. See you then, *Caterina*."

Her head jerks back—probably as much at the name she shares with her mother as at the surprising confidence in my tone. A small smile of admiration springs to her lips. "All right, kiddos, try not to kill each other when I'm gone." Cat takes a step away and elbows Austin in the ribs. "Take care of my girl, Michaels."

She walks down the hall toward her own locker and I watch until she disappears into the crowd. "Thank you for maintaining my ruse," I tell Austin. "Much like you, she seems to think I am sheltered and in need of protection."

He chuckles, a deep, rumbling sound that for some reason makes me uncomfortable. Turning away, I grab the dial of the lock with shaky hands and try to remember the combination Cat taught me. Austin closes his hand over mine. "You're not gonna need any books today."

Confused, I twist to look at him with a frown. "I'm not?"

He shakes his head. "Not where we're going."

It takes me what feels like a full minute to realize his intention. Then I gasp. "But you promised Cat you would get me to class." He nods, not at all looking guilty for his blatant deceit—he must practice it far more frequently than I do—and I shake my head. "You lied!"

"Yeah, sweetheart," he says in a slow drawl. "I did." Austin pulls a piece of paper from his pocket, unfolds it, and hands it to me. With a devilish grin he says, "Challenge two presented."

A glance at the paper reveals the words *Lethal Xperience: Rush Theme Park* written above a steel contraption built with impossible twists and turns, looming at even more impossible heights. A group of unfortunate people strapped to the death-defying object peer up from the page, strangely enough with joy on their faces.

My gaze shoots back to his. He laughs at what I can only assume is my panic-stricken expression and reaches out to nudge my open jaw closed with his knuckle. "It's a roller coaster, Princess. It's fun. Are you allergic to fun?"

Fun I can handle, I want to tell him. *Death, not so much.*

"B-but class," I say, weakly waving my hand at the rooms around us. "Isn't leaving school grounds during the day against the rules?"

He huffs in exasperation. "Alessandra, you only live once, and to be honest, *you're* not living at all. You promised you'd give me a week to loosen you up. Are you backing out already?"

I loathe the truth in his words.

Needing to concentrate—and to not be distracted by Austin's temptingly sinful grin—I squeeze my eyes shut.

Does it really matter if I break a few modern-day rules?

My time here is finite. Four days have passed since I arrived in the twenty-first century, and I have already passed my first marker. Shouldn't I spend the remainder of my time embracing every moment, not bored behind a disagreeable desk, listening to concepts I cannot fully comprehend?

I bite my lip, unsure if I am more excited or shocked at my own thoughts—or if they are even truth or merely an excuse to be alone again with Austin. I glance at the emptying hallway.

With a teasing wiggle of my eyebrows and an eager smile at my tempter, I take off running.

. . .

Austin gets out of the truck and stretches, the hem of his faded blue T-shirt lifting. A strip of bare flesh—the same flesh I openly gawked at yesterday—peeks from underneath, but even though my eyes got their fill then, I steal another quick, swoon-worthy glance. Then, with a mouth gone dry, I turn away from the enticing sight and gaze upon my death instead.

Across the crowded parking lot sits Rush, an outdoor wonder otherwise known as an amusement park, evidently home to much more than just the Lethal Xperience. As I gaze out...and *up*...from the relative safety of my seat at the wide array of supposed enjoyment, I come to the decision that people of the twenty-first century have entirely too much free time on their hands.

Where I come from, in the rare moment when we are without duty, we create art or sing songs or even talk. We do not search for creative ways to defy nature and call it *fun*.

Austin opens my door and chuckles. "Let me explain how this works. In order to ride the roller coaster, one must get out of the vehicle. It doesn't come to you."

I suck my teeth and wonder again how I can find such arrogant behavior appealing. It must be a sickness.

"Hi-*larious*," I mumble, a sarcastic expression I overheard Cat tell her father last night. I did not quite get it then, but it sure feels as though it fits now. Austin smirks. Heaving a sigh of resignation at my fate, I step onto the cracked asphalt.

He grabs my hand, most likely to ensure I don't wander off or make an escape. But the heat of his skin centers me, bringing all my attention away from my frazzled nerves and onto my pounding, frantic pulse.

The towering structures grow in size with each additional step we take toward the gate. When we reach the front, Austin behaves like a gentleman for once and purchases our tickets, and I crane my neck up.

My, that is high.

I imagine my cousin asking, *What have you gotten yourself into now, girlfriend?* And the truly horrible part is that I don't even know how to answer.

What *have* I gotten myself into?

I still firmly believe that Austin will never let anything happen to me, but it is quite clear we view danger very differently.

A hand touches the small of my back, and suddenly he is

ushering me inside.

Without stopping or even slowing his stride, he grabs a map from a vendor and flips it open. "So Lethal Xperience is at the back of the park. We'll hit that first and then make our way up to the front."

He seems unaware that the length of his legs far exceeds my own. As I frantically attempt to match his stride, I must pant or wheeze because he finally looks down at me, no doubt pink-faced and wide-eyed both from the sensory overload surrounding us and my huffing at a near jog to stay beside him. He grins. "Try to keep up, Short Stuff."

I grit my teeth with determination and somehow keep myself from muttering, *Yes, Master.* But the thought still makes me smile. Cat must be rubbing off.

We pass a circular ride filled with fake horses going up and down. Giggling and drooling children clap their adorable hands from their belted saddles while a spirited tune blares overhead. Just past that is a miniature roller coaster made to look like a giant, happy centipede. The child in the front seat waves to his mother as the cart dips, and his squeal of joy tails behind him. It's too bad that not all roller coasters can be five feet tall.

Then I get a wicked idea.

Austin believes I am a child, naïve and boring, and, it would seem, without any humor. This second challenge is supposed to be about fun, and nothing—not even the lead role in a prestigious play with a crowd of a thousand—will give me more joy than turning the tables on him, even if only for a moment.

Looking back at the children's ride, I grab Austin's elbow and say innocently, "Is this not the roller coaster you are looking for?"

He stops rather abruptly and peers at me through squinted eyes. "You know, it's like you *look* normal..." He trails off, points a long, tan finger at the centipede ride, and in a tone dripping with condescension explains, "Less, Arthropod Picnic is a kiddie ride. It's made for pint-sized ankle-biters ages three and under."

I try my best to look disappointed. I do everything I can to contain my mounting delight. But after no more than a few brief moments, I let forth a victorious giggle.

Realization dawns on his face. "You think you're funny, huh?"

When I nod, he chuckles. He leans back on his heels and lets his gaze travel over my body. Humor dissipates as my skin prickles to life. On Austin's slow ascent back up, he pauses to look me in the eye, and an emotion crosses his face. It's so fleeting—gone and there in an instant—that I cannot catch it.

"So, you think you're ready to play at the big girl table now." The left side of his mouth kicks up in a grin. "We'll just have to see about that."

The apparent taunt and Austin's added wink spur me on.

This is my chance to prove to him that I'm not the timid girl I once was. To prove to myself that I'm no longer the child of my youth but a *woman* ready for the future.

I sashay toward a person dressed as a shiny nugget of gold posing for pictures with children, feeling Austin watching me, his gaze on my every step like a physical touch. My legs feel wobbly under my skirt, but an energizing spark ignites in my blood. I glance over my shoulder, confirming I have his complete attention, and then with an outward shrug (and an inner dance), I reply with every ounce of confidence I can muster, "Yes. We *will*."

Austin's smile widens. The sounds and patrons of the park fade away, and it is as if we are the only two around. I don't know what is happening…I scarcely even recognize myself in this moment. Being with Austin does that. It turns me into someone else.

And I like who I become.

I watch his slow saunter, my body poised with tension. I don't know what is going to happen next, but I wouldn't trade the delicious expectation for anything. Austin doesn't stop until he is right in front of me, close enough that I have to look up to meet his demanding blue gaze, and so close that warmth fans across my face as he says in a low voice, "Careful, girl. You're playing with fire."

"I've been *careful* my whole life," I tell him, surprising myself with the resentment ringing in my tone. But it's the truth. "And you know, I think it's about time for me to be a little…" I bite the corner of my bottom lip, searching for exactly the right word to describe the emotions and thoughts that have surfaced the last few days. When I find it, I smile and wiggle my eyebrows suggestively "*Wild*."

Austin sucks in a breath. He searches my eyes, and I boldly stare back, praying that he cannot see my knees shaking. Then, obviously concluding that I meant every word, he flashes his devilish grin. "I can work with that."

Chapter Sixteen

The coaster chugs up the steel tracks inch by inch. Anticipation, fear, and unbridled excitement roil in my gut. Without thinking, I reach out and latch onto Austin's arm. He gently threads his fingers through mine, and I chance a look over.

His eyes are focused on me.

"Here it comes," he says. His words and the gentle squeeze of his hand make my stomach dip.

I don't turn back to watch the end of our slow ascent. Instead, I lock my gaze onto the enigmatic boy responsible for bringing me here, for unleashing this other person that's been trapped inside me for so long...

And we fall.

"Ahhh!"

The wind steals the rest of my scream, but I am quite sure it continues long after we plummet to the earth. And then again as the Lethal Xperience shoots us back up, only to send us on not one, not two, not *three*, but four consecutive twisting, turning, stomach-flipping loops.

My cheeks feel sliced in half from the width of my smile.

The coaster comes to a sudden and jolting stop with a resounding *whoosh*, and Austin asks, "Wild enough for you?"

I shake my head. "No. But this park has excellent potential."

He laughs and helps me out of the web of belts and locks the attendant placed around me. People in modern times may be crazy, but they aren't stupid. And for that, I am eternally grateful.

"What next?" I ask as we exit the ride and walk through a cluttered gift shop.

Austin stops in front of a counter and points at a wall of screens. "First, we get a memento of your daredevil experience. Then we snatch a funnel cake from the snack shop outside."

"Food?" I ask incredulously.

Perhaps my stomach *is* a bit empty, and the sweet aroma wafting from the Snack Shoppe we passed did make my mouth water…but I'm way too twitchy to eat now.

I want to ride another roller coaster.

Or jump off that tall crane in the sky in the center of the park.

I tell Austin this, and he shakes his head with a smile. "All in good time. But honey, I'm a growing boy. You don't mess with a man's stomach."

The disappointment of defeat lasts only until he procures a bag from the woman behind the counter and hands it to me. I've always had a soft spot for gifts. I take a peek inside and grin. "Hey, that's us." Then I glance back up, confused. "But I don't recall a photographer sitting on the tracks. How did someone take this?"

"They mount the camera on the ride itself," he explains, his expression a mixture of amusement and confusion. Judging from that expression it would appear that this should be common knowledge. Oops. "It snapped that during our first free fall."

Impressed, I carefully slide the picture out of the bag and stare at the captured image: Austin and me, our gazes locked, sharing a secret grin.

Something inside my chest catches.

He clears his throat. Prying my fingers from the photograph, Austin slips it back inside the gift bag, then snaps his fingers. "So, food."

With a determined nod, he takes two brusque steps in the direction of the exit. Unfortunately, as he does, the pocket of his jeans catches on a rack of California-inspired souvenirs, sending a shower of overpriced goodies to the floor. Shooting the woman manning the counter an apologetic glance, he stoops to replace a few on the stand. Then, popping back to his feet, he flees the shop without another look back. My gaze widens in delight.

Austin Michaels is flustered.

And he's flustered because of *me*.

A peculiar feeling of empowerment whispers through my veins and across my skin. Matteo may not have ever loved me, and it's very likely I will return home after this time travel adventure to become a cold man's bride. But right now, in this moment, in this time, I made a boy as beautiful and aloof as

Austin the Incorrigible Flirt actually nervous. Now *that* is an accomplishment.

Positively giddy with my success, and with a joyous skip to my step, I rush to catch up.

As it turns out, funnel cakes are a gift straight from heaven. It must be true, because there is no way a mere mortal could fry bread in such a lovely pattern, sprinkle it with the lightest, sweetest sugar, squeeze warm chocolate fudge across the top, and then finish it with a dollop of fluffy, cloud-like whipped cream. Oh, and a bright red cherry. It is just not possible.

I take another bite and moan in ecstasy.

"That good, huh?"

"I commend your stomach," I tell him around a mouth stuffed with the treat. My manners have all but disappeared by now, but I am finding it very difficult to care. "There are no words for how good this is."

Austin breaks off a sugar-dusted piece and pops it into his mouth. "My mom always brought us here after our first ride. Jamie and I would stuff ourselves with crap and then take off again. Half the time we took turns getting sick, but we never messed with the tradition."

I give him a gentle smile. The softer look is back on his face. I don't want to say the wrong thing and make his walls come shuttering back up. But then he looks at me with eyes lost in memory, and I cannot help myself. "Tell me about her."

Austin slouches in his seat. "She was great." He plucks a napkin from the silver dispenser and starts shredding it, and I wonder if I've pushed too far. Just when I decide that I have and that he's not going to elaborate, he says hoarsely, "She had this amazing singing voice. Mom, I mean. Jamie and I can't sing to save our lives, but she…she sang every Sunday at church—even when she was sick. Until"—he swallows—"well, until she couldn't anymore."

My eyes prick with tears, hearing my own mother's sweet singing voice in my memory. The loneliness I feel over missing her, missing all of them, is nothing compared to Austin's pain—he has lost his mother forever. I jiggle my foot beneath the table, wanting, needing to do or say something to help shoulder his grief, but not knowing what. This is the *real* Austin, the one hidden beneath all the sardonic expressions, careless attitude, and outrageous flirtation. A boy who fiercely loved and misses his mother, and three years later remains locked in pain. I try despite my inadequacy. "And your father—"

"Is an ass."

I inhale a sharp breath. Austin's clipped, automatic, venomous reply steals any chance of me asking him to explain.

But I don't have to.

He shakes his head and says, "Do you know that asshole was in Sacramento during Mom's last week? It was just Jamie and me with her. The hospice people came and went, and Grandma was there, but we were the ones who took care of her. We gave her ice chips; we sang off-key and told her stories. We put the pillows under her head and jumped every time her breathing stopped. Dad came home for the very end, when she was practically in a coma, but not when it mattered. Not when she needed him." He draws in a ragged breath and narrows his eyes. "It's always about the job for him, the *people*. My dad cares about everyone in the state of California *except* his own family. And it took Mom dying in her bed without him for me to finally see it."

The sudden silence after Austin's rare verbal onslaught is deafening.

My heart pounds in my chest. As horrified as I am by the images his words put in my mind, I know I have to keep him talking, let him know that he can trust me. Admittedly, part of it is for selfish reasons—by confiding the truth about his past, I can at last solve the mystery. But mostly I want it for him. I doubt he ever speaks about this with anyone. The flush of his cheeks, the erratic rise of his chest, and the tick in his jaw are all proof of that.

So I wrap my hands around his clenched fist and say as gently as I can, "Cat told me you changed after your mom died."

I don't give voice to my suspicion; I want Austin to do that on his own.

At first, he doesn't say anything. He just stares at our joined hands. Then, after a long moment, a faint, rueful smile twitches on his lips. "I actually used to idolize the dickhead. Can you believe that?"

He laughs; a harsh, derisive sound that causes me to flinch.

"I thought the man could do no wrong, so of course I couldn't, either. I *had* to be perfect—I was Taylor Michaels's son. But once Mom was gone, I realized it doesn't matter what I do. It won't make him care. The perfect family façade he wants everyone to believe is bullshit...and I'm done being a part of the hypocrisy."

His thumb skims across the edges of my hand, trapping, then releasing my fingers—an unconscious touch seeking comfort. The scrape of his nail across my flesh induces a warm tingle, and a peculiar sense of déjà vu envelops me, but I ignore it. Now is not the time for my baffling responses.

When Austin lifts his eyes back to mine, I notice the blue of his irises has deepened, less like the ocean and more like the dark denim of his jeans. "It started as a way to get a rise out of him, you know? To see if it'd get his attention, what he'd do. But then everything changed. People who used to kiss my feet because I was the golden boy's son suddenly expected the worst of me. And I gave it to them." His jaw ticks, and he pops his neck.

Knowing that it was around this same time that Kendal also broke his heart makes his confession all the more poignant. No wonder he guards himself—and his heart—so much. In some ways, he's a lot like Cat.

"It's easier this way," he continues. "Not caring how I measure up or if I'm good enough to meet anyone's standards. I just let it go and do what I want now." He shrugs. "Beats the shit out of pretending to be someone I'm not."

He says it like it's not a big deal when it's anything but. For me, his declaration is life changing. I know he isn't talking about me—he doesn't know the real me or my struggle between society's expectations and my own desire for passion. But his words, however crudely spoken, fit me just the same. They stay with me through the rest of our snack and as I emerge with a back-to-normal Austin into the warm January sunshine, ready to tackle our next exhilarating ride.

We stop when we find a crowd gathered in front of the Snack Shoppe. The lively tune blaring from the center soon explains why. As Austin guides us along the edge of the cheering audience and away from the street performance, I find myself dragging my feet. Where a moment before I couldn't wait to test my new bravado, now I am intrigued by the music. I grab Austin's arm. "Could we watch for just a moment?"

He sighs with exaggeration, as if he is granting me a favor, but nods. Eager, I politely push my way into the audience to catch a glimpse of the singers. Though I have yet to see the main vocalist's face, the sweet notes of her voice leave no mistaking she is a woman. And her enthusiasm, judging by the dancing crowd around me, is contagious.

A tall man blocking my view checks his watch and yells something indecipherable at the woman by his side. Providentially, they leave, granting me my first clear shot.

My gaze lands on the source of the voice, and I gasp in wonder.

The woman is enthralling to watch. Her genuine zest for life *is* evident in the lilt of her voice, the warmth of her smile, the energy with which she moves…and the shocking pink hue of her hair.

Pink hair. *A soft-rose color.*

Reyna's second marker.

With the sudden feeling that my time here is running out and still thinking about Austin's words from the table, I grin and ask loudly enough so he can hear me over the music, "Austin, can we make a stop on the way home? I need to go shopping."

Chapter Seventeen

"Alessandra?"

My cousin's frantic shriek jerks me from staring at my shocking reflection. Two days have passed since our day at the amusement park. Two days of drifting through the endless school day, knowing my time in the twenty-first century is only one sign away from ending. Two days of hearing Austin's confession of his past repeating in my mind. And two days of hiding the black shopping bag stuffed with clothes at the back of Cat's closet, wondering when I would get the courage to wear what was inside.

This morning I decided that day is today.

It's time I abandoned myself fully to this process. Going along with everyone's wishes has always been my *thing,* my way of ensuring their constant approval. But I am here. In the future. In the land of opportunity where women can stretch their wings and make mistakes. I craved adventure, I craved more, and after wasting two days wishing I could be more like that enthusiastic performer at Rush, I'm going for it.

I turn off the tap as the doorknob on the locked door of the bathroom shakes. "I hear you in there, you know," Cat says as I dry my hands on the soft towel hanging near the sink. "Do you have any idea how much I've been freaking out since you didn't show at lunch? I covered for you on Monday, but I don't know if I can do it again. They're gonna call my parents."

Worry and disappointment strain her voice.

When she sees me, I'm sure that concern will grow.

The door thumps as if Cat is leaning against the wood. "I've been wracking my brain wondering where you could've gone or what you were doing—though it doesn't exactly take a genius to figure out who you were with." The door shakes again and she knocks twice. "Less? What's going on? Open up!"

A hollow cavern in my stomach flutters. After enlisting Austin's help in my complete makeover, and then basking in the pure rush of *finally* doing something wild, it never even crossed my mind that my disappearance this afternoon would affect Cat.

I meet my dark eye-lined gaze in the mirror. Monday's stunt already kicked her overprotective vibe into full force. Confiding the truth about Austin's challenge now would not be wise. But while I may have to withhold certain aspects of my stay, I want to share this moment with her. Whether she approves of my actions or not will be plainly obvious the moment I open the door.

My hands tremble as the fullness of my apprehension sets in.

The doorknob rattles, and I walk toward it, smoothing the sides of my newly donned modern top along the way. I place an open palm against the frame and draw a steadying breath.

This is it.

Unlocking the door, I say in a shaky voice, "Come in."

"Oh my G—"

Fortunately, Cat's astonished yelp cut short her blasphemy as her widened eyes rake over me. Strangely enough, her reaction is nearly the precise response I had anticipated.

To ensure she gets the entire effect, I lift my arms, displaying my exposed elbows, and fluff my hair as I turn in a slow circle. "So…what do you think?"

When I make a full rotation and face her again, Cat squeezes her eyes shut. She shakes her head and then opens them again, wide. Then she laughs.

"What do I *think*?" She tentatively reaches out and pinches a lock of my hair between her fingers. "I think what in blazing Hades did you do?"

The stupefied expression on her face gives me a twinge, and I glance at the captured strand in her grasp. The bright color makes me grin.

"Less, I've been scared out of my mind since lunch, wondering if you were hurt, lost, dead, or back in the sixteenth century, and you…you…" She releases her grip and wraps her hands around my head, yanking it down so she can study my hair better. "And you've been getting a makeover by Dr. Seuss?"

"It's called highlights," I explain, unable to contain my excitement. I do not know this Dr. Seuss she is referring to, but

I *have* shocked my un-shockable cousin. That alone is cause for celebration. "When I couldn't choose between the shades, the lady at the salon just let me do them all. This is Cotton Candy Pink, over here is Electric Amethyst, and this one strip here is Atomic Turquoise. I admit that one is a bit bold, but I just could not resist adding it. Isn't it fun?"

My cousin presses a palm to her cheek. "Well, it is certainly that." She moves her hand to her forehead as if checking for a fever, then settles a closed fist over her mouth. After a moment, she asks, "And I suppose Austin is somehow behind this experiment?"

"No," I answer emphatically.

Austin may be at the root of most of my adventures, but this one was just me...which makes me all the prouder for it. If I ever wanted to prove I was more than a dutiful, rule-abiding daughter, this did it.

At Cat's skeptical look, I clarify. "I asked Austin to bring me to the salon, yes. And he took me shopping Monday. But the clothes, the makeup, the hair, *and* the nails were all completely my idea."

"Nails?" Cat asks with a laugh. "I'm almost afraid to look."

Giddy to show off the extent of my transformation, I wave my To-Teally-Hot-coated fingernails in the air. "Aren't they delightful? I am painted from head to toe with color."

"It's like a rainbow threw up," she says dryly. She pushes away from the doorframe and walks backward toward her bed, unable to stop gaping at me. Plopping onto the soft mattress, she raises her hand, indicating my wardrobe. "Dare I ask what happened to the strict ban on elbow showing and gentlemen's trousers?"

I lift a jean-clad leg for inspection and shrug. "I believe I may've overreacted upon my first encounter with them. The sensation was just so new and shocking. But that is what I am here for, is it not? To experience life and do things that I cannot in my own time?"

Almost begrudgingly, and blinking repeatedly as if she still cannot make sense of me, she nods.

I've avoided telling Cat about finding the second sign, afraid that once I admit it aloud it will make it true. But that's just it—it is true. And admitting it may help explain what she obviously believes to be my crazy behavior. Joining her on the bed, I fold my legs like one of the delicious pretzel snacks I consumed in her kitchen. The complete freedom modern clothes provides for mobility is definitely a plus. "I found Reyna's second sign."

Cat's sharp intake of breath and wide eyes is her only reaction.

"The soft-rose songstress was a vibrant singer with bright pink hair and a zest for life," I say. "And watching her captivate an audience—captivate *me*—well, it woke something inside me, Cat. In the sixteenth century, all I do is live by established rules, follow expectations, and look perfect. I can never simply let go and do what *I* want. And seeing that girl out there living her life with such joy, it made me wonder if maybe she wasn't just a marker but also a suggestion. A role model for how I should spend the rest of my journey. When I return home, I won't be able to dye my hair on a whim, wear trousers, or go shopping unchaperoned with a male who isn't a relative." The lyrics to a song from my cousin's iPhone, another modern convenience I will not have when I return but will miss, plays in my mind. "Just once I wanted to be the girl who says, *what the hell?*"

Cat's response is a surprised bark of laughter. "Wow. Okay, note to self: keep Alessandra away from mass media." Tucking her legs under her, she sits up tall across from me. "Less, I hear what you're saying. I get it—remember I visited your time two months ago, so I know what it's like where you're from. And the clothes *do* look great, and the hair is…uh, well, fun. But, girl…" She touches my hand. "You scared the ever-loving snot out of me today."

At the worry shining in her eyes, I lower my lashes.

She's right. Regardless of how excited I am to be here, and how eager I am to discover all that life can truly hold, there is no excuse for upsetting my loved ones. Running my fingers along the rough texture of denim, remembering the similar dark blue of Austin's eyes during his admission at the Snack Shoppe, I confess, "I suppose I got swept away with the possibilities of adventure. But it was wrong and selfish of me to cause you concern."

"Yeah. It was."

At the blunt words, I look up. Cat flashes me a frazzled grin. "But you know what? I'm not your mama. And really, it's not that I care what you do; it's your journey, and you should spend it how you want. But I need to make sure you're safe while doing it. This world—my world—is totally different from what you're used to. And I'm not even talking about cars and phones and electricity. You can't even imagine all the ways you can get in trouble or lost around here."

I wrinkle my nose. "But Austin was with me the whole

time."

"Yeah," she says, shoving a section of hair behind her ear. The skin around her eyes and mouth tighten as if she is about to say something unpleasant. *This cannot be good.* "About that."

My entire being stiffens, waiting.

Cat waves her open palms in the air. "Don't get me wrong, if you're gonna be gallivanting around town, I'd much rather you be with someone you trust than by yourself. And it's not that there's anything particularly wrong with Austin." She pauses, tilting her head back and forth, obviously conflicted about something. She bites the corner of her lip and says, "It's just that he doesn't really get where you're coming from. Or how, er, *new* all this is for you."

I get the distinct impression that was not what she had intended to say. Ever since Austin and I started spending time together, she has acted strangely.

"Look, if you're bored with school and want to be doing something else, I can take a few days off," she continues. "You're only going to be here for a short time, anyway, and skipping school is, like, a rite of passage. There are tons of places I'd love to take you." The flash of excitement in her eyes transforms back to worry and I wonder if she is finally going to reveal what has been bothering her. Her teeth trap her lower lip and release it as she says, "But I'm not sure it's the best idea to be hanging around with Austin quite so much."

Time seems to stop for a moment. And the sole thought in my head is that I can't lose Austin.

Without him, the exciting, passionate side of me that I always knew existed yet refused to let out will vanish. He's the one who brought it out; *he's* the one who gives me the courage to embrace it. But even more than that, the thought of spending the remainder of my time here without all his challenging taunts and devilish smiles causes a crushing heaviness to settle over my chest.

Cat's gaze sharpens, and I realize I'm rocking back and forth. I loosen my grip around my knees and let them sink back onto the mattress.

Forcing a casual smile, I say, "I promise you, Austin is harmless."

"Harmless?" Cat says incredulously. "I mean, it's not like I think the boy's gonna do bodily damage or anything, but that's not exactly the description I'd choose. We are talking about the boy who got you—the textbook definition of Renaissance *propriety*—to break a bazillion rules, dye your hair like an Easter egg, and dress like a quote-unquote courtesan. Though"—she tilts her head—"it does kinda prove what I'm really worried about." Her eyes pierce into mine, and I hold my breath. "You like him, don't you?"

Clarity dawns. For Cat, a girl hurt so badly in the past, it makes sense that this would be what terrifies her the most. I rub my hands together and release a breath, pondering her question.

A few days ago, my answer would have been easy: an automatic and resounding *no*. But that was before my conversation with Austin at the Snack Shoppe.

So how do I feel about him now?

Well, there is no escaping the fact that the boy drives me crazy. That he somehow simultaneously inspires me to want to tear his eyes out and wrap my arms around him. Or that his past brings forth my sympathy, and just one of his smoldering looks ignites a delicious fluttering in my belly. Austin pushes me. He questions me. He makes me laugh. We're practically strangers— I've only known him for a fraction of the time I knew Matteo— but there is still something achingly familiar about him. It is as if his soul calls to my own, almost as if we met in another time.

No. Even though I did not come here wishing to lose my heart, denying my affection for him now would be a lie.

I lift my eyes. Cat gives me a knowing look, and I'm tempted to lie. The last time I thought I felt this way, it turned out quite unfavorably. It would be easy to save myself from the embarrassment I suffered with Matteo and feign indifference— thanks to my unfortunate skill for telling falsehoods of late, my cousin would no doubt believe me. But I can't, I *won't*, mislead her about something like this…not when she is trying so hard to do the same thing with her feelings for Lucas. So I shrug.

"Austin is different than you believe. When it is just the two of us, away from school, he is…" I frown, unable to complete that thought. "Actually, I cannot say he's sweet. The truth is that he is still incredibly arrogant. Perhaps even more so. Not to mention horribly ill mannered. Half the time I wish to throttle him."

I frown, realizing I've gotten severely off point, and clasp Cat's knee. "*But* there is more to him, too. During our time together, I've gotten to see the real boy he hides behind that cavalier facade of his, and I am telling you, Cat, Austin's heart is good."

As I say the words, a tidal wave of emotion loosens within

my chest. I wrap my arms around my waist in an attempt to keep it all inside.

Austin *is* good—though I doubt even he believes so.

I give my cousin a trembling smile, unfamiliar sensations coursing through me, and Cat catches her lip between her teeth. In a soft voice, she says, "But it's not Austin's heart I'm worried about."

Elbows on her lap, chin in her hands, she levels me with eyes brimming with concern. "I understand if you want to spend your remaining time with him, and that's cool. Just please promise me you'll be careful. And I don't mean with *him*—though I'm not gonna lie, cluing me in on any future adventures or ditching excursions would rock, and probably save me from going prematurely gray in my twenties. But I mean with your feelings. Less, we both know your stay here is temporary. It's been almost a week already. One day soon, maybe very soon, you're going to leave him. And you saw what happened with Lorenzo and me. Trust me when I tell you that the pain is just not worth it."

My heart clenches—not at Cat's sentiment but at her fervent belief in it. What I wish more than anything is for my beloved cousin to understand that while the pain of potential heartbreak may not be worth it, actually living life *is*.

Regrettably, I do not have a chance to explain that because the doorbell rings. Cat lifts an eyebrow in question and I shake my head. I was not expecting anyone to call. The one person I know here aside from her is Austin, and he was heading home to bring Jamie to rehearsal.

Cat pushes herself to her feet, and I follow down the rug-covered hallway. She pauses in the atrium and stifles a yawn before opening the front door.

On the other side stands a handsome, smiling, book-toting Lucas.

Cat practically chokes on her sharp intake of air.

Biting off an amused grin, I look to the heavens and nod in acknowledgement.

Without taking his eyes off Cat, Lucas says, "I saw you weren't in French, so I thought I'd drop off what we did." He glances in my direction as he brandishes the book in his hand like evidence. He blinks, then looks again. "Cool hair."

"Thank you," I tell him, although he's already returned his gaze to my cousin. "Is that your car in the driveway?"

Lucas glances at the sleek black car behind him. "Yep."

"And you are able to drive yourself?" I ask to clarify, ignoring the probing look from my cousin. "You do not need a driver?"

"No." A crease forms on Lucas's brow but he shakes his head. "I'm seventeen and passed the test last month. No driver necessary."

"Wonderful." From the corner of my eye, I see Cat's gaze grow wide with recognition of what I'm about to propose. Before she can interject, I rush to say, "I have a rehearsal this afternoon at The Playhouse, and Cat here was just saying how she wished to watch. We were about to call our driver." My smile grows as she wrenches my wrist. *At least I discovered a way to use my lying for good.* "Perhaps you could take us there instead?"

Seeing Lucas now, I'm ashamed to admit it's been five days since he passed all my tests. It's even worse that I've spent all of them focused solely on myself. But Cat was correct earlier in one regard: the sand in the hourglass marking my stay is dwindling, as is my time to help her trust her heart again. It is as plain as the matching dimples in Lorenzo's and Lucas's cheeks that fate had a hand in this meeting. And the infatuated sparkle in Lucas's warm brown eyes proves their job was well done. Cat may be scared to admit her own feelings, but I believe after a solid nudge, she will be well along the way to the path of love.

And if nothing else comes from my time travel journey, that will be enough.

• • •

Thanks to my quick-thinking maneuvering, and Lucas's more-than-willing consent, we ride to the theater with Cat riding shotgun and me in the roomy backseat. The uncomfortable quiet between them lasts longer than I would like, but slowly, surely, Lucas draws her into conversation, and soon they are lost in laughter and discussion. As he pulls into a parking space, I can't help but smile. Reyna would be proud.

The two of them take their seats in the cool shadowed house of the theater with the rest of the spectators, and I traipse up the stairs to the scuffed black stage. The balding, pudgy gentleman I have learned is Mr. Williams, our stage manager, rushes from the wings, gaping incredulously as he flies to my side.

"Wh-wh—" he stammers, a vein throbbing on his sweat-coated forehead. "What did you *do*?"

I look behind me and then down at my outfit, knowing I look no different than any of the other performers here. If anything, I actually fit in better in jeans, and it must be said they are much more comfortable in the frigid chill of the playhouse. I rub my hands over the rough denim, then scratch my head in contemplation, and realize he is referring to my hair.

Twirling around, loving the feel of my long, dyed tresses catching the wind and fanning behind me, I say, "Oh, isn't it beautiful?"

He narrows his beetle-like eyes and huffs. "What it is *not* is Shakespearean!"

Oh, drat. I hadn't thought of that.

As he mumbles ungentlemanly remarks and flings accusatory glares at my person, I fight to hold onto my previous joy. Darting my eyes at the growing crowd around us, I notice Kendal among them. Of course.

Stiffening my shoulders, I share—as assertively as I can through a throat obstructed with dawning dread—that the dye is only semi-permanent, which the stylist assured me comes out after several washes. (As amusing as it would be to see the look on certain people's faces, I could not chance returning home to Mama this way—she'd drop into a dead faint and then send me to church for practicing witchcraft as soon as she recovered.) Unfortunately, Mr. Williams doesn't seem to think a few washes is fast enough.

I hear a snicker and instinctively know who it is. Who other than Kendal would take delight in this moment? Reid materializes beside me and places a supportive hand on my elbow.

Mr. Williams lifts his hands. "When Marilyn sees this—"

"Oh, chill, Mark, it's no biggie."

All eyes shift to Maggie, one of the hairdressers I met last week who doubles as Mr. Williams's assistant. She fluffs her artfully coiffed blond hair and says, "The night of the dress rehearsal, I'll mix up a quick batch of bleach and shampoo, work it through, and all that gorgeous color you see before you will disappear in moments." She shrugs. "It'll be a shame, but I do it all the time."

The tension formerly forcing my shoulders up into my ears deflates, and if it would be at all appropriate, I would kiss the woman.

Maggie's words seem to appease the hairy, scrunched-up monster otherwise known as Mr. Williams's eyebrows. They settle back into their rightful place, and he shuffles off, muttering something about inconsiderate actresses. Reid plucks a strand of my pink hair and says, "I happen to like it. Totally matches that perky, bubbly smile of yours."

Kendal walks behind him and lifts a finger to her mouth, pretending to retch. Reid turns to see what I'm glaring at, and she gives him an innocent smile. When he turns back, she mouths the word *freak* and disappears offstage.

Clearing my head from her vile influence, I say, "Thank you, Reid. As always, your flattery is appreciated."

"Hey, it's not flattery; it's the truth. I'm counting on that smile to light up the stage during our scene." He leans in and mock-whispers, "It's our secret weapon."

He flashes his childlike grin, and the familiar blush I've grown to loathe heats my cheeks. There is no denying he's handsome. And I defy any woman to hear a kind word from a gentleman, especially a handsome gentleman, and not preen just a little. But as I stare at my costar's upturned lips, the only thing

I can think about is Austin's tempting version. One hard-earned smile from him is worth at least a dozen of Reid's easy ones.

Reid continues to watch me, as if waiting for me to respond in some way. But I don't know how. Other than a handful of dance requests from gentlemen at a lifetime of balls, Matteo was my first real experience with male attention. And if his abrupt turnabout to Novella was any indication, my feminine responses with him left much to be desired.

Although my lack of knowledge in this regard doesn't quite matter now—for it is not *Reid's* attention I wish to cultivate.

Pity Austin doesn't seem as interested in being my suitor as this charmer.

Luckily, Marilyn Kent saves me from making a further awkward fool of myself. The side doors to the theater bang open and conversation around me stops. Briskly walking across the floor to the lamplit table, the *click-clack* of heels punctuating each precise step, Marilyn commands every eye on stage to follow her progress like the world-famous director she is. And it's not until after she takes her seat, sets down her clipboard, and takes a long sip of water that she lifts her head to survey her awaiting cast. When her shrewd gaze lands on me, she pauses.

My mouth goes dry, as if suddenly filled with the puffs of white cotton Cat keeps in the bathroom. I fight the urge to blink, scared to miss a twitch or tick that will give me a clue as to what she could be thinking, and curse my burning eyes.

What if Ms. Kent doesn't know about Maggie's magic solution, or worse, doesn't care? Could my first—and potentially only—touch of spontaneity result in her asking me to abandon my dream and leave the workshop?

Finally, her mouth curves into a faint smile. And when she calls out, "Let's begin," my heart stops its attempt to leap from my chest.

One of the young assistants looks at her clipboard. "Reid and Alessandra, you're up first."

Relieved, and to be honest, a little light-headed, I walk to center stage. Lightheadedness turns to full wooziness as, between Marilyn and her various assistants, I am beset with thousands of minute details: where to stand, where to look, when to enter, what my character is feeling. The past few rehearsals were spent sitting around a table reading our lines, but this is the first time I'm actually onstage, surrounded by the beginnings of an actual set. I glance out into the dark audience where I know Cat and Lucas are watching, needing just an ounce of her unending strength.

As overprotective as she can be, my cousin is my rock, the one thing that remains constant and familiar as I continue acclimating to this crazy world. And she's always been my number-one fan.

Convinced she's imparted all she can for now, Marilyn calls us into place. I chance a quick wave out into the audience, and a lone whistle answers from the darkness. With renewed confidence, I take my mark.

· · ·

Standing atop my makeshift balcony, reciting the lines I now know by heart, I realize I am no longer the same aspiring actress from my audition. With my new hair, new clothes, and new attitude, it is as if I have taken on two separate roles: the one of Juliet, and the side of me that Austin has let loose.

When Reid and I conclude the third run-through of our scene, Ms. Kent nods in approval. Reid squeezes my hand as we exit the set.

"You *are* a natural," he tells me once we reach the wings. He folds his arms across his chest and tilts his head. "I knew you were good during the read-throughs before, but man, it's like you were born for this. On the one hand, I'm glad to hear the rumor mill was right for once. In Hollywood, that's not normally the case. But then on the other hand, you're forcing me to bring my A game."

Catching enough of his meaning to understand, I shrug a shoulder and give a teasing grin. With a friendly pat of his arm, I say, "I'm sure by opening night you will find some way to keep up."

Reid's eyes widen as if I surprised him—I know I continue to surprise myself daily. But before he can issue a retort, an intern grabs him for an interview. It is with obvious reluctance that he leaves, stopping halfway to the exit door to shoot me an amused grin, and I laugh at his retreating back. This twenty-first century role is getting easier by the day. Proud of my accomplishment, I turn to watch the next performance.

"No way in hell it's coming close to yours," Jamie says, appearing out of the darkness. "You were awesome out there. Kendal was practically spitting nails at all the praise Kent gave you." She wraps me in a hug. "It totally made my day."

Filled to near bursting with the praise I've spent years yearning for, I squeeze her tightly, then turn to watch the actress in question. Kendal may have wanted to play Juliet for the workshop, but her assigned role could not fit more perfectly. She is portraying Katherina from Shakespeare's *Taming of the Shrew*, a description that appears apt for both girls. In fact, I'd think the Bard had her in mind when he wrote the play…except that Ms. Kent does not appear quite as certain.

"No, no, no," she says after correcting Kendal for at least the tenth time. Marching onto the stage, face pinched in frustration, Marilyn stops in front of her. With hands on her hips, she says, "Miss Matthews, there is no question that you play the bitch role with flair, but there's more to Katherina than PMS. You must dig deeper. What is she *feeling* in this scene?"

The entire theater grows deathly quiet to hear how Kendal will respond. Jamie has confided that Kendal has a reputation for not always handling criticism gracefully, a trait I have witnessed for myself in our drama class. Tuesday's class was all about improvising, a skill with which our teacher's pet seemed to struggle. The fact that I didn't, and in fact earned praise from Mrs. Shankle, only solidified my place as her enemy.

Hayley reminded me after class that auditions for the musical begin next week and pushed me again to try out for Tiffany. Figuring Reyna would send me back long before the final production, I told her no. But standing here in my new clothes with my new hair and receiving such praise, I'm tempted to change my mind.

On stage, Kendal's hands flex and then unclench, and I can't help but feel a tug of sympathy. Despite her horrid behavior toward me, I take no joy in watching our director publicly scold her. Had she not been so talented, perhaps it would be a different story, but she is. Her impressive ability to unleash anger with a moment's notice and project her voice to the rooftops is inspiring, and it is apparent, at least to me, that she is trying her best.

She answers Ms. Kent in a voice so soft I can scarcely hear it, but what little I do hear sounds strained. She shifts her weight, and the spotlight hits eyes glazed, shockingly, with repressed tears.

Marilyn sighs and dismisses her, promptly calling for the next set of actors, and as Kendal strolls off stage, her shoulders droop in disappointment.

Jamie looks at me and flattens her lips in an uncomfortable grimace. "That was not as much fun as I would've thought."

I nod in agreement, and when Kendal draws nearer to where we wait in the wings, I take a step out of the shadows. "Good job out there."

Her head snaps up, eyes wary from being caught so distressed. Behind us, Marilyn begins the onslaught of details for the next scene, asking the actors, "As you enter the Forest of Arden, what do you think you are *feeling*?" and Kendal ignores my compliment, choosing instead to twist around and watch.

I exchange shrugs with Jamie, unsure of how to proceed or what else I can say, but I needn't have bothered worrying. A moment later Kendal turns and meets my sympathetic gaze with one of pure scorn. "I know," she tells me, her voice ringing false with confidence.

Then she saunters away with a dismissive lift of her nose, knocking my shoulder without apology as she passes.

Chapter Eighteen

I walk into French class ten minutes before it is to begin, still reeling from drama. Even though I am sure to be gone long before the musical actually begins, and even though it is unheard of for anyone to outshine Kendal in Mrs. Shankle's eyes, I gave in to Hayley's good-natured badgering and agreed to try out, not for one of the *nerds*, as was kindly suggested by the class pet, but for Tiffany. My hand shook as I signed the audition list, amidst Hayley's whoops of victory, Austin's quiet smile, and Kendal's fierce glare, but the wave of unprecedented confidence that overcame me was amazing.

Weaving through the crowded aisles to get to Lucas, I smile at the lingering sensation and ignore the whispers that follow in my wake like pups nipping at my heels. It has been the same all morning. These are not the same whispers that trailed me when I first arrived, the ones about who I was, why I bolted at every look, or the way I spoke so strangely. These are curious, appraising, and even openly admiring. And though I do not loathe receiving such attention, even while still being quite unsettled by it, I'm completely without recourse for how to respond. For at least the tenth time since the school day began, I find myself asking what the modern me should do.

Lucas raises his head from a sketch and grins at my approach. I stop at the empty desk beside him and with a flick of my multi-colored hair, plop into it, suppressing the urge to laugh at my own actions. The part of enigmatic teenage rebel is such a contradiction to what I truly am that it's fascinating.

"Someone's the talk of the school this morning." Lucas winks, and the gesture reminds me so much of Lorenzo that my breath catches in surprise. Of course, the familiar lilt of his voice adds to the overall effect. "And here I thought I was the mysterious Italian transfer."

I grin and bat my mascara-coated eyelashes. "*Moi*? Mysterious?"

He gives an exaggerated look at my torn jeans and large slashed shirt, which is tied at the small of my back and hanging off one shoulder. The exposed band of my violet tank on my shoulder matches the color swept across my eyelids. Whenever I catch a glimpse of myself in a reflective surface and see all the skin I have on display, I can't help but imagine Mama's shock.

My stomach clenches. This is the longest I have ever gone without seeing either of my parents, and the separation has been tugging on me with each passing day. Strangely enough, the knowledge that I am one sign away from returning to them is both a reassurance and a source of turmoil.

"Yeah, you," Lucas says. "Between showing up sweet and

innocent on Friday, skipping out twice this week, then arriving today like this, you've got the school gossip working overtime. Mark my words, woman. Before long the entire hallway's gonna be filled with multihued classmates. Hell, even I'm considering it." He rakes his hand through his soft blond curls and asks with all seriousness, "How do you think I'll look if I go blue?"

The image of his hair as blue as the animated creatures in the movie I watched the other night appears vibrant in my mind, and I laugh so hard, I snort.

"Oh, quite dashing," I tease when I recover, and Lucas smiles. "And as for the others..." I shrug. "Let them wonder. It just so happens that I am a *very* complex woman."

The fact that I nearly get through saying that with a straight face makes me laugh again. Just nine days ago, my own family would have found that declaration hysterically preposterous. I would have, too. Now, I am not so certain.

Lucas rolls his eyes. "Complex, huh? An exasperating trait you share with your housemate, then."

He glances at his sketch and retraces a drawn line with his pencil. Realizing that this is the first time that the two of us have really gotten to talk without Cat's presence, I lean across the aisle and ask, "You like my, uh, housemate very much, don't you?"

He lifts his head and looks at me through the thick fringe of his lashes. "You must think I'm pathetic, huh? The way I chase after her?"

Shocked by the question, I widen my eyes in horror. "Of course not!"

He laughs at my outburst. "Well, that makes one of us."

Yesterday turned out to be about twenty steps forward and five giant steps back in Lucas and Cat's growing relationship. Their shared banter and affectionate looks lasted throughout the long rehearsal and well until we were halfway home from the theater. But then it was as if Cat remembered what she was supposed to be doing and retreated again. When Lucas pulled his car into her driveway a little after nine o'clock, Cat exited with little more than a mumbled thank-you, and she refused to talk about him for the rest of the night.

Squeezing Lucas's arm affectionately, I say, "Things may not have ended precisely as I had hoped, but it looked as though you two did enjoy each other's company."

"Thanks to your obvious plan." He gives me a depreciating smile. "You know, normally I don't need help in the hookup department, but then Cat's not exactly normal, either." He blows out a breath and tousled strands of hair lift around his face. "That girl is so damn confusing. But no matter what she does, I just keep getting further hooked."

As the classroom fills around us, I lean my cheek on my hand. "Lucas, what is it that first caught your attention about her? That made you want to chance her…perplexing, changing moods?"

He grins at my question, and I cannot help thinking that the description of my cousin sounds eerily similar to Austin.

Lucas turns at his desk to face me. "When I found out I had to move here, I hated it. We've lived in Milan for years, and I was happy there. I had a life; I had friends. You're from Florence, so you know how beautiful it is. But Dad's company transferred him, and I didn't have a choice. Then I met Cat two weeks later, and, I don't know…"

He shifts his gaze over my shoulder, and his handsome face clouds with some unknown emotion. I scoot to the edge of my chair, eager to hear his side of the first encounter, curious if he felt any of the shocking rightness she did.

Lucas shakes his head. "Look, I'm not an idiot who's gonna say it was love at first sight or anything, but meeting Cat was different. Yeah, she's gorgeous, she's smart and funny, and she went out of her way to hang out with my sister. But it was more than that. When we danced…there was, like, a connection." He winces. "God, that sounds like a bad teen movie. I'll turn in my man card the first chance I get, but I'm telling you, I've relived that night over and over again, and it was there. And I know *she* felt it, too. Alessandra, for the first time since I found out I had to move, I had a reason to want to be here. To feel like this is where I belonged."

Again, the shocking similarity between his relationship with Cat and my own with Austin cannot be ignored. Over the past week, Austin has given *me* a reason to be here—many of them, in fact. It is almost as if the fates made him especially for me.

Feeling closer to Lucas than I ever have before, I nod heartily in agreement, hoping he'll continue. Maybe through his experience, he can offer insight into my own perplexing emotions.

He shrugs. "But then she ignored my calls and fell off the face of the earth. I thought maybe it would be different when school started, and we'd get back on track, but for some reason she's fighting it. If she wasn't interested anymore, that'd be one thing…" He trails off and kicks the leg of his desk with his heel.

"I should probably just cut my losses and get over it, but I can't."

Wanting to offer encouragement, I place my hand on his forearm and squeeze. "I'm glad to hear it." Then, careful not to reveal too much of my cousin's past or betray her trust, I say, "Cat has had…a somewhat difficult life. Perhaps it takes her a little longer to open up than others, but I promise you it will be worth it. You're right, she *does* care for you." Lucas's chest expands with a drawn breath, and I give him a reassuring smile. "I'm as certain of that as I am about the awesomeness of my hair."

The skin around his intense brown eyes relaxes, and a soft smile tweaks the corners of his lips. "And no one could deny that it is awesome."

"Exactly."

We share a grin, and I relax against the cool wooden seatback. Then he says, "Speaking of your awesome hair, was it really Austin Michaels's idea?"

I huff. "I asked Austin to bring me to the salon, but the idea and the choice of colors were mine."

Lucas nods. "I figured that. You don't seem like the kind of person to be talked into something you didn't want to do." He playfully punches my shoulder. "You seem pretty tough to me."

Sounds around us muffle as the door to the classroom closes. Mademoiselle Dubois strides across the tile floor, calling out a joyous, *"Bonjour!"*

We both turn to face the whiteboard, and Lucas sighs the sigh of a student ready for the end of the day. As a class, we answer back, *"Bonjour,* Mademoiselle Dubois."

But as the lesson begins and I mindlessly take part,

conjugating endless verb tenses, my thoughts remain on Lucas's last words.

I *am* tough. I'm not an innocent little girl anymore simply being led around by her nose. All of Austin's adventures are things *I* want to do. And I'm loving every minute of it. Since my arrival, my entire world has shrunk down to the thrill of wondering what Austin will suggest next, anticipating that rush of freedom, and counting the minutes until I can see him again. This afternoon's excursion includes the Rollerblades I discovered last week.

My gaze flits to the large clock on the wall. Just a few more hours to go.

• • •

Sea salt stings my cheeks, and the crisp scent of the ocean consumes my senses. All around me are sand, water, sky, and surfers. The early-morning sun seeps into the top of my head, warming me from the inside out…along with my temperature-raising tour guide. Austin's legs are encased in the same wetsuit from our Jet Ski adventure, except now he has the top peeled down, exposing his strong, toned chest and hard, flat stomach.

He catches me staring and smirks. However, instead of being embarrassed, and giving in to an even *more* embarrassing blush as I usually would, I stare back without flinching, drawing strength from the secret knowledge that his unapproachable bravado is as much an act as the role I performed onstage a few days ago. When I do not cower or lower my lashes, Austin swallows heavily. I watch his Adam's apple bob and then look up to meet his cool blue gaze. "Where do you want me?"

For some reason my words cause his gaze to widen significantly. I glance down at the foam board he placed onto the sand for my practice, unsure why my question is so baffling. This is my first introduction to his special world of surfing; I've never attempted it before, so I do not know if I should sit, stand, kneel, or dance across the long stretch of board resting on the sand.

I look back up, and Austin clears his throat. "Excuse me?"

Wrinkling my nose, I point to the board. "Should I stand up or lie down?"

"Uh, lie down." He scratches the back of his neck and hollows out his cheeks, and it isn't until he clears his throat again that I get the potential double meaning to our conversation. And *then* I blush. Not surprisingly, that brings a ghost of a smile to Austin's lips. "On your stomach."

The rough sound of his voice sends shivers racing across my skin. Goose bumps prickle in their wake, and though they are concealed beneath my own wetsuit, I still feel exposed. I splay my limbs across the board and sink my fingers into the soft sand, watching his tall shadow fall across my own. Despite the layers shielding me from his keen vision, I can't help feeling that he can clearly see what the sound of his voice does to me.

"The first thing you need to learn," he says with just a trace of huskiness remaining in his voice, "before you even get out on the water is how to paddle and pop up." He places a foot on either side of my hips and leans down to clasp both of my hands in his. The bulk of his body hovers in the air just above my own, and suddenly that is all I can think about. "Paddling is a lot like crawling, pulling one hand after the other through the water, cupping and scooping. Good, just like that."

I nod weakly in acknowledgement. Words right now are impossible. He continues guiding my arms in the proper technique, and my eyelids flutter shut.

I take a breath and inhale Austin.

The scent of citrus on his breath as it fans the loose hair around my face and the scent of salt, sweat, and clean soap that wafts from his body. The kiss of his bare skin grazing my back, burning through my wetsuit as he dips forward to instruct me, the intoxicating sensation of his strong hands engulfing mine. And finally, the restrictive feel of his legs straddling my hips.

Austin continues in a steadier voice, seemingly not as affected by my own proximity. "When you're out there, I want you to dig in deep. Really propel yourself. Then, when you're in position"—he takes my hands and places them on either side of the foam board—"grab your rails and shoot to a strong push-up, hands and toes touching the board."

Again, he places my body into the correct alignment, handling me like a child's pliant doll. The coolness of his fingers sliding and making circles around my bare ankles sends a jolt to my stomach. When he moves his hands to grip my waist, helping to take the pressure of my weight off my hands, my head grows light, as if filled with air.

"It's, uh, important," he says, voice a tad rougher than before, "that you don't go to your knees...when you pop up. Just snap right to a crouch. Here," he adds, releasing me somewhat abruptly onto the board. "Watch me."

The loss of his warmth leaves me slightly dazed. Swallowing, I push myself up to a sitting position and try to concentrate on Austin's lean body snapping into position. But I seem to have lost the ability to focus on anything.

Austin pops to his feet again, and his eyes lock with mine.

I do not know what expression he sees on my face, but it causes his confident smirk to fade.

In the distance, shouts ring out from other surfers riding the waves, but here, on this patch of sand with Austin, I feel isolated.

One of us moves first, I am unsure which, but soon my knees are sinking into the sand, and I am tipping my head back to look into his eyes. The brilliant blue color has deepened again.

Awareness fills the thin sheet of air between us. I lick my lips without thinking, and he lowers his eyes to watch the flick of my tongue. I have never in my life been wanton, but the feminine empowerment I feel as he exhales a shaky breath makes me want to do it again. So I do. Slowly this time, gliding my tongue over my bottom lip.

A low growl is my only warning before Austin's hands thrust into my hair. "I warned you about playing with fire."

Breathlessly, I say, "And I told you I'm tired of being careful."

He nods once…and then his mouth crashes onto mine.

Firm lips devour me, and I drown in the rush of feeling. In all my late-night dreams of what this moment would be like, I never expected it could be like this. My body collapses, and one of his arms locks around me, smashing my chest against his.

My first kiss is not the slow, sweet build-up I witnessed between Cat and Lorenzo. This is aggressive. This is passionate. This is Austin.

The shocking sting of teeth biting into my lower lip causes me to gasp, and Austin uses it to drive his tongue into my mouth. My knees buckle. If it weren't for the splay of his hand on my lower back and the pressure of his fingers wrapped around the nape of my neck, I would sink to the sand.

I hang in the moment and briefly do nothing. Everything that is happening is so shocking, so unexpected, and so deliciously wonderful that I cannot think, cannot breathe. Then the taste of orange hits the back of my tongue, reminding me of the orange soda Austin drank on the way here, and I give myself over to the embrace. Good girls may not kiss like this where I come from, but I am here now, and there is no greater adventure then the feel of Austin's lips on my own.

Suddenly he breaks away.

The heat in his eyes as he stares down at me is enough to melt my wetsuit. His shifting, unusually vulnerable gaze has me wanting to wrap my arms around him and bring his mouth back down to mine. But then the walls he chooses to hide behind come back up. They shut me out as effectively as if he had slid on a mask, and my arms dangle to my sides, weighted.

"So," he says, pushing to his feet, "back to surfing."

Acting as though nothing happened, Austin slides his arms through the slick fabric of his suit and zips it over his chest, the cold, metallic closing sound symbolic of his own attempt at retreat. But what he doesn't know is that this time, I refuse to let him hide.

To quote an expression I heard a teacher use yesterday, I have Austin's number now.

Today may've begun as just another one of his challenges, but now it is so much more. Licking my lips and tasting orange, I vow that before the day is done, I will know the *real* Austin a whole lot better…and experience kissing him a great deal more.

Chapter Nineteen

The turbulent waves crash all around me and I would be lying if I said I wasn't terrified—this seemed like a much safer proposition on shore. After practicing on the sand until I perfected my pop-up, Austin handed me a pair of surfing booties and gloves to keep my extremities warm in the cold winter water. Then, after donning his own booties (he just rolled his eyes when I asked about his gloves), he grabbed the board and guided my prone body to a "calm" stretch of ocean between the breaking waves.

If this is calm, I do not believe I will ever be ready for agitated.

Who would have thought that a God-given ocean could be more frightening than a man-made, death-defying roller coaster?

It is imperative that Austin not see my distress. I want him to think me brave and confident. I want him to be proud of me—*I* want to be proud of me. So I sit up tall and grip with my thighs as another swell rams into my board.

"Feel that?" Austin asks, and I blink rapidly in reply. *Of course I felt that.* "This isn't much different than how it'll be when you're really surfing; you're just gonna be on your feet. Nothing to it, right?"

I give a thin-lipped smile and nod, then turn to watch the surfers in the distance. Austin said he chose this spot so we would not get in their way, but a side benefit is that I am without an audience. Instead, I can be one.

"Now watch that guy," he says, pointing toward a boy just popping up onto his board. Austin changes his grip on my board and sits up taller in the water. "He saw the wave coming and started paddling hard. As soon as he felt the surge, he shot up to his feet. Wait for that feeling—like someone's behind you, giving you an extra push. If you pop up too early, you're just gonna fall off the back of the wave."

I glance at the churning, swirling water. That does not look at all appealing.

"See how his knees are bent?" he continues, and I raise my head. "And watch his turn—all he does is take a slight step back near the fin, and that lifts the nose of the board. Now he has leverage so when he leans to the left, the board knows where to go. Then he goes right back to the center. It'll be the same for you—like a dance. Take a step back, twist your torso just a bit, and then return to center and ride the wave. Make sense?"

Absolutely none. "I think so."

Austin grins. "Look, this is fun, but you have to relax. It's just you and the water out here. No one's watching. Well, except me."

Though his attempt at encouragement causes my stomach to tighten more, it isn't solely from nerves. Out here in his element, Austin is altered. He doesn't completely give himself over and become the hidden boy that I know lives underneath, but he is softer. More caring. Sweeter, even. His patience with me has been boundless and he's proven that he is worthy of my trust.

"Okay," I tell him, taking a breath. "I'm ready."

He smiles one of his rare, hard-earned smiles and I feel as though I can do anything. "There's my girl." Heat infuses my cheeks in spite of the cold, but to my surprise (and satisfaction), Austin doesn't take back his words. Chuckling softly, he pats the back of my board. "You're pretty tiny, so when you get into position, I'm gonna ride back here to give you some confidence and help steady the board as you stand up." He glances out to the waves. "Ready to practice catching a few easy ones?"

As ready as I will ever be.

"I trust you," I tell him, lying down as he instructed, belly to the board. "I know you will take care of me."

When he does not immediately tell me where to go or what to do next, I twist my neck around, curious about the delay. Austin stares back with a disconcerted look on his beautiful face. After a beat, he coughs, then in a strange voice says, "Thanks."

Hmm, not exactly the reaction I had expected. I know I am not the only one who feels this way about him—his sister Jamie believes he hung the moon. Puzzled, I set my elbow on the board and begin to sit up. "Austin—"

He abruptly looks off at the ocean. "Look, here comes a

good one. Let's go chase it."

Recognizing a diversion ploy when I see it, I grant him his privacy and throw all my energy into following his instruction. I paddle hard, cupping my hands and pushing myself through the tossing waves of the water, loving the feel of power over the elements. When I get into position, Austin climbs on the back of my board, and I turn around and lie down facing the water's edge. My foot brushes against the inside of his thigh, and my stomach flips, remembering the heat of our kiss. Then a spray shoots up and hits me in the face, bringing me back to the present. I wipe the moisture from my eyes.

A bird calls overhead. My heartbeat accelerates. The energy of the ocean ignites the blood in my veins, and I quiver in anticipation. The swell rises below me and propels my board toward the shore, and I pop up just as Austin taught me. I grin, knowing he is seated right behind me, steadying me, and I bend my knees.

Oh, Signore in heaven, I'm actually doing it!

Words cannot describe the feel of the wind on my cheeks and the sensation of oneness I feel with God's creation. Needing to see Austin's reaction, to know if he's proud of me, I look back…and my legs wobble.

Time slows to the beat of my heart in my ears. Austin's eyes widen. I face the shore again and throw my arms out, trying to rectify my balance—but the effort comes too late. My board flies up in the air, I pitch forward, and my chest hits the water with a loud, agonizing splash.

Pain radiates throughout my body. My body sinks as though made of lead, and the only thing I can think is, *I cannot swim.*

Why didn't I think about this before? The answer, as embarrassing as it is, comes all too soon. I was too eager, too trusting…too naïve. But I will not let my folly end my adventure in such a way.

I kick out my feet and throw my hands up, trying to paddle in the water as Austin taught me on land. Holding my breath, the pressure mounting in my head, I lift my eyes and look for the surface.

Water churns. Bubbles shoot past my face.

My lungs begin to burn.

Then a strong arm wraps around my waist and hauls me up.

"I got you," Austin says, holding me high as I gasp and choke on precious gulps of air. He pushes through the water, holding me close, and then lifts me. A wave crashes below me as he pats my back, repeating, "I've got you. You're all right."

Cradling my head in the nook between his neck and shoulder, he runs through the foamy water, carrying me as if I weigh nothing. He doesn't stop at the packed edge where the water and sand meet, but brings me all the way up onto the soft sand, away from any onlookers. I sputter and drag in more air as he lays me down and brushes away the long strands of hair stuck to the wet skin of my face. When I can at last inhale and exhale again with a bit of normalcy, he glides the back of his hand across my forehead and over my cheeks. "Alessandra, are you okay?"

Ignoring the loud buzzing in my ears, I manage a weak, "Y-yes."

He shakes his head. "I don't understand. I mean, I know getting tossed off your board can feel like you're trapped in a washing machine, but the water wasn't even that deep. What happened out there?"

I gnaw on my cold lower lip, scared to admit the truth and knowing that I must. A shiver rocks through me. Looking up into Austin's worried eyes, I confess, "I can't swim."

Those worried eyes narrow in disbelief, then he closes them and releases a frustrated breath. "That's something that would've been good to know *before* we got into the ocean."

"I know," I say through chattering teeth, feeling dreadfully stupid for what I'm about to say. "To be honest, I did not think of it." Bewildered eyes fly open at my admission, and I hasten to add, "I-I was just so eager to partake in your world, a-and I guess I didn't think I would fall."

"Everyone falls at some point." He rakes his hands through his wet hair. "I even have a freaking life jacket in the back of my truck. If you would've just been honest with me, this wouldn't have happened."

I shake my head, though whether he can tell through the rest of my body's tremors, I am not sure. "I promise you, I did not withhold the truth on purpose—I truly am that ignorant. In the face of the big, bad ocean, I forgot I cannot even tread water."

At my self-deprecating laugh, Austin finally looks at me. I offer a weak smile, and the anger burning in his denim blue eyes quickly dims.

He pulls me into his arms and begins rubbing my arms vigorously. After a moment, he exhales a long, steady breath. "Sorry for being such an ass. But you scared the shit out of me."

Relieved he is no longer angry, I lean in to his embrace, my entire body relaxing. I would be content never to leave this position. Inhaling the scent of salty sea, I say, "I scared myself, too."

His chest rumbles under my head, but his quick laugh turns into a sigh. "Well, that was surfing. Guess it's time to head on back."

At that, I lift my head. "But why?"

"Uh, because you can't swim? Or maybe because you just wiped out?" He leans back and looks into my eyes. "Princess, you can't seriously be saying you want to go back out there."

I pause to do a quick internal inspection: lungs working, head growing increasingly unclouded, heart rate normal…well, as normal as could be expected when I'm near Austin.

"While wearing the life jacket you mentioned, yes. Surfing was fun. At least it was until I fell into the ocean and believed I would die," I tease, hoping that confronting the problem head on will ease the tension.

For a brief moment that felt like forever, I *did* believe I was in trouble out there. But I also meant what I said before: I know I am safe with Austin, possibly even more so now. His attentiveness after my fall proved that.

Bestowing upon him my most dazzling smile—the one that got my brother Cipriano to do anything I asked—I say, "I would like to try it again."

Austin turns and stares out at the uncontrollable ocean, his compressed lips the exclusive indicator that he heard my request and is considering it. A wave rolls and crashes on the sand. With eyes still trained on the line of surfers in the distance, he says, "You know, I believe there may be a shredder in you yet."

And the proud gleam in his eye when he does turn back gives me all the confidence I need.

Chapter Twenty

Headlights dance across the streets of West Hollywood. Unlike at home where curfews reign and roads are quiet, California comes to life at night. Not that it isn't alive during the day, but despite the growing late hour, people here gather. Bright lights buzz. Colorful, flashy cars race one another, squealing and stirring up the night air. A gust of it skims over my bare shoulders, sending a shiver down my arms. I pull on the hem of the red dress I bought a few hours ago with the money Cat generously made me carry and wonder, not for the first time, if perhaps I should've gone with a different style. One with slightly more fabric.

Behind me, music pounds the darkened windows of Lyric, the crowded club Austin suggested for the rest of tonight's challenge. The vibration tickles my back. I look to my left to see if I can spot Cat past the line of people awaiting entrance, and instead catch Austin's eye a few feet away. He flashes me one of his devilish grins, and just like that, my body temperature rises, dulling the chill.

"Cold?" he asks, subtly bobbing his head to the loud music coming from inside.

I shake my head, then grin. "Well, perhaps a little. Cat and Lucas should arrive soon, though."

After the second time I left school without telling her, Cat asked if I could keep her apprised of any new misadventures. When Austin suggested we come here, I immediately grabbed the cell phone she'd thrust at me this morning, knowing I should inform her. But as the phone rang in my hand, I realized this provided an excellent chance to further my own goals as well— assisting Cat in following her heart with Lucas. Of course, when issuing the invitation to meet us, I didn't confide the additional member I hoped would be joining our party.

Sickly sweet perfume claws at my nose, a distinct, un-Cat-like scent. A group of girls around my age slinks past on their way into Lyric, all four of them poured into dresses much shorter—and tighter—than my own. One of the girls, a slender brunette, puts a hand on the arm of the heavily muscled gentleman manning the door as her friends take their place at the back of the line. He rolls his dark eyes as the door opens behind him, sending music bursting onto the sidewalk.

The tallest of the group, a gorgeous redhead wearing the highest heels I've ever seen, saunters back toward us. She slides a dismissive look over me before feasting hungry eyes on Austin. "Save a dance for me, handsome?" The flirtatious lilt of her voice sets my molars on edge.

The brunette near the door snickers, and she and the others

exchange knowing smirks.

Jealousy pitches and roils in my gut. Anger burns in my blood. This girl is stunning, sexy, and wise to the ways of this century. She is everything I am not, and it's clear that she rarely hears the word *no*. But though she may be accustomed to obtaining male attention everywhere else she goes, she won't be sinking her red-lacquered talons into this one.

Before I can open my mouth to say so, however, Austin pins me with a look that says he knows exactly how I'm feeling. He bites off a smile, then with eyes trained on me, tells the temptress, "Sorry, but I'm only dancing with one girl tonight."

The heat of his stare ensnares me, and a moment later, she walks away in a huff. Another group enters the building, the foursome among them, and the sound of the club softens.

We are alone again.

Inexperience has me wanting to look away from the intensity in his eyes, to break this silent moment we seem entrapped in, but the stronger part of me denies the weakness. I vowed earlier that I'd find a way to experience Austin's kiss again, and right now, I cannot think of an opportunity more perfect to do so.

I take a step on the trembling high heels I also bought today, with the now-dwindling money in my borrowed purse. But every cent spent is worth it if it brings me closer to his lips. My chest feels as though a hummingbird is caged inside, the beat of its wings sending my pulse into an erratic rhythm. Austin watches my approach with hooded eyes, his long body casually leaning against the cold brick building of the club. His gaze traces the lines of my dress, the length of my bare legs, and the straps of my red shoes. When he looks back up, our eyes meet. My breath hitches.

"Less, is that really you?"

The astonished question asked in my cousin's familiar voice breaks the magical spell. I blink and look over Austin's shoulder to see Cat strolling up behind him. She gives my outfit a wide-eyed appraisal and laughs. "Wow, I'd say you're definitely acclimating"—she glances at Austin—"to America. You look hot."

Despite her horrendous timing, I lower my lashes and inwardly do a joyous twirl. Austin assured me that my previous jeans and shirt would've been suitable for our venture, but I wanted something more daring, so I asked him to take me shopping once our surf lesson was over. And I am glad I did. If the redhead inside is to be my competition, I want to look every bit the woman I have become.

Cat nods her head toward the beefy doorman guarding the main entrance. "So you guys ready to head on in and shake it?"

"Um, actually," I say, stalling as I open my handbag and withdraw my phone, "not quite yet."

I read the glowing time display and sigh impatiently. Just as I thought—Lucas is late.

Upon returning the phone to my bag, I lift my head to find Cat staring at me through narrowed eyes. "Less, what did you do?"

Just gave fate a little nudge.

Fluttering my lashes in total innocence, I say, "Nothing bad."

She purses her lips. "Yet somehow I don't believe you."

The sound of a rock skittering across the pavement grabs her attention, and the tension in her lips softens. I don't have to look behind me to know the reason.

"Hey, guys, sorry I'm late. Parking was a beast." Lucas sidles up to our group, and Cat elbows me in the ribs. He meets my gaze in a brief friendly greeting before bestowing his warm smile on my cousin. "Ladies, you look beautiful."

Cat smooths nonexistent wrinkles from the skirt of her dress. I can almost feel the hum of tension between them. "Thank you, Lucas." She looks to the ground, then back up and motions toward Lyric's entrance, an almost desperate edge to her voice as she asks, "Everyone ready to head inside?"

I withhold my sigh, knowing that she has been hurt before, but send up another silent prayer that she will soon choose to leave that in the past. I take a step toward the door and come to an abrupt halt when Lucas says, "Actually, Cat, I was hoping I could talk to you first."

Hope surges through me. With a grateful glance to the heavens, I turn to see Lucas tapping what appears to be an odd-shaped painting against his thigh.

Cat swallows nervously. "Me?" She grabs my arm, yanking me back as I try to give them privacy, and shoots me a look that clearly says, *Stay put.* Shrugging, she says, "Sure, what's up?"

Lucas scratches the back of his neck, glancing at Austin, then at me. I offer him an encouraging smile. With a short laugh, he presses on. "Look, I know you're probably used to guys falling all over you. You're beautiful and funny, and you're talented as hell. You can have anyone you want, and there's no doubt you deserve someone better than me, but that's not gonna stop me from trying, anyway."

My cousin inhales a deep breath, and my previous hope turns into pure joy as I realize Lucas is finally declaring his feelings. *Thank you, Signore.*

"Cat, the night I met you," he continues, "everything clicked into place for me. The move to the States was suddenly a blessing instead of a curse, and life made sense again. I won't pretend to understand why you're so determined to fight the feelings I know you have for me, too, but I just wanted you to know that I'm here." He takes a step forward. "I'm not going anywhere." He takes another step and brushes a strand of hair away from her face. "I felt something between us the night of your party, and I feel it between us now, and I'm not gonna give up. Not until you tell me to."

My heart melts, and I steal a look at Cat. She is as enraptured by Lucas's words as I am. I bite my lip to contain my excitement.

Lucas holds out what looks like a small painting. "This is for you."

Bewildered, Cat takes the odd painting. When she opens it, I realize it's a box, containing a row of sharpened pencils, much like the ones she has on her desk. She bites her lip and looks up. "Art pencils?" Lucas nods, and she asks, "But why?"

"To let you know I see you. That I care about you. Hopefully when you do your next kickass sketch, you'll use these and think of me."

Her gaze drops to the box again, and she traces the cover with a trembling finger. "*Madonna and Child with Apples and Pears.*"

Even though the painting has yet to be created in my time, I know the name. It is the painting that launched my cousin's fascination with the Renaissance. It's what inspired the tattoo that she has on her hip and the piece that most likely prompted her to become an artist herself.

"How did you know?"

"I pay attention." Lucas smiles, and when Cat raises her head in confusion, he explains. "You have a copy of that painting in your art folder. I noticed you look at it whenever you get frustrated in the middle of a project."

He shrugs his shoulders as if his gift is nothing special, when I know that to Cat it means everything. Probably even more than his declaration. And when the lightest glow blooms across her cheeks and a smile breaks across her face, my heart soars.

All is going as planned.

"Thank you, Lucas," she whispers. "I love it."

She reaches back to hand me the present, and before I can even wonder why, she closes the distance between them, wraps her arms around his neck, and presses her lips to his. Delighted at the turn of events, I bounce on my toes and open my mouth in a silent cheer of joy, still grinning when she steps back a moment later and rubs her thumb over Lucas's lips. He presses his forehead against hers and closes his eyes.

After giving the happy couple a moment, I playfully bump my cousin's shoulder, completely pleased with my success. "Now I'm ready to shake it."

Cat laughs. She twines her fingers with Lucas's and pulls him toward the entrance. Austin waves his hand forward, amusement shining in his eyes. "After you, Cupid." We slip inside the dark, hazy club.

Inside the dark, hazy club, it takes a moment for my eyes to adjust to the dim light. When they do, I'm surprised to find that instead of an overcrowded room, we are in a small hallway. The walls are black, the carpet red. On one side, a weary woman waits behind a sign asking for patrons' jackets, and on the other, tucked just inside the door, stands a bright-eyed woman behind a cracked wooden counter. Cat grabs my elbow and pulls me to a stop.

"That was quite tricky inviting him tonight," she says, giving me an indulgent grin. I follow her gaze to Lucas, talking with Austin a few feet behind us, a dazed look still on his face. "You're determined to see the two of us together, aren't you?"

"No." Clearly unconvinced, Cat pins me with a look, and I rest my head on her shoulder. "Determined to see you happy."

She looks at Lucas's present, shuddering with an indrawn breath, and I smile. She deserves to be happy—even when she refuses to make it easy for me to make her so.

Cat places a swift kiss on the top of my head as the guys join us. Opening her purse, she puts away the pencil case and pulls out her wallet.

Austin waves her off. "Tonight I'm buying."

His authoritative voice carries over the pulse of the music pouring from the curve in the wall ahead, and Cat lifts her hands. "Hey, I'm never one to pass up a free ride." She deposits her wallet back in her bag and shoots me an approving nod. "Thanks, Austin."

Settling a searing palm on my waist, he leans over to give the woman behind the counter a handful of cash. "We're all under eighteen," he tells her.

Nodding, she grabs a strange object and shoves it onto a dark pad. "Hands, guys."

As Cat lifts hers and receives what appears to be an instant tattoo on her skin, Austin doesn't remove the hand he has around me. In fact, he presses closer. Heat from his palm scorches the thin cotton of my dress, and my body melts back against him.

I don't know if it is the stuffiness of the enclosed room or the feel of Austin's hard chest behind me, but perspiration prickles at the nape of my neck. He thrusts his other arm out to receive the ink tattoo, and the scant space left between us vanishes. The scent of his newly applied cologne envelops me. My senses heighten. My silly heart dances in my chest.

"Alessandra?" Austin asks a moment later, the dark notes of his voice laced with satisfaction. I look up, and he lifts his chin at the woman behind the counter. "She needs your hand."

I swallow hard. *And I need a massive fan with which to cool my heated flesh.*

In lieu of one, I exhale a strong puff of air, lifting the dampened tendrils off my face, as I raise a shaky hand. "Of course."

Once we have all received *stamps* declaring us underage — Cat explained the concept the other night at dinner when I mistakenly asked for a glass of wine — we follow the red carpet down the hall and cross the threshold into Lyric.

A lit-up stage at the back of the room catches my eye. Bodies sway on the darkened floor before it, moving in cadence to the powerful beat of the live, screaming band. Overhead, a series of tracks and small boxes bathes the entire space in diffused shades of amber and red. And running the length of the wall nearest us is a glossy mahogany bar. Cat steers me in its direction.

"Boys, we'll be right back." The look in her eye, more than the suspicious tone in her voice, says she's up to something. "Just have to make a quick stop in the ladies' room."

As we walk away, Lucas heads for a set of unoccupied chairs edging the dance floor. He pulls four together and then sets a black boot on one of the rails. Leaning an elbow on the thin ledge holding various bottles and plastic cups, he turns his attention to the hypnotic pulse of the dance floor.

Austin remains where we left him, following my progress with curious eyes.

Cat laughs softly. "Girl, he's got it bad." She makes a clicking sound with her tongue. "Who would've thought my little cousin would land bad boy Austin Michaels?"

"Not so little anymore," I reply without thinking. When her grin turns into a full-fledged smile, I realize I did not deny the rest of her statement.

"Touché," she says, maneuvering us around a fallen chair. "The point is that the boy wants you for more than just a project partner...or whatever it is the two of you do when you say you're studying. And right now you're so keyed up wanting him *back* that you're about to pass out where you stand. Breathe, girl. Oxygen is a good thing."

I roll my eyes but take a deep breath, anyway. Interestingly enough, it does seem to help.

When we near the restroom doors, our supposed destination, Cat pulls to a stop. Swinging her hair to the beat of the music, she gives the area a quick scan and, with short, randomly spaced steps, starts inching closer to an open space at the bar. Not quite understanding why, I follow along, jerking my head to the music as well—though sadly not nearly as rhythmically.

"Uh, Cat," I ask a moment later, "what are we doing?"

"Shh," she replies tersely, doing another sweep of the space around us.

I wonder if she is unaware that the ladies' room is located right behind her.

Then her gaze sharpens, and I twist around to see a blond waitress talking with a man behind the bar. Before I can ask what she finds so fascinating, two boys walk up to us wearing low-slung, oversize jeans and matching suggestive grins.

The modern word *ew* leaps to mind.

The one closest to Cat leers and, sliding a hand through unnaturally shiny black hair, asks her, "You looking for me, honey?"

She steps back and sneers. "Hell, no, but your mirror is." She wiggles her shoulders in a display of disinterest, then waves an exaggerated farewell. "Buh-bye now."

Their grins fade, replaced by matching expressions of detachment. The thought flitters across my mind that they must coordinate these bizarre façades at home. The previously silent boy—the one closest to me—shrugs. "Your loss, baby."

I am unable to conjure a fitting reply.

Muttering ungentlemanly curses under their breath, the duo moves on, heading toward a group of girls propped against the wall. This time, however, the response they receive is much more welcoming.

As they strut to the dance floor in pairs, Cat says, "Guess there's no accounting for taste." I wrinkle my nose. The look we exchange is equal parts incredulity and bewilderment.

At the other end of the bar, an inebriated woman yells out, "Two rum and Cokes!" before promptly falling backward, having missed the stool behind her entirely. With a telling huff that says it is not the first time this has happened, the male bartender jumps to attention, leaving a tray of approximately two dozen freshly poured drinks, and Cat exclaims, "Finally!" With hands darting out so fast they blur in the dim light, she snatches one of the short glasses off the overloaded tray and shoves it at me. Bright red liquid sloshes onto my hand.

"Here," she says in a rushed voice. "Before someone sees, down this." I hesitate and she rolls her eyes. "Dude, I just watched the guy pour it—it's a shot. I think a double, actually. It's alcohol, and you, my friend, look like you could use it. But be quick. There's so many they won't notice right away, but eyes are everywhere in these places."

I stare at the glass of ruby red alcohol and sigh. Having grown up in a time where drinking wine at meals was the norm, I know the effects alcohol can produce, and perhaps it *will* take the edge off my frazzled nerves. Releasing a centering breath, I look down and laugh—the hand holding the stolen shot is the same one bearing the stamp.

Whatever happened to sweet, innocent, rule-abiding Alessandra? The answer comes and I grin: Austin happened. And I wouldn't trade it for anything.

Before I can second-guess my behavior, I tilt my head back,

part my lips, and swallow the alcohol.

The burning is instantaneous.

Tears fill my eyes. My chest tightens, and a cough explodes with such force, it feels as if my lungs are rebelling. This alcohol is not weakened, such as the cups of wine I have always consumed in Italy. This is full strength. And it is *potent*.

After plucking the glass from my hand and thumping it onto a nearby tabletop, Cat slings an arm around me and pushes me into the women's restroom. The area is blurry through my watery eyes, and as I sputter for breath, I watch her crouch-walk before the stalls until she finds an empty one. When she does, she kicks it open and pulls me inside.

"In and out, girl, in and out," Cat instructs, demonstrating the God-given ability to breathe. I nod weakly. That is, after all, what I have been trying to do. But as I stare into her calming eyes and drag oxygen through my nose—in, two, three, out, two, three—the burning in my throat recedes.

And glorious lightness enters.

"Oh," I say, startled, as the peculiar feeling seeps from my neck and down my spine. My legs tingle as if the bones supporting them have softened, and I wiggle my newly sensitized fingers. "Well, that is splendid."

Cat grins. "Yeah, you definitely don't need more than one. But feel better?"

I nod and then continue nodding as I realize my head no longer feels as attached to my neck as it did a moment before. "Quite so."

An unpleasant sound erupts from the neighboring stall, and the air becomes tinted ever so faintly with the appalling scent of vomit. Cat says, "That's what can happen when you have more than one. And that's our cue. Ready to dance now?"

"Absolutely."

Modern dance moves remain a mystery—where I come from dances are coordinated couple affairs—but with the liquid fire surging through my veins, I feel as though I can excel at them all…though one more taste of that marvelous elixir couldn't hurt.

Even with the alcohol numbing the edges of my anxiety, I still feel flustered knowing that Austin is waiting for me. Tonight, after our kiss, everything feels different. And I'm entirely out of my element. Just one more drink should calm the lingering butterflies in my tummy and the hammering of my heart. Contrary to what my cousin thinks, I *can* handle another one. I'm not the little girl she still sees me as, and if she will not help me, I'll simply acquire it myself.

If Cat can be sneaky, so can I. We are blood relations, after all.

Giggling, I stumble out the swinging door.

Cat laughs. "You, my dear, are what we twenty-first-century peeps call a friggin' lightweight."

Raising a pointed finger, I feel the words of disagreement sitting on my tongue. But then I see an opening. "Perchance you are right. I think a glass of delicious water will be just the thing. Go ahead and tell the boys I shall be right there."

"Less, it'll just take a minute. I'll wait—"

"No," I interject, a tad too forcefully. I widen my eyes and smile broadly. "How difficult can it be? Let me do this on my own; I promise I will not tarry."

She eyes me for a moment, undoubtedly because my grasp of modern lingo is slipping in my alcohol-kissed state, and she doesn't quite trust my motives at the moment—and well she shouldn't. But then she shrugs. "All right, but be careful. And don't accept any drinks from strangers—you never know what someone could put in it."

She walks a few steps away and pauses as if rethinking her decision. At the bar, the blond waitress returns and says, "Hey, Mike, you missed a shot of Red Snapper—I needed twenty, and you only gave me nineteen."

At that, Cat takes off, disappearing into the crowd.

And I make my move.

"Excuse me, kind sir," I say, stopping a gentleman wearing a bright blue band—and no stamp—on his way to retrieve refreshment. "But could you please procure a short glass of red elixir for me? The one I had was quite scrumptious, and I believe I'd like another."

The corners of his whiskered mouth twitch as his eyes do a leisurely sweep of my dress. "Sure thing, darling, I'll fix you up."

Remembering Cat's words, I touch his leather-clad elbow and frown. "Now, I must watch you procure it. Apparently it is possible for you to put something unpleasant inside."

The twitching gives way to a side grin. "Why don't you stand right there and watch me? I promise not to slip anything in it. Scout's honor."

He holds two fingers up in some form of a salute, and, not wanting to be rude, I salute back.

Watching the entire transaction for any misdealing, my mouth begins to water. And a few moments later, the kind gentleman returns with my drink. "One shot of Goldschläger for the lady in red. Wasn't sure what your 'red elixir' was, but this'll do you right."

"Goldschläger," I say, testing the name on my tongue. The slurred sounds make me smile, and I say it again. Then I lift the drink to eye level and gasp. "Why, it has tiny specks of gold floating in it!"

He puts his hand over mine and lowers the glass. "Yeah, it does. But try to be more stealth-like, sweetheart…this is kinda illegal."

Grimacing at that truth, I stoop my shoulders, close my eyes, and gulp the golden liquid. The taste of hot cinnamon courses down my throat. Warmth chases after it, heating my chest, my limbs, and pooling in the center of my stomach. My shoulders do an involuntary shake—a *shimmy*, Cat calls it—and I lick my lips.

A taste of pure heaven.

Cool fingers pry the glass from my fingertips and I open my eyes. "Thank you," I say…or try to say. Oddly, my lips feel numb. The whiskered gentleman grins, and I ask, "What is—" But my breath catches, and an unseemly loud hiccup sound rises in my throat. I wait for my cheeks to flame in mortification at my grossly unladylike behavior, but they do not respond. It appears embarrassment does not exist in my current pleasant state. "—your name?"

"Daniel," he answers with a grin.

"Well, Mister Daniel, that was rather tasty. How much"—my words catch again, but thankfully, no additional emissions spring forth—"do I owe you?"

Covering his mouth, which does a horrible job of hiding his chuckle, he shakes his head. "Believe me, it was my pleasure. But take some advice. If I were you, I'd think about stopping for the night."

"Yes, sir," I say, nodding at his sage wisdom. "That…was all I wanted."

Daniel laughs outright this time and then wishes me a good night. He heads in one direction and I go in another, trying to recall where it was that I left Austin. Alas, doing so with a fuzzy head proves to be problematic. I narrow my eyes in the direction I believe he is in, hoping the action will somehow help things, and zone in on a cascade of long red hair.

My eyes widen, and my nails bite into the flesh of my palms. It's the girl from outside.

Plowing through the crowd, racing to Austin, the only thought in my head is getting her away from him—and reminding her precisely who he came here with.

Just as I arrive, Cat looks up from her conversation with Lucas. Her jaw drops as I grab the girl's shoulder and spin her around. "Retreat, you bitch," I tell the girl, applying the derogatory name that Cat and Jamie use so often. People used it in my time as well, but I never cared to utter such a vile, contemptuous term. Until now, that is. "Austin is *mine*."

Chairs screech as Lucas and Cat bolt to their feet. The redhead angles her hip, and her friends appear out of nowhere. Austin pulls me to his chest.

"Ladies, let's not get crazy," Lucas says in a calm voice, taking a position to my left. My cousin comes around to my other side and grabs my hand as Lucas continues, smiling in such a way as to highlight the dimple in his cheek. "We're all here to have a good time. Obviously there's some kind of mix-up, but we don't have a problem, do we?"

"Looks like Tie-Dye here's the one who has the problem," the brunette friend says, referring to my hair and looking at me as if she smells something foul. "And if Kasey needs us, we're here to solve it."

Bending at the waist, she gestures at the other girls in tight dresses flanking her. I close one eye and tilt my head, puzzled. Why would the redhead need any help? The solution is not one that requires assistance—she must simply leave the premises. And perhaps buy a longer dress. What is so difficult about that?

Then I realize in the midst of that strange reply, the redhead's friend inadvertently slipped me her name.

Kasey. The vixen's name is Kasey.

I inhale a steady breath through my nose and square my shoulders, ready for battle.

But before I can give utterance to the jealous rage roiling inside, Austin lowers his mouth to my ear. The warmth of his breath on my flesh weakens my resolve—and my knees. "Princess, I can smell the alcohol on you," he says in a low voice meant for only me to hear. "And I know this isn't you...though I ain't gonna lie, this possessive streak of yours is a turn-on."

He presses an open-mouthed kiss to the sensitive skin right under my jaw, and my heartbeat stutters.

Across from us, watching our whispered conversation with disdain, Kasey shrinks her eyes into little crescent-shaped slits. Austin shifts behind me, and the scent of his yummy cologne invades my senses. My eyelashes flutter, and I decide I don't really care about the shape of Kasey's eyes.

"So since this isn't you," Austin continues, his nose skimming the column of my neck, "and you're not really in control of your brain at the moment, why don't you let me handle this…*situation* before your drunk ass gets us kicked out?"

My euphoria from his touch fades at his choice of words. That was not exactly the romantic banter of a Shakespearean sonnet. But not wanting to leave tonight without my promised dance, I nod my consent.

He steps away, bringing with him his warmth and bodily support, and I sink into a chair. Propping my head on my hand, I motion for Cat and Lucas to sit.

"Somebody had more than water," my cousin says as the two of them take their seats. "Just tell me you didn't do anything stupid."

I shake my head, and my elbow falls off the tabletop. Righting myself, I assure her, "I was completely safe. I asked a kind gentleman to get it and watched him the entire time." Recalling the taste of cinnamon, I say, "This drink had lovely flakes of gold in it."

"*Goldschläger?*" Cat asks with a laugh. "So that explains *that* performance." She looks away and juts her thumb to where Austin stands with the redhead—Kasey, the bitch. "Don't worry; I had my eye on her the whole time. If you hadn't shown up when you did, she would've gotten the hint soon enough. But then, watching you do the equivalent of peeing on the boy and staking your claim was pretty awesome."

"I concur," Lucas chimes in, and they share a grin. He takes

Cat's hand in his and places them on the tabletop.

Despite the dawning fact that I will regret a few of tonight's more illicit choices in the light of day, the sight fills me with joy. At the very least, my amusing exploits are bringing the two of them together. Smiling at the sparks flying between them at last, I shift my gaze and watch the fearsome female foursome slither away.

Austin smirks as he strolls up to our table. "You know, all that unleashed estrogen's got me needing to burn off excess energy. And I think I made someone here a promise." Offering me his left hand, he asks, "Dance with me, Alessandra?"

The intoxicating sound of my name on his lips has me jumping from my chair. I lunge for his hand and end up jostling the table, sending a plastic cup of brown soda gushing over the surface. Cat laughs, and I stick out my tongue teasingly.

Walking to the invisible line dividing the bar from the dance floor, Austin turns to Lucas and says, "Hey, man, in case Ms. Inebriated here gets in another scrape, do me a favor and keep close, all right?"

Lucas flashes me a grin and agrees. I'd like to argue their concern is unneeded and unwarranted, but even I know that's untrue. It would seem that Cat was right—I *am* a friggin' lightweight. But I take solace in the fact that I do not care, for soon I will be in Austin's arms.

The band changes songs, and we step onto the packed floor. Entwining his long fingers with my own, Austin tugs me toward a back corner, away from the crowd of dancers and near a shadowed row of half-empty tables. My feet carry me forward, following where he leads, as a sensation that feels like falling fills my stomach. My head spins, and it's becoming difficult to catch a breath—but none of it has a thing to do with the alcohol I consumed, and everything to do with the boy stopping under the glow of amber light and pulling me in his direction.

I lift my head and stare into the deep blue of Austin's eyes, hoping this delicious feeling never ends. He takes our entwined hands and places them behind his neck, then catches my other hand and drapes it along the first. The movement crushes me tighter against the firmness of his torso.

The only other time I was this close to a boy, I was kissing him. And that boy was Austin.

Callused fingers slide down my bare arms, and shivers explode in their wake. My own fingers curl into the soft wisps of hair at his nape. Locking his hands together at the small of my back, Austin begins swaying our bodies to the slow, exhilarating beat of the music.

"I've never done this before," I tell him. I don't know why I do, but it feels important that he know.

He grins. "Don't worry, I'll be gentle."

A blush erupts under my skin. Austin's grin widens, seeing the power his words have over me, but I'm not embarrassed. I'm tired of trying to hide how I feel. "I know I don't have to worry," I say. "You're always good to me."

Austin's mischievous grin fades as his gaze holds mine. His fingers contract, and he draws me even closer.

I lose myself in the music, in the words, and in Austin's strong embrace. The buzz of alcohol and the close proximity of his body electrify my blood, and my head grows heavy. Resting it against his shoulder, I strengthen my grip by clasping my wrists. If I could live in this moment for the rest of my life, I would.

I press my lips along the warm column of his neck, and he sucks in a sharp breath. His body tenses, and I wonder if I am being too forward. But then he releases a low noise in the back of his throat and spears a hand through my hair, possessively splaying the fingers of his other low on my back.

One song bleeds into another like this, the next with a noticeably faster tempo, but we do not change position. I nuzzle into the crook of his shoulder and breathe him in.

I feel Austin hesitate, and with reluctance I lift my head.

"Alessandra—"

The glide of roaming fingers on my backside causes me to jump, cutting off whatever Austin was about to say. I widen my eyes at him in surprise, but then register the dual pressure of his hands where he left them minutes before—one threaded in my hair, the other spread low on my back.

Whipping around to discover just who had dared to take such liberties with my body, it doesn't take long to catch the arrogant smirk of a man taking his seat at the now crowded table behind us. The desire once thickening my blood from Austin's proximity transforms into molten lava.

I have been dishonored.

I don't think past that; I just act, fueled by Goldschläger.

Marching the three and a half steps to their table, I fist my hands on my hips and do my best to level the brute with an aggressive, haughty look—it aids me greatly that he is seated and we are now at similar heights. Heedless of the man's mocking, lifted eyebrow, I plow ahead.

"Excuse me," I snap, not feeling at all guilty for interrupting their table's conversation, "but the beauty of this world is that I don't have to accept such vulgar behavior—especially not from distasteful little men like you." I have no clue where the word *little* came from, for the man is *far* from that. Nevertheless, I carry on, throwing my shoulders back and folding my arms across my chest. "You, sir, defiled my person with your unwelcome advance, and from now on I ask that you—uh, I ask that you..."

And it is about this time that I lose steam. I've never been very good with insults, and I already used the word *bitch* once this evening. Palming either side of my head, I long for another insult to come, preferably one that will make sense in this generation. I very much doubt calling the man a knave or miscreant will have the desired effect. But then an expression I learned from a humorous movie of musical, rock-band children zaps into my brain, and I snap my fingers. "I have it!"

Paying no heed to the derisive snorts from the table, I shove a forceful finger into one of the man's brawny biceps and shout as loud as I can, "Step off!"

In response, a muscle ticks near the man's eye. He glances down at his arm, and then gradually, deliberately taking his time, back up at me.

An outbreak of tingles surges over my skin, but this time they are not from the effects of alcohol, Austin's kisses, or even from the venom in this miscreant's eyes. They are from the pure thrill of standing up for myself and for all womankind.

Unfortunately, Austin cuts short my dance of victory by whisking me into his arms and carrying me toward the club's side exit.

"But wait," I say, pounding his shoulder and fighting his hold. "I wish to continue our dance."

He ignores my protests and lengthens his stride. I twist around in his grip just as he kicks open the door and manage to see Lucas acting yet again as peacekeeper, this time with my foul offender.

Then Austin hauls me outside.

Chapter Twenty One

Austin doesn't stop walking or even let me go until we are halfway down the street.

Unlatching the rear gate of his truck, he sets me down and cages me in with his arms so I cannot escape. Not that it was my plan to do so. Being this close to him in relative privacy is almost as good as dancing.

Chest heaving, Austin lowers his head to my shoulder, muttering a string of curses under his breath. Confused over his winded reaction—he carried me farther than this on the beach earlier today without any difficulty—I run my fingers through his soft black hair. "Austin?"

He nods once, as if to let me know he is still coherent. But he does not lift his head. Moments pass to the sound of his labored breathing and the whistle of the passing cars before he finally raises his eyes to mine. At the emotions swirling within their blue depths, I gasp.

Austin stands there, letting those emotions wash over me, before asking in a voice laced with surprising tenderness, "Alessandra, who was that girl back there?"

His rough, disappointed timbre and the sadness in his gaze let me know that he isn't talking about the brazen redhead; he is asking about *me*. Unsure of the exact reason, my heart begins to pound, and any lingering effects of the alcohol burn away.

"Don't get me wrong," he says, raking a hand through his already disheveled hair, "I'm glad you told that dickhead where he can stick it. Once I realized what he did, I wanted to rip his fingers off myself for even thinking about touching you. But all of that back there? Confronting him, the showdown with the girl before—that wasn't just the alcohol talking. And it wasn't your newly dyed hair. That was you." He releases a weary breath. "And you've changed."

My shoulders stiffen, even as I fight the urge to be defensive. After all, wasn't my changing what he wanted all along? Swallowing around a thickened throat, I find my voice and say, "Of course I have changed, Austin. This is the new me, the one *you* inspired. It was you who issued the challenge to shake me up. And everything you told me at Rush the other day about your dad and your past and not caring anymore? You were right. Being perfect all the time is exhausting! Some days, it's hard for me even to lift my head off the pillow. I've spent my entire life trying to be everything for everyone, but this…this is so much easier."

I take a breath in preparation to speak again, and in the space of a second relive the arguments the new me found herself in tonight. While I wouldn't deny the confrontations were terrifying, the freedom I felt to speak my mind in both of those moments was nothing short of liberating.

I give Austin a reassuring smile and wonder why the action suddenly feels forced. Brushing it off as exhaustion, I add, "And your way is a lot more enjoyable."

Yet for some reason, the words ring hollow in my ears. And from the slant of Austin's rueful smile, he hears it, too. A nagging inner voice breaks in to ask, *But is it really more enjoyable?* And grudgingly, I admit that perhaps I'm not as certain as I'd like Austin to believe.

In many ways, the gifts of independence and choice in this century *have* been thrilling…and I have discovered much about myself in the process. But at the same time, I've hurt loved ones, behaved just as horribly as my old nemesis Antonia ever did back home, and done things for which I have not always been proud—consuming illegal drinks being just one of those things tonight.

As if he can read my thoughts, Austin takes my hand in his. "But Alessandra, everything I said that day in the park was wrong."

Astonishment colors the thick air between us. I blink, certain that my sense of hearing must be failing. Austin would never admit to being wrong about anything, much less about a philosophy he's built his entire life around. Blowing out my cheeks, now even more confused than I was when he hauled me from the club, I release a forceful blast of discharged air and ask, "You were?"

He releases a long, low sigh. "I *thought* it was easier this way," he clarifies. "When I stopped caring what people thought about me—what my dad thought about me—I felt invincible. The pain of never being good enough for him or the fact that he was never there couldn't touch me if I didn't care to begin with."

As the wretched words fall from Austin's flawlessly sculpted lips, the solid walls he erected to guard himself topple down, just like at the audition, the Snack Shoppe, and this afternoon on the beach when he kissed me...and I'm left staring into the soulful, vulnerable blue eyes of the *real* boy behind the mask. My chest constricts and all I want to do is hold him. "Oh, Aus—"

He places two soft fingers over my mouth, silencing me with an apologetic look that begs me to let him continue. "From that first day in class, I saw in you the person that I used to be, and I hated it. I wanted to wake you up, make you change. I decided it was my job to teach you how wrong you were for not living the way I thought you needed to." He scoffs. "As if I know so much about the world.

"But *you*, Princess, you were the one who was right that day at my house—I'm not living, either. All I'm doing is hiding. And being with you this week, watching you and seeing how trusting and honest you are, how much you care about everyone... Alessandra, it changed something in me."

Austin bends his knees so I no longer have to look up to see into his eyes, and he tucks a strand of loose pink hair behind my ear. Cradling my face in hands roughened from salt water and surfing, he glides his thumbs across my cheeks and says, "Baby, you're not the one who needs to change, and definitely not for a chickenshit like me. You're *perfect* the way you are, and I'm an asshole for not realizing it sooner."

I sit in stunned silence; my face presses into the warm

comfort of his palm as the words *you're perfect* wash over me again and again in spine-tingling waves.

Austin Michaels thinks I'm perfect.

And if that is true, then it has to mean he cares for me.

Drawing on every ounce of courage I've attempted to build within myself during this time-travel adventure, I grip the hard muscles of his arms and say, "But Austin, you *did* teach me. In the last ten days with you, I learned more about what it means to live than I have in the last sixteen years. But even more, you make me feel as though you can see all the tiny pieces of who I truly am inside, the real Alessandra that no one else knows—the woman who lives behind the girlish act of perfection I wear for the world. You may not agree with me all the time, and you exasperate me far more often than I'd like, but you respect me...and Austin, that means more to me than you'll ever know."

When I finish speaking, I realize I am trembling, but it's not from the night air. In the distance, I hear the faint sound of music seeping from Lyric, but neither that nor the cars whooshing past just a few feet away on the street breaks the roar of silence between us.

Though I did not profess the full extent of my affection, I have no doubt Austin knows how much I care for him. And as his silence lengthens, I begin to think that perhaps I was mistaken. That he does not feel the same, and that he is now preparing to let me down gently. Pondering that thought, I fortify my heart for another man's rejection, but even while I do so, I cannot regret sharing my feelings.

My faith remains in the truth I have fought so hard for my cousin to believe: the pain of not having Austin return my feelings may be excruciating, and it may not be worth the turmoil of heartache, but choosing to take a chance and living life *always* is.

Austin interrupts my somewhat dark and profound introspection by dipping his forehead to touch mine. And just like that, all thoughts are whisked away, and my senses are filled with the scent of mint.

With our gazes connected, we share a breath, one now sharpened with the same sting of awareness from the beach. My pulse quickens with the realization that this does not feel like rejection…this feels like desire.

And I'm so ready to experience another one of Austin's kisses that I almost explode from the anticipation.

His darkened gaze drops to my mouth for a long moment, and the skin around it prickles to life, already tasting him. But instead of lowering his head and capturing my lips, he looks into my eyes. The fullness of my yet unspoken affection reflects back at me.

Then, with eyes so dark they blend into the night, Austin whispers, "I do see the real you, Alessandra." He smiles. "And I think I'm falling for the girl I see."

Chapter Twenty Two

I awake the next morning fresh from a dream that consisted of nothing other than Austin's sweet words of affection and the exquisite feel of his kiss. It was the best dream I believe I've ever had. My perfect bubble of happiness surrounds me throughout my morning as I eat breakfast and get ready to go to Austin's house, where we will (finally) begin work on our Modern Leadership paper. The paper that started it all.

It's incredible knowing that, were it not for our American government class or for Miss Edwards, Austin and I would be relative strangers. We would've never had the chance to see past our initial impressions of each other. He would have never issued my challenge, and I would still most likely be scared of my shadow—acting in the winter workshop, yes, but too timid to audition for the school musical or to reach out and fully experience all this life has to offer.

Miss Edwards may very well be the best teacher in the

history of the world.

A knock on the door has me jumping from the table, ready to greet the day, and Cat lifts her hands in mock surrender. "Enough with the giddy grin already. All this freaking sweetness is giving me a toothache."

Her tone is light, but I sense the worry behind her words. Assuming it is more of the same, concern over my heart breaking at the end of this journey, I brush it aside. I refuse to let fear dictate my actions. Laughing instead, I widen my grin and lift my chin at the front door. "Then I am to assume you are not at all giddy at the thought of seeing Lucas this morning? If I remember correctly, Austin and I were not the only couple caught in a compromising position last night."

Cat transfers her gaze to the closed door, and even in profile, I can see the smile lighting up her face. I snicker, and she mutters a playful, "Shut up." Her almost bashful tone makes me even happier.

Shortly after Austin bestowed his second life-altering kiss, the unromantic sound of two throats clearing, followed by various snickering catcalls, broke out behind us. Austin lifted his head, and when I looked over his shoulder, there stood Cat and Lucas, not at all appearing apologetic for ruining our moment. So when Austin and I drove past Lucas's car a half hour later and found the two of them locked in their own embrace, we had no pangs of remorse for honking the horn and whooping loudly.

In spite of the teasing, I am happy for them. Last night Lucas stepped up his game, as Cat would say, and the payoff is a cousin who finally owns her feelings. I watch as she speeds across the floor and throws open the door.

"Hey, beautiful," Lucas says, pressing a lingering kiss to her cheek.

Cat bites the corner of her lip, losing the battle to keep her enormous smile hidden. "Hey, yourself."

Lucas's playful grin turns into a smug smile as he takes her hand in his. Lifting his eyes to mine, he asks, "How's the head, Alessandra? The last time I got as sloshed as you were last night, I was an absolute waste of space for at least two days." He shrugs and flashes his dimpled grin. "But it did keep me sober. I believe my days as a high school drunkard are behind me."

Cat snorts. "Yeah, I don't think even a hangover could cut through the lovesick daze she's been walking around in. Come on, lover girl," she says, nodding her head toward Lucas's car in the driveway, "your brooding bad boy awaits."

. . .

Austin lays our books out on his kitchen table, making a point to brush my fingers with his. It becomes a game between us, who can steal the most innocent touches. I laugh when he overtly slides his hand along the exposed skin on the back of my neck when he walks to the refrigerator, and when he wiggles his eyebrows suggestively as he pops the top on his can of soda, I shake my head.

"You are incorrigible," I tell him, even though I am secretly delighted. I love seeing Austin minus his walls of protection.

"That I am," he says with a devilish grin. "And you love it."

Choosing to leave that statement unanswered, I open the spiral notebook I brought with me and write *Modern Leadership* at the top of my page. "Seeing as though you are the expert in this department, and that I have been a very diligent participant in your challenges, I submit to your extensive knowledge, Mr. Michaels. Where shall we begin with the topic of Leadership in Government?"

An older man with dark black hair and blue eyes steps out of the closed room near the kitchen, the same inauthentic smile from the photos at Austin's beach house plastered upon his face. "Did someone say government?"

A muscle in Austin's jaw twitches. "Just working on a paper for school, Dad."

"For school?" Mr. Michaels asks, his tone colored with amused incredulity. "My son is actually doing his homework. Never thought I'd see the day." He shoots me a wink, attempting to include me in the joke he has made at his son's expense, and every protective bone in my body hums in alert. "You know, you happen to be in the presence of a state senator, darling, and my son, well, he isn't exactly well-versed in politics." He strolls over and grabs the assignment Miss Edwards gave us. "Maybe I should help you with this paper."

The overconfident note in his voice, the blatant barbs aimed at Austin, the snapping tension between father and son, and Austin's palpable discomfort in the man's presence prompts me to yank the paper from his hands.

"I appreciate your offer, sir, but as I'm sure you are aware, your son is incredibly intelligent. He has a brilliant plan in place," I say, not at all sure what Austin's plan for our paper is but not caring at the moment, "and I think we're fine here."

Austin stares at me, perhaps in shock, as I conclude my brief but—in my opinion—powerful speech. I smile with pride.

Hello, world, meet Alessandra D'Angeli Forlani, the twenty-first-century version. I may not have to change everything about me, but standing up for my loved ones is one trait from this experience I'll gladly keep.

Back home, I never could get away with speaking to an elder in such a manner but here, in Cat's world, Austin's father simply shrugs his shoulders and plasters an even bigger false smile on his face before walking out of the room.

"Whatever happened to my prim and proper princess?" Austin asks with that heart-stopping smile of his, stalking toward me with purposeful strides. He squats down in front of me and hands me a bright red can.

"She got herself an excellent tutor."

Chapter Twenty Three

The next few days meld together in a series of Austin's kisses, workshop rehearsals, and heartfelt conversations with Cat. Now that Lucas has breached the last line of her defenses, she is happier than I've ever seen her. Even happier, dare I say it, than she was in my time with Lorenzo. I still sense that she is worried and possibly even keeping something secret from me, but I trust that she will confide in me when she is ready. As for myself, I drift through the days in a blissful stupor, one that is not missed by my amused costars, nor one far-from-amused one.

"Oh, joy, it's the happy couple again. Everyone grab your barf bags."

Austin breaks away from our kiss, piercing his ex with a glare. To say Kendal is not pleased with the romance budding between us is putting it mildly. The accolades I received after my audition for Tiffany yesterday only added insult to my list of crimes in her eyes. But even the wicked witch's sharp-tongued barbs cannot shatter my contentment. Leaning around Austin's embrace, I look across the busy Roosevelt Academy hallway and offer my adversary a pleasant smile. "Good morning, Kendal."

She rolls her eyes and walks away in a huff, which is not at all surprising.

"I'll see you in drama," Austin tells me, pressing one last kiss against my lips. "And with Kendal there, you can be sure it'll be full of that." He tugs a strand of my hair, then steps back into the chaotic stream of students, walking backward so he can keep his eyes trained on me until the crowd swallows him.

With a contented sigh, I grab my purse from inside my locker and close it, then head off to lunch.

Cat is already waiting inside the cafeteria, two books signaling the seats closest to her are reserved. I of course take one of them, and when Lucas appears moments later, he takes the other, the one just beside her, spinning the chair and straddling it. I shoot my cousin a grin.

Peeling the wrapper off a granola bar, Lucas slides his arm around Cat and says, "Looks like Angela is meeting with Jenna tonight about her sweet sixteen. I figured I'd tag along to help. I've been told my opinions on fabric and napkin samples are very useful."

"How metrosexual of you," Cat says with a laugh, poking him in the ribs with an elbow. "And dork, if you want to see me, all you have to do is say so. You don't need a made-up excuse to come over."

The look Lucas pins her with clearly says that up until this past weekend, he *did* need such an excuse, and my cousin has the decency to look guilty. "Well, at least not anymore," she clarifies. Then she smiles at me. "Less, why don't you invite Austin, too? We can all hang out, order pizza, and watch a movie or something."

Just a modern-day double date, I think with amusement.

Sinking my teeth into a crisp carrot stick, I nod. "This afternoon I have a short rehearsal at the theater before our extended dress rehearsal tomorrow, but I'll ask him if he can join us after."

Lucas slides his elbows onto the table. "It's about that time, huh? Cat told me opening night's only two days away. Are you getting nervous?"

I shake my head and give him a smile that only comes from doing what I've always wanted but never dared to believe possible. "No," I tell him. "I'm exhilarated, I'm eager, and perhaps a touch impatient—" I nudge Cat's foot under the table, and she barks a laugh. "But I'm not nervous. For some reason, it feels as if I've been waiting my entire life for this role."

• • •

Later that afternoon, I stand on my mark on the set of Juliet's famous balcony, reciting the opening lines of the famous scene to my handsome costar…and continue seeing Austin's face instead.

It's been the same problem all day. Seeing blue eyes where there should be brown, tousled hair in lieu of styled, and the sound of Austin's tempting whisper canceling out the screams, echoes, and questions of the crowded halls. In school I was not overly concerned, for I will unfortunately be gone long before any test scores are revealed. But here it is different. The theater is my forbidden dream come to life, one of the purposes for which Reyna sent me here, and I have to find a way to concentrate.

Sighing in frustration as I stumble over a line, I decide that this must be what falling in love feels like…

…and then my heart races, and I do an imaginary fist pump as I realize that if that is so, then this is exactly what Juliet felt every time she thought of her Romeo!

I ask to begin the scene again, and when I do, I bring the knowledge that I am in the middle of my own true-life love story to my performance. Utilizing the feelings stirring within me, I proclaim to Reid as Romeo the very words of forever love that I wish I could say to Austin. The new-to-me, yet centuries-old tale becomes real in a way it never has previously, and once again, I find in Juliet a kindred spirit.

Before I know it, Marilyn lifts a hand, signaling the end of the scene.

"Very well done, Alessandra," she proclaims from her lamplit table—or *the throne*, as my fellow actors have grown to call it. "And Reid, you were fantastic as always. As the both of you know, our entire production builds to this final scene, and I could not be happier with how it's coming together."

Feeling the glow of praise shining in my warm cheeks, I watch Ms. Kent take a long pull from her ever-present water bottle. Then she points a finger and proclaims, "This scene is going to receive a lot of attention in the media this weekend. I hope you're both ready for the accolades."

I want to yell from the rooftops just how ready I am, but

deciding that my exuberance may be a bit much, I instead issue my heartfelt gratitude and follow Reid into the curtained wings to wait for Austin. Jamie's scene is coming up, and I know he won't find a seat without first finding *me*. In fact, I'm counting on it.

The very moment we're offstage, Reid takes me into his arms and twirls me around in a circle. "I told you that smile of yours is our secret weapon!" Setting me down but not letting go of my hands, he says, "Alessandra, I wish you could've seen yourself out there. I don't know what happened; it seemed like you were a little lost in the beginning—it was probably just nerves. But after that, you totally owned it. You took an already spectacular performance and made it even better. I bow down to your talent."

I laugh as he does just that, taking our joined hands and raising and lowering them in mock adoration. Knowing precisely what it was—or rather *who* it was—that bettered my performance only makes my smile grow larger.

When Reid straightens, he still does not let go of my hands. Sliding his thumb along the underside of my wrist, he says, "You should know that receiving praise from Marilyn is pretty much like money in the bank, so I declare that the two of us must celebrate. Wherever you want to go, Ms. Future Star, I'll take you…well, except for maybe Paris. You do have school in the morning."

He flashes that easy smile, and the knowledge comes to me that this is about more than celebration. This is Reid once again wishing to court me. That truth settles in my gut and brings with it my first real twinges of guilt.

But for mere twinges, they are powerful.

I've never encouraged Reid's attention, but I've also never been direct about where my interest and affection lie. The day of our first rehearsal, Austin made a puzzling, false claim that he and I were in a relationship, but even then, I knew it wouldn't deter Reid. He is someone who thrives on a challenge. At every rehearsal since, he's proven that, maintaining his own unique brand of lighthearted flirtation. And if I'm being honest, I've even enjoyed our innocent banter—but it no longer feels so innocent.

I care about Austin; Austin cares about me. I don't wish to do anything that will harm our budding relationship, nor do I wish to hurt Reid's feelings. He has been a good friend to me here, and no one who has suffered heartache wishes to bestow that upon another.

Smiling affectionately—but not *too* affectionately—I squeeze the hands still clasped around my own. "That is a very generous offer, Reid, and I am grateful for the compliment, but I fear that I already have plans for the evening."

That easy smile fades a fraction, but then quickly perks back up. "Oh, yeah? Who with, that guy from the other day?"

"Yes," I say without hesitation. "And his name is Austin."

Heavy footsteps echo behind me. Even before I turn, I know whom I will see. My heart beats faster as I watch Austin walk across the scuffed floor, sharp eyes targeted on Reid. He comes to a stop beside me and slides a hand across my waist, settling it over my stomach, causing it to plunge again. The sensation is not unlike the roller coasters he took me on at the park, only safer. And much more thrilling.

I press into Austin's side and shiver at the affection in his stare. Turning back to Reid, I nod again, knowing I need to be clear. "Yes, Reid, my plans tonight are with Austin, as they are most nights. Because the truth is…" I look into Austin's eyes and return the words that I did not get to say last night. "I'm falling in love with him."

Austin's blue-eyed gaze glows with warmth as his mouth lifts into a knee-weakening smile.

"But I will see you tomorrow," I say, turning back to Reid with reluctance. "And thank you for a splendid rehearsal."

"Hey, that's what I'm here for." Reid gives a casual shrug of his shoulders, but I notice the tension in his posture, and twinges of guilt jab again at my insides. "You guys have a great night. I'll see you tomorrow, Alessandra."

"Tomorrow," I repeat, but I'm unsure if he hears me, for he's already walking away.

A silent, awkward moment hangs in the air. Then Austin says, "So, we have plans," bringing my attention back to him— back where it belongs. "And when exactly were you thinking about telling me this important information?"

"As soon as I saw you," I say, placing my hand over the comforting beat of his heart. "I figured you would be here with Jamie, or I'd call you when my scene was through. But if you already have plans for the evening, you don't have to come. Cat and Lucas just invited us for pizza and a movie at the house, nothing as exciting as one of your challenges."

"Anything with you is exciting, Princess." He moves his hand beneath my thick hair and plays with the wisps at the nape of my neck. He brushes his lips against mine, just a tease, then

lifts his head and grins. "And it just so happens I like pizza"—
another light brush—"and movies." His mouth presses more
firmly this time for a prolonged, lingering touch, and then he
shrugs. "And I guess the company is decent enough."

"Oh, is that right?" I ask, trying to feign insult, but mostly
succeeding in sounding breathless. "Only decent?"

He glides the tip of his nose against mine. "Mm-hmm."

I pinch the taut skin at his waist, and he chuckles. The
sound does glorious things to my insides. Then, *finally*, Austin
strengthens his hold around me, crushing me to his chest, and
tilts his head, capturing my lips in a long, searing kiss that has
me clinging to his shoulders.

Chapter Twenty Four

The glow of the television flickers across Cat's face as Lucas and she battle each other. "I'm not watching *Entertainment Tonight*, *TMZ*, or anything on E!," my cousin says as she wrests the remote from his grip. "As far as I know, Mama Dearest is laying low on the scandal scene, and I don't need any gossip-spewers destroying that lovely illusion. I'm sure I'll learn all about her latest embarrassment soon enough."

Lucas and I share a look. This isn't the first time Cat has brought up her mother when we've watched television at night or happened past a row of newspapers and magazines in a store. And it appears as though the longer time ticks without any salacious news, and the happier Cat grows in her relationship with Lucas, the more on edge she becomes. It's as if she believes she's only allotted so much happiness in life and is waiting for a villain to reveal the turning point.

Such as she experienced during her journey to the sixteenth

century.

Lucas shrugs his shoulders, clearly more concerned with the girl beside him than what is on television. "Not like I'd ever watch that garbage, anyway, *dear*."

Cat sticks her tongue out at his teasing tone and shoves his chest when he leans in to nibble the side of her neck. I smile, impressed with his diversion techniques, and Lucas tosses me a grin as he slides his arm along the back of the sofa.

"Or ESPN," my cousin continues, her tone much lighter than before as she scrolls through the options on the menu screen. "And all those testosterone-filled, boy-like sports channels are obviously out for oh, so many reasons. But— aha!—see, here you go." She presses select and the screen switches to a man with a comically wide smile, acting as host and mediator between two sets of boisterous, screaming, and frankly somewhat frightening, people lined up behind a long desk. "You can never go wrong with the good old Game Show Network."

A bright red x blazes on the screen, accompanied by a startling *bong* sound, and the entire audience boos in empathy. "*Family Feud*," she says with a nod. "An American TV classic."

Lucas rolls his eyes but pulls her into his arms, snuggling her close as they watch the bizarre program. Unaccustomed to the garish colors of the set and the chirping noises emitting from the speakers, I begin straightening the coffee table between our two sofas and attempt to ignore the adorable couple opposite me. It is not that I begrudge them their affectionate display; I'm just impatient for Austin to arrive so that I can have my own. I find that I've become addicted to his presence, and the last few days have only added to my obsession. I stack empty soda cups and toss in the crumpled napkins littering the smooth mahogany tabletop, and grin when I spy the half-empty box of pizza.

If Austin doesn't arrive soon, I'm going to have one hungry boy on my hands.

The skin on my backside tingles at the memory of his playful swat. And when the doorbell finally rings, following another red x and loud *bong* from the television, I spring to my feet.

It's about time.

Taking off at a near sprint, I call over my shoulder, "I'll get it!" As I hasten my pace, my sock-encased feet lose traction on the smooth hardwood floor. I slide into one wall, push off, and grab the corner of another to keep from crashing again, and the disembodied sound of Cat's laughter trails behind me. "Don't go hurting yourself now."

I roll my eyes but slow down, for even I notice my behavior is bordering on frantic. And I'm not quite sure why. Based on appearances, there is nothing to be anxious about. The four of us are simply going to relax—*hang out*—in Cat's home, enjoying one another's company. It will be much easier than any one of Austin's nonstop adventures. But it doesn't change the fact that everything about tonight feels significant, important. Almost as if I've crossed some invisible line and begun a new chapter in my time-travel tale. And that is why this is such a defining moment; this evening I will truly experience a typical night in the life of a modern teen, one who happens to be falling hard for the enigmatic boy waiting for her.

I glide to a stop in the atrium and check my reflection in the mirror over the entry table, looking for anything unseemly or out of place, any food lodged between my teeth. I pat my hair and straighten unseen wrinkles in my shirt. Smiling at the crimson stain on my cheeks, aware that this time my characteristic blush is not from embarrassment or discomfort but unbridled excitement, I throw open the door.

But it's not Austin standing on the threshold.

Cold night air rushes in. I feel it, but that is not what brings about my goose bumps. The sound of Cat's and Lucas's laughter floats from the living room. They are just down the hall, yet it suddenly seems as though they are miles away. And when the visitor's identity finally breaks through my thick wall of self-denial, the rest of the world fades away.

Reyna.

Pressure mounts behind my eyes. I clutch my arms around my waist, and the row of bracelets on my wrist *clink* together with my tremors. I want to ask her, *Why are you here?* and, *Why now?* but my voice is strangled by the hopes and dreams that I know now will never come to be. Besides, I already know the answer.

She's here to take me home.

Before I can tell Austin good-bye. Before I even learn if I won the lead in the school musical. And before my big performance in the workshop.

Did I miss the third sign?

I wrack my brain, trying to remember what she said the third sign would be and wondering how I could've missed it. But then, I know why. I was living in the moment, swept up in all this life has to offer—and ignoring what I knew was coming all along.

And life will imitate art. That was the final sign. But art has always been Cat's domain, not mine. How would I have known to look for it? When did it happen? The very fact that Reyna is here now, after sundown, proves it was today. But what was it?

Fisting a hand over my mouth, I try to conceal my sob, wanting to be strong. For a moment, I believe perhaps my strength can make a difference, that if I act calmly I can somehow change her mind. But my attempt to hide my dread is useless—as useless as begging time to stand still—for nothing can stop the desperate moan building in my chest. It echoes off the cold, hard surfaces around me and reverberates in my ears.

The television in the living room silences.

"Alessandra," Reyna says, her voice low and unforgettable. "You look well."

She dips her head, and I notice her long raven locks are disheveled. Almost as if she rode on the wind itself to get here. I wouldn't be surprised if she had.

I shake my head at the wistful thought and swipe at a falling tear.

Reyna studies my face carefully, and my nails sink into the flesh of my palms as I will myself to be brave. I've been here for fourteen glorious days. That is more time than I ever hoped possible a few weeks ago. My weak and senseless tears will do nothing to change my fate. What I need to do—what I *ought* to do—is show Reyna my appreciation, and let her see that her magic was not in vain. That I've grown during my short stay in the twenty-first century and become the strong woman I claimed to be back in my own.

But the thought that I have yet to achieve the goal in my vision and may never see Austin's face again crushes any shred of bravery I have in me.

Swift, purposeful footsteps behind me let me know I'm no longer alone with our visitor. Cat's rose scent envelops me as she wraps a supportive arm around my waist and squeezes me tight. Her shoulders stiffen with the confidence I wish I had in this moment.

"Reyna, I'm surprised to see you so soon."

Cat's tone is confused as she looks to me, perhaps wondering too when we missed the third sign. Wrongly, we had both thought I would at least have until after the performance; maybe that is why I grew so lazy in my watch. But unlike when Reyna appeared to bring Cat home to *her* own time, the gypsy's arrival tonight should not have come as a shock to either of us—if only I had kept searching for the markers.

Reyna hitches a dark eyebrow. "Alessandra knew that I would return when the third sign was revealed."

I release a shaky breath and look to my cousin. "And *Alessandra* failed to pay attention."

More footsteps approach. Cat glances back at Lucas, then meets my eye. In her misty brown depths, I can read the message almost as if she spoke the words aloud: *the show is over.* Alessandra Forlani is no longer. Lucas is about to meet Alessandra D'Angeli, time traveler. And how he will react to the true me is anybody's guess. Reyna may be filled with gypsy mojo, but short of erasing Lucas's memory, there is no way he can *un*hear or *un*see what is about to occur. I would know, for the memories of the first time I saw Reyna, and of when Cat disappeared, have haunted me for the last two years.

I squeeze my cousin's hand for encouragement—about as much communication as I can offer in my speechless state—and give a faint smile. I do not envy the explaining she will have to do when I'm gone.

Cat doesn't appear too eager for the conversation, either. She takes a deep breath and turns back to Reyna. "When did life imitate art?" she asks. "I figured that wouldn't happen until she was on stage. Opening night isn't for another two days."

I didn't think the iron vise around my chest could tighten any more, but I was wrong. Hearing aloud how close I came to recreating my vision from the tent brings me to the point of agony, and another moan escapes.

Reyna pins me in place with the knowing look in her eye. "At rehearsal today, Alessandra, did you not connect with your role of Juliet? Find in her a kindred spirit? Understand her better because of your own emotions?"

I nod, remembering that rush I felt once I'd made the connection—and how much I looked forward to experiencing that again in front of a spellbound crowd. My lifelong dream was just within my reach, so close that today the wispy tendrils actually brushed my fingertips. I could feel the heat of the spotlight, hear the packed audience's thundering silence as they hung on my every word. I came so close to experiencing the surge of their applause. Cat and I had been sure that this was why Reyna sent me here, that the theater is where *my real strength lies.*

Wasn't that the point of her cryptic message?

As if I she can read my thoughts, Reyna asks, "Alessandra, your time *was* spent living adventures and experiencing the world of possibility, was it not?"

The fullness of her prophecy whispers in my mind— *the adventure that you seek is full of possibilities, but always remember where your real strength lies*—and I suck in a breath.

I may have been wrong about the second part of the message, which, if I'm to leave now will forever remain shrouded in mystery, but thanks to Austin, I more than fulfilled the first half of it.

Scenes from the last week chase the haunting words: my arms wrapped around Austin as we flew through the water on his Jet Ski, the sting of salt water biting into my cheeks. Holding his hand at Rush as the roller coaster slowly made its upward trek, and the security I felt as we plunged back to the earth, knowing I was safe as long as Austin was by my side. The way the waves pounded my board as he taught me to surf, and earlier, the scorching heat of his legs as he straddled my hips on the shore. And eclipsing each of the memories, though they all tug at my heart, is the exhilarating rightness of my very first kiss.

Cat's brow creases as she watches me, no doubt seeing the emotions roll across my face. "Adventures? Less, what is she talking about?"

I shake my head, now not being the time to tell her about Austin's challenge. She huffs a breath and steps closer to our unexpected visitor. "That doesn't matter. Reyna, you said in your letter that you were leaving her in capable hands, and you trusted that I'd know what to do. And I do. Give her forty-eight more hours. Let her do her dress rehearsal tomorrow, and experience opening night, and then take her back."

My eyes widen at my cousin's bold request. Reyna purses her lips, and Cat, perhaps sensing her tentative acquiescence, moves even closer. "She's got this."

I just stand there, a passive observer in my own fate as they discuss my future. Where is the brave girl I claimed to be, the girl I've become the last week? The girl who stood up for Austin with his father and defied Kendal by auditioning? Apparently the thought of returning home has scared her away, for all I can do now is watch silently and pray that Reyna will say yes to Cat's request. I doubt I'll ever have enough time with Austin or in this world, but right now two more days feel as though they are a lifetime.

Lucas shuffles his feet behind me, reminding me of his presence. I can't even begin to wonder what he must be thinking. But I do not turn around and ask because Reyna suddenly bows her head. My breath catches, and Cat clutches my hand.

"As you wish," she tells Cat, her eyes trained on me. "She may remain until after the performance. I shall be waiting for her at the portal at midnight."

She doesn't need to explain. A flash of the chaotic theater of etched handprints and stars leaps to mind. TCL Chinese Theatre, the location where I first arrived.

Relief fills me to bursting as her words and their meaning sink in…and maybe a touch of something else, too, for as Reyna turns and walks away, I finally find my voice.

"Can I stay…forever?"

The words are out before I can even think about what I'm

proposing, what it'll mean. Cat stares at me as if I have lost my mind, and perhaps I have, but I can't take back the request. Nothing in my entire life has ever felt as right as staying here.

My heart aches with the admission. It feels like a betrayal to my parents—to *Mama*—to wish to stay where they aren't. But what is truly waiting for me at home? A family whom I love with every piece of my breaking heart and whom I miss more than anything in the world, yes, but also a brother who lives in another city and parents who are growing older with each passing day, currently on the marriage hunt for me. Once I return, it will not be long until they make me a match, a suitor who at best will not be Austin, and at worse will be cold and indifferent. And after leaving the shelter of my familial home, I will be thrust into a life filled with propriety and rules, expectations and limitations.

I have become too comfortable with the ways of this world. The freedom I am granted, the choices that I have. Here is where I've come to be the woman I always wanted to be, and can have the life I always dreamed of. Here is where I can create my own destiny.

I don't know where I'll stay. I can't expect Cat's father will just take me into his home and accept that I no longer have one of my own. But those are details for later. *If* Reyna agrees.

A very important *if.*

She takes her time turning back. I stand frozen in place, waiting to gauge her reaction, conjuring up a thousand possibilities. But when she does turn, I am unable to read her expression.

Seconds tick by in anticipation. Not knowing whether I

pushed too far is worse than any outburst.

A car drives down the street. The engine rumbles; its headlights illuminate the porch where we stand, lighting our alcove like the noonday sun, then driving away, shrouding us again in darkness. My cousin shifts on her feet. Lucas coughs.

Finally, just when I think I cannot take the silence any longer, Reyna asks me, "Is your request in earnest?" just as Cat leans close to my ear and whispers under her breath, "What are you *doing*?"

My gaze darts between them, but I do not answer. I can't. It took everything I had in me even to make such a proposition in the first place. But as I remain silent, I can't help but feel as though I failed somehow when a flash of emotion crosses Reyna's face. It takes me a moment to decipher it, but when I do, any shred of hope I held for my future is dashed.

Disappointment.

The smooth skin around Reyna's eyes tightens. "Alessandra, staying here would affect much more than just you." Her stare drills into me. "Such an act would change *history*."

As she emphasizes the final word, the amber color of her eyes seems to glow and swirl in the darkness, lit this time not from a passing car but from a mystical source within. The girl inside me who still believes in things like signs and hidden meanings wants to believe it is for a reason, that she is sending me a silent message of some kind. But when she speaks again, I realize that is simply the childish, wishful stirring of my imagination. And perhaps a touch of slanted moonlight.

"I am truly sorry," she says, "but a decision like that is not within *my* power."

Her emphasis, this time on the word *my*, catches my attention. I furrow my brow, marveling over what she could mean, what force could be at work in this situation that is greater than she is.

Signore?

The fates?

As I consider the possibilities, my eyes leave hers, closing for just a moment. And in the second it takes for my lashes to lift, Reyna disappears. No windswept storm to ride on. No whispered chants. Simply gone.

And I burst into tears.

Chapter Twenty Five

The crunch of boots on gravel causes me to lift my weary head. I'd recognize that unmistakable tread anywhere.

I'm still standing in the open doorway to Cat's house, the cold night air settling around me like a torn, tattered blanket that suffocates all the same. Until now, the only sound to pierce the thick silence has been my sobs, my cousin's sharply whispered "not now" to Lucas's obvious bafflement, and the lonely drone of a car engine fading into the distance. All have formed a depressing yet completely fitting accompaniment to my misery. But as the *thud* of Austin's confident, purposeful footsteps joins the nighttime symphony, my agony reaches a new low.

The automatic porch light switches on, bathing his raven head in soft light, making him appear every bit the fallen angel I once proclaimed him to be, and I realize this may be—no, it *will* be—one of the last times I'll ever see his handsome face. Ever hear the deep notes of his voice. Every fiber in my being wants to prolong this moment, to savor it and commit it to memory so I can take it out and relive it in the years to come, but for some reason I'm finding it difficult even to look him in the eye.

"What's going on, Princess?"

Those deep notes I've grown to love so much hold a touch of concern and confusion, and that's what finally prompts me to meet Austin's gaze. And when I do, my breath catches at the pure joy—rather than his characteristic cool indifference—shining in his eyes.

Well, that is, until he sees my face.

Then fury, swift and ferocious, replaces it, and the ease with which he took his first steps up the driveway shifts to edgy, tense strides as his long legs devour the distance between us.

"What happened?" he barks at Cat, simultaneously sweeping me into his arms. He glides his thumbs under my eyes, wiping away the tracks of my tears, and then places a feather-light kiss on my forehead. Before I can relax into the tender caress, he raises his head and swings around to Lucas. "Someone better start talking. Now."

Lucas holds his hands palms up. "Hey, man, don't look at me. I'm as lost as you are."

Austin narrows his eyes but nods, then turns and targets Cat with his wrathful stare. I latch onto his arm. "Austin, neither of them is the reason for my tears."

"Then what is?" he asks. A confused, hopeless look crosses his face. "Tell me, please, so I can fix it. I can't stand seeing you like this."

His eyes bore into mine almost pleadingly as his hands rub

my arms, and I open my mouth to tell him, but what can I say? The truth is too complicated.

Austin notices my hesitation, and his back stiffens. He takes a small step away from me. "Unless I'm the problem?"

Walls that have taken two weeks to topple erect themselves in an instant, and a fresh onslaught of tears spring forth. I shake my head at how right and how wrong his question is. A half laugh, half cry bubbles up in response, a mucus-filled, disgusting, blubbering sound that is not at all appealing.

His eyes widen. The protective façade falls away, and just before he pulls me back in and tucks me against his chest, I catch him mouth the words *help me* over my head.

Under my ear, the comforting sound of Austin's heartbeat calms my own, and the feel of his strong hands rubbing soothing circles on my back makes me want to burrow into his skin. Warm breath fans across my cheek as he whispers, "I'm an idiot. It's all right; I shouldn't have asked that. I'm here. Whatever it is, I'm here."

And therein lies the true problem, for soon Austin and I will be separated indefinitely, and he doesn't even know it. And instead of focusing on his consoling words or the gentleness of his voice, the only thing I think is, *You might be here, but I won't be for long.*

I don't know what to do next. Should I tell him about Reyna and where I come from, and risk having him not believe me? Or do I feign a brave face—or at the very least, a non-crying one—and pretend we have forever?

I decide the best I can aim for is somewhere in the middle and throw my arms around his neck. My emotions have a mind of their own tonight, but I will do everything I can to make the most of the little time we have left. My hands lock behind Austin's head, and the thought crosses my mind that maybe if I never let go, I can somehow bring him home with me.

The image of Austin in my world of rules and regulations, pretentions and propriety makes me laugh—which really comes out closer to a splutter—and I snuggle my face into the soft folds of his cotton shirt. Inhaling the crisp scent of mint and soap that will forever be entwined with his memory, I say, "No, Austin, you aren't the problem. You are everything that's right. And I am so glad you're here."

His chest expands with a relieved breath and I hear the sound of his lips forming a smile. He places a kiss on the crown of my head, then cups my face in the palms of his hands. "Where else would I be? I go where you go, simple as that."

I lower my lashes to hide my reaction, and a third hand, smaller and feminine, pats my back—Cat. I look over my shoulder to see her sympathetic smile. If anyone can understand what I am going through right now, she can. We share a look that needs no words, and with reluctance, I step out of Austin's arms.

"So anyone gonna tell me who that woman was?" Lucas asks, looking between us. "Or maybe what the hell that was all about, worlds of possibilities, portals, and changing history?"

He shifts his weight from foot to foot, and Austin's body tenses. "What woman?"

Lucas ignores him and takes a step closer, lowering his voice as if worried someone will overhear. "Because either someone slipped some funky mushrooms on our pizza tonight, or that woman just disappeared into thin air. And last time I checked, that wasn't possible."

Austin wraps his hand around my elbow and repeats his question, this time more aggressively. "What woman?"

His jaw clicks with frustration as he waits for me to answer, and I realize there is no way to avoid answering him. I shift my gaze to Lucas, watching his hands flex and clench at his sides, his body poised as if preparing for a battle he does not understand, and exhale a resigned breath.

I look at Cat. "We need to tell them."

She closes her eyes and nods once.

This will not be easy.

"All right, guys, let's go inside." She takes Lucas's hand and leads him to the door. "I think you're both gonna want to sit down for this."

My cousin doesn't stop in the living room where we sat before, but continues down the hall to her bedroom. "In case anyone comes home early," she explains as I walk in after the boys. She shuts the door behind me and locks it, testing the knob to ensure our privacy, then slides her arm around my shoulder. I rest my head against hers.

It's time the boys hear the truth. I only hope they believe it.

• • •

The air conditioner whirs overhead, sending shivers down my arms. The springs in Cat's heavenly mattress squeak, protesting under the amassed weight of four bodies. Austin squishes the feathers of her pillow in his hand, and the scent of rose fills the air. I must admit, all those nights I spent lying awake at home, fantasizing about the first time I would ever share a bed with a boy, I never dreamed it like this. Unmarried. Fully clothed. And with an audience.

The awkward trepidation and uncertainty, unfortunately, was always part of the fantasy.

Lucas looks at me and plunges his fingers through his curls. We've been sitting here for a full minute in silence, perhaps longer, neither Cat nor I sure of where to begin. How does one tell someone such a fantastical tale? Then I remember my cousin confided this very thing to me two years ago (interestingly enough, also in a bedroom) during her own time-travel jaunt. I further recall how hard it was for me to accept the truth. I'm not even sure I fully believed it until I saw Reyna appear on the street, watched her clothes transform from the drab servant outfit into her costume of veils, and witnessed the two of them go inside the green tent and vanish a short time later.

But as often as I have played back Cat's confession that night, marveling at the way destiny works, I never thought I would be on this side of the conversation.

The mattress dips as Lucas shifts, and I hear his breath catch.

"Cat, is that *you?*"

Ripped from my memories, I shift my gaze to where he is staring and land on Lorenzo's painting. *Well, it looks like we found our opening.*

"Uh, yeah," Cat says, turning to me. "It's kind of an interesting story."

She hesitates, perhaps waiting for me to jump in, but if such a thing as being an expert on explaining time travel exists, or at least a seasoned speaker on such a topic, my cousin would be it. I wave my hand, indicating she should go on, and she rolls her eyes.

"All right, then." She tucks her legs underneath her and settles in like she is about to tell us a bedtime story, and proceeds to tell Austin and Lucas about her magical, fantastical trip back to the sixteenth century.

During the telling, Lucas's eyebrows creep so far up his forehead that they nearly meet his hairline. Austin blinks his long, beautiful lashes, then fixes his deep blue gaze on me. His thoughts remain hidden in their depths, and I hug my legs to my chest, wishing I had some of Reyna's powers so I could determine what he is thinking.

After explaining how it was she came to arrive in my time, she pauses, then looking at me, says, "And that's where I met Less."

One, two, three—

"Wait, what?"

At his outburst, Austin's thoughts no longer remain hidden. Blatant incredulity is written all over his face, and even though I have been exactly where he is now, most likely questioning and doubting the very same things he is—such as my cousin's sanity or if this is all a joke—I can't help wishing he would just accept the truth without question. That somehow, he would just *know*.

But that, I suppose, would be too simple.

Instead of answering him, Cat strolls over to her desk and opens a drawer. As she pulls out a bright purple binder and flips the thick pages inside, Lucas watches her every movement. He hasn't said a word yet, not even a grunt or disbelieving snort, but the squiggle between his eyebrows implies he shares Austin's concerns about her sanity.

Austin isn't watching my cousin, however. He's watching me. And afraid of what I will see when (if?) he finally does accept the truth, I cast my eyes to my lap.

Cat plops down in the middle of the bed, seemingly unfazed by their obvious doubt. Only those closest to her know how she hides her insecurities, and knowing her as well as I do, I see the slight tremor of her fingers, the tension in her shoulders.

"When I came back home, I didn't think anyone would believe me." She laughs. "Hell, I didn't plan on ever *telling* anyone, either, but just in case I needed to, I collected proof."

"Proof?" I ask, wondering why she never mentioned this before.

She flinches, and my apprehension escalates. I know she didn't forget to show this to me—she kept it a secret on purpose. But why would she feel the need to hide?

Tapping her manicured nails on the binder's cover, she focuses her gaze on Lucas instead of me. "You see, as if the ability to travel through time wasn't crazy enough, my gypsy girl let me bring my backpack with me. And along with much-needed toothpaste, deodorant, magazines, art supplies, and various electronics, I had my camera. Whenever people weren't looking, or sometimes even when they were, I snapped shots."

She opens the binder and begins flipping through pages of buildings, outfits, and food. I spot the familiar sight of Mama's profile, and my heartbeat stutters over the gaping hole her absence has left. Then Cat stops on a page containing a picture of me covered in green goop, and blood rushes to my face.

"We all agree this is Less, right?"

The boys nod, and Austin's lips twitch with amusement. I flash Cat a disgruntled look. *Could she not have chosen a less embarrassing photograph to prove her point?*

Cat grins and flips another page, and then it is time for her breath to catch. I look down and discover why.

It's a photograph of Lorenzo.

Lucas jerks and grabs the binder. She places her hand on his arm. "Lucas, meet Lorenzo. Lorenzo *Cappelli*, your Renaissance ancestor, and the artist who painted me there."

Almost as one, four sets of eyes shift to the painting.

A muscle pops in Lucas's jaw, and I can't imagine what he is presuming. Cat bites her lip and picks at a nonexistent hangnail. "Luc, I know how it looks, but nothing happened. It was completely innocent. Most of that painting is artistic interpretation."

I bite my tongue, deciding it best I not share my suspicions about all that Lorenzo glimpsed that day, and look back at the binder, pondering what else it contains.

Cat begins flipping pages again, an obvious attempt to refocus Lucas's attention when she says, "But that's not the painting I wanted to show you. He did one of Less, too."

Now *my* eyes widen. Austin sits up straight and cracks his knuckles. When my cousin points at a page, he strains his neck to look over her shoulder, trying to smooth his facial muscles. But I see the tension snapping just below the surface. Knowing I never posed for such a painting, nor have any intention ever to do so in the future, I say, "That's not possible."

Lucas huffs. "Seems like there's a lot of that going around."

Cat lifts the book to her chest. "This is different. This is a painting Lorenzo did right before you got married, or, err, *get* married. He did it as a wedding gift to your bridegroom or some craziness."

The word *bridegroom* hits me like a bucket of cold water. Austin visibly recoils.

Sure enough, she lowers the binder and exposes a printed replication of a portrait of me, sitting on my beloved fountain in my family's courtyard. I am dressed in a gown Mama recently had done up for me, my current favorite, a light green surcoat with the most beautiful embroidery.

I grab the book from her hands, searching the page for a clue as to when this could've been painted and who I am to marry, hoping to find some mark that will show it is years from now. But I look the same as I do today. I lift my eyes, and Cat nods at my unspoken question. "The date said 1507."

The book falls from my fingertips. "But when I return it will be 1507." Even to my own ears, my voice sounds hollow and far away.

She presses her lips together in a thin line, and realization hits me.

"But you knew that," I say. "The first day I arrived, I told you what year it was when I left. Which means you knew all along that I was to marry soon."

Cat looks at her bedspread. That is what she has been hiding. All this time she has known what waited when I returned. Betrayal washes over me...and then fades as quickly as it comes.

What good would it have done for me to know the truth any sooner? Would I have changed one moment of the last two weeks? If anything, had I known what lay ahead, I most likely would have focused on that, on my future as a bride, and not on my time here.

With Austin.

I feel the weight of his stare as I ask her, almost scared of her answer, "Do you know whom it is that I am to marry?"

Cat shakes her head. "The title of the painting didn't say. It just said it was a gift to your bridegroom. I planned to do a full ancestry search soon, to find out what happened to everyone. You, Cipriano, your parents, Patience, Lorenzo." Her eyes dart to Lucas and back. "But I haven't had time yet with Christmas break. I found this doing a quick Google search right after I got back. But if you want, we can go to the library tomorrow and find out before you leave."

Of course, my mind immediately conjures the worst potential suitors in Florence, and how lonely a life with any of the men would be—but I still have to know. "Yes," I say, even as my stomach roils. "I would like that."

Austin's eyes have remained on me for our entire exchange, sitting in relative silence, not even commenting on the fact that I am (apparently) soon to become a sixteen-year-old bride, something quite unusual for his time.

Cat does what I haven't been able to do since I heard the word *bridegroom*—she looks at Austin. Closing the binder, she takes Lucas's hand and pulls him off the bed. "We're gonna go in the bathroom and let you two talk."

From Lucas's expression, I have no doubt their conversation will be an interesting one as well.

Austin waits for the telltale *click* of the bathroom door, then interlocks our hands. I stare at the contrast between his thick, roughened fingers and my smooth, slender ones. He lifts our joined hands and places a knuckle under my chin so he can look me in the eye. "So it's true?"

I give him a halfhearted smile. "You always say I speak like a historical novel."

The side of his mouth lifts in a grin, and hope flutters in my chest. "You do."

I fight the urge to squirm and look away as he studies my face, and when his mouth tightens, every cell in my body tenses for his response.

"You know, as crazy as it is, it kinda makes sense. In a surreal, mind-boggling sort of way."

Deeming it too good to be true, I ask, "You mean...you believe her?"

Austin slowly nods, almost as if he, too, is surprised. "I do. I mean, at first I didn't. The buildings in Cat's pictures don't look much different now, and the rest could've been from a really good Renaissance fair. But that painting of you...and seeing your face when you heard about getting *married...*" He breaks off with a low curse. Then he closes his eyes and opens them, the blue so deep I could drown in them. "Yeah, I believe you. But that's not why you were so upset. You always knew where you were from, so something else must've happened before I got here. What?" He narrows his eyes. "Why was that woman here tonight?"

Willing myself not to cry again, I crush his fingers in my

grasp and whisper, "She came to take me home."

Austin bounds off the bed and paces the length of the room. He stops, starts again, and then pulls me up with him. Gathering me to his chest, he curls his shoulders around me as if he can protect me—as if he can stop fate just because he wills things to be different—and says, "That's not happening."

His voice is sharp, with a determined edge of steel, and if I weren't so heartbroken, I would kiss him.

Instead, I lay my hand on his cheek. "It's all right. Reyna granted me a forty-eight-hour reprieve. I have until after opening night." I swallow hard, pushing my emotions back down my thickened throat. "But—but then I'll have to leave you."

Austin takes my hand and walks back to the bed, placing me on his lap as he sits down. "Baby, I just found you…you really think I'm gonna let her take you away from me? We'll figure something out, I promise you that."

"But how?"

I startle from Cat's sudden appearance in the bathroom's doorway and look up to meet her troubled gaze.

"I mean, Austin, this isn't politics. You can't just argue your point here. This is fate. Destiny." She wiggles her fingers in the air. "Magic." She shrugs. "It's kinda hard to fight."

"No, Austin's right." Lucas glides past her and sits in the rolling desk chair. "The two of you aren't alone this time. There's four of us now and only one of her. We'll start with that ancestry search Cat was talking about; maybe we can find something there. That was Reyna's big argument, right?" he asks me. "That you'd change history if you stayed?" I nod, and he grins. "Then there you go. Let's find out who's in your lineage and what great things we'd be changing if you stayed. There has to be a loophole."

Austin clasps his arms around my waist from behind. "I'm great at finding loopholes."

It is tempting to let go and be swept away by their excitement, but the boys do not understand the magic we are dealing with. I look at Cat, who gives me a gentle smile but voices the question we're both thinking. "And if we don't? If there's not a loose thread to pick, or a flaw in her logic?"

Austin's fingers sink into my skin. "Then I'll go back with her."

I must have heard that wrong.

I twist my head around, certain there's no way he would be willing to give up this world that I desperately want to stay in, all for a girl he just met. But the emotion in his eyes tells me that he is, and that my ears are working just fine.

Austin resettles me on his lap, clasping his arms around my back so I will not fall, and once he is sure I am comfortable, asks, "What does this century have for me that yours won't? Electricity? My dear devoted dad? My superior academic record?" He gives me a droll look, and even with the trauma of the day, I find my smile.

"And Jamie?" I ask, knowing how close the two siblings are.

As anticipated, sadness rolls across his face, but it is quickly replaced by resolve. "Yeah, you're right. If I leave—and I don't think I'll have to, but if I do—I'll miss her. But my sister's a fighter, Princess. And she's all grown up. More importantly, she's not *you*."

I hear the bathroom door creak behind me, and I picture my cousin's mouth hanging ajar. But nothing, not even Reyna, could get me to look away. Austin bends his head so close to mine and lowers his voice to just above a whisper as he says, "I don't think you're getting it. I told you I'm not letting them take you away, so you better get used to this face. One way or another, Alessandra, I'm yours until you get rid of me."

My heart swells, and I cling to his words like the lifeline they are. "Well, you better get used to mine," I tell him, "because I'm *never* getting rid of you." Then I seal my promise with a kiss.

Chapter Twenty Six

The ancestry search had to wait until morning. Shortly after absorbing Austin's words, Jenna arrived home from touring potential sweet sixteen venues with Lucas's mom and sister in tow, and as eager as we all were to fight fate, we decided it best we start fresh in the morning. So at nine o'clock in the morning on the day before I am to leave the twenty-first century forever, I join my boyfriend, cousin, and friend at the Beverly Hills public library to research their past—and my future—in an attempt to find a fatal flaw in Reyna's divine logic.

To admit my hopes are pinned on a very slim chance would not be an overstatement.

"Slumming it with the rest of us lowlife, school ditchers, huh?" Austin teases Cat, grabbing the seat across from her. "I didn't think you had it in you."

She lifts her head out of a book. "What can I say? My early ancestors set a horrible example."

I jab her in the ribs with my elbow, and she winks, though the gesture seems a tad…strange.

I knew last night that she was worried, feeling guilty for keeping my marriage a secret for so long, but I told her I understood. I can't imagine what it must have been like, knowing what my future held and watching me fall more and more for Austin. No wonder she fought against us so much. But I thought that we had moved past that.

Frowning, I shake off the lingering sense of unease. I've been overly anxious all morning, imagining conflict where there is none. I guess fighting fate will do that to a girl.

The library is deserted and quiet, and we've received more than a few inquisitive looks, wondering why we are not in school. Austin, a professional at making excuses for such things, explains we are gathering research for a class project. Luckily, the woman behind the desk seems to accept his explanation without question. After all, as he told me when I expressed my disbelief earlier, "Why would anyone believe we'd skip *here*?"

I take a thick volume I found on Lorenzo's life from the top of my stack of books, hoping it will contain a clue about the painting he did of me. It is still strange to think about how well-known he has become in the last five hundred years. If things do not go the way I wish and Reyna sends me home tomorrow night, I'm unsure if I should ever tell him the extent of his fame…he could grow quite insufferable. I smile, thinking of my friend, and crack the spine of the tome.

A half hour and no huge discovery later, I glance up, eyes weary from strain. Austin does the same and shifts his gaze between Cat and me. "I can't believe I didn't notice how much you two look alike."

"You didn't know to look for it," I suggest, sitting straighter in my chair.

I've long thought Cat and I shared certain attributes—it is one of the reasons I so easily believed she was my father's niece, Patience, when she first arrived two years ago—but I have yet to hear anyone else say the same. Turning in my seat, I beam at my cousin and observe the deep etches on her forehead.

She nods. "Yeah, I see it, too."

The difference between my thoughts and her statement is that Cat's voice catches with sadness as she says it, and instead of smiling at me with equal delight, her gaze flits back to her open book.

Realizing my previous concern was not paranoia, I ask, more than a little hurt by her disappointment in resembling me, "Cousin, are you all right?"

She closes her eyes tight and snaps, "I'm fine."

Obviously not, but I dare not say so and risk her ire again.

When Cat opens her eyes, she tosses me a quick smile. "I'm sorry. I didn't mean to jump on you. I guess I'm just a little stressed that we're not gonna find anything, but that's all it is." Then she looks back at her book, effectively shutting me out.

I have not known my cousin long—nine days during her journey, fifteen now for mine—but during that time she has never lied to me. Well, if not counting the numerous times she claimed to be Patience, but even then, she was never very good at it. Cat never needed to lie about anything important because I have always accepted and loved her unconditionally... which makes her insincerity now even more surprising. And disconcerting. Call it intuition, a familial bond, or just keen observation, but something is definitely bothering her. And it is something she doesn't want *me* to know about. Another secret.

Lucas looks at me over Cat's bowed head and shrugs, then reaches for his chirping cell phone. He's been calling and e-mailing his contacts back in Milan all morning for assistance. He gets up from our table and rushes down the aisle, past the frowning librarian, to accept the call outside. Austin lifts his chin in Cat's direction, urging me on.

I close my hand around the wooden seat of my chair and scoot closer. The screech of the legs against the floor brings another scowl from the woman behind the desk. Despite Austin's assurances, I am beginning to think she has her doubts about our alibi.

"Cat?" I ask, wincing at the slight waver in my voice.

"Yeah?"

She turns another page and lifts the book up. What she doesn't lift is her eyes.

Not a good sign.

I shove my hair behind my ear, then rub my hands along the rough denim of my jeans. In all the questions I assumed I'd be asking today—and I imagined a lot—I never expected I'd have to ask this…or that I'd ever dread the answer.

Feet bouncing beneath my chair, I gather my strength and blurt out, "Do you not wish for me to stay?"

Austin stops writing. Cat drops the book from her hands. And I wait in fear.

The same doubts I had when I first walked up to her door come creeping back. Could she have been pretending this whole time? I think back to her excited greeting and the way she welcomed me so readily into her home, and doubt that can be true. But if she did miss me, and did want me here, could it be that I pushed too hard about Lucas?

I frown, thinking back over the last week. The two of them have seemed so happy now, especially once she settled his fears about his ancestor lookalike.

Finally Cat looks up, stopping my runaway assumptions and ponderings. "Of course I want you to stay, Less."

Relieved breath rushes out of my lungs, even though I hear a distinct *but* left unsaid.

She puts her elbows on the tabletop and massages her temples with her fingers. "Of course I want you to stay," Cat repeats, "but I can't help being scared. Last night Reyna said that if you stayed here, you'd be changing history. Basically you'd be wiping out a whole line, right? So what does that mean for me? What if we find out today that *I'm* part of your line, Less? Does it mean that if you don't go back, then I'll just... cease to exist?"

Silence follows her speech.

Chapter Twenty Seven

I don't know why I never thought of this before.

No wonder Cat has been so on edge all morning.

I stare at her steepled hands, the long, slender fingers so much like my own, and wonder how I could have missed the signs. From the first moment I saw Cat step out of the carriage that brought her to my home two years ago, I have felt a strong connection with her. Everyone loved her, of course—Mama, Father, Cipriano—but it was the two of us who bonded so quickly and so well. I teased her that we were blood relations and I could decipher her thoughts as well as my own, and perhaps this is why. She comes from my own blood.

For the past twelve hours, my only concern has been myself...well, myself and Austin. Not once did I stop and truly think about how my decisions would affect those who come after me. Cat is right. My actions tomorrow night could erase an entire lineage, including the descendant sitting beside me whom

I've grown to love as a sister.

"Oh, Cat, I am so sorry," I tell her, reaching a hand out and then hesitating and drawing it back. "I-I didn't know… I didn't think—"

"Princess, it's all right."

Austin's words hang in the air. Astonished he could dismiss the subject so lightly, I gasp. Cat blinks—I only assume as baffled as I am—and we both turn our attention toward him.

"Excuse me?" she asks, dropping one of her hands to the table. It lands with a *smack*. "You did not just say it's all right. I mean, I'm sorry for getting all heavy and freaked about my own demise, Mr. Laidback, but you know, some people actually value their lives."

Austin shrugs, letting the insult and her sharp tone roll off his shoulders. "But you're not part of Alessandra's line. No demise to freak about."

With an incredulous look, Cat's head falls into her other hand, as if the day has already exhausted her, and it isn't even lunchtime. Feeling similarly drained, I rest my elbows on the table. "And how can you sound so sure?"

"It's easy. She's related through her mom, right, because of the name?" he asks calmly, already knowing the answer. On the ride here this morning, we filled the boys in on all we knew, including how her birth mother's last name of Angeli is the Americanized version of my real last name D'Angeli. I nod and Austin continues. "But your descendants would have your last name. The last name of whatever guy you *married*."

Austin's lip curls around the last word as he says it.

As Cat stares blankly ahead, obviously absorbing the

information, I search my mind for any holes in his reasoning. But it makes perfect sense. My body sags under the enormous relief, and my head falls onto the tabletop. "Oh, thank heavens."

Cat releases a shaky laugh. "You can say that again."

"Oh, thank heavens."

She laughs again, only this time for real. "Now you're learning." I hear her sigh and then feel the weight of her head press against my shoulder blade. "Girl, I'm sorry I've been such a bitch all morning. I was just scared, but I wanted to help, and I didn't know what to do."

"You could have begun with telling me," I say, my voice muffled by the tabletop. I lift my head, and Cat sits up; I turn so I can look in her eyes. "You do know that as much as I want to stay here, I would never even think about doing so if it meant hurting you, right?"

"Of course I know that," she says. "That's why I didn't tell you. I wanted to find out for myself if it were true, and then only tell you if I absolutely had to." She grins. "We only needed one family member hyperventilating in the bathroom this morning."

I cringe, envisioning her doing just that while I grabbed a bowl of those delicious multi-colored circles for breakfast. "From now on," I tell her, holding my little finger out as she'd showed me once. "We are a team. No more secrets."

"No more secrets," she repeats, hooking her finger with mine. As we tug, the tension between us drains away.

Austin nudges my foot under the table, attesting to that fact that while I may not have all the answers yet, I at least have the people I love in my corner, helping me.

One disaster averted, I think, nudging him back. Then I dive back into my book, my thoughts remaining on the rest of my possible descendants.

A few minutes later, Lucas returns with a broad smile. "I've got intel."

He flips a chair around and sits down, setting his phone and an open notebook in front of him. "That was a friend of mine back in Milan. Figured they may have better resources on Italian history there, so I asked him to check things out for me. Basically I had him focus his search on any future world leaders, scientists, or Nobel Prize winners that were in your line. I thought that could be our loophole for Reyna—if no one affected history in a big way and you choose to stay, you can argue that any children you have here have the potential to do more for humanity."

Lucas shrugs and sort of rolls his eyes, as if his idea is nothing more than a shot in the wind. But right now his theory is our best—and only—option.

"No, that could work," I say, leaning forward in my chair with renewed optimism. "What did your friend find?"

"It turns out we got lucky. Records from the sixteenth century aren't that easy to find for just everyday, regular people, but the guy you married was in government, so my friend was able to find a trail."

Out of everything Lucas just said, one detail stands out from the rest as if it were lined with the many-hued lights that illuminated the streets of West Hollywood. It appears Austin agrees for he asks, "Wait, you know who she marries?"

I flinch at his use of the word *marries*.

Whenever the topic of my potential spouse has arisen so

far, Austin has always been very careful to use the past tense, as if we were discussing something that happened long ago and has no effect on us now. And in a way, he is right. For him, these things are history, and depending on what we discover today, we may have the chance to change any of these things from happening.

But everything we are learning are also things yet to come for me. My possible future. And the fact that Austin didn't just ask who I *married* makes me think that for him, things are now getting real in a way they hadn't before.

Lucas hesitates before picking up his notebook and narrowing his eyes to read his tight scrawl on the page. "Domenico Bencini," he reads before lifting his eyes to me. "Ring a bell?"

My stomach clenches, but whether it is from surprise or fear, I do not know.

In my mind's eye, the image of a tall man enters, his dark brown hair shot with gray. The premature color makes him appear older than his thirty-two years, but from the air in which he carries himself, the proud angle of his jaw, this man revels in that fact.

The D'Angeli and Bencini families have long been a part of the same social circles, attending the same dinner parties and events, so of course I know Domenico. I recall even being subjected to a dance with him at a recent ball. (Luckily, my feet recovered with time.) And although the two of us never really held a conversation other than the most basic of pleasantries, I have always thought him…amiable enough. Quiet. Reserved like Father. Only where Father is kind and has a wonderful sense of humor, Domenico is, well, boring.

Could it have been a love match that brought us together?

I try to picture myself kissing him and shiver in disgust.

No, definitely not.

"Domenico enters into government?" I ask, not completely surprised. He wasn't a member when I left, having just reached the required age for some of the smaller offices, but the senior Bencini has long been in service and has groomed his eldest for the same his entire life.

"Yeah." Lucas consults his notebook again. "The *Tre Maggiori.*"

My eyes widen, and Lucas turns to the others to explain. "My friend said they were the highest executive offices of the Florentine Republic, which is why we lucked out. Because this guy was so powerful, his birth records were saved, along with some of his personal letters, which made our job a lot easier."

Austin's stiff nod makes the hair on the back of my neck rise, and I almost ask Lucas to stop. But then uncontrollable curiosity takes over, and I say, "Tell me what you learned."

Lucas grabs his notebook, settles back in his chair, and begins telling us—telling *me*—all about the life I may or may not ever have. "From what we can tell, Alessandra never had any children. It was common back then for fathers to declare their children, especially their sons, in the records as early as possible just in case they ever wanted to hold a public office. And in Domenico's personal letters, there are also several mentions of—" Lucas looks away and scratches the side of his neck. "Miscarriages."

My hand flies to my throat.

I always imagined myself with a large family. At the very least, two children like my parents had. A daughter named Lena with my auburn hair, pointy chin, and sense of wonder, and a son named after my father, Marco, with his dark eyes and strong sense of duty.

As the reality of Lucas's words crash around me, I cannot help but mourn that dream and the children who will never be. At least not in that life.

Beside me, Cat blows out a breath. "Wow." She squeezes my hand and glances at me but then quickly away, instead choosing to look at Austin sitting across from us as she says, "Well, I guess we found our loophole."

Even in my disoriented state, I register his hope-filled nod of agreement.

Cat grabs Lucas's notebook out of his hands and reads over his notes. "I mean, if Less doesn't have any… I mean, if the line ends with her, then history can't change that much if she stays." She glances up. "Right?"

This last question she directs at Lucas, who mumbles a soft, "Bingo." Then he lifts his chin in my direction and asks, "Alessandra, are you okay?"

I open my mouth and then close it, my mind an endless tumble of thoughts. But in the midst of my confusion, I know there is still one thing I have yet to learn. So instead of answering I ask, "Did Domenico's letters say anything about me?"

When Lucas's first response is to bite the corner of his lip, obviously hesitating, I regret the impulsive question.

"There was a brief mention here or there," he says, dragging the words out as if reluctant to reach the end of what he has to say—another bad sign. "There are a handful of letters he wrote to you when you were staying with your family. Apparently your father became very sick, and you moved back home for a short time to help your mother take care of him"—he clears his throat—"before he died."

Father.

As I try to grapple with this impossible reality, Lucas stops to scratch the side of his neck…and I realize that there is even more to the dreadful story. *The story of my life.* "What are you not telling me?" I force myself to ask, my heart still with my father.

Lucas leans back and runs his fingers through his hair. "There's also a letter to your brother about…about how *you* died."

Cold fingers of dread creep down my spine.

I swallow the fear and push it back where it belongs, roiling in my stomach with the rest of my emotions. It sounds like someone else's voice coming out of my mouth when I ask, "How?"

Lucas folds the top corner of his page, not looking at me. "He told Cipriano that you contracted a fever shortly after returning home from your father's deathbed and died of the same breathing ailment a few weeks later."

I nod, not exactly sure why because none of this even feels real—it is as if we are discussing a character in a book. But I need to react somehow. "And how old was I when I died?"

"Thirty-five."

Lucas says it matter-of-factly, no hemming or hawing over the cruel facts that took my life, and I appreciate his honesty. It was what I asked for, after all.

Thirty-five. It may not be a terribly long life, but it is longer than some. My cousin Patience's parents died much younger than that from an epidemic. And while it does not sound as though I lived the great life of possibility that I could here, the Alessandra in the history books seems as though she lived a good life. She was taken care of, provided for, and had a husband who wasn't altogether awful. She had connections and society.

And at least for a short time, she had her family.

My heart begins to hurt.

It's strange. I know I just heard about my life, or rather my future (past?) life. I know that I am sitting at a table in a library in the twenty-first century, trying to find a way so I can stay here. I know there's a chair under me, a ceiling overhead, and friends all around. But inside, I feel numb. Almost as if I'm in a dream, or watching the world outside myself. My thoughts are fuzzy, and I can't seem to grasp what it is I should do next.

I want to hug my father, even knowing that doing so is probably what got me sick in the first place. I want to comfort the strong man who always comforted me, who always sang me songs when I had a cold and bought me dresses to cheer me up. I want to go back home and make sure he knows how much I love him…but will my presence change the outcome or save him? Will I be doing it for him, or for me?

Closing my eyes, I lower my head into my opened hands.

Choosing the right path is suddenly much more difficult than I imagined it would be.

"Stop it," Austin says, his raised voice startling me. "I see what you're doing. You're reverting to that girl you used to be, aren't you?"

"No, I—"

"Yeah, you are. I get that you love your father. I mean, it's no secret I hate mine, but I love that you care so much about him. But you're doing it again, worrying about everyone else and what's best for them. For once, can't you think about what *you* want? Or do you even know?"

"Austin, it's just not that simple."

"Yeah, it is," he says, his voice suddenly desperate. "And if you can't figure that out, all this"—he sweeps his arms out, taking in the library and beyond—"will be gone. Reyna's holding a ticking clock, and it's getting louder. It's so freaking loud it's like a time bomb, counting the seconds until you're gonna be forced to choose. And you *will* have to make a choice, Alessandra. There's no getting out of it. So tell me, what do *you* want to do? Stay here with me?" he asks. "Or go home to *Domenico*?"

The desperation in his eyes turns to fury, and I swallow hard. Heat flushes through my body as my blood pounds through my veins.

I've never seen Austin this angry...*I've* never been this angry.

"Do you truly think I would choose that insufferable man over you? This isn't about *us*. It's about the man who gave me life. I can't just forget about him or the rest of my family. My mother is my best friend. My brother is the most amazing man I know. I love them, Austin." Then his words sink in. I reach out to grab his hand. "And what do you mean stay here with you? What happened to you coming with me?"

He scoffs. "And watch you marry someone else?"

My head jerks back in shock. "Marry? I wouldn't marry him. Not if I had a choice—not if you were with me."

Austin laughs, a cruel sound with a distinct edge that sends quivers shooting down my spine. "I hate to break it to you, Princess, but I've been sitting here doing my own research. You really think your parents will let you be with me? A stranger with no family, no money, no land?"

A vein bulges in his throat as he closes his eyes. And pain lashes my stomach. He's right. My parents love me and would never do anything to hurt me, but a girl in my time does not have much choice in these matters.

Cat knows that most of all.

"Don't you see, Alessandra?" Austin asks, opening his eyes again. "The only way we could be together is if we started our own lives, away from your family. So it *is* a choice between Domenico or me. You can either choose what we have together, the excitement I've seen in you the last few days, and fight for that…or you can do what you've always done. The *right* thing. The *expected* thing. Go back home to Domenico." He pauses. "And get rid of me."

In Cat's bedroom, I promised him that would never happen. But I didn't know everything then, didn't realize the lives that could be affected by my oath.

I take a breath. "I just need time to think."

"Then it's too bad that's one thing you don't have." And with that, Austin gets up from the table and walks out.

Chapter Twenty Eight

The beam of light shining down on me is just as bright as I envisioned in Reyna's tent. I draw a deep breath, winded and spent from the rest of the scene, and look down at Reid as Romeo as he delivers his line on the stage before a packed theater. This is it, the last lines I may ever speak as an actress, and as I feel the energy in the room, hear the silence as the audience hangs on our every word, the realization is bittersweet.

"Sweet, so would I, yet I should kill thee with much cherishing," I say, the words almost painful as I say them. My chest is so tight, it squeezes my lungs, and I draw a shuddering breath. I can't believe I may have to give this all up tonight. "Good night, good night!" I tell Reid, and quite possibly this world. "Parting is such sweet sorrow, that I shall say good night till it be morrow. Sleep dwell upon thine eyes, peace in thy breast!"

And with those words, I step back through the set acting as

my bedroom window, and away from the spotlight.

As Reid says his final speech, I jog down the makeshift staircase, skimming my hand over my hair, the color of which is back to the same old boring auburn shade it was when I arrived (thus appeasing the hairy, scrunched-up monster otherwise known as Mr. Williams's eyebrows). My sweaty palm slides across the wooden banister, and I skip the last step, making it to the side of the curtain just as Reid walks off, applause already rising behind us.

"You were amazing!" he says, grabbing me around the waist. His smile is full of life and humming with the force of all we accomplished. "You ready to take your bow, Miss Forlani?"

I nod, unable to find words. He leads me out onto the stage, and the crowd's praise and ovation swell into a thunderous wave crashing around me. I close my eyes and soak it in. The love, the adoration, the acceptance. This moment is everything I hoped it would be when I cried out for adventure in my courtyard. Yet it doesn't feel complete.

The absence of Mama, Father, and Cipriano is like a living entity beside me, reminding me that I am straddling two worlds and will soon have to make a choice. And not being able to share this moment with the boy I've grown to love in *this* world nearly crushes me.

Here it is, opening night, and I'm standing on an enormous stage overlooking a sea of people. I just gave the first and perhaps final performance of my life, and Austin may not have even seen it. It was possible he left after Jamie's scene, no longer feeling the need to stay for mine. I couldn't look down from my perch on the balcony and know for certain he was watching in the audience, smiling and sending me encouraging thoughts. I can't hear him now in the front row, yelling my name or letting out a sharp whistle. It isn't that the roar of the applause and the congratulations from my fellow actors isn't wonderful. But without Austin to share it with, it feels empty.

Cat and Lucas both suggested I give him space to calm down and to think, so I did. Twenty-four hours and counting of space. As tempted as I was to pick up the phone or ask Lucas to drive by his house, I didn't. And when I saw his father's assistant picking Jamie up from dress rehearsal, I didn't stop and ask her where Austin was or what he was doing. I knew.

Avoiding me.

As I exit the stage and make my way down the hall to the dressing room, I notice Kendal standing outside the door. Ever since Mrs. Shankle posted the cast list for *Back to the 80s: The Totally Awesome Musical!* and the class saw my name listed beside Tiffany's—and Kendal's next to Eileen's, one of the *nerds*—we have given each other a rather wide berth. A part of me thinks I should step aside, give the role to her since there's a good chance I won't even be around for our first rehearsal— but the part of me that still believes in miracles, that is awed at winning the role and eager to play it, holds me back.

But even though I may not be willing to step down, there is something my adversary needs to know before I meet with Reyna. My steps quicken with determination, and Kendal's eyes narrow in suspicion. "What do *you* want?"

Her snarky attitude is almost enough to make me keep on walking, but instead I bite the inside of my cheek and press on. "Kendal, I thought you should know that you did a wonderful job out there tonight. I have never seen the role of Katherina performed so well before."

Of course, I have never seen the role of Katherina performed before ever, but she doesn't have to know that. Plus she really *did* do a good job.

She scrunches her mouth and studies me—for so long I begin to wonder if anyone has ever truly given her a compliment. Then I see something I never thought I would. Kendal's shoulders seem to relax…a smidgen…a very *small* smidgen…and her lips curve into what may be considered an actual smile.

"Thanks," she says. Another miracle. She shrugs. "You did good, too." Then, as if her praise wasn't enough to stun me into total speechlessness, she adds, "I'm looking forward to working with you on the musical."

And I burst into tears.

Kendal steps back, as if it is contagious. I almost laugh. For some reason, her unanticipated act of kindness took all of the fear I have about my meeting with Reyna, all my heartache over my fight with Austin and wondering if I'll ever see him again, and all of my confusion over which path I should choose to fight for, and brought it to a blubbery head.

"I am, too," I tell her through sniffles, although my future still hangs in the balance. "It will be an honor to share the stage with you again."

Kendal eyes me quizzically, no doubt considering rescinding her extended olive branch on account of my apparent madness, and I decide it best that we part before I do something completely crazy like hug her. I bid her farewell, and watch as she walks confidently—and perhaps hastily—away, down the emptying hallway. Then I shuffle into the cluttered, deserted dressing room.

Romeo and Juliet was the last scene performed in the workshop. While I stood in the wings, watching each performance and waiting to see if Austin would sneak backstage and find me, everyone else came in here, threw off their costumes, and changed, and then hurried to the awaiting media room for post-performance interviews. Ms. Kent expects me to make a stop in there as well, and I know that I should—hearing their accolades will be nice, although perhaps not quite as fun to hear their criticism—but right now, I need the quiet.

All around me, cast members' discarded costumes hang off surfaces. Balloons and teddy bears sent by their well-wishing relatives and admirers cover the counters. And the cloying scent of *far* too much perfume clouds the air. I pad across the floor, careful to sidestep a dulled prop sword, and stop in front of the brightly lit table with the cardstock sign labeled *Alessandra*.

Amongst my scattered hairbrushes and makeup sits a dozen beautiful red roses in full bloom with an envelope floating above it, inscribed with Jenna's swirly handwriting: *Congratulations, Alessandra!* Another card, this one sticking out of a bouquet of friendly white daisies reads: *Who owned that stage?*

I smile as I open the cards my loved ones sent me, telling me how proud they are and how much they care. There's even a small piece of folded parchment from Reyna, simply saying, *Well done.* But search as I do under the piles of makeup brushes and bottles of hairspray, there isn't a single note from Austin.

In the mirror, my reflection stares back at me with dead eyes.

I have lost him.

A movement in the glass behind me captures my attention. I blink as an enormous bouquet materializes in the glass.

"Delivery for Juliet."

My heartbeat stalls at the familiar deep timbre, then sets off again, hammering the now erratic pulse against my breastbone. I whirl around, breathless with hope.

"Austin?"

The vase of blossoms lowers. "Hey there, Princess."

My fingertips tingle, and I clench them at my sides so I don't just bolt into his arms—there's too much I need to say to him first.

I swallow and wet my lips, open my mouth...and don't know where to begin.

It's not as if I haven't thought about this moment every second since he stormed out of the library yesterday. I've rehearsed the same words over and over again—the words I wish I would have said then—so many times that they've now become meaningless. Yet now, standing here with him, none of it seems to be enough. So leaving behind my beautiful, well-prepared speech, I simply say, "Hello, yourself."

Austin shifts his weight. "Look, Alessandra." He thrusts his fingers through his hair. "Yesterday... Yesterday I—"

He breaks off, cursing under his breath, dumping the vase of blooms on the nearest table. With four long strides, he covers the distance between us and takes hold of my shoulders. "Yesterday I screwed up. I never should've left you like that. I just kept thinking about that guy putting his hands on you and I couldn't stand it. The thought of losing you..." He swallows hard. "But when I was watching you tonight, I—"

"You watched my performance?" Everything about Austin's speech has been perfect, but knowing he witnessed me up on that stage means more to me than any pretty promise or apology ever could.

His brows furrow. "Well, yeah. Of course."

And that's all I need to know.

Unclenching my hands, I do what I've wanted to do ever since I saw him walk through the door—ever since I met him, if I am to be completely honest. I leap into his arms, clamp my legs around his waist, and capture his lips in a kiss meant to show him exactly how much I've missed him. How much I am falling in love with him. And how much his being here for me means.

Austin hesitates only a moment, a surprised breath fanning my lips before he crushes me against him and returns the kiss stroke for stroke, moan for moan, and nibble for delicious nibble. When he wrests control of it, sucking my bottom lip between his teeth, my bones seem to liquefy, and I melt into the strength of his arms.

He presses a hot line of open-mouthed kisses on the column of my throat, and I tilt my head to give him better access. He licks the sensitive spot just under my ear. The rasp of stubble on his chin grazes my skin, and I shiver, never wanting this moment to end.

But all too soon, Austin leans back. I moan a protest, and he grins, a mischievous glint alight in his eyes. "Now *this* isn't how a proper sixteenth-century Ice Princess is supposed to act."

I laugh and lock my ankles around him tighter. "Then I guess it's a very good thing I'm not one anymore."

Then, just to prove I mean it, I kiss him again.

• • •

"Knock, knock." Cat pokes her head around the open dressing room door and asks, "Everyone decent?"

Austin sits up from his slouched position on the sofa and wraps his arm around my waist. Tugging me tighter against him, he mutters under his breath, "Unfortunately," and I slap his chest with a grin.

Cat frowns as she steps through the doorway, then looks back at Lucas and shakes her head. "Damn, I knew we waited too long."

I smile at their teasing and the scandalous implications, then laugh when I realize a few weeks ago, I would have been completely horrified. Nestling myself farther into the warmth of Austin's embrace, I pat the empty space on the sofa beside me. "On the contrary, dear cousin, your timing couldn't be more perfect."

Austin slaps hands with Lucas in a manly sort of greeting. "Though I ain't gonna lie, another hour with her all to myself wouldn't have sucked."

I bite my lip and lower my eyes to the ground. The problem is that I do not *have* another hour. And the fact that the playfulness of Austin's tone and gesture didn't quite reach the deep blue of his eyes lets me know that is a fact of which he is well aware.

Apparently, so is Cat. A strange noise rises in her throat. I look up to see her fiddling with the hem of her shirt as she knocks her knees gently against mine. At first, she doesn't say anything, choosing to let the silence say it all. Then, "Guess it's about that time."

Tension crackles in the room. It seeps into my muscles and makes my head feel heavy.

Cat looks to Lucas, Lucas to Austin, Austin to me.

The tick of an old clock on the wall hits my ears—*tick, tick, tick, tick*—and my pulse slows to keep time with the lonely, terrifying beat.

I try to swallow, but suddenly it feels as though my throat is coated with cotton.

Austin coughs and locks eyes with Lucas, communicating wordlessly. Lucas nods. "I'll drive," he says, digging his car keys out of his pocket and twirling them on his finger. That he has to try so hard to look at ease makes everything so much worse.

Austin mumbles his thanks and stands, then turns around and offers me his hand.

Staring at his open palm, I hesitate...and shake my head. "No."

Austin's hand jerks back, then lurches out to grab mine. *"No?"*

Squeezing his fingers, I lift my gaze. The flash of incredulity in his stormy blue eyes is nearly my undoing, so I turn to look at my cousin and Lucas, seeing equal astonishment in them.

"I need to do this on my own," I explain.

"No way," Austin says, barely allowing me to finish. "Not happening. I'm going in there, and if she—"

"Hey, Marilyn needs you."

We all jump at the intrusion as Reid stops midway into the room. His body tenses as he quickly surveys our faces. "Am I interrupting something?"

"Yeah, man," Austin says, pulling me to my feet. "You kinda are." He loops his arms around my waist, staking a visual claim. "Tell Marilyn Alessandra is busy at the moment."

At the dismissive tone in Austin's voice, Reid crosses his arms. He has changed out of his Romeo costume, and the buttons of his long-sleeved shirt strain against the hostile gesture. "I think the girl can answer for herself, don't you?" He strolls the rest of the way into the room at a leisurely pace, belying the tick in his jaw, and stops just in front of us. "Alessandra just gave a kickass performance on opening night of a workshop directed by a famous director. Local reporters want to interview her. It's part of the business." He grins. "Or maybe you're too threatened to let her out of your sight."

Austin's fingers dig into my sides. I rub my temple, willing the building headache away, and eye the clock. It's eleven twenty. Only forty minutes until my showdown with Reyna—I barely have enough time to get across town as it is. What will she do if I never show up? Will I just disappear wherever I am, before ever having a chance to state my case?

I pry Austin's hands loose and turn to face him. "Give me a minute." Before he can argue, as he looks like he wants to do, I press a soft kiss on his lips and step away. "Reid, can I talk to you in private?"

With a smug look, Reid says, "Lead the way, pretty lady," and follows me to the far corner of the room.

Once we are away from the others, his easy charm and smile come back. He grabs my hand and says, "I meant what I said—you really were amazing out there tonight."

"Thank you," I tell him, grateful for the compliment. "You were, too."

And he was. Marilyn couldn't have found a better Romeo in all of Hollywood. Even Austin, who performed wonderfully on the day of my audition, does not have the polish Reid has, gained from years of practice.

As I look up at Reid, reliving our scene together and the way he delivered his lines in his *historical* costume, I'm shocked to realize who it is he has reminded me of all along: Matteo. Well, Matteo before he betrayed me.

The two gentlemen share the same good humor and charisma, the effortless way they carry themselves. Once, Reid was the exact sort of man I thought I wanted. Now I know what it is that I *need*. A man who challenges me, a man who lifts me up and is not afraid to call me on my failings. Who makes me want to be the best version of myself that I can be, and knows exactly how to encourage my growth until I get there.

A man like Austin.

Reid's childlike grin fades as he watches me closely. He glances at Austin, standing where I left him by the sofa practically vibrating with restraint, and back at me. "So he does it for you, huh?"

I smile and say, "Yeah. He does it for me."

He sighs and then in the smoother, refined voice he uses on stage says, "'Tis a far, far better thing I do then I have ever done."

Confused, I wrinkle my brow, and Reid shakes his head. "Never mind. Go be with your man. I don't know what's going on but obviously, something important is going down. You go take care of whatever it is, and I'll head back to the room and play up my egocentric reputation. I'm sure I can find some excuse to keep their attention." He grins. "Maybe start a few rumors about my indie film coming up."

Relieved, I throw my arms around him for a quick hug, glancing again at the clock over the door. *Eleven thirty.* "Reid, thank you. This really means a lot."

"No problem," he whispers, squeezing me tight. He exhales and slowly steps back. "You better go." He looks over my shoulder toward my friends. "Looks like your crew's getting restless. And besides, I have reporters to distract."

And with that, Reid leaves the room.

I'm sorry to see him go. He has been a good friend. But before he has even disappeared through the doorway, Austin's arms are back around me. He touches his forehead to mine. "Can I drive you there and just not go in?"

I curl my palm around his cheek. "I'd never be able to get out of the truck."

"Then at least take our driver," Cat says, joining us at the doorway. "If you insist on doing this by yourself—and don't get me wrong, I hate it, but I guess I get it—then I'll go home with Lucas." Her chin wobbles ever so slightly, so faint that anyone else would probably miss it. But not me. "Time's already getting short, and you don't want to waste any of it hailing a cab."

Then my cousin sniffs, her eyes fill with actual tears, and I'm out of Austin's arms and into hers, breathing in the familiar scent of her rose-scented shampoo.

Her shoulders tremble. "It's not fair," she says, voice breaking. "I can't say good-bye to you again." She steps back to look at me. "I already talked to Dad and Jenna. Thanks to the acting genes Mama Dearest passed on, I concocted an amazing story explaining why you were hanging around for the next two and a half years. They already agreed, and Jenna's taking you shopping for your new bedroom suite, so you better come back to us." She gives me a watery grin. "Trust me; you don't wanna go messing with that woman and her plans."

I laugh, then cover my mouth as it turns into a sob. "I'll do my best, believe me."

Lucas slides his arm around Cat's shoulders. "Take care of my cousin," I tell him. "You know, just in case." I blink away tears and attempt a smile. "She wants everyone to believe she is tough, but underneath her warrior exterior, my cousin is all heart."

"I know," Lucas says. "And I will. But you'll be here to remind me of that."

I only wish the conviction of his words matched the pitch of his voice. "I hope so." He nods and takes Cat's hand, stepping to the back of the room and giving Austin and me our last few minutes of privacy.

Austin puts a finger under my chin. "Don't you dare give me one of your Wizard of Oz–like speeches. Our American government project's due next week, so you have to come back." He grasps my shoulders in his hands, as if he can convey his determination and conviction with his grip. "If you don't, I'm just gonna hunt this gypsy down and make her bring me to you.

Because this," he says, pointing a finger between us, "isn't over. Believe that."

Tears course down my cheeks, but I nod, anyway, wanting to believe it so badly. Then I press my lips to his, perhaps for the final time, and hold on tight.

Chapter Twenty Nine

The portal is just as I remember, sitting in the exact spot I suspected in front of the famous Chinese theater. On the crowded sidewalk in front of it, people brush past the seemingly innocent green tent without a second glance. No raised brows, no disbelieving glances, not even a questioning look as they dash off to wherever it is people choose to go at such a late hour. Either they are unaware of the immense power and significance that is right in their midst, or Reyna has cast some type of spell, cloaking it from prying eyes.

But I see it.

A side flap shifts in the breeze stirring from the cars on the road behind me. It seems to be calling to me, beckoning me closer, as much as Reyna's crooked finger did that day in my courtyard. And just like then, I am alone, with hope in my heart for my future, and a healthy dose of apprehension for what lies ahead.

I pull out my cell phone and watch the time switch over to midnight.

Showtime.

Straightening my shoulders, I run my palms along my Juliet costume. I had no time to change before leaving, having spent so much of it waiting in the wings and then not wanting to waste a second on my appearance once Austin, Cat, and Lucas joined me in the dressing room. But now that I think of it, my apparel is rather fitting. I am dressed similarly to the way I was when I first entered this space, only my costume today is the twenty-first-century version. Embellished and reinforced, made stronger, by all the conveniences of the modern era.

Much like me.

An impatient horn blares behind me, and I jump into action. As I cross the distance to the portal, walking over stars carved into the ground, I'm reminded of the words I uttered to Reyna just before sitting at her table, taking a chance on an adventure. I told her I was no longer the timid girl she once knew, and even though my words were admittedly nothing but false bravado, now they hold true. I am not without fear, but courage is taking action despite the fear. Knowing what you want, what you are meant to do, and proceeding despite any knots in your stomach or rocks stuck in your throat. It is walking boldly into the unknown with your chin held high… even if it quivers.

Pushing through the open flaps, I enter the tent. They close behind me, sealing me into darkness.

I shall not be afraid. I shall not be afraid.

I kick off my shoes and fling them where I think the side is, calling out, "Reyna, I'm here."

"I can see that." The bored-sounding reply comes just behind me, and my heart leaps into my throat.

Twisting around, I find a shadowy outline. Reyna must have been waiting for me by the entrance, watching my approach.

Grateful for the dark that hides the embarrassed flush of blood rushing to my cheeks— wondering if Reyna saw any hesitation in my eyes that could hurt my chances of staying—I square my shoulders. "I have come at the hour we agreed upon to tell you that my desire has not changed. I wish to stay."

She stares back at me with eyes that seem to defy the dark, that need no candle to illuminate them. She does not say a word as she studies my face, and the weight of her intent appraisal feels heavy on my skin. I fight the sudden urge to sink farther into the shadows or smile too broadly to overcompensate for my unease.

I stand strong. And finally, she nods.

Careful not to read too much into the all-too-common action (she could have been silently agreeing that I deserve to return to my own time, or even deciding what to have for dinner once I do), I allow my shoulders to relax an inch.

"Come."

With her edict, Reyna walks toward the back of the tent, candles along the ground flaring to life and leaving a glowing trail in her wake. The earthy, familiar scent of pine brings me back to the last time I was here. Back when I was so scared of the unknown. And now I am here again, asking for more of the same.

As she sits behind the small table lit by the sapphire candle,

I smile at how much I truly have changed into the girl I once claimed to be.

And that's why I must remain.

If I return to my life in the sixteenth century, it will be easy to fall into old habits, following others' expectations of me and living the life Lucas told me about in the history books. My efforts will be consumed with hosting government balls and spending as much time as I can comforting my father before he dies.

That life, while sad, would not be a horrible one, which is the reason I hesitated in the library. My marriage to Domenico might not be based on love, but he would provide me with a good life. A decent life. One that, until I met Cat and Austin, was all that I could have asked for.

But instead, I choose the adventure. The unknown. The future.

"You believe your time here has changed you," Reyna says as if reading my mind.

The rasp of her voice makes it difficult for me to read the intention behind her statement, and I cannot tell if she is disagreeing with my assessment or merely sharing a fact. *Do I answer?*

Then she continues before I can. "You wish to alter the fabric of time because of this transformation, but I already told you a decision like that is out of my power. What do you think has changed in the last two days to make that fact any different?"

Perhaps your suspicious use of the word "my" the last time you said that...

The more I have pondered it, the more I know there is something Reyna is not saying, something that she is hiding. And something she wants me to figure out on my own. But for now I just say, "I have learned the details about the history—*my* history—that you say my decision will affect."

I may not know who holds the power to alter history, but I do at least know that my decision will not start a war or wipe out an entire lineage.

Inhaling a pine-scented breath, stealing a moment to center my thoughts and galloping pulse, I look at the open seat opposite her. It is tempting to sink into the support of the wood, to relax the rigidity of my spine. But as I prepare to fight the most important fight of my life, I need to feel the solid ground beneath my feet, rooting me as I say, "I know about my marriage."

I pause, and Reyna waves a hand for me to continue, the gold bracelets on her arms *clink*ing gently as she does. The candlelight catches the gold, making them shimmer.

Staring at the soft shine of her jewelry, I say, "And I know that I remain childless"—I swallow past the pain those words cause—"at least in the sixteenth-century. Which means my lineage ends with me. My choice to remain here will not affect medical advancements or cause a political upheaval. I know that my father…" Here is where my voice finally breaks, but I cannot give in to the sadness now. I must plow through while I still can. "I-I know of his illness. I even know of my own death."

My legs are shaking so badly now that I surrender to temptation and drop into the empty chair. But even so, I raise my head and meet Reyna's gaze squarely.

"The truth is that even if I were to return to my own time, things could still change. I am a different person now, I might make different choices. I'm no longer content living my life timidly and being an observer. I want to be an active participant. The life I lived in the historical texts was a fine one, but I want *more*."

A wonderful surge of energy rushes through my veins the more I speak, but I truly have no idea where my speech is coming from. Words are pouring out of my mouth without my giving them permission to do so, and I'm uttering beliefs that I have not even fully formed until they are spoken.

But as my thoughts take shape, my confidence builds.

Leaning my elbows onto the table, I say, "Reyna, my sixteenth-century life was spent putting other people's desires before my own. You know that—you were there. But this experience taught me that while doing so on occasion may be noble, I made myself into a martyr. Now it is time for *me*, for me to follow my own heart and passions." Hoping she can see the depths of sincerity shining in my eyes, hear the conviction ringing in my voice, I say, "I'm stronger here. And it is in *this* century that I belong."

The silence after I finish speaking is heavy. It taunts me with its shadowy edges, causing me to wish my words back from the air and start again.

Maybe I went too far.

Has anyone ever stood up to Reyna before?

To fate?

Asked the stars to realign themselves just for their own purposes and then arrogantly expect them to listen?

I begin losing feeling in my limbs from abject terror of the divine…but then I see it. Under my wide-eyed scrutiny, Reyna's close-lipped mouth twitches.

That miraculous ghost of a smile holds for a moment, and then an actual burst of laughter explodes from her mouth.

Were it not laced with her rough undertones, I would not trust my own eyes and ears.

"Well done, Alessandra," she says, clapping her hands twice. "You *have* grown."

It feels as though the world has tipped, and I don't know how to react to this new side of Cat's gypsy girl. I decide to go with gratitude. "Thank you. I, uh, I'm glad you think so."

She chuckles softly and strikes a match. The smaller white candle beside the sapphire one flares to life. A shadow dances across her face. "You have more than fulfilled my expectations and your destiny," she tells me, indeed sounding pleased. "But I must ask one more question."

And I slump. Foolishly, I had thought that the hard part was over, but the sudden graveness of her request causes a hummingbird to knock against my rib cage. Drawing on every drop of courage left in reserve, I say with only a slight waver, "All right."

Reyna's eyes flash over the flickering flames. "Is your desire to stay based upon your affection for a certain young man?"

Here is the real test. Intuitively I know that my answer here matters more than anything else I have said. And while everything in me wants to rush to answer in the negative, I sit back and truly ponder her question.

It is a fair one, and truthfully, one I should have expected.

For the last two nights, I've stayed awake at night thinking about the second half of the vision I received during Reyna's initial spell—the faceless boy with dark hair who held me in his arms. I thought about how my spirit seemed to respond to Austin even when he was still driving me insane, and I realized that *he* was that boy. I thought I was calling out for adventure, and I was—the first part of the vision, the glimpse of me onstage, proved it. And the reality was everything I pictured it would be. But I was also calling out for a chance at love.

So it would be a lie to say that Austin has no bearing on my decision tonight. He is, after all, the first man to inspire the true stirrings of love in my heart. But I know as well as I know my own name that he is not the sole reason.

"No," I tell her with certainty. "Austin is wonderful, and I *do* care for him, but I want to stay here for *me*. I want the life I can live here. I want to be the person this place has made me. And I want to continue growing into the person I know I can become because of the freedoms and possibilities this century allows."

Reyna drums her long, black-painted nails along the matching tablecloth, and I realize that is the first sound I have heard other than the soft *clink* of her jewelry and our own voices since entering the tent. Having grown accustomed to the noises of Cat's world, I know that even in this short time, I should have heard the wail of an ambulance, the screech of tires, and at least a dozen impatient car horns coupled with yells of annoyance. I tilt my head, straining to listen, but hear nothing. Not even the melodic bubbling of a fountain that would signal home. It is as if we exist in our own dimension, being neither here nor there.

Pinpricks of trepidation prickle on my skin as I wonder if my arguments have all been for nothing, that I am already on my way back to my own century. But Reyna has never given me reason to suspect she would mislead me, that she would have me explain my reasons simply to yank my dreams away. The powers of fate and destiny can be overwhelming and scary for certain, but Reyna has proven herself time and time again to be on our side. One of the good ones. A friend.

I close my eyes and begin rocking back and forth in my chair. The creak of the aged wood lulls me. And I decide to choose trust even in the middle of so much fearful uncertainty.

But then Reyna asks, "Tell me, Alessandra, do you remember the message I left you with?" and my eyes snap open.

It takes a moment to notice the small smile playing upon her lips. When I do, the air around us shifts. Holding onto hope that I'm finally going to learn my fate, I repeat the words I can probably recite in my sleep—and probably do. "You said that the adventure I seek is full of possibilities, but that I should always remember where my real strength lies. Though that is what confuses me. You came to Cat's home prepared to send me back before I even performed on the stage. Is that not where my strength lies? The stage?"

"No, it is not." Reyna reaches across the table to grasp my hand. She uncurls the fingers I've formed into a fist and traces a long line down the center of my open palm. "Your true strength lies in yourself."

I pull back my hand and stare at the series of squiggles. "I do not understand."

"You say you are stronger here," she says, and I can hear

the smile in her voice, "but that strength has been inside you all along. Your strength lies in your heart, in your selfless caring for those around you. When you trust that inner voice, when you let go of expectations and follow that loving heart of yours, Alessandra, you're able to move mountains. Cat and Austin can attest to that. If you had found a way to embrace that strength in the past, in your own time, then that would be where you should return. But if the trappings of the modern world and the opportunities here are what you need to become your true self, then that has always been an option. You just had to realize the possibility and grasp it." She pauses. "For the right reasons."

She lets her words sink in and then clears her throat delicately. "All you needed was to *challenge* yourself to figure it out. And to help you do so, I might have given you a little push in the right direction."

I note the inflection on the word *challenge* and the sharpness of her gaze, and it clicks in my mind. "You are Miss Edwards."

She winks. Rubbing my tense forehead, I ask, "So the other night when you said that the decision was not in your power, you meant it was in mine?" She gives me a knowing smile, and I shake my head in amazement. "This was certainly much easier than I expected."

Reyna chuckles. "Alessandra, I have learned that our world is filled with two kinds of people: old souls, and people who were born before their time. You, dear girl, are the latter."

My chest swells, knowing that is as close to a compliment as I may ever get from her. I lower my gaze to the table and land on the white candle. "So that is it?" I ask, wondering why she lighted it if so. "No spells to perform? No magic tricks?"

She shakes her head. "Once you walk out of this tent, history will be forever changed. So you must be sure that this is what you want, for once history is altered you cannot go back."

Amazement and profound relief that I—formerly timid me—actually took a stand for what I wanted and *won* consume me. But then I remember everyone I am leaving behind.

How is it possible to feel so much happiness and sadness at one time? Can a heart withstand such turmoil?

I know this is the right decision. My parents are grown, and my father has always told me to follow my heart.

You are a good girl, Alessandra, with a good heart. Follow that, and you shall never be led astray.

The memory of his words brings fresh tears to my eyes.

This is what my heart is telling me is right…but that doesn't keep it from shattering. Never again will I feel Mama's arms hold me. I will not hear her singing or the lilt of my father's laughter, or see the crinkle around Cipriano's eyes in the very rare moments he shucks his overwhelming sense of duty and smiles.

I brush away a tear as it glides down my cheek. "What will my family believe happened to me?"

Reyna purses her lips and considers me. "I suppose we can handle it any number of ways. It was my intention for them to awake in the morning with the belief that you ran away for love. But if you wish something different, I am open to your suggestions."

I do wish something different, but I have asked for so much already. It seems selfish to request anything more—and what I want may not even be possible. But I have to try. "If I wrote a letter telling them good-bye," I say, "could you get it to them?"

Reyna snickers. "You are just like your cousin. I transport the pair of you across hundreds of years and rewrite history, and you think me unable to perform the simplest of tricks." She shakes her head with a grin. "Yes, I think I can manage sending a letter."

Mumbling to herself about skeptics, she reaches into the small dresser behind her and pulls out a piece of parchment and a pen. After sliding the materials onto the tabletop, Reyna says quietly, "I will give you a few minutes alone. If you need anything, just call."

I watch her disappear into the dark. Then, holding the pen in my hand, I stare at the paper. I think about all the things I wish I could have told my family before I left, things I want them to know and remember about me, and as the words come for my final good-bye, salty tears splash on the thick paper.

Dear Mama, Father, and Cipriano,

I know my disappearance may come as a shock. But please know that I am stronger than I ever gave you reason to believe. It is because of your love and endless faith in me that I am now able to step out in faith, choosing a life filled with love, hope, and possibility. Do not doubt that I have loved every moment of my life, and a portion of my heart will forever remain behind with you.

I cannot explain where I am going. I cannot even tell you how you can reach me to reply to this letter. Just know that I am safe and that I am happy. Father, I am finally following my heart. It is my fervent prayer, if fate and Signore will it so, that we shall all meet again someday. Until then, know that I am forever thinking of you and missing you.

Your loving daughter and sister,

Alessandra

Postscript: Tell Lorenzo I shall miss my childhood friend, and that "Goddess Victoria" wishes him well. Also, tell him to continue painting...he has more admirers than he could ever dream.

Chapter Thirty

Back on the streets of Hollywood, I close my eyes and savor the sounds of the future. The wail of the ambulance, the honks of disgruntled drivers, and the squeal of tires provide a beautiful melody of my new home. The very things that terrified me when I first arrived, standing in this spot crowded with painted creatures and ill-mannered people, are the very things that will be a part of my everyday life. And I can't wait.

Confidently strolling to the curb, I tell Cat's driver that I would rather find my own ride, and with reluctance, he agrees. But he does not drive away. Grateful for the caring way he watches me, I take a few steps, thrust my hand into the air, and let a whistle rip. Almost immediately, a yellow taxi pulls over.

Yes, I can do this.

Grinning wide and proud at the driver in the black car behind me, I slip into the backseat of the cab. The smell of food lingers inside, just as it did for my first ride, but this time it is almost pleasant. The cloth seat is comfortable and dry, the. ground under my feet not sticky.

A very good omen.

I rattle off the address, and the driver eases into traffic. As the streetlights and sights I once found scary fly past, I think about my last moments with Reyna.

Once I completed my carefully worded letter to my family, she took it in her hands. She did not read it but merely folded it in half, then folded it again, forming a perfect, neat square.

Then, she thrust it into the flame of the white candle.

Of course, I screamed—I worked hard on that letter and it was my only chance to tell my family good-bye. But she merely grinned, assuring me this was how it worked. *A magical form of delivery*, she said, and I had no choice but to trust her. She is the expert, after all.

Once I calmed down (though to be honest, my tender heart may never fully heal, always having a hole where my family should be), Reyna led me to the entrance of the tent. She told me where to find an account that had been set up in my name for college, a modern-day version of a dowry I suppose, courtesy of the stars.

Then, staring deep into my eyes, she said, "Never forget your strength, Alessandra. Follow your heart, and you will always find your way."

Hearing her reiterate my father's words, although I never shared them with her aloud, was my cosmic sign that everything would be all right.

Of course after that, she shoved me out of the tent.

I laugh quietly at our gypsy girl. Reyna is impossible to

figure out. She never seems to act the way I expect, and she loves speaking in incomprehensible riddles, but underneath all the veils and mystique, she is a kindred spirit. And I will dearly miss her.

The taxi slows to a stop, and the driver glances at me over his shoulder. "Here you go, miss." He looks back at the bright red meter beside him and says, "That'll be twenty-five fifty."

I smile, knowing exactly what he means. Then I pat my lap and remember I am in my costume. With a sinking in my stomach, I open my purse and find my cell phone, a pack of gum, and a pair of dark sunglasses. But no wallet.

It is well and good that I understand modern currency now, but it still helps to carry it.

Sighing, I lean forward and ask, "Sir, do you mind waiting for a moment? I somehow forgot to put any money in my purse, but I know the person inside will be happy to help."

The man chuckles under his breath. He yawns and rubs a hand over his eyes. "No problem, honey. This kind of thing happens all the time."

I guess if nothing else, it is reassuring to know I'm not the only forgetful person in this century.

I thank him profusely for his understanding and hop out of the backseat. Jogging to the front door, my only thought is yelling from the rather high rooftop that I am here to stay. Before I even think about the time, my finger shoots out to depress the doorbell. And as the very loud *ding*s chime inside, I stare at the intricate carvings in the glass, impatiently shifting my weight from foot to foot, peering inside for signs of life.

Finally, a dark figure appears on the other side. I know the moment he realizes who is at the door because Austin's slow pace transforms into a run, and then his front door is open, and I am in his arms.

Soon I will go home and twirl around the room, dancing with Cat in celebration, and tomorrow we'll invite Lucas over so he can stuff me full of pizza, but right now, this is exactly where I need to be.

Leaning away, I manage to say, "Guess you're not getting rid of me," just before his mouth descends upon mine, and any other words I would have said fade into oblivion.

Austin lifts me into his arms and buries his face in my neck, breathing roughly and squeezing me so tight it is as if he wants to meld us together. "I told you to believe, didn't I?"

He sets me down and brushes the hair away from my face, gazing at me so reverently that my heart clenches. In this moment, I know that every heartbreak was worth it to get me here.

"Austin, I've always—"

A quick interrupting *beep* of a horn reminds me that we are not alone.

"Oh, yes," I say. "That would be the taxi driver. It appears that in my fancy modern day purse, I forgot to pack anything remotely useful. Such as *bucks*."

Austin looks at me strangely, obviously not getting my private joke from the first day I arrived. "You know, Princess, I don't think we need my challenges anymore. I can already tell life with you is going to be adventure enough." Then he smiles, a shiver-inducing grin that has me wanting to pull him right back into my arms, and says, "Be right back."

As he runs down the driveway to pay the kind gentleman driver, I glance up at the stars and issue a silent *thank-you*. I look down to see the man wave his hand out his opened window, reverse down the drive, and be swallowed up by the moonlit night.

"Now, where were we?" Austin says when he returns, sliding his hands around my lower back and tugging me close.

He lowers his head for another kiss, and as much as I would enjoy giving him that very thing, I lay a palm against his chest.

"Before we get to *that*," I say with a grin of my own, "there is something I need you to know."

Austin runs his fingernails over my back, his gaze curious, but he doesn't say anything.

I take a breath.

"I've *always* believed, Austin," I tell him. "At first, I believed solely in the power of destiny and fate. Then, magic. But I've learned during these last few days that there is something even more powerful than those things." Austin raises an eyebrow, and I grin. "Choice. True happiness is something we create ourselves with our own choices: whom we want to be with, whom we let into our worlds, and how we choose to spend what little time we are given in this world. And I, Alessandra D'Angeli Forlani, choose this life, *this* time." I press my lips against the curve of his delicious mouth, then draw back just far enough to whisper, "And I choose *you*."

Acknowledgments

I've always heard that second books are hard. Pressure mounts, a blank page looms, worries descend. Since *A Tale of Two Centuries* is technically my third book, I figured I'd be spared the drama. (*insert snort laugh here*) Yeah, I was wrong. So many people stepped up, providing encouragement, support, commiseration, and love. So many times over the past year I've shaken my head and then looked above, thanking God for all that He's given me. What an amazing ride this has been!

My Super Sweet Sixteenth Century found an audience with enthusiastic, wonderful readers, and not letting them down was forever at the forefront of my mind. I'm a reader first, so I know how many fabulous books are out there, and I'm so grateful and honored you chose to read this one. I hope Less, Austin, Cat, and Lucas gave you a fun and flirty escape from the real world. Thank you for reading!

Speaking of readers, my Flirt Squad rocks my world. This

group of enthusiastic readers and bloggers made what could've been a terrifying, lonely, stress-filled debut year an absolute joy. They encourage and inspire me daily, are made of all things sparkly and awesome, and I've formed AMAZING friendships with them. A few in particular though went above and beyond, so here's a HUGE Flirt Squad shout out to Ali Byars, Alicia Marie Ezell, Amy Fournier, Anubha Agrawal, Atmika Singh, Caitlyn Santi, Cassie Frye, Ciara Byars, Cynthia Bolasina, Daisy Richeson, Daphne from Winged Reviews, Denice Cordero, Denise Zaky, Diane Abbas, Erleen Alvarez, Gabriela Ledesma, Gaby Navarro, Hawwa Alam, Hikma Saleem, Jana Cruz, Jared Mifsud, Jenna DeTrapani, Joie de Lire, Justine Bowman, Katlyn Charlesworth, Kelsey Ketch, Kelsey Simpson, Kyra Morris, Laura Nuez, Mandy Reupsch, Megan Tuckerman, Myra White, Nobonita Chowdhury, Paige Bradish, Samantha Weck, Sara Ahmed, Staci Murden, Vi Nguyen, and Zoe Leonarczyk. Thank you, thank you, thank you! I love y'all!

Shannon Duffy, Trisha Wolfe, and Rose Garcia worked magic with this book, making me laugh with their comments, and smack my head against the desk catching my silly errors. Mindy Ruiz rocked so hard, answering random questions and advising me on fun activities for Austin's challenges. And as always, emailing with Cindi Madsen, Tara Fuller, Lisa Burstein, and Melissa West kept me sane. The five of us debuted together, and I look forward to a long future of shared releases. Seriously, if it weren't for these eight incredible ladies, I probably would've bitten off all my nails and eaten gargantuan amounts of ice cream. Oh wait…

So much love to Stephanie Kate Strohm and Fiona Paul.

You ladies ROCK!! Jenna DeTrapani, Heather Self, Amber Troyer, Lisa T. Bergren, and Tiffany King, I'm blessed to know all of you. The crew at Houston YA/MG and West Houston RWA have taught me and inspired me more than I can say. Hugs, love, and gratitude to Lauren Hammond and Pam van Hylckama for believing in me and in my writing. My literary cheerleader, Tara Gonzales, my ninja goddess, Heather Riccio, and the angel in my corner, Kelly P. Simmon, work miracles, fill me up, and make me happy dance. I honestly don't know what I'd do without you ladies.

Stacy Cantor Abrams and Alycia Tornetta—there are no words. But, I shall try (*grin*). For all the emails, for all the texts, for all the encouraging and hilarious comments about Austin's muscles and Alessandra's hair, thank you. For taking this story and making it better than I ever imagined it could be, thank you. For always having my back, thank you a thousand times over. I love you, I trust you, and I'm blessed to call you my friends. Liz Pelletier, thank you for giving my writing a home. By providing such a welcoming family at Entangled, I felt comfortable to take this story where it needed to go. Mwah!

And last on the page but first in my heart, my family deserves an entire book filled with thanks. My mother-in-law, Peggy, is a constant source of encouragement, my godmother-in-law, Joann, gifted me with my first ever book club visit (it was a blast!), and my cousin, Brookelyn, never fails to make me smile. My parents and brother live next door and help me in too many ways to name, so I'll just say THANK YOU!!! My daughters, Jordan and Cali, are my biggest fans and publicists, making sure to tell anyone and everyone their mama is a writer. Their enthusiasm and support mean the world to this homeschooling mama's heart. (Girls, I love you to infinity and beyond!) And finally, my husband, Gregg, is my rock. He came up with this title (good job, hun!), helped me figure out character arcs and plot holes, gifted me with hotel rooms away twice during drafting, and continues to tell me that he believes in me. He is the inspiration for every love story I write and is proof that a HEA can be found in the real world as well as fictional. SHMILY, baby!!

**Travel back in time to where it all started
with Rachel Harris's
My Super Sweet Sixteenth Century
Available in stores and online now!**

On the precipice of her sixteenth birthday, the last thing lone wolf Cat Crawford wants is an extravagant gala thrown by her bubbly soon-to-be stepmother and well-meaning father. So even though Cat knows the family's trip to Florence, Italy, is a peace offering, she embraces the magical city and all it offers. But when her curiosity leads her to an unusual gypsy tent, she exits . . . right into Renaissance Firenze.

Thrust into the sixteenth century armed with only a backpack full of contraband future items, Cat joins up with her ancestors, the sweet Alessandra and protective Cipriano, and soon falls for the gorgeous aspiring artist Lorenzo. But when the much-older Niccolo starts sniffing around, Cat realizes that an unwanted birthday party is nothing compared to an unwanted suitor full of creeptastic amore. Can she find her way back to modern times before her Italian adventure turns into an Italian forever?

Things I know about Reece Malcolm:

1. She graduated from New York University.
2. She lives in or near Los Angeles.
3. Since her first novel was released, she's been on the
   New York Times bestseller list every week.
4. She likes strong coffee and bourbon.
5. She's my mother.

Devan knows very little about Reece Malcolm, until the day her father dies and she's shipped off to live with the mother she's never met. All she has is a list of notebook entries that doesn't add up to much.

A offers a whole new world to Devan—a performing arts school allows her to pursue her passion for show choir and musicals, a new circle of friends helps to draw her out of her shell, and an intriguing boy opens up possibilities for her first love.

But then the Reece Malcolm list gets a surprising new entry. Now that Devan is so close to having it all, can she handle the possibility of losing everything?

Chapter One

I was in show choir the day I found out Dad died in a car accident. We were singing "Aquarius" right before, which means I'll always associate Dad being gone with the moon being in the seventh house and Jupiter aligning with Mars.

Dad and I weren't close, not lately at least. Maybe really never. I tell myself it's because Dad wasn't the kind of guy who seemed to get close to people, but honestly I'm afraid I inherited that from him, too. Sometimes days would blur by and it would hit me that Dad and I hadn't talked at all. So I know it's dumb that I cried for about three days straight after it happened, if you can even keep track of time during something like that. Mourning should be for kids who have a billion happy memories, like Disneyland and learning to ride a bike and whatever else dads are supposed to do.

Still, I don't think I'll ever be able to listen to the cast recording of *Hair* again. Or go to a planetarium.

Now it's three months later, and I'm on a plane to L.A. Technically Burbank, but thanks to Google Maps I learned that Burbank might as well be Los Angeles. It's very close. That probably sounds like a good thing, but I'm more than a little convinced L.A. is the epicenter of everything superficial and overly tanned.

My mother's lawyer is next to me. Until the plane went up up up into the blue(ish) St. Louis morning sky, he'd been tapping out messages on his BlackBerry. Now that it's off, he fidgets with it, and occasionally he picks up the pamphlet about safety. Since this is my first flight, I'd read it with way more interest. But after trying to imagine myself zipping down an inflatable slide into the depths of the ocean, I figured maybe it was okay to limit my knowledge as far as disastrous possibilities were concerned.

With regard to the airplane, at least.

"Your mom tells me you're a junior in high school," the lawyer says pretty much out of nowhere. I guess he's finally bored with his powerless device.

"Stepmom," I correct. Knee-jerk reaction by now. People always mean Tracie.

He takes a sip of coffee. "No, your mom."

I realize he *is* talking about my actual mother. It washes over me that he actually *knows her.* As her lawyer he probably knows a lot about her. Unlike me, he doesn't only know her as a name on a book cover, a name I plug into Google on a regular basis. "Didn't speak much to your stepmom."

"Don't feel special," I say without thinking, though he

chuckles.

"It'll be good," he says. "To be with family at a time like this."

I shrug. No one said anything about me right after Dad died. Not just, specifically, who had custody of me and where I would live, but hardly anything about me at all. Kids in musicals without parents always ended up okay— Annie got Daddy Warbucks, Cosette got Jean Valjean, Christine got stalked by the Phantom, though she did get to make out with Raoul—but I doubted anyone would show up and rescue me. (Or make out with me.) People swooped in around Tracie. But even though I didn't know how to function without a dad any more than she knew how to function without a husband, no one offered to help me figure it out. So when all the legal stuff finally got sorted and the lawyer showed up, that much didn't seem like a surprise. Or even a bad thing.

Until I heard where I was going.

"Must have been tough on you," he continues. "Dad here, mom in L.A. I felt bad enough when my wife and I divorced and I left the Valley for the Westside."

I nod to him as politely as I can manage given what's going on and how early it is. I guess he figures out I'm not up to talking because he turns his attention to the catalogue of bizarre items available to purchase while in the air.

After what I figure is a respectable wait, I get out the iPod my best friend Justine gave me as a good-bye gift. It's loaded with musical theatre cast recordings (the only music I ever listen to, which, okay, is ~~maybe a little~~ totally geeky, but it counts that I know that, right?). I scroll to *Little Shop of Horrors*, which we performed in together back in April. Only about three notes in I'm barely managing not to cry, so I switch it off.

"Did you have to come because you're a lawyer?" I ask. His name is Roger Berman but I don't know if I'm supposed to call him Mr. Berman or Roger so I just don't call him anything. "Or did my— Did she just not—"

"Want to leave the house this month?" Roger Berman laughs. "That's always a safe bet with Reece, isn't it? I guess if you write like that, you're allowed to be a hermit sometimes."

6. She is a hermit sometimes.

"Well, yeah," I say, as if I'm some expert on Reece Malcom. Her talent probably *does* allow her a lot. I wonder if my talent will ever allow me anything. So far it kind of feels like the opposite.

"You know how she is," he says in a conspiratorial tone, us bonding about what a kooky recluse my mother is or whatever. "I wouldn't make anything out of it."

I have this fantasy of responding that since she ignored me my entire life and *then* didn't even bother to leave the house, there's probably a *lot* to be made out of it. But I never say things like that.

And, anyway, Reece Malcom has clearly explained things to her lawyer in a way that makes us seem like a perfectly normal mother-daughter combo that just happens to live half the country away from each other. I'm not going to ruin her planned illusion.

I've thought about meeting her. Of course. It's not just that I had the clichéd evil stepmother who couldn't stand me. It's not just that a lot of times—well, most of the time— Dad acted like I didn't exist. Okay, sometimes I thought about nothing but leaving them for my mother. But I never wanted Dad to die. No hypothetical versions happened this way. I wanted a real reunion, not being forced on her. That was the worst part of this. Maybe. It's almost amazing how many bad parts one thing could have.

When the plane lands at Burbank Airport (the only other slightly scary part of flying besides a tiny bit of turbulence is touching down, but, really, it was just a little bump and then we're back on the ground like we never left), I guess I did hope she'd be waiting for us the second we passed through security. But I just follow Roger Berman into the bright sunshine to the baggage carousel like this is exactly what I expect.

I seriously can't even explain how clear and crisp the sky is, the bluest blue I've ever seen. I feel like Dorothy waking up and walking into the colorized Oz, though it's not a witch who's dead, it's someone who shouldn't have been, and it wasn't a tornado-induced falling house, it was a thunderstorm-induced five-car pile-up.

And, anyway, I'm not a blue skies and sunshine person. Life is just life, no matter the weather.

I realize the lawyer is on his BlackBerry, and a woman's voice rings out of the speaker just enough that if I were a dog my ears would prick up. I bite my lip to keep from asking if it's her. A normal kid would recognize her own mother's voice.

"Where are you? No, we'll wait; it's fine, Reece. Great, we'll see you then." He clicks off the phone and smiles at me.

"I'm sure you're not shocked she's running late."

"Oh, um." I nod. "Right. You don't have to stay with me or anything."

"Actually, legally, I do," he says. "And it's no problem. She'll be here soon."

My heart shoots into my throat at that full realization.

"So, um, like, what happens if this doesn't work?" I ask. If I wasn't wanted there, and I'm not wanted here, I should at least know what's next.

"You being in L.A. full-time?" he asks. "We can cross that bridge if we come to it. I know Reece is . . . well, Reece. And L.A. probably seems overwhelming to you, I get that. But I'm sure it'll be fine."

7. Reece is Reece, which never really describes someone likable.

We're quiet for a little while. I keep scanning the crowd, even though if she were here I'd know it. Not like I'd get some Mother Detection Spider Sense, just that she'd find Roger Berman.

It's weird how different people are here. I've never really left Missouri (driving over the river to a concert choir showcase in Illinois doesn't, in my opinion, count), so maybe this kind of thing is obvious once you've traveled. But the crowd around the outdoor baggage claim is more tanned, and definitely better dressed, and everyone looks younger. Not like I'm going around asking ages, but it's the kind of thing you can just tell.

"You a writer, too?" he asks. He's a very random person for a lawyer. "That kind of thing hereditary?"

"Definitely not. I mean, *I wish.*"

"Don't we all." He looks out to the line of cars stopped at the light across from us. "Speaking of."

I follow his gaze, but I don't really know what I'm looking for. A black BMW pulls right up to the stretch of curb lined with cars making drop-offs or pickups, and she jumps out of it. I've only seen one fuzzy little picture (Reece Malcolm is practically unGoogleable), but there's no doubt this is her. I tell myself to really suck down this moment, get every detail because I'll want to remember it forever. So it's weird that she's just this person, one out of lots and lots at the airport.

"Thanks, Roger," she says, no eye contact with me at all. "Sorry I'm—"

"Ten minutes late is practically on-time for you," he says. "Early, even." He hands over a folder to her, the one my birth certificate is in. I saw it when we went through security and I had to show ID. "Give me a call if you need anything."

"I always do," she says in this voice that's, somehow, halfway between monotone and perky. I've imagined my first conversation with my mother many times, but she never sounded like that in my head.

"Devan, good luck." He shakes my hand and gives me a warm smile. "L.A.'s not so bad, I promise."

"Thanks." I try to return the smile. Really he only had to bring me here, but he's been nice the whole time.

She sort of barely turns to me as Roger Berman walks away, which is my first chance to actually look at her, even if it's a lot like staring into the sun. She's taller than me, though not by much—which I guess I didn't expect—and her hair's much better: glossy and chestnut brown, not the mousy shade mine is, hanging to her shoulders. I guess we're built the same, sort of curvy, thin-not-skinny.

And, very depressingly, she's wearing faded jeans, a fitted T-shirt, and fairly grungy Converse Chuck Taylors, while I'm in cropped jeans, a red and white shirt with tiny pearly buttons, and white flats. Up until this moment we haven't been able to share my life, but can't we at least share a duty to style?

She gestures to my suitcase as well as my backpack that I rested on top of it. "Are those all your bags?"

"Um, yeah, I—"

She grabs them both and deposits them in her car's trunk. "They take the no-waiting or -parking rule pretty seriously. Come on."

I get into the car's passenger side and buckle myself in, wondering if I'm being dumb to expect maybe not a hug but at least a hi?

My mother hops into the driver's seat and squeals off from the curb. "Sorry I was late. I'm sure Roger filled you in that it's not exactly an uncommon occurrence."

"Yeah. Um, thanks," I manage to squeak out. "For picking me up."

"Oh." She adjusts her sunglasses as she merges across a few lanes of traffic. "Yeah, of course."

I look out the window as L.A.—or Burbank?—flies past us. I expected the palm trees and sunshine, but I thought everything would be blanketed in smog and way more glamorous than a bunch of strip malls and car dealerships.

A cell phone rings as my mother pulls onto the freeway, and she sighs loudly and gestures to her bag, which I realize is at my feet. Also: soft black leather, amazing detailing, very enviable. Immediately I put a lot of hope into that bag.

"Can you grab that?" she asks. "Sorry."

I reach into her purse tentatively but luckily locate the ringing phone right away. She doesn't take it when I hold it out, though.

"Who?" she sort of barks. I feel like I might never get used to her tone.

I check the screen: brad calling, and let her know.

She holds out her hand to take the phone, clicks to accept the call, and holds the phone to her ear. "Yes, I got up in time. I can't imagine you're calling for any other reason. Yes, she's here, and— No, I haven't. Your priorities are very strange." The last one is the only thing she's said so far that doesn't sound rushed and vaguely annoyed. I wonder who Brad is to earn a nice moment from Reece Malcolm. "I'm hanging up, all right? I'm completely breaking the law right now— If I knew where it was I'd be using it. No, don't— Brad. I'll take care of— Fine, fine. Right, you, too."

She clicks off the phone and tosses it onto my lap. "I don't know about the laws in Missouri, but here you can't hold your phone to your ear while driving," she says. "Not that I follow it. Are you hungry? Are you even up for food? I hate flying."

"Flying's okay," I say, while I try to gauge if I'm hungry or not. My stomach makes interesting decisions when I'm stressed out. "I guess I'm hungry. If you are."

"I don't think it works that way," she says. "But, yeah. Let's stop."

This is beyond weird. Long-lost mother finally sitting next

to me, and we're discussing cell phone laws and lunch. Once we're off the freeway, my mother parks behind a hamburger place she claims is both "a-ma-zing" and the closest to her house. I follow her inside, wondering how hamburgers can be a-ma-zing, but this place is actually super fancy with red vinyl chairs and shiny chandeliers and a bar displaying—for whatever reason—a stuffed swan. But the only thing I'm trying not to stare at like some kind of stalker is my mother now that she's taken off her sunglasses. Her eyes are brown, just like mine. I wonder if she already noticed, or if it even means anything to her.

"Are you sure you're feeling all right?" She looks up at me. "We can take this to go, if you'd rather."

"No, I'm fine, sorry." I force myself to look at the menu, in case her concern stems from me gawking at her. "Just tired." I nod as a waiter walks up to get our drink order. Two Diet Cokes. I know it's lame to get excited, but I like having it in common with her. Also, when you're a self-identifying choir and musical theatre nerd, you pretty much accept that some a lot of things that excite you are going to be lame.

By the time the waiter brings our drinks, I still have no idea what I want, so I just let Reece Malcolm order two things for us to split. You know you're desperate to bond when fancy hamburgers are your best plan.

It's quiet again while we wait for the food, and the silence continues once we're served, outside of Reece Malcolm saying, "See? A-ma-zing."

To be fair, she's right.